HIDDEN COLOURS

A Novel by
Nillu Nasser

HIDDEN COLOURS
Copyright © 2018 by Nillu Nasser
Cover Art Copyright © 2018 by D. Robert Pease

FIRST EDITION SOFTCOVER
ISBN: 1622537831
ISBN-13: 978-1-62253-783-9

Editor: Jessica West
Interior Designer: Lane Diamond

EVOLVED PUBLISHING™

www.EvolvedPub.com
Evolved Publishing LLC
Butler, Wisconsin, USA

Printed in Book Antiqua font.

BOOKS BY NILLU NASSER

All the Tomorrows
Hidden Colours

For my parents,
who are born helpers.

1

Nestled in the far-east corner of Treptower Park, past the abandoned funfair with its rusting dodgems and the Ferris wheel overcome by climbing ivy, stood a midnight blue and bronze tent. It didn't look like much — particularly tonight, when the inky sky blotted out the stars — but each evening at the stroke of seven, the circus came stutteringly to life.

From the moment the circus materialised, it transformed the landscape. Once in full flow, the emerald grasses vibrated with the rhythm of the house band. The winds carried peculiar scents far afield. Nostrils twitched when exotic odours replaced altogether familiar ones. Walking deep into the park, the waft of smoking sausages on summer barbecues or the tang of wet autumn earth disappeared, leaving only the scent of sawdust, sugared almonds and a fog of incense.

This was a circus for all seasons. Whether birds chirped in the park, great gusts of wind rocked the boughs, snow crunched underfoot, or thunder pulsed across the Berlin skies, the big top beckoned like a mirage. If curious individuals followed their feet towards the tent, they found sticky trestle tables outside it, where adults clinked glasses and children slurped pink concoctions through winding straws.

Here and there, between the patrons, clusters of performers lingered in full costume: young women in shimmering leotards with plumes of feathers attached to their rears; a clown with a magnificent bowtie that seemed to increase and decrease in size as you watched; stilt-walkers who roamed the lawn in between faded dinosaur figures and could be confused for great oaks. Neither the performers' faces nor their accents stemmed from Europe. A strangeness pervaded this circus, an other-worldliness. The circus people gathered at the banks of the River Spree to play stones, a ritual to dispel their nerves. They disrupted the calm surface of the river with a flurry of ripples, and became animated at the sound of an eerie gong to summon them to their starting positions.

Tonight, a sparse crowd filled the tent amidst a jumble of fairy-lights, sawdust and clattering seats. Close to half of the stands stood empty. The immigrant circus, as it was known locally, was no longer Berlin's newest curiosity, but no matter. The spectacle didn't dim. Three girls in long flowing skirts paced through the tent, holding jasmine-scented incense sticks aloft, their hair in swinging pony-tails. Parents shushed their excitable, popcorn-popping children. A group of women celebrated a hen night and attracted the attention of four boozy men sitting in the row behind.

The microphone boomed as Emir the ringmaster, rotund and buoyant, his moustache thick like a bristle brush, entered the ring. He plumped out his ruffled shirt and tipped his tatty top hat. "Ladies and gentleman, boys and girls, welcome to the circus. We'll dazzle you, we'll enchant you, we'll make you rub your eyes in wonder. You'll be transformed by what you see. It's showtime!"

The performance commenced with a display from gleaming horses which galloped into the ring unaccompanied. The audience gasped when the three girls in their midst set aside the incense sticks and climbed onto the rafters. They leapt and, for a moment, appeared to pause in flight before landing on the bare-backed steeds, racing around the ring until beast and beauty became a whirr of hooves and skirts. Wild applause whipped through the big top.

There followed a giant man, more nimble than he looked, leading a troupe of goats in a merry dance, and the goats danced in pairs, courting each other, and seemed to waltz and tango, such was their magic. Next, a woman slid down aerial silks, bending her limbs at impossible angles with the gracefulness of a willow tree before cocooning herself and disappearing a breath later.

So, the evening hurtled forward at break-neck speed, the circus-goers cheering and quietening by turns as the artists turned their tricks into spectacle.

High above the unfolding acts, Yusuf shook with nerves, as he did every night.

Emir reclaimed the microphone, his voice a foghorn of exuberance. "Next up, it's the man—nay, the star—you've been waiting for! He can leap. He can somersault through the air. He can land like a cat. Our resident acrobat, Herr Yusuf Alam!"

Not for the first time, Yusuf wondered whether the performers should change their names to be more palatable to this audience.

Less strange.

For Yusuf and the motley troupe who had become his family, the circus wasn't merely a performance. The big top that flared above them might have been an inanimate object, but it symbolised the chance of a new life. After he'd fled Syria, he hadn't thought he'd ever find another home, until the circus found him. The performers forged new ties because without each other, they had nobody. The circus had become a lifeboat, as if they were still making the treacherous journey across the globe away from disease, war and uncertainty. As if the twinkling lights of the tent amounted to the North Star.

If only the city kept her arms open.

He'd arrived in Berlin two years ago, an alien being adrift in a foreign landscape with its own stinking history of violence and hatred. Grief knotted with gratitude at the centre of his chest. Two years had passed since he'd seen his mother and filled his belly with her stewed curries that stained his fingers. Two years since war threw their lives off track and imposed its will on them as if they were nothing more than flies.

"And here he comes!" said Emir the ringmaster, drunk on energy.

Yusuf locked away the errant thoughts that flooded his mind and slipped into his acrobat's skin. He smoothed down his costume and stepped out onto the beam, high above the spectators. The moment of jumping always overwhelmed him. Each time he jumped, his experience divided into two halves: the fear of falling and the joy of flying. Sometimes, when he leapt through the tent with his acrobat's grace, the weightlessness of flight—for a nanosecond— removed the burden of his memories. Tonight, not even the thought of momentary release helped. He didn't want to do this. He scanned the crowd. The faces of strangers blurred into a mist. His heart clamoured in his chest.

Will I ever be safe?

He wobbled. The roar of the wind at the top of the tent echoed in his ears as he regained his composure. He balanced, body taut. Better to pause and let the crowd imagine him falling for an instant. He blinked to shake the image from his own mind, his legs suddenly like jelly.

Yusuf leapt, and when he did, the spectators held their breath — a suspended moment, like after the shells landed in Syria. He somersaulted through the air, spinning like a top, and a shower of stardust raced after him, microscopic particles twinkling in his wake. He gave himself to the freedom of the fall, although he quivered with fear and his people were dying, still. When he landed, dust swept into the air, reminding him of the dry earth at home, which sometimes became wet with rains or blood.

The audience burst into applause.

2

A billowing cloud of sawdust floated to the ground. Yusuf stood in the glare of the spotlight and bowed low to the stands to acknowledge the crowd's rapturous reception, though he didn't care for the wild applause. He longed for a greater connection than this, to be rooted in this country and bonded to its people, to shed the skin of his own ragged history. Pearls of sweat pooled between his shoulder blades. He bowed once more, lycra slick against his skin, to those who had no idea how lucky they were with their white faces, here in the most powerful country in Europe.

The house band swung into action in a rousing melody of Middle-East poetry meets Berlin hip-hop. Inside his body, cavernous parts echoed with the energy of the music, igniting a sense of urgency in him. Yusuf's blood ran quicker with the beat and he darted to the edge of the arena. The tambourine, goblet drum and fiddle vied for attention with Najib's beat-boxing, lips alive at the microphone, dead eyes above.

He sent a silent message to Najib. *Focus.*

Right now, it was showtime. This magical, fragile home of theirs couldn't afford any complaints. The circus needed to excel. They needed all their concentration, all their tricks and spirit to outperform their competition and attract visitors.

Emir the ringmaster clapped his hands, and the lights blacked out. The tent fizzed with anticipation. The lights flared and in came the twins, sequinned from head to toe, riding bareback on their horses, dove-tailing, leaping, turning slow, sensual flips, though their father would have turned in his grave. Zul the Clown bumbled into the ring, feigning flatulence to the hilarity of the children, his polka-dotted flat cap turning on his head of its own accord. Next, a lute rang out through the air, sweet and clear, as Amena, Aya and Aischa returned. Resplendent in the new costumes they had sewn, they performed a folk dance with spinning skirts, casting threads of gold into the air. Meanwhile, Esme—pretty in a ruched moonlight gown, her hair shrouded by a headscarf—offered warm chunks of *manoushi bread* and *baklawa* to the audience.

Onwards continued the show, like clockwork.

The girls danced not five feet away from him, round and round, and their movements hypnotised. Yusuf's eyes blurred and he retreated into a memory of his mother. He recalled the comfort of her calloused hand on his face, how it would linger there as if he were a child and not a grown man. How he missed her, even surrounded by his new family. His mother had wanted him to be a surgeon or a lawyer. She'd stayed in the land of their ancestors, too old and tired to make the journey, too reluctant to give up her past. She didn't know how her remaining son contorted himself into shapes and spun through the air to please strangers. Even now, he could almost feel the vice-like grip of her fingers on his arms, the salty tears threading a pathway across the creases of her skin. Her parting words to him had been branded into his psyche.

Do what you must to survive, but never forget who we are.

He owed it to her to make a go of this life. All around him, his fellow performers dazzled with colour, song and razzmatazz, spirit and skill. He knew happiness here, especially with the circus in full motion, with his newly-made family in a flurry of activity around him and the satisfaction of a seamless show. Here, in the tents, the performers controlled their world.

Soon it would be time for the finale when the performers flooded the arena once more: the acrobats, clowns, stilt- and tightrope-walkers, leaping horses and dancing goats. The world would shrink to a point inside the big top, and all around there would be the energy of a dozen planets and colours stolen from Allah himself. It would feel like a wedding in Syria, when the village came together and his face hurt from smiling, his feet ached from all the dancing, and his cheeks flushed with heat. The finale was when the circus most felt like home, when they were together like they belonged. Misfits and broken people who had only become whole once they found their way together like magnets.

Suddenly, a shout pierced through the serenity of the lute.

An audience member called out, puncturing the dream-like trance of Amena, Aya and Aischa's dance. Again it came, brash and unapologetic, a dose of reality crashing into the fantastical realm they had toiled to create. Anxiety bubbled in Yusuf's stomach and his eyebrows snapped together as he strained to hear the precise words.

The man lurched forward in his seat, red-faced and drunk, although they didn't serve alcohol here. "Go on, you monkeys! Dance!"

Yusuf's skin prickled with fear. The disrespect shown to his friends—to them all—wounded him deeply, but they could neither censure nor retaliate, powerless as they were.

The man hadn't yet finished, and the audience around him looked away, aghast. "Dance, dance 'til you drop, then we can put you back in your boats where you belong. Rats, the lot of you!"

Yusuf itched with the need to restrain him, but how could he when bound by the rules of gratitude for being allowed to live in this country, and by the rules of hospitality to a paying member of the audience? He looked to Emir's impassive face at the side of the ring. How far would they allow insults to go before taking action?

The girls continued dancing as if they were dolls, not real flesh capable of hurt. Esme—an Afghani girl, who was sweet on Yusuf—stood closer to the fray. The man's shouts startled her and she dropped her tray of food over herself and into an audience member's bag. Her moonlight dress dimmed, and she flushed and stooped to undo the damage, all the while whispering apologies to the woman she knelt before. The man crowed and settled back into his seat, pleased with himself.

A ruckus like this set them all on edge and chased the magic away. Bad enough that circus attendance had been dwindling. Worse, disturbances such as these had increased and had resulted in additional scrutiny from the Interior Ministry. With any luck, no one with any clout had been there to witness it. The Interior Minister's aide, all corkscrew curls and a hooked nose, had been an increasingly regular visitor to the circus in recent months, and that in itself had raised concerns.

Yusuf swivelled and blinked to adjust to the glare of the lights.
Damn.

His heartbeat accelerated and his palms grew sweaty. There sat Rex Silberling himself: Interior Minister, the Chancellor's right-hand man, and architect of the circus. Tonight, his aide flapped next to Silberling as he sat still and grim-faced in his house seat, power rolling off him in waves. She motioned to Silberling's security men not to intervene in the disturbance: the drunk man had already settled down.

Yusuf sighed. Politics turned on a pin. They couldn't risk displeasing Silberling, lest he withdraw his patronage. Lest he decided to invest his energies elsewhere.

His mind spun through a reel of the latest indignities the circus had suffered: their own waste found strewn in the tent; the horses released from their paddock at night; crude images of buxom girls in compromising positions graffitied on the sweets wagon; the laughter of teenagers running away in glee.

But his circus family—refugees all—had survived worse. The band's energy leapt a notch, and the plaintive sound of the sousaphone jolted Yusuf into action. Never mind the disrupter in the crowd or the frowning presence of Silberling. It was time to take to the stage. In they all ran, beasts and performers alike, springing, turning, waving to the crowd, singing for their supper. Silberling, too, became merely one of the audience as the performers threw batons into the air and the goats danced and skirts became a whirr of colour. The girls threw small squares of tissue paper into the stands, which, in the blink of an eye, transformed into sapphire butterflies flecked with copper. The men blew into their cupped hands and bubbles emerged and floated away, growing ever larger, until they popped over the heads of the audience in a burst of raindrops.

"Isn't this just fantastic?" said Emir into the microphone in the midst of them all, his shirt straining across his belly as he hopped in excitement from one leg to another.

The final moment approached, in which Emir pulled a lever that released a flurry of multi-coloured foils over the audience, never failing to make the children squeal with delight, a parting surprise the girls would later painstakingly gather up for tomorrow's performance.

He pulled the lever, but it stuck fast. Emir tugged it again to unleash the nets at the top of the tent. An avalanche of paper balls covered in stark print came turning through the air. Emir's mouth gaped and he cried out, dismayed at the unwelcome surprise. Not one of them had noticed the change in the contents of the nets that morning. They'd been secure in the knowledge that all had been prepared for tonight's show.

The performers stuttered to a halt.

The band momentarily lost its rhythm.

Silberling's security men emerged from the shadows.

The audience clutched at the dirty projectiles as they tumbled through the air and onto laps. Silberling, too, unfolded his spidery legs and reached for a paper ball, as if it were a fortune cookie to be read. He unravelled it, eyes hooded as he read the page, mouth curled in displeasure.

Yusuf's ribcage contracted, as if the air had suddenly become thinner. He didn't need to read the words — the sabotage spoke for itself — but he couldn't help himself. He grasped a ball, unpeeled it, and read:

Dirty rat.

And another.

Thieves. We don't want you here.

Around him, the performers stood still, faces painted in alarm. Emir, ever ready with cheer, appeared dumbstruck. With every moment, the buoyancy in the tent fizzled out. Circuses were stitched together from fantasy and could not survive the intrusion of the real world, the shades of grey and black and blue that track human existence.

"Follow my lead!" said Yusuf to Zul the Clown.

They ran around the arena, and the rest soon caught on, scooping up the offensive words, teasing the children, offering a peck on the cheek here, a handshake buzzer there, doing their best to ignore the expletives nestled on the page, the clues that to some they were not equal to the shit on their shoes.

Inside, a leaden darkness settled over Yusuf, despite the cheer he showed in the tent.

As the audience emptied the stands and the final sounds of the band died out, Emir excused himself, and his moustache drooped. "You understand, son. My heart can't take such shocks."

"It'll be okay, Emir. Leyla will make you one of her world-famous soups for supper and all will be well."

"You may be right." The older man pushed through the heavy curtains of the tent, looking all of his fifty-seven years.

Yusuf turned and found himself face-to-face with Silberling.

"Goodnight, Herr Alam," said the gravel-voiced minister. His stare, predatory and cold, sent a jolt of electricity through Yusuf. "You understand, these little disturbances cannot go on?"

Yusuf's throat thickened. How could it be that Silberling offered neither praise for the revelries nor solace for the night's injustice? The man remained as cold as a fish. Far be it for him to explain something so obvious to a superior.

"I'm sorry," said Yusuf with a stutter. Even this foreign tongue that he'd taken pains to learn came to him less easily when he stood before Silberling, as if by the very virtue of being himself Silberling made others smaller. "I'll pass that on to Emir. We'll do better next time."

Silberling wrinkled his nose, and Yusuf became aware of the mild stench of bodily exertions and stale popcorn underneath the cloud of incense and sawdust. With a nod, the minister took his leave, striding into the night accompanied by his team to where his state car awaited him.

He'd met men like Silberling before. Hadn't his father been such a man, before it all came crashing down? Can't they be found on every street, in every country, there where the wine flows, backs are patted and decisions are made? Some wore suits, others wore *kurta*, some carried guns, and some a briefcase, but the undercurrent of energy remained the same, and the hunger in the eyes.

There, in the majestic tent full of possibility, oceans away from the troubles of his past, amidst the sweat and the sawdust, despite their talent and commitment, Yusuf knew the circus and its people to be pawns in a game of power and perceptions. Yusuf couldn't trust Silberling even though the circus, in essence, belonged to him. Without the circus, Yusuf would have been lost, and Silberling could so easily take it all away.

3

Rex Silberling liked to think of himself as a knight in shining armour. The Chancellor appointed him as Federal Interior Minister in the aftermath of her decision to provide a million Syrians with refuge from the war. Rex admired her bravery but the swell in anti-immigrant sentiment—particularly after the sexual assaults in Cologne—didn't surprise him. No one liked to think their country had changed overnight; change could come too quickly.

Then Rex had a brainwave that propelled him into one of the highest offices of state: the immigrant circus. His idea took on shape and colour, like an origami bird. Not that Rex was an idealist. No, he harboured no such illusions. He was a pragmatist. Germany couldn't afford a repeat of its history; it had taken decades to move beyond the shadow of Nazism, and the country couldn't fall prey to the nationalist surges across the globe. As the grand dame of Europe, Germany had a duty to lead or risked being toppled from her throne.

What better way to ease tensions between the local population and refugees than by encouraging interactions in a frivolous setting while also enabling a livelihood, sense of community and a path to citizenship? It didn't worry him that those absurd left-wing rags complained the immigrant circus reeked of exploitation. They always cried foul over something or other. This was about results, not sensitivities. A brave new world.

Rex knew his strengths. He could sell oil to the Saudis. He grew the idea of the immigrant circus in gleaming boardrooms in which powerful, elegantly-suited men nodded sagely while secretaries tended to their every need. The Chancellor was taken with it. What an initiative! The immigrant circus would be a flagship integration project across Europe. It wasn't without risks, of course. But were it to go well, they might win over those pesky nationalists. Rex had an uncanny ability of transplanting himself in other men's minds, of understanding even the basest notions. If the Chancellor was willing to settle a large group of immigrants just a stone's throw away from the Bundestag, the foul-smelling, uneducated lot couldn't be that bad, could they?

Once the circus had the right backing, it took flight and transformed into a real life breathing organism, its tents erect and bold at the heart of Berlin. The performers happily accepted their roles, awash with shame and gratitude. The circus tent's blue and bronze fabric stood stark against the sky, a beacon to visitors across the city, like a minaret functions on more exotic soil. Rex pushed away his nagging concern at any similarities with the human zoos of the nineteenth century, where crowds had ogled black people, bearded ladies and conjoined twins.

He really did have a lot to unpack with his therapist the next time he saw her.

Still, as his political mentor used to say, *good things don't last*, and in politics, two years is a long time. Marvellous though the idea had been, Rex had a panther's instincts. He sensed it might be time to gift his patronage to another project, and tonight had proved his point. The immigrant circus was no longer the newest attraction in town and even Berliners, those most cosmopolitan of all the German people, had grown tired of it. Their curiosity had dwindled into apathy. The past six months had been marked by fewer ticket sales, grumbling neighbours, and an uptick in the number of assaults on the circus performers.

The orbs of hate that had fallen from the rafters at the circus indicated a pattern Rex couldn't ignore. He knew when to cut his losses. The nationalists had grown in strength, and had surprising staying power. They'd be bolstered by similar movements dotted across the globe. Their list of grievances demanded that their needs were placed above those of migrants. Such were their numbers that they could fell governments. Or worse. Even in the West, he'd seen how politicians and journalists had paid for their ideas with their lives.

No one had ever accused Rex of bravery.

He wouldn't die for his ideals.

He'd built his reputation on sensing the mood of the nation. It would be easy enough to convince the regional governing bodies that this little experiment had run its course. The voting public's attention and compassion had moved onto other concerns, judging by the recent swing in polls.

He stood, and his dog Jessy cocked her ears, alert to his every movement. She padded beside him, and he placed a gentle hand on her collar to restrain her from slipping through the door he opened.

"Corinne, come," he said, calling his aide. "We have work to do."

His aide swept up her papers and hurried inside. Her corkscrew curls formed a particularly unruly frame around her face this morning.

Rex nudged Jessy's rump towards the desk and shut the door. Yes, it might be time to polish his environmental credentials. After all, voters only had the capacity to care so much.

The next evening, as the moon rose behind a bank of clouds, Rex strode into Mutter Hoppe, a brasserie in Berlin Mitte. He liked the hearty, old-fashioned food here, and he could count on it to be quiet enough for business meetings. As usual, Frauke, the waitress with a barrel-like waist, met him at the door to lead him to his reserved table. The dark wooden booths were perfect for what he had in mind: privacy and, if he spread himself out widely, a little discomfort for his guest. A useful combination for getting what he wanted while staying out of earshot of any passersby. It wouldn't do to be recognised or overheard.

When he saw Marina Schmidt already seated, Rex smiled. Arriving second signalled his importance. Ever dependable Corinne, hovering outside with his dog, had done her work well.

"Frau Schmidt." He nodded, and held out his hand for a cursory handshake.

She fumbled in her purse for a moment then her clammy palm met his cool one.

Was she frightened by his person or his role as Interior Minister?

"Herr Silberling. You're much taller in person than you appear on television."

Rex waved a hand dismissively. There could be no illusions that the two of them were equals. "Appearances can be deceiving, my dear." The endearment dripped off his tongue. She might be editor of *Berliner Allgemeine Zeitung*, a newspaper boasting the city's highest circulation, but she was still a little girl in comparison to him.

He slid into the booth and splayed his legs, one on either side of hers, and placed his folder of documents on the table. "You refused my invitation to the circus tonight."

"I would have loved to come, Minister, but I hadn't yet given the green light on tomorrow's edition. I hope you didn't mind."

Her hair brushed against his hand. He blinked, surprised once again at how power brought out an awkward coquettishness. He was emotionally loyal to his wife, but the odd dalliance with the opposite sex re-established his prowess as a man. It'd been years since a woman had given him the brush off. It almost made him wish for a challenge. He harboured no vanities that Marina was attracted to him—in fact, Marina and her girlfriend were one of the most committed relationships on the Berlin high society scene—but there could be no doubt she hankered after his favour.

Little wonder, when her newspaper leaked revenue. The losses it had accrued could hardly be sustainable.

He fixed his china blue eyes on her. "Have you visited the circus before?"

She shook her head.

"A shame. It really is very good."

He'd expected as much. If Corinne's research stood up to scrutiny—and she hadn't failed him yet—Marina Schmidt's reluctance to visit the circus aligned with her views. Funny how predictable people were when you learned to look for the signs. A horse-rider, whose bank account told of regular donations to animal rights charities, Marina had an instinctive dislike of the circus, and she had a gaping financial hole to plug. There was no doubt: Rex needed to control the press and Marina Schmidt was the right woman for the job.

Frauke returned with menus.

"A bottle of your finest Côtes du Rhône, thank you." Rex waved her away and turned his attention back to Marina. "You've heard of the trouble, though?"

Marina frowned. "Grumblings, perhaps. The usual stuff. Foreigners taking away our money, the state spending millions on them, thieving. Nothing out of the ordinary."

"Crime is on the rise. This week, the circus was targeted again. The police tell me it's only a matter of time before the situation escalates. It's not what I want."

"What can I do for you, Minister?"

"Follow the story." He arranged his features into a friendly expression. "Can the circus be saved?"

Frauke returned with the wine and poured it, offering it to Rex to taste. He swirled it in his glass to check its viscosity, breathing it its aroma, before sipping some and letting it linger on his palate. He nodded his approval at Frauke, and they waited while she finished her task.

When she had gone, Marina's astute eyes searched his face. "The question is more, do you want to save it, Minister?"

She was smarter than he'd given her credit for. He knew the limits of his own department's energies. Should he throw more resources at the circus in the face of growing opposition, or abandon it and shore up his support? His resolve grew. Better to control the narrative and the outcome. Marina formed an integral part of his plan to accelerate the inevitable decline of the circus and close it down before the next election round. That way, he would save face when he brought the axe down and protect his international regard.

He needed to be careful how he expressed himself here. It would be folly for any of these manoeuvres to be traced back to him. In fact, Corinne—whose unswerving loyalty matched Jessy's—would be doing the running from here on out. Plausible deniability remained one of his guiding principles. The most effective politicians learned to weave lines that allowed them to twist in any direction.

It all boiled down to this moment. Rex enjoyed this part of the game, the way his ambition unfolded, almost as if it were a game of puppetry. He leaned towards Marina, speaking in hushed tones, as if they were friends. "There's only so far you can nurture the public's better instincts. I fear the tide has turned. I trust you to do what's best for the city," said Rex. Flattery was a powerful tool. "I think this project has run its course and, of course, the Chancellor will be disappointed, but what can you do when the people remove their support?"

Marina's fingers opened and closed around her pen: she had a journalist's instincts despite being stuck behind an editor's desk. "I need to be clear, Minister. What are we talking about here?"

Time to seal the deal.

He'd expected more subtlety. "An evidence-based story on crime and the circus, Frau Schmidt. We are so used to second-guessing our instincts in this country. And while we guard against the horrors of our past, we can't be afraid to act in the best interests of our nation just because we are worried about being seen as xenophobic. I'm asking you to do what you do best. Courageous, no-nonsense journalism. Just run it by me first."

"What's in it for me?"

Rex grew impatient. Outside, Jessy barked, as she did when separated from him for too long. "You get to keep my ear. There might be some funding in it too. Channelled to you through a suitable project, obviously."

She leaned forward. "What timeline are we talking about here?"

"Three weeks."

"And the circus people? What happens to them?"

He sipped his wine and swirled it around his mouth before answering her. "That's my problem, not yours."

She nodded. "Of course, Minister."

He placed a crisp fifty Euro bill on the table between them, and pinned it in place with the half-empty wine bottle. Then he eased himself out of the booth.

"Goodbye, Frau Schmidt."

"Minister, your folder," she said.

"What folder?" he called over his shoulder, a smirk on his lips. "That's not mine."

At the door, he turned to find her leafing through the documents Corinne had collated: police records outlining crime in the immediate vicinity. The evidence was woolly but Marina Schmidt had a knack for presenting stories in just the right way.

4

Ellie Richter had a string missing from her DNA. Her mother swore it. At a time when the world pulsed with fear, Ellie refused to hide away. She had always been that way, ever since she had been a tiny girl with ginger pigtails and alabaster skin dotted with a generous spray of freckles. It was why, at four years old, she roared at a growling dog twice her size, though she should have been quaking in her boots. It was why, at nine years old, the school bully made the mistake of stealing her lunch only once. His nose smarted for days after their encounter; his ears rang with the story of Ellie's fists for his whole school career. Ellie's courage made her a great reporter, if only her editor would give her some freedom. That tenacity had also often landed her in trouble.

At lunchtime, she escaped the *Berliner Allgemeine Zeitung*'s offices on Friedrichstraße to eat lunch on the lawn outside Berliner Dom. Tourists meandered past in sunglasses and shawls as befitting early spring. The cathedral's sage green dome reached into a sky filled with wisps of cumulus clouds. Sedate organ music drifted out from open doors into the warm Berlin air. Ellie dug her bare toes into the springy grass and picked at the cheese and grapes she had packed that morning.

This brief hour in the middle of the working day, when she could take refuge in the nooks and crannies of the city, soothed her. Especially when her new job, despite her striving, failed to live up to her ideals. What had happened to the investigative journalism she'd dreamed of in college? Her job at *BAZ* had the potential to be wonderful. A local paper with a thriving readership that packed enough of a punch to be syndicated nationally. A shame then, that the assignments Marina gave her prompted groans Ellie could barely conceal. They stifled her, like slick oil on a seagull. Ellie didn't want to be just another lackey; she wanted more.

She cast a glance at her wrist watch, weighing up when she had to be back in the office. If she rode fast, she could stay a little longer. Her phone vibrated in her bag. Ellie sighed and dug it out, tossing pens, her journal and a flask of water onto the lawn in the process.

"Hello?"

At the other end of the line, Tom, her boss's assistant, huffed. Ellie could hear the bustle of the news desk in the background. "Hi, trouble. I thought I was having a bad day, but yours is about to end in hellfire, judging by Marina's body language."

She and Tom had quickly become firm friends, and it paid to have an ally at work.

"Dude, what now? I'm at lunch. Can it wait? I'll be back in the office in a quarter of an hour."

"No, I'm afraid not. She's just read your latest copy and there's steam coming out of her ears. She wants you in right away, before her editorial meeting at 2 p.m."

Ellie bristled and checked her watch.

"Okay."

"Good luck!" Tom disconnected the line.

"Just great."

In the distance, the organ blared. Ellie gathered up her things, her heartbeat a drum in her ears, before pushing her feet into her Dr. Martens. Then she slung her bag across her body and tossed her remaining lunch in the bin. Her bike waited just beyond a canopy of trees, where she'd secured it to railings. She fumbled with it, and as she did, a man stumbled into a pedestrian, a slam of bodies, one against the other. He apologised in heavily accented German. Her journalist's brain filed him away like a snapshot: above average height, a mop of artfully dishevelled hair above a chiselled, bearded face, striking grey eyes and protruding ears. The man strode past, as comfortable with his aloneness as she was with hers. Then she mounted her bike and joined the stream of cyclists, pushing her legs hard to make good time.

It was going to be a long day.

Ellie clumped through the office, her hair a sweaty mess at her nape. She flung her jacket on her desk, ignoring the buzz of her phone and the journalists scurrying to meet tonight's deadline.

"You're cutting it fine, aren't you?" hissed Tom.

"I came as fast as I could." Ellie smoothed down her skirt.

"She'll have five minutes, tops. Try not to make her angrier." He nodded towards the inner sanctum of Marina's den.

Inside, grey paint contrasted with exposed red brick. Past editions of the newspaper dotted the walls, stark headlines preserved behind shiny glass, a testament to Marina's prowess as an editor. She'd become the first female editor of *BAZ* at the age of forty-one, and her reign had outlasted any of her male predecessors. Pictures of Marina with the city's best and brightest decorated her desk: Marina with Katharina Witt, the figure skater; Marina with the late Helmut Kohl and the Mayor; Marina arm in arm with the chairman of the Pergamon Museum, all shiny white teeth and alcohol-glazed eyes. It paid to network in this world.

In the corner of the room, on an oval meeting table for six, sat Marina in a crisp white shirt, rolling her eyes. "You've got balls, I'll give you that much."

"Sorry I'm late," said Ellie.

Marina's thick brunette hair had been blow-dried artfully into smooth waves that fell across her shoulders. In her late forties now, her skin betrayed the signs of heavy smoking. Lines criss-crossed around her pursed mouth. She was always happier with a cigarette between her fingers. Right now, her fingers drummed a beat on the glass. She motioned to the space across from her. "Sit."

Ellie sank into a seat.

Marina let rip. "I read your latest copy—let's see—an hour ago now, and I'm still seething. That wasn't the angle we discussed. Why do you insist on being difficult? You'd do well to remember you're not out of your probation period yet."

Ellie could be pretty certain that Tom and the rest of the newsroom could glean what was happening by the tone of Marina's voice through the thin walls. Trust her to always raise the prospect of Ellie not passing her probation.

Ellie chewed on her lip. "I wrote an earlier draft, but it seemed a bit, you know, on the nose."

"On the nose?" Her face contorted.

"Lacking in depth." Ellie held her breath. One–two–three…

"For the love of God!" Marina pulsed with impatience. She flung up her hands then made a concerted effort to restrain herself. "The board needs the paper to sell, not to educate. If you want to write upmarket copy, maybe this isn't the place for you. You need to up your game, you hear me? Sales have plateaued, advertisers are running God knows where, and we just can't afford to keep someone who can't read the writing on the wall. One chance, Ellie. You can be good. You just need to try." A pause. "Are you listening to me?"

"Yes," said Ellie, laying her palms against the table. She had been trying. What Marina meant was she just needed to be agreeable and follow instructions. Why did she find that so hard? One day, she'd be able to tell her where to stick it. She could've written the article Marina wanted in her sleep. The words weren't the problem: Marina keeping her on a leash was. However much she had wanted to admire the older woman, or even see a mentor in her, their instincts couldn't have been any further apart.

"One chance, Ellie."

Marina had a tough reputation, and Ellie had been subject to her wrath more than once, but in five and a half months, she'd never been this close to the precipice. She'd have to work hard to earn back Marina's trust for now. How lucky she'd been to get a job at the most popular newspaper in the city, and one with a national circulation, in the first place. She couldn't get fired, not when the internet had all but pushed print media out of existence.

"Okay. I understand."

Marina's expression opened up. "Good. Right, read these." She handed Ellie a paper file.

"What are they?"

"Papers about crime levels in Treptower Park."

Ellie opened her notepad, pen poised. At last, something meaty. "We're doing a crime story? Isn't that Benedikt's remit? I don't want to step on his toes."

"This isn't really his bag."

"Oh." She meant this didn't need the big guns. Frustration bubbled just beneath the surface. Just once, Ellie wanted the chance to shine. "What do you need?"

"I need you to link this crime to the immigrant circus. Seven hundred words by Wednesday."

Ellie gulped. "The Treptow Circus?" She was no stranger to the circus. It was situated less than a mile from her parents' apartment. To her, it had always been a story waiting to be told. She just hadn't been expecting to link it to a story on crime. A Wednesday deadline left her less than a week.

"Most of what you need should be in that dossier. If you can get some personal anecdotes, that would give the right emotional tone."

Ellie fidgeted. "Anecdotes about the immigrants' pasts? Little pen pictures of who these new Berliners are?"

Marina's brow furrowed. "Not quite, Ellie. This is a crime story. I want anecdotes of those who've been impacted. *Real* Berliners disgruntled at what is on their doorstep."

Ellie visited the circus regularly. She didn't need to investigate what was on their doorstep. She already knew: a magical world that represented both possibility and tragedy. She could never tell if the performers were happy or sad. She closed her notepad. "*People* are on their doorstep."

"No, crime and poverty are," said Marina. A nerve twitched in her neck.

Ellie chased away the clouds gathering on her face, eager to show willingness, although her resolve to please Marina dissolved with every passing second. How could Marina be so resolutely against the circus? Why the insistence on these specific parameters for the story? Even Marina gave her journalists a little wriggle room.

Unfazed, Marina pushed on. "If we owe loyalty to anyone, it's the locals. They're worried about the alien culture. The strange men and the strange smells, the tearful women who don't look them in the eye."

"So this is about compassion?" Ellie's gut churned.

The oddities of the immigrant circus hadn't alienated her; they had drawn her in. So much so, that Ellie often visited alone, although that might have seemed peculiar to nosy onlookers. She'd take her seat and watch the performers put on masks. They leapt and danced and guided their animals in tricks while the house band transported her to a faraway place, and she slurped a milky pink concoction strewn with nuts called sherbet, common in the lands of the immigrants themselves.

Marina had hit her flow. "Of course this is about compassion. I love this city. Who said this pet project would be a good idea? Aren't you worried about the infiltration of Islam? I can't imagine what the spend must be on the circus. We should send a signal to the Government that they were unwise. Think about where else they could funnel that money. What about funding for online technology, electric cars or building up our art and museum collections? How about investing in cancer cures and amping up our military presence at home and abroad in the fight against terrorism? Or bringing the Olympics to Berlin, expanding our astronaut program or artic exploration? We need to help ourselves before we help others. Besides, it's cruel making animals perform. They have rights."

Could she hear herself, the way she had prioritised things over human lives? Ellie wanted to blurt out in disgust, but she held back. It wouldn't do to poke her boss in the eye so soon after her latest fiasco. Instead, she said merely, "The circus has become part of Berlin." How could any good come of the immigrants feeling unwelcome?

"Only for hippies and liberals." Marina fixed Ellie with a hard-eyed stare. Her pupils glinted like flint. "Don't forget the disgruntled and the fearful, the lost and the angry. They drive our readership. We're a newspaper, not an encyclopaedia. You know how it works."

Ellie was starting to. Her mood hung about her like a gloomy cloud.

Tom rapped on the door, signalling Marina's two o'clock. Editorial had lined up outside the glass door. Marina stood, brisk and dismissive. She pulled on a chic jacket with tapered lapels. "I used to be like you once. So eager to make strides that I cast everyone in the role of enemy or competitor. Don't make me your enemy, Ellie. You've got talent. I'd rather you see me as your mentor."

Ellie didn't respond.

The editorial team filed in, a noisy rabble of jocularity and rustling paper. Ellie took her leave, wondering all the while when the truth had become an alien concept to an award-winning journalist like Marina. Ellie knew there was more to unravel at the circus than just a story of crime. Their untold histories and uncertain futures pulled her into the dusty tent on the hottest summer days, when the city presented her with an array of pleasures but the booming music and colourful fabrics of the circus beckoned.

Ellie's thoughts scattered around her mind like the pieces of a jigsaw waiting to be put together. She couldn't yet decide what was more important: her career, her moral compass, or simply following the truth.

Marina had made one thing abundantly clear: Ellie teetered on thin ice.

5

Although the role of de facto leader of the circus–
due to age, culture and personality–naturally fell to Emir, today
Yusuf stepped into the breach. It often happened this way, an
unremarkable sharing of the burden, normal for this new family of
his. With their blood relations for the most part absent, the circus
family filled the chasm and ministered to each other's suffering.

Most days, Emir wore his responsibility well. It went hand in hand
with being ringmaster: buoying the troops through the sunshine and
rain, here in this land far from their homes. Always benign, Emir had
become the father figure the performers had lost, or the one they had
always wanted. Yusuf loved and respected him for his generosity of
spirit, and for the steadying hand he brought as an older man within a
young troupe. The sight of his tatty top hat around the circus, or the
wiry hair that Leyla transformed into a halo before a show, meant that a
kind word or a keen ear was always within reach.

Emir was integral to the mood of the show. Without his
showmanship, the links between the acts fell flat and the dazzle of
the circus dampened, as did the crowd's reactions. But when his
nerves were frayed, the joyful energy he expended in the ring
transformed into something else entirely: a frenzied angst which in
turn depressed even the most spirited performers. It was then that
Yusuf would gently take the reins.

"It's only a matter of time before they close us down, son," said
Emir, his coarse hair unkempt.

This man was more a father to him than his own had been.
"Don't worry about that. You concentrate on being well for tonight,
and leave the rest to me."

These little disturbances cannot go on.

These past few days, Silberling's voice had stalked Yusuf's dreams. Even so, veiled threats didn't paralyse Yusuf with fear. He understood the disquiet that gathered in Emir like a storm, the setbacks that wreaked havoc with his digestive system and, sometimes, his heart. But Emir was an old man who had fought numerous battles. Why should he have to fight again on the cusp of old age? He shouldn't be here, bereft and separate from all he cared for, with the exception of his beloved Leyla. He should be sitting in a sweets shop in Afghanistan, with his grandchildren playing on the street outside not dead in a ditch.

Yusuf gulped down the rising bile in his throat.

Sometimes the circus morphed from a fantasy world to a bubbling cauldron of grief. The surfacing of one person's pain became a touchpaper for everyone else, a doorway to their own hells. Yusuf's nostrils filled with impossible smells from his last months in Syria: acrid chemicals that stung his throat, rotting corpses and burning bodies. He tasted hunger, the rawness of his stomach lining. He remembered children crying from chemical gas dropped by planes everyone saw but no-one claimed as theirs. Fathers digging sons out of the rubble and clawing sand from their throats. Faces looming, covered in dirt, wet from the sea or from tears. Grief rising like a wave through his body. He fought to keep the ghosts at bay, the faces he loved and would never see again.

It didn't do any good to dwell. In these moments, overwhelmed by the deep well of his grief, he heard his mother's voice again and again. *Do what you must to survive.* He took his pain and fear, and instead of paralysis, he used it as fuel. It galvanised him to do better. If the immigrants did their best to be exceptional, if they were good and followed all the rules, they would be safe. If they were loved, they would be safer still. How better to secure their status in their new home than to put on a show Berlin would never forget?

So he toiled.

Yusuf made a worthy apprentice ringmaster, when Emir required it. The young people gravitated towards him and he possessed the requisite energy and gravitas. In another life, he thought perhaps he might have been a teacher. He wondered sometimes if he was an old man trapped in a twenty-seven-year-old's body. It had taken no time at all for him to learn the expressions of his new family, not when vulnerability stripped away masks, when war had given him a new compass. Maturity had come to him ahead of time, in the arms of grief.

He'd spent the morning with the young circus hands, who too often lost focus and needed a firmer hand. Working with the children gave him renewed purpose. Perhaps he couldn't erase his own troublesome memories, but he could help the children gain confidence and set them on a brighter path. He recognised the need in them for someone like him. He wanted to give them something to live for, someone to depend on. Grief followed an unholy pattern, and untended to, it could spiral out of control. In the girls, more often than not, it unleashed an unbearable sadness; the boys grew angry instead. Dawud and Simeon in particular, thirteen and fourteen years old respectively, had been sparring of late. Tensions had reached a high amongst the boys, perhaps due to boredom or anxiety at the recent microaggressions against the circus. But Yusuf had a plan. He would be a listening ear and a guide, but the children also needed responsibility. It was time for them to graduate from being part of the circus crew to developing their own acts.

In circus life, exposure lead to experience. Merely watching didn't lead to expertise. Tightrope walkers, acrobats, even clowns, all had to start somewhere. Yusuf set a small group of young girls and boys to work spinning plates. He coaxed them to display their skills in a comedic fashion, mixing tricks with deliberate breakages and exaggerated reactions to entertain crowds waiting for the show to begin. The sun warmed their backs as they practiced. Dawud and Simeon looked sullenly at one another at the start of the session, but soon their discord became competitive as the practice plates fell and they experimented pulling faces.

"You'd be better off helping Leyla with the cooking than juggling," said Simeon, pleased at his own progress. He had a smart tongue and even quicker reflexes.

Dawud swivelled and flung plates at Simeon as if they were frisbees. "You've got such a big head, I'm surprised it fits in the tent." Ever the sullen one of the group, Dawud could be hard to reach but sometimes, when the rest of the performers drifted away, he'd tell Yusuf the ghosts of stories about the friends he'd once had.

A practice plate veered out of Dawud's hand in an awry fashion. Golden-haired Mirjam, a mere nine years old, ducked too late and yowled as the plastic disc hit her on the nose.

Yusuf knelt to squeeze the little girl's slight shoulders. "Are you okay, little one?"

She frowned at him.

"Look what you did," said Simeon. He planted two palms on Dawud's chest and shoved hard.

Dawud tripped and fell, but sprang up a moment later, his fists ready to pummel Simeon.

Yusuf separated them. "That's enough, boys. Just when I thought you were doing so well. Dawud, a slip of concentration like that can have big consequences in circus life. You could hurt yourself, a team member or one of the crowd. If that hand been a real plate, Mirjam's nose would be gushing blood right now."

Dawud avoided Yusuf's eyes and dipped his head to his chest.

"Both of you, keep your tempers in check. We're a family." He glared at them, then softened, remembering how easily emotions had flared in his own youth, how he wouldn't have survived without allies and guides. "Right, we'll pick this up later. Go call the others. I need everyone in the tent in ten minutes."

They raced off, in competition with one another once more. Yusuf shook his head. He hadn't been able to penetrate their walls completely yet, but he would. He stooped to collect the discarded equipment. Then he checked the perimeter of the circus tent, using his weight to drive the stakes deeper into the dry ground, as he'd been trained to do in the early days when he'd passed the auditions for Silberling's programme.

A quarter of an hour later, his circus family gathered underneath the big top: Zul, the Clown of Aleppo, who had always known the promise of the circus and who'd not dismissed Silberling out of hand; Najib, the hardest to know of them all, even now tapping a beat with his foot; Old Sayid the maestro, who had vomited on the seas until his body ejected only bile; the twins; burly Osman, who tended to the animals and had lost his sons; Amena, Aya and Aischa, sisters in spirit who had been captured and tortured by Yemeni secret police because of their videos documenting the progress of the Arab Spring; Dawud, Simeon, Mirjam; and two dozen others, who performed, carried out chores, managed the rigging or performed administrative jobs. Yusuf called them to attention with two sharp claps of his hand.

He spoke in a mixture of German and Arabic. That covered the bulk of the refugees from Syria and Afghanistan. Osman spoke Pashto and acted as translator for the Yemenis, where required. Usually, Emir delivered a pep talk, but today the job fell to Yusuf. "Tonight, we are going to excel. We may have had some knocks, but we train hard, we know what we have to lose, and we know how to put on a show. There's no room for lapses of concentration. Dig out your best smiles, every inch of charm. I'll be coming to see each of you individually in training. Get to it. Push hard, but leave something for the big top tonight. I want the tent swept, the seats gleaming, and costumes dazzling. Young ones, with me. I want this city in the palm of our hands."

They dispersed: the ones who had come to this trade, not with circus in their blood but who had learned it, painstakingly, and now understood the allure of this world of make-belief and camaraderie. Broken people plucking pearls of talent from the strings of their DNA and making the impossible possible.

"Roll up, roll up!" Emir's voice boomed through Treptower Park, carried on the wind through the sun-bleached dinosaur models, remnants of failed fairgrounds now consigned to history. "Come, old friends, and new! Our tricks will delight and surprise you, even shock you."

They came, more than Yusuf had anticipated. It relieved him that Emir's free day had reinvigorated his spirits. Esme circled the wooden trestle tables outside, offering tickets, exotic juices and sweet treats for sale. Yusuf headed into the tent, and for a moment it seemed he'd travelled through a portal into a new land. The circus tent gleamed from polish and elbow grease. Man, woman and child had worked their fingers to the bone to provide tonight's spectacle. The ground beneath his feet reverberated with deep bass notes underlying the frisky tune played by Old Sayid's house band. Stars made from delicate silver fabric lined the upper parts of the tent.

Strings of fairy-lights had been strung through the rafters. They twinkled in the dark, blazing just for this brief hour or two when the circus came to life.

Yusuf breathed in the sawdust and scent of popcorn and Eastern treats. From the corner of his eye, he noticed Rex Silberling arrive together with his entourage and slide into his house seat. Knots formed in the pit of Yusuf's stomach. He'd heeded Silberling's warning. They'd worked harder than ever before.

To the left of him, Amena helped a child with pigtails onto a saddle. A stallion kicked at the ground, eager to take the girl around the ring. Osman, an incongruous bald-headed giant atop stilts, zigzag-ed through the arena. At centre stage, the plate-spinners showed off their tricks, dressed in simple tracksuits of shimmering blue. The growing audience tittered at their antics as the young performers feigned disappointment at missed catches, sending ceramic crashing to the floor atop a carefully laid tarpaulin that would be rolled away before the main event. Little Mirjam was the star of the group, throwing her wares up to nearly double her height, dressed in a long-sleeved leotard, ballet shoes and a slick of lipstick. Her importance equalled Emir's; in the circus, there were no hierarchies. Even Eastern masculinity, dominant often in the ancestral homes of the refugees, had been neutralised here, as if the circus tent possessed magic all of its own.

So it began. The oohs and the aahs, and the perilous feats of agility they had first learned under the tutelage of the Chinese State Circus, an exchange of skills orchestrated by the German government that had involved a year's intense, disorienting programme of circus skills and language training when they'd first arrived on German soil. Their bruises and broken bones now came not from war but from performance, from willing rather than inadvertent participation. The lean diet they ate to build strength seemed rich in comparison to what they had become accustomed to. Not one of them would have chosen to return to their blood-soaked ancestral homes.

The crowd involuntarily bobbed in their seats to Najib's beat-boxing. The spotlight widened as the band struck up a Berlin hip-hop beat and Najib jerked into action, delighting the children with handstands and break-dancing, his body at times almost parallel to the ground. Emir conversed with the crowd, a microphone curling from this ear to his mouth. The audience gasped as he juggled batons encased in fire, his hands an effortless blur. At the top of the arc, the fiery batons transformed into colossal icicles, before sparking into fire once more as they neared the round ball of Emir's belly.

"Watch out!" said a boy in the stands, jumping up and down in his seat.

"Don't worry about me. I'm a superhero!" said Emir.

Next followed Esme's doves, which cooed as they pattered up one side of a miniature seesaw and glided down the other. They came to rest on her arms, apart from the naughty one which always preferred her head and charmed the crowd most of all. A little girl in the front row pointed to the dove, and Esme darted over to carefully show off her animal friend, which seemed to coo in the little girl's ear, before Esme exited the ring to a smattering of applause.

Hot on Esme's heels came the stallion and his stablemate, thrilling onlookers by turning on the spot, and disappearing in a mist. When the horses reemerged, they cantered around the ring with Amena, Aya and Aischa riding pyramid on their backs, not a wobble between them. Next, Osman's pygmy goats jumped over fences and wove though slalom poles that rearranged themselves like an enchanted maze, earning cheers. To end their act, the goats sat obediently on stools, crossing their legs as if they were in a Parisian café and not a circus ring. The audience tittered.

Yusuf bloomed with pride at their feats of imagination and strength, such that when his turn came, his fear rescinded into the background, even when he hung upside down like a bat and only his feet held him to the trapeze. The crowd went quiet, as if the merest peep would cause him to fall. Only when he had spun through the air with gut-churning speed and landed on the ground did they clap, and he was glad he'd managed another performance without incidence.

"More, more applause for our resident Spiderman. Who else can fly through the ring like him? Not Zul the Clown, that's for sure," said Emir, adjusting his tatty top hat and revelling in the excitement that fizzed around him.

Zul the Clown tumbled into the ring — he who had once been the Clown of Aleppo, and before that a bookish accountant known for his mild nature and extraordinary number recall. He'd taken to clowning as the war deepened and bookkeeping no longer seemed necessary, when bombs rained down all around. His clowning had brought smiles to children whose childhoods had been stolen. He continued, even when his own family died, until the day orphaned Mirjam took his hand, and asked him to be her friend and take her somewhere far away. So Zul the Clown of Aleppo became Zul of the immigrant circus, and he was cheered by the joy he brought to others, and Mirjam filled a place in his heart that might have grown cold and hard after the death of his son had she not been there.

Tonight, he arrived in the ring dressed in an evening gown and clown shoes, a faint smile on his lips, drawing attention with his stillness. His lips and eyebrows had been painted a stark white, and bright rouge adorned his cheeks. He'd mastered his art of connecting to the audience through mime. He clowned through language barriers and won fans in seconds, whichever routine he attempted. This evening, he poked a hairy leg through a split in the dress and cocked an eyebrow, his miming exquisite. Every time an eyebrow rose, his dress changed colour: first moss green, then coral pink, olive, and petrol blue. Zul looked down, surprised at his costume, at the cinch of the fabric across his narrow hips, and the cut of his neckline. The audience roared with laughter.

Next, Zul's face became hypermobile, his energy boundless. He waved at the children.

They waved back.

"Bobobeebimboop," he said, swinging his arm in a great arc and cupping a hand to his ear.

The children caught on quicker than the adults. "Bobobeebimboop," they said, beaming.

Zul's bulbous nose grew bigger still. He looked cross-eyed at the crimson red splotch as he stumbled and tottered across the ring in his enormous shoes, causing children to erupt into fits of laughter. After a few moments, Esme appeared, ethereal in a sea-green shift dress and matching headscarf. Zul preened in his dress and attempted to mimic Esme's allure, failing disastrously. He leant forward for a kiss and fell flat on his face. He followed her around the ring, emulating the sway of her lips and tripped in his shoes. He shook his bosom and looked disappointed to find nothing there.

Then he stopped short.

His surprised drawn on eyebrows followed the progression of something beyond the crowd on the outer rim of the tent. Old Sayid the maestro noticed his hesitation. He waited for a long moment for Zul to resume. When he didn't, Old Sayid started up the swinging beat of the band, cutting short the wheelbarrow farce Zul had intended to close his act with.

Yusuf frowned, a sense of foreboding deep in the pit of his stomach. The whole troupe had worked so hard for tonight's show. There could be no question of failing; he would hold the threads together, no matter what it took. He darted forward in the direction of Zul's gaze.

A scuffle at the eastern perimeter of the tent.

Two faces twisted in anger.

With a thud, Yusuf recognised the sparkling tracksuits and clumsily gelled hair. Simeon and Dawud brawled, oblivious to the commotion they caused, anger transcending any sense of shame or decency. They pushed hard, alphas vying for ascendency, though they were only boys and should have been in their mother's arms, in bed, or at school, anywhere but here. They fought, behind the turned backs of the audience, who strained to see what new marvel would be presented in the ring.

Please! Don't jeopardise what we have built here.

Keep up the pretence that we are whole, that we can be good.

Yusuf's lungs pumped as he ran, and he wondered whether Silberling was already tracking him, judging them all, not on their merits but on their value to him.

Thirty seconds and Yusuf would reach them.

Please, boys, don't do anything stupid.

Nearly there. He'd take them outside for some air, then they'd come back for the finale and forget all about this tussle. Tomorrow, he'd find a way to show them they weren't alone.

His heart lurched.

Something glinted in Dawud's hand: white, an irregular shape held between his fingers, gleaming against the velvet innards of the circus tent.

A thrusting motion.

"No!" Was that his own voice or someone else's?

The blood drained from Yusuf's face. He ran towards the boys with futures blackened by tragedy.

6

Yusuf ran as fear snaked through him.

Let them be okay, he thought as he neared the boys.

In the arena, Zul the clown started up his farce accompanied by laughter.

Yusuf fell to his knees in the dirt behind the stands. Simeon lay in a heap on the floor, his legs crumpled as if he were a mannequin, not flesh and bone. A long shard of ceramic lay buried in the boy's chest, and a red flower bloomed across his tracksuit. His warm blood pooled on the ground in lumps as he bled into the sawdust. Yusuf's heart hammered against his ribs. He searched for a pulse in Simeon's slack wrist, not really knowing what to look for. He shuddered. He'd been certain that any discord between the boys had been buried that morning. What could have happened? He should have realised not to leave them alone together.

Simeon moaned beneath him.

Think, man.

Above him stood Dawud, perspiration dotting his skin, his anger spent. "I didn't mean it, I swear," he said. The words tumbled out, a shrill defence of the unforgivable.

Yusuf glanced up, throwing out sharp words in fury. "You fool."

Dawud stumbled back, and Yusuf blocked him out. Simeon had to be his first priority.

A woman with ginger hair and a spray of freckles crouched down beside him. Vibrant green eyes radiated concern. This wasn't a tourist; she looked German. "He needs an ambulance."

"Can you?" said Yusuf, looking around for something to stem the blood flow.

"Right away." She leapt up, clumsy in her boots, fumbling for her phone as she went.

Aischa appeared behind him. She thrust a scarf into his hands, moon eyes wide with panic. "Here."

Yusuf took the scarf, pressed it against Simeon's wound. The boy's nut-brown eyes rolled in his head. Fourteen was no age. *Please let him be okay.*

A handful of spectators closest to the commotion twisted in their seats, half-standing, mouths aghast as if they had never seen its like before. Then all at once, performers formed a circle around them, using their bodies to protect the boys from prying eyes. Here were Amena, Aya and burly Osman, grief etched into the lines of his face. They looked on, as helpless as he. What now? Yusuf's own panic surfaced. He pushed the blackness aside and focussed on the Simeon's face. He felt again for a pulse, like he'd seen on the dubbed American detective shows Doris watched. The ones that pretended justice always won out.

Nothing.

His mind flashed back to another time in the dust, dust all around, his broken brother in his arms. A roar gathered in his mind, a whooshing he couldn't escape.

Simeon coughed.

Relief flooded Yusuf and the swell of fear subsided, although it lurked still, black and uncompromising at the edge of his sanity.

The German woman came back and touched his shoulder. "The ambulance is on its way."

"Thanks." Yusuf motioned to Aischa to continue applying pressure to Simeon's wound. Blood, as dark as a beetle's shell, had stained her scarf black.

She fulfilled her duty with solemn diligence, hands trembling.

"We should call the police," said Osman in his deep baritone.

"First Simeon. Then we deal with Dawud."

Dawud shied away and crouched in a ball next to the popcorn stand. He vomited into the sand, great heaving ejections of bile and tears. He stood alone; his crime had rendered him friendless. If only he'd used words or his fists. Anything but a weapon.

Yusuf beckoned Amena closer. His mind whirred. "Tell Emir to close the show. Any reason–it doesn't matter–just not the truth. Send the crowd out from the front."

She rushed away, her long hair swinging in a ponytail.

Despair tightened Yusuf's chest. The glittering edge at his neck itched. How could he protect them now, these boys adrift in a strange land without their parents and aunts and uncles, without their siblings and friends? Boys, more lost than even he. It hadn't even been a year since Simeon had fled Yemen. The boy had escaped a war that had left the country in the grip of cholera and on the brink of famine. To die here, not of old age but of a stab wound, was cruel.

Where was the ambulance?

Yusuf pushed away the thought that emergency services responded with less urgency for a refugee boy than they would for native Germans. The world couldn't be so bleak. "Osman, stand by the entrance to direct the ambulance crew. No one else comes in that way."

Osman dragged Dawud to his feet and took him outside to await the ambulance. He pressed the boy into his rugged chest and held the sobbing child fast. Beside them, the heavy velvet-lined tarpaulin gaped open and Yusuf imagined Simeon's soul passing through.

The house band stuttered to a halt. "Ladies and gentleman–" Emir's voice filled the tent. "This evening's performance must now come to an end." A cry of disappointment washed over them. Emir continued, soothing, jovial, apologetic. Old Sayid instructed the band to strike up a never-ending merry loop at odds with the dying boy, and the crowd dispersed.

"I want my mother," said Simeon in his native tongue, his pallor a sickly hue, his eyes glazed.

The German woman knelt next to him, stroking his hair, talking to him all the while, though she didn't understand his words nor he hers.

"Be strong, Simeon," said Yusuf.

He willed Death to stay away. Just this once. As if prayers had ever worked before. Who had failed these boys? The country they had fled, their dead or absent parents, the country they had made their home, or the makeshift family that had come together around them like a car cobbled together from old parts? Would Silberling punish them for what happened tonight?

The circus tent emptied, and the last remnants of magic of the night fled. One by one, the performers learned of Simeon's plight. They gathered around him, a circle of love, while Aischa and the German woman tended to him. Eventually, in came Osman through the curtains, a sombre giant, his arms wrapped around Dawud. They led the ambulance crew to Simeon. The medics pierced the circle, stern faces dressed in red, the colour of death and danger. They moved aside the kneeling women and began work, calm and methodical, asking questions all the while, attempting to undo the damage Dawud had caused.

The spectacle was over.

Yusuf slipped away through the rain, past the waiting ambulance with its flashing light and the silhouette of Silberling behind the darkened glass of his car. He braced himself against the wind, pushed on past swaying trees to the tiny, lightless box he called home, and wept.

Yusuf awoke naked in his bed. His costume lay in a ball on the cold floor beside him, still caked with Simeon's blood.

Simeon.

He rolled out of bed, grabbing a threadbare towel for his hips and shower gel that smelt of Western men to him, as if certain scents indicated a higher civilisation.

He was thankful for the meagre apartments provided to the immigrant circus by the German state. They curved in a semi-circle around the big top, more akin to battlements than a home. Last night, the apartments had rocked with the high winds, as if they were boats on the ocean. Erected as hastily as the circus tent, they had no foundations to speak of. A safe haven, but perhaps also a reminder of their precarious situation as immigrants. None of them had papers yet; their status could be rescinded at any time. Still, immigrants were a grateful sort of people. Who ran from the arms of untold horrors and demanded more than a hovel to recover?

The block was comprised of little more than a series of interconnecting cubes arranged on one level beneath a canopy of trees. It had been stacked in three rows. Single occupants lived in the smallest cubes at the front of the building, with space for a bed, a chair and a light. Next came larger cubes for pairs: lovers, siblings or friends. Often the loneliness became so unbearable that even strangers decided to share a bed. The largest cubes comprised the rear of the building, reserved for families of three or more. Rarely did families survive the journey to Europe intact, and so the large units stood empty as a reminder of loss or as communal spaces to unwind, pray or dine together, as if they could erase the memories of the families left behind.

Yusuf sighed as he trod wearily along the slim corridors, making out voices every now and then through the paltry wall divisions. Some doors he passed had been decorated with pictures or dried wreaths, others painted a bold colour in defiance of the rules.

He washed and scrubbed himself clean in the communal showers, before rinsing his costume and wringing it out. Simeon's blood disappeared down the drain, pink and diluted. Then he fastened the damp towel around his waist and hung his costume over the shower railing before padding to the far corner of the dwelling where Doris Kaun, the only German in residence, lived. Her door stood ajar, but he knocked anyway.

"*Herein.*" She smiled gently, and put down her tea on the worktop.

"You young men, so proud of your bodies that you forget to clothe yourselves. You should have seen me in my heyday." She hugged him briefly. Her silver hair brushed his chin. "Sit. The kettle's already on–I'll make you some tea. You must still be in shock."

"How is Simeon? Have you heard?"

The kettle whistled. "He's not out of the woods yet, but he is young and you did well to apply pressure to the wound. The doctors think there is every chance he'll live."

Yusuf slouched with relief, as if worry had pulled him taut. "And Dawud?"

Doris poured out the boiling water onto a peppermint teabag and pushed the steaming mug towards him. Her voice cracked with age. "I vouched for him. I've emphasised the trauma in his past but his future here hangs in the balance."

It was Doris's job to help the refugees settle in, to be their listening ear. Talks with her had been instrumental in improving Yusuf's grasp of German, and in helping the performers feel anchored to their new home. She coordinated their integration lessons in the German language and law and culture, provided information on voluntary initiatives such as Kreuzberger Himmel which had sprung up in response to the surge in refugees in the city, and offered a hand of friendship. In exchange for her efforts, Doris received food and board. Widowed, with fiercely liberal instincts and her children grown, the job suited her.

The toilet flushed, and the bathroom tap sloshed. Yusuf spun in his chair.

"Sorry, I should have said I have a visitor," said Doris.

Yusuf hadn't even noticed she had poured out two cups of tea in addition to her own. The door opened and a woman entered the living room. He shuffled in his chair and rearranged his towel, suddenly feeling self-conscious about his state of undress. The woman tucked a strand of her long ginger hair behind her ear as she approached them in her clunky boots.

He froze. "You."

Doris looked from one to the other. "Of course, you met each other last night. Yusuf, this is Ellie from the *Berliner Allgemeine Zeitung*."

"Ellie Richter. Nice to meet you." She held out her hand to shake his, unfazed by his nakedness.

Heat rose to Yusuf's cheeks as he grasped her hand in his. He frowned. "You're a journalist?"

Her eyes sparked with intelligence. "You're an acrobat."

He smiled. "Thanks for yesterday. For calling the ambulance for Simeon, for staying with him."

"I hope he's going to be okay," said Ellie. She turned to Doris. "Maybe I won't stay for the tea after all. There's a lot going on right now for you all."

"If you're sure?" said Doris.

"Certain. Thank you." Ellie swung her satchel over her shoulder and closed the door behind her.

Yusuf raised his eyebrows. There was little point in speaking to journalists. Too often they already knew what they wanted to hear. "What's she doing here?"

"She's doing a story on the circus. She wanted some background information, that's all, and to speak to some of you."

A frisson of fear embedded itself in Yusuf's belly. He'd learned over the years to ignore his instincts at his peril. Basking in attention during a performance made sense to him: he could control that environment. Nothing good, however, could come of increased media attention on refugees. The narratives they endured always came slicked in negativity. The best way to be happy in a new land was to fly under the radar. "That's why she was there yesterday?"

Doris nodded. "It's not a great time for media attention, but who knows? Maybe some good will come of it. Bigger audiences, more understanding. Silberling's ever ready to stick the boot in when once, he would have leapt to the circus' defence. He's a slippery eel, that one. I'm sure he's realised the election will be here in the blink of an eye."

"Will he make things difficult for Dawud?"

"I don't know. The department is investigating. Simeon refused to talk to the police." Doris placed a calloused palm on his hand.

Yusuf's sadness crashed over him like a wave. "Dawud needs us. They can't send him back. He won't make it. I can't let that journalist stir up trouble."

"It's going to be okay." Doris reached out for him, pulling him into a hug, but Yusuf remained stiff, a husk that love couldn't penetrate.

Syria might just be a memory for him now, but his experiences had forever honed his senses. Yusuf could sense danger out on the streets of Berlin by the prickle on his skin, the guarded looks of strangers, and the way men bristled and women crossed the road. Try as he might to plant his roots in Berlin, it could never be home. Not while his kinked hair, brown skin and foreign accent marked him out as different. While the refugees performed on stage like monkeys to the script assigned to them.

Monsters lurked beneath the veneer of progress in this city. Ghosts accompanied him when he passed old buildings. The crumbling stone and creaking wood in Berlin shuddered with the weight of the past, when millions of ordinary people had met a brutal end simply because they suddenly didn't belong.

And still, the world turned.

7

Ellie pulled Doris's door shut, and listened to the muffled voices inside for a moment. Her heart skipped faster, remembering Yusuf's athletic physique, the towel slung low on his hips. Hadn't it been Yusuf she'd seen outside Berliner Dom, wearing his solitude like a comfortable old coat? How many times had she seen him perform at the circus, at great heights, without taking in his chiselled face, the sadness in his grey eyes?

What a story had landed in her lap. She couldn't be sure if her own affinity for the circus would help or hinder. Her parents lived a stone's throw from Treptower Park and she knew this space like the back of her hand.

On paper, the location for the immigrant circus couldn't have been more perfect. She'd heard her father tell the land's history many times. Before the fall of the Berlin Wall, this part of the city had been the home of an amusement park sponsored by the East German state. After reunification, the land fell into private hands, and was abandoned to the elements after its owner was caught smuggling a haul of cocaine into Germany in the masts of a Flying Carpet ride.

The circus had sprung up almost overnight a few years back, as if it had materialised from a tear in the sky. Treptower Park's colossal Soviet War Memorial stood on the same grounds, a shrine to men lost in the Second World War, its focal point a soldier, sword in hand, a child in his arms and a broken swastika at his feet. The placement of the circus nearby sent a powerful anti-fascist message. Had the state's flagship integration project really failed? It made the story even more juicy.

Marina would be thrilled if Ellie turned in an eye witness account of the violence between Dawud and Simeon, set against the drama of the circus in motion. This story wouldn't fade into the reams of other information that seeped into the world each day. It would stand out nationally and cement her position at *Berliner Allgemeine Zeitung*.

Still, Marina's lack of nuance as an editor irked Ellie. How could anyone fail to pity Simeon and the path that had led him here? How could she turn her back on the haunting sadness in the performers' eyes? Last night had convinced Ellie that the human story of the circus deserved to be excavated. Perhaps she'd stumbled across an opportunity to showcase some compassionate, complex journalism. She longed to be more than Marina's blunt tool.

To that end, she tossed out Marina's idea of pen pictures of crime victims, and devised a three-prong approach to form the basis of her story: the papers Marina had given her; interviews with circus performers; and, possibly most interestingly, a visit to a local Imam about his community outreach work. Perhaps her curiosity about the real story here would even earn her brownie points with Marina.

She strode down the hallway in her boots, rummaging in her bag for her list of interviewees and their flat numbers. The walls rattled as she walked. With steel beneath her warm exterior, Doris had refused her permission to speak with Dawud and Simeon, and the ringmaster Emir had been unwell. Instead, she had offered to arrange other interviews. After few false starts, Ellie found flat 23, where Osman Malik resided. She rapped her knuckles against the door. The door opened a notch, and through the gap came a pink nose, which Ellie thought at first belonged to a dog, until the accompanying bleat informed her otherwise.

She jumped back. "What on earth?"

A broad, hairy hand reached through the gap and pulled back the creature. "Sorry. They won't hurt you."

They?

The man swung the door wider and the stench of excrement and unwashed flesh hit her. Ellie peeked past the man's considerable girth to where three small goats lay sprawled on blankets. The fourth reached past the man again to prod her hand with a cold pink nose.

The man laughed. "She thinks you may have brought her some food."

"I have cheese sandwiches for my lunch."

"Hold onto them for dear life." The shadows underneath the man's eyes betrayed his tiredness. He waved his broad hands with a flourish. "Please, come in to my humble abode. Doris asked me to tell you a bit about myself."

"I'd appreciate it, Herr Malik."

He puffed out his chest at the mark of respect, and Ellie warmed to him, despite the stink, the skittish goats and confined space. Who was she to judge? Maybe those subject to the worst twists of fate made the best humans; bad luck eliminated the pride that made men brutes.

Inside, Osman's room measured perhaps three metres squared. There were no windows, and only a single lamp hung from the ceiling. A slim bed occupied one corner of the room, and Ellie struggled to imagine Osman in it. She'd grown accustomed to seeing him balance his giant body on thin stilts. Here, he seemed a caged animal. On the wall hung a small, stained tapestry in bright blues and yellows.

He caught Ellie appraising it. "A gift from my wife."

"It's beautiful."

Ellie perched on a lonely chair in the room, placed furthest away from the goats. One clanked its teeth against a drum filled with water.

Osman motioned to the animals. The cadences of her mother tongue were unrecognisable when he spoke it, as if he had invented a hodgepodge language all of his own. "Are you scared of them?"

"I've seen them at the circus. I didn't expect them to be here. Frau Kaun, the warden, allows this?"

He flashed a mischievous grin. "As long as they behave. They have their own barn but it comforts me to have them with me."

"Last night must have been difficult for you."

Osman splayed his hands. "We are family."

"How about your own family? I can record?"

He bobbed his head.

She pressed record on her phone and placed her notepad with her prompts on her knees. Being prepared made her more confident.

Osman drifted off, occupying a space and time thousands of miles away. "My wife died when the boys were young."

"Are your children here with you?"

"Amar is 23. Bilal is 19. Bilal is stronger than his brother. The muscles on that boy! He helped his brother after the waves rocked the dinghy. I could see their heads, but it was chaotic. I lost sight of them."

Ellie's breath caught in her throat. "I'm sorry."

"Don't be. Bilal would never have left his brother behind." A ghost of a smile passed his lips, and he rubbed his bald head. "They'd be telling me now, 'Papa, your home stinks. What would Maa say?' I always say, when my boys return, the goats will go back to the barn."

The happy ending hung between them, and both knew it was impossible Osman's sons would return. "You're from the Middle-East?"

"From Yemen. At first, I was stubborn. Who would want to leave their home? We slept underneath furniture in case of an air strike. Then our neighbour's house disappeared overnight. All that was left was a hole in the ground. That night, we escaped with what we could carry, and took shelter underground. Still the bombs fell and the bullets whizzed." His voice broke, and he seemed to shrivel in size. One goat snuck close to its master where he slumped on the bed. Osman twirled his fingers in its coat. "I needed to keep my boys safe. They are all that is left of my wife and me. We moved three times. The fighting and the cholera got worse. How could I protect my family? What could I feed them? And so we came. To start a new life. Even before we made the journey we were swindled, time and again. I would pay smugglers with what little I had, and there were promises, but the men would never return. We began to lose faith. And then, a man came and told us to be ready. I hid my fear from my sons. I knew how dangerous the journey would be. We'd heard stories of boats sinking, of families freezing to death trying to cross borders. But what choice did I have? Now, there is only one mouth to feed."

Ellie willed herself not to cry. Osman's tragedy was so great that it seemed selfish to make it her own. "What was your trade in Yemen?"

"A butcher. These days, we barely eat meat. It's unhalal and expensive–unless it's pork." He laughed. "The Germans and their sausages."

"Good old stereotypes." She smiled. "Don't forget the cabbage. And this new life in Berlin, how do you find it?"

Osman's face clouded and he bit his lip, revealing teeth blackened from tobacco or lack of care. He shrugged. "We are safe, but it isn't home. People like me are not important creatures."

Ellie leaned forward, forgetting the goats. "Why do you say that? Hasn't the government made you feel welcome? Haven't the people been considerate?"

"In my country, we bring food to new arrivals. We welcome them into the community. We don't take no for an answer. If they are quiet, we talk until they begin to talk themselves. It is love."

"And what have you found here?"

He shrugged. "At first, I couldn't speak the language." He'd not yet mastered the rhythms, the hard consonants, and he chose each word with care. "I can communicate adequately now but my native accent sticks. We do not share the same linguistic roots, or even alphabet. Speaking to Germans can be daunting. I worry they will be impatient with me."

"I think mostly they would appreciate how hard you've worked to learn the language."

"Perhaps. I think my appearance makes it harder." He gestured to his large frame. "I'm a big man. It's hard to forget my presence, even when some people would rather not see me. It would be better to blend in. It would be easier."

Ellie resisted the urge to negate his experiences because they made her uncomfortable. She wanted to convince him this city could be a utopia, somewhere for him to realise the dreams that had been stolen from him in the land of his birth. But how could you start anew after losing your wife and children? So instead, all she said was, "I see."

"Do you? I look at you, and I see a chance my children never had, just because they happened to be born elsewhere. I wonder what they could have been. I'd give anything to hold them once more." He sank his head into his arms.

He hadn't even had a chance to say goodbye to his boys. She remembered being nineteen, with life stretching out in front of her. She had felt bullet-proof. How unfair for his sons to have faced their mortality so soon.

Osman wept, loudly, unapologetically, and the goats flocked to him.

What comfort could Ellie offer him? As she left, she laid a hand on his shoulder, and two stories took shape in the folds of her mind: one a story of misfits, grief and happenstance; the second a story of the other, of crime and recriminations.

8

In the weeks that Yusuf considered leaving Syria, he escaped his family home, where pictures of his brother adorned the walls. The war had worsened. He slumped at the roadside, searching for a map to his future, the dust from mortar and shells clawing at his lungs. Smugglers crawled out from every crack, searching for ways in which to line their coffers, mining tragedy and dreams as currency. He had stashed away most of the required money to pay the smugglers. The remainder could be borrowed. But how could he abandon his family, and if he did, where would he go?

He wouldn't be the first to flee.

Friends had made the journey across borders and continents before him. Yusuf couldn't be sure how their stories had ended, but he'd listened to their deliberations about where to seek asylum from the horrors of war. Only the foolish and naive set their sights on Turkey as an end destination. There, civil society deteriorated, and refugees could be certain of an inhospitable government, squalid conditions and empty bellies.

His childhood friend Hamid had said as much. "$1,500 to cross the border to Turkey, and for what? I'd rather die in the sea trying to reach other shores than die in Turkey, starving and without a chance. I'll go to Denmark, and when I have the right to remain, I can call my parents to join me." Hamid's brown eyes sparked with fierce determination, but when he left to meet the smugglers, he quivered like a boy half his age, and Yusuf knew his decision had been far from easy.

Western Europe shone like a mirage for those willing to inch further across the globe. Austria, Holland, Sweden, Norway, and Denmark had all been possibilities, but for Yusuf, Germany topped the list. There, refugees waited only three months for a permit to work. He wanted to be a teacher, and Germany's free university studies and low unemployment made that a possibility, not to mention its growing economy and protection of human rights. Who wouldn't want assurances they would be treated with dignity after all they had endured?

He'd even heard stories of how some citizens greeted refugees with applause when they arrived on German soil. But that was before the assaults in Cologne and the Christmas Market attack in Berlin, as well as the countless flares of violence that had occurred in Europe, where once citizens had assumed they'd been so safe.

So he'd travelled to Europe in an unholy stop-start relay of dank flats, dark lorries, and a sea journey that made him rue the day he had left Syria. His story was not unusual. He closed his eyes and sank into the flickering memories that tracked across the nebulous pink inside his eyelids: stinking bodies huddled together in the dark, reeking piss pots in the corners of rooms, lumps of valuables strapped underneath clothing, and the ever-present threat of violence and rape. They had no choice but to trust strangers. Even sleeping grew difficult, without allies to watch over you.

He met corruption at every turn amongst the smugglers. Some slunk away in the night with his money. Others made promises and never returned. Men with dollar signs in their eyes and masks they wore away from their own families. Such men could be found within border control and the police too, of the countries through which Yusuf sought passage. The journey aged him, and his dreams retreated beyond his grasp.

When he finally reached Berlin and found himself squeezed into the open cubicles in the temporary refugee camp at Tempelhof airfield with thousands of others, he couldn't imagine focusing on study. His mind raged like a choppy ocean. He needed time to recoup, to find his feet in this new land. Eventually, word reached him from an asylum officer of auditions for the Treptow Circus project. It seemed like the answer to his prayers: a home to call his own, a purpose, and a way to form bonds with others like him, who had a chance of a permanent home in Germany. The physical rigour of circus training suited him more than intellectual vigour.

He'd been right to come to Germany after all.

Gratitude didn't thread its way into the hearts of all the circus refugees; a few carried a sense of entitlement that Yusuf struggled to understand, which caused uncomfortable clashes in the common room at the residences.

At lunch that afternoon, many of the performers broke from practice and preparations inside the tent to eat together, speaking in huddles about what had occurred between Simeon and Dawud the night before. The room, large enough to accommodate fifty people at once, benefitted from large windows that made it bright and airy, unlike the bedrooms. It served as a space to eat and relax. At one end of the room, eight pock-marked tables stood in a long line, adorned with an odd sequinned runner Leyla the cook had found at a Berlin flea market. An assortment of chairs had been neatly tucked in. The other end of the room contained floor cushions in olive green on a floral rug, and a large L-shaped sofa in grey velvet. Posters of key words and tenses in German dotted the walls, as visual aids for the integration classes that took place there three times a week, encompassing German language, culture and law.

Yusuf lay on the floor, a towel hooked around his left foot, his leg perpendicular to his body as he stretched out his calf. He and Zul had been speaking in hushed tones when a ruckus erupted at the buffet.

He looked up and sighed to find Najib hovering over a tray of food he'd deliberately knocked to the floor, judging by the stance of his body, legs wide apart, arm hovering in the air, his expression uncompromising. With Emir nowhere to be seen, it fell to Yusuf to smooth things over. He heaved himself up, and made his way over to Najib, taking care not to tread in the chutneys, cheese and grilled chicken he'd pushed over.

Leyla, wife of Emir, hurried to clear up the mess, her great bosom heaving as she crouched on the floor with a washcloth.

"That was unkind," said Yusuf, using a napkin to scoop a mound of food off the floor. "Leyla spent time cooking this for us. What's wrong, brother?"

"Always the same food here. Who isn't fed up?" said Najib with a scowl.

"Something is bothering you." Yusuf placed a hand on Najib's shoulder but Najib shook it off.

"Like you care."

"Of course I care. We are family here," said Yusuf, although Najib happened to be his least favourite person in the circus, and he'd learned to be wary at the prickles that often arose from nowhere.

"I was by the television tower on Alexanderplatz this morning. Do you know how much money those living statues make when they just stand there all day? I had a bowl out, and a sign asking for money. I can't live on what we earn here. A man gave me Monopoly money–the cheek of it!" His nostrils flared, and he dug in his pocket for a clutch of small, brightly coloured notes, before making a show of tearing them in half.

Yusuf rolled his eyes. Beneath them, Leyla picked up the discarded food, and Najib still knew no shame. "Why can't you just be grateful for the chance we have here? We have enough to be happy."

Najib stiffened in anger.

Sensing trouble, Zul approached. "How many times have we asked you not to beg? I'd report you if it wouldn't harm us all by association."

"Pah," said Najib. "My family lived like kings in Syria. We lost everything. Why should I be a pauper now?"

He rubbed his hand over the stubble that sprung up on his face despite his daily shaving. The beard and well-developed muscles, together with his lack of youthful innocence, had given rise to rumours that he was significantly older than the seventeen years old he'd proclaimed himself to be when he crossed the border into Germany. Without him, the residences would be more peaceful, but he had passed the circus auditions with flying colours as a result of his dancing and musical talents.

"Our monthly allowance is more generous than in other receiving countries. I'm grateful for what we have," said Yusuf.

Leyla finished cleaning up, and stood heavily, addressing Najib. "Son, one day you will learn that what you earn in this life is never yours to keep. We can take nothing to our graves."

Najib shrugged. "You are closer to your grave than I am to mine."

"That's enough!" said Yusuf.

Leyla blinked back tears. Zul placed his arm around her shoulders.

Yusuf ached for her. Feeding the circus could be a thankless task, but while Leyla might not receive the applause of the crowds, her role remained integral to the refugees' wellbeing. She managed their food budget skilfully, weaving in the odd culinary surprise to their weekly menus, with never an unkind word, despite the monotony of her task. Her selfless, sunny personality contrasted with Najib's, who sowed discord wherever he stepped.

Leyla was right. They were, after all, the lucky ones. How many more had perished at home or at sea? How many people reached safer shores only to be turned away? Yusuf couldn't understand Najib's nature, how he insisted he deserved more, how he made waves and rocked the peace of their new home, never once being perceptive enough to read the dismay that his presence caused to those eager to make the most of their opportunity. Even Yusuf, who might have bonded with Najib, given their shared history as Syrians, found himself avoiding close interaction with him whenever possible.

"You overstep the line," said Yusuf. "She doesn't deserve that."

"Who are you to school me when you let Dawud get away with what he did?" said Najib.

Yusuf shook his head. "I'm not protecting him. I told Doris what happened."

"And yet you and Emir refuse to let me tell the police what I saw."

"If Simeon doesn't want to tell the police who is responsible, we can't take that choice away from him. And maybe Simeon is right. Dawud's just a child. You've seen him. He's sick with regret. He's learned his lesson."

"Can't you see your double standards? You're angry at me and yet you all protect him."

Yusuf sighed. They needed to come together as a community if they were to heal from last night. Instead, even more fault-lines materialised. By now their conversation had drawn eyes from across the room, and he had no idea how to diffuse the situation.

"Come now, let's pray together," said Leyla, looking up from the crook of Zul's arm. "People who eat together and pray together, stay together."

"You don't understand. Why should we play fair by the system?" said Najib, wringing his hands together, imploring them to understand, to not cast him in the role of the black sheep. "I fought as hard to be here as you all. The system is rigged. Just look at France. You need to be a superhero, to actually scale buildings like Spiderman, to gain citizenship. Maybe I would be better at following the rules if I thought we had a real chance of being granted permission to stay."

"Maybe it's the other way around. Maybe by breaking the rules, you are the one that is going to close the coffin on this opportunity," said Zul, thumbing his nose at Najib. "You want everything for nothing."

Najib clenched and unclenched his fists, leaving small red welts on his palms where his nails pressed into his skin. "Why should I apologise for wanting more for myself? Why should immigrants be made to feel lesser people just because they want to live better lives? Why shouldn't we be able to go and stay wherever we want to?"

Doris walked into their midsts, bringing with her an aura of calm. "Dearest Najib, I understand you're angry, I really do. Life is not fair, but believe me, the German state isn't perfect, but it is doing as much as it can."

Najib spun around to face her. "This is our common room, Doris. You shouldn't sneak up on us."

"Leave her alone," said Yusuf. "She's just doing her job."

"I came here to check on you all after what happened last night," said Doris.

Najib ignored her and directed his venom at Yusuf. "Doesn't the global order ever frustrate you? How the Europeans and the Americans always assert dominance over the rest of us?"

"I can't say I've ever thought about it," said Yusuf.

The lie left a bitterness in his mouth, but what good did it do to challenge centuries old dominance? It was the way of the world for some to be born with a silver spoon in their mouths and others to suffer. He didn't think it fair, but then Najib would complain about the sun and the moon if he could.

"I'm not stupid. I know we all get dealt different cards in life. The question is, how are you going to play yours?" said Najib. "People like you always toe the line. You're too scared to step beyond it, but you'll see, you'll end up in the mud like the rest of us."

9

Rex considered his greatest strength to be his ability to lock away his emotions and get the job done. For that reason, on the night of the stabbing while he awaited news of the boy's fate, the political serendipity of the incident didn't pass him by. Not that he wished the boy harm. Rather, Rex's vanity didn't allow for him to be painted as the bad guy, and the night's ills reassured him he acted with good judgement in his plan to close the circus.

He spent the day working on matters of state, with Jessy slumbering by his side, looking at worrying anti-Semitism trends and agreeing to increase police presence at the nation's synagogues. Corinne brought him up to speed on cyber threats from foreign agents, and he chaired a round-table of key people combatting terrorism. He loved the variety of his job on a daily, even hourly basis; he loved the importance it attached to him. The responsibility might be great, but he'd been born for a role like this. His parents, his teachers, even his wife had told him so, not that he'd needed to hear it. Ambition was threaded through every cell in his body.

In the late afternoon, when the dog grew impatient and needed to empty her bladder, he whistled to her, slipped his jacket on, and said his goodbyes to Corinne.

"Minister, are you sure it's wise for you to undertake this meeting? Should I not go in your stead?"

Corinne had been with him since the early days of his political ascent, and though her salary paled in comparison to his, there was no one whose judgement he trusted more. Still, he couldn't send her in his place, not into a possibly volatile situation. He owed her more than that. Besides, controlling all the pieces was his forte. His instincts told him that his political survival depended on how he handled the growing rumbles of xenophobia, and he needed to assess for himself whether each pawn in his plan functioned as it was supposed to.

"It's a few words, Corinne. If I'm accused of anything untoward, then I'll say I was walking Jessy. Besides, when do you ever leave here before ten? Go home, for once."

"In that case, this is where I've asked him to meet you," she pointed to a red x drawn onto a map. "It's not covered by cameras, and off the usual tourist route. Are you sure you don't want me to call your driver round?"

The fewer witnesses to this meeting, the better. Corinne's file had provided him with all the ammunition he needed. "No, you can dismiss him for the day. Best keep this between just the two of us."

He walked from his office in the Interior Ministry to the hollowed out spot of Tiergarten not far from the Holocaust Memorial. The sky hung in silver threads above them, strewn with puffs of candy-floss. Soon, the sun would set, and the tourists that milled around the tombstones of the memorial would disperse. Beside him, Jessy trotted happily, her long tail wagging as she went. Weimaraners had originally been bred as gun dogs for aristocrats, and even now as Jessy walked beside him, noble in gait, full of purpose, it struck him how suited they were to one another.

Situated a short walk away from the Reichstag and the Brandenburg Gate, the Holocaust Memorial was startlingly visible. Up close, the sheer mass of stone and voids created by the pillared grid stood as a testament to the six million Jews murdered by the Nazis. Ironic then to be on his way to meet a far right extremist, and a Holocaust denier at that.

Rex shook his head. To not use your intellect constituted a high crime. What drove men to refute naked truths, however horrifying or unpalatable they might be? How could they possibly surmise that the Third Reich only sought to deport Jews when a deluge of historical evidence spoke otherwise? How could school children visit the concentration camp at Sachsenhausen and grow up to be men who denied the existence of gas chambers?

Still, the ecosystem of mankind meant that even stupidity had its uses. A bitter taste invaded his mouth. Politics could be a grimy business. So, Rex found himself alone with a neo-Nazi in a corner of Tiergarten not overlooked by cameras, under a cluster of maple trees.

Karl Klein, leader of a militant group and publisher of colourful pamphlets fuelling anti-immigrant sentiment, waited under a canopy of leaves, propped up against a tree trunk with gnarled roots. He wore a faded terracotta t-shirt, which exposed his bulging forearms.

"Evening," said Karl, holding out his hand.

Jessy growled at his sudden movement.

"Ssh, Jessy," said Rex, shaking Karl's outstretched hand.

"A nice evening for a walk." Karl ran square fingers through his lopsided fringe.

Wariness danced underneath Rex's much prized image of power and overt masculinity. He didn't consider himself physically at risk. He had Jessy with him, after all, and she could be a ferocious thing when the situation called for it. He valued his own life too much to place himself in danger, but meeting Karl unsettled him.

Corinne's file included photographs and revealed a man who hid his beliefs beneath a façade of normality. Karl blended into his environment, much like Rex did: hiding his predatory impulses in plain sight. This was no shaven-headed Nazi. His dogged nature, willingness to get his hands dirty, and a talent for recruiting others to his cause had endeared him to those prominent in the far right. He'd risen higher up the ranks than the mere thugs. Neither did he speak like one. Karl's silver tongue contrasted with the man Rex knew him to be. A man who had once punched a young Afro-German woman in the face, breaking three of her teeth. A man with strong links to the alt-right at home and abroad, and whose social media showed a mastery of the dark web. A man who had riled up his youngest recruits with so much bile and bravado, they had set a Turkish supermarket alight. A man who was even more dangerous because he couldn't outrun his future. The police case against him had finally reached a tipping point.

He was just the person required to stir up trouble for the circus.

"We're not here for small talk, are we?" said Rex. "Let me get to the point. The Treptow Circus is in trouble."

"And you've seen the error of your ways in supporting that rabble?" Karl cocked a half-smile, revealing pearlescent veneers that hid a history of menace.

Rex looked away from the man, and shielded his eyes against the dying sun. Across the vista of Tiergarten, students lounged on the grass and office workers recouped their energy after long days staring at screens. How refreshing to live one day at a time, rather than plan like a chess master. What might his life have been had he taken another path? He sighed, and let Jessy off her lead. She hovered, unwilling to go far with a stranger so close to her master.

Rex turned to Karl. "Tell me, do you ever think about the human impact of your...business?"

Karl laughed, but Rex didn't reciprocate, and Karl's sheen of charm evaporated on the wind. "Being soft is a luxury for those who have it all. But people like me, we have something too. We shatter taboos. We have energy and vitality. We are not scared to speak truth to power. We are creative and not trapped by the structures the elite build."

Rex rolled his eyes and his voice became steel. "Those very structures are closing in on you."

Karl pushed himself off the tree trunk and drew near. Amber eyes watched from the undergrowth just beyond, ready to pounce. The two men stood face to face, the neo-Nazi a full head shorter than Rex.

"A good lawyer will see me off," said Karl.

Rex looked down and could see his own eyes reflected in Karl's sunglasses. He noted, not for the first time, the advantages that came with being a tall man. He could crush this imbecile like a cockroach. He released his words through gritted teeth. "Don't count on it. You're scum. You deserve to be locked up."

"Then why are you here, Herr Minister?" Karl laughed, flashing his perfect teeth.

"I'm nothing like you," said Rex. Conviction raced through his body, making him stand taller still.

A hint of a raised eyebrow. "You carry on believing that."

The thin band of civility which held Rex together beneath his air of polish snapped. "Shut up, fool. It's only a matter of time before you're in prison again."

Karl bristled. "You're lying."

"The case against you used to be wafer-thin. You were shrewd enough to cover your tracks. But arrogance has a knack of tripping people up. You're getting sloppy. And your victims aren't as frightened as they used to be. Funny what the promise of extra protection does."

"You bastard." His words whipped through the still air around them.

Jessy came bounding over, and Rex, calm and collected, slipped on her lead. "Remember who you're speaking to before you say something you regret."

Karl took off his sunglasses, and Rex's china blue eyes met his bloodshot ones. "Well, the gloves are off, aren't they?"

"I suppose they are," said Rex. "But then, you have so much to lose, Karli. That is what your little sister calls you?"

Karl grew pale, and his eyes became narrow slits in an expressionless face. In the corner of his mouth, a nerve twitched.

Bingo, thought Rex. "She's only fifteen, right? Your parents are so old now. They won't be around forever, and your father's gambling debts are already out of control. What's Julia going to do without you?"

Karl clenched his fists. "You leave my sister out of this. She's not me. She's not in my world."

Rex continued, unabashed. "She has such talent. It'd be a shame to let that go to waste, to let her despair about you propel her away from the path she's on."

Karl winced. "What do you want?"

Beside Rex, Jessy's body stretched taut like a wire, every nerve ending assessing the threat.

"I need a blunt tool. That's all."

"And if I get caught?" Karl's defiance peeled away. All that remained was pleading.

Rex shook his head, like the executioner's guillotine. "I'm afraid that ball is already rolling. The choices you made long ago are catching up with you, Herr Klein."

"You can't keep me out of prison?"

The wolf had morphed into a lamb. Part of Rex felt sorry for the man. "No, I cannot. But if you help me, I'll see to it that Julia gets into the best art college and secures an apprenticeship of her choice."

"No, that's not enough. An apprenticeship is not enough. What happens when that ends? I need to know she'll be able to look after herself."

"Fine. I'll see to it that there's a job waiting for her on the other side. I have a wide range of contacts. She can take her pick. You'll never have to worry about her again."

Karl held his gaze. "I have your word?"

Rex bowed his head, low and deep. "Of course."

"Okay, we have a deal," said Karl.

"One more thing."

"Yes?"

Rex passed him a slip of paper. "Everything from this point forward goes through my assistant. If we are publicly linked, our deal is off."

Karl replaced his sunglasses on his nose gave a mock salute. "Yes, Sir." Then he reached into his pocket for a small flask and took a swig before sauntering off into the park.

10

Yusuf missed his mother, perhaps more than anyone else. Even more than his dead brother. She was the summer's day to his father's winter nights. She carried her own burdens with grace, shielding the boys, ever-ready with a steaming plate of food, a gentle touch to ease his childish hurts. Not even his father's rages could have driven Yusuf out of the family home while she was there. Her faith sheltered them all–until the day his brother Selim died.

Just when he thought he'd overcome the worst, Yusuf's mind would leap to those dark hours. His breaths started coming in short puffs. His eyes clouded over until he faded from the present.

Doris pierced through the mist. Cool hands found his bare shoulders.

"Breathe, Yusuf. You'll be okay." Doris pulled back his chair and bent him forward so his head hung between his knees.

He drifted back and his body was his own once more, in Doris's apartment. Tears formed in the corners of his eyes. "I'm sorry."

"Don't be," said Doris. Her brusque manner hid her concern.

He didn't tell her how much he'd come to depend on her. How her touch, even briefly on his shoulder, or a hug, filled that cavernous part of him that missed his mother.

She sat, and he wished she'd stayed near. "There's been so much discord recently. I've invited everyone for coffee, cake and a film in the common room, but I know you and your dislike for television. Would you like to come regardless?"

Not one of the performers could have afforded a television set of their own, and the children especially enjoyed watching the communal one. Doris, a devoted cinema goer, often treated them to showings of films that had been at the Berlinale. Yusuf usually spent time in the common room for the sense of kinship, not for the television with its flickering pictures and loud advertisements. How wasteful to spend hours glued to fictions they would forget a few days later.

Of course, the television could have been a portal to the world, to unspoiled paradises and reams of knowledge, or a way of finding out what continued to befall his mother and his people at home. Except Yusuf already knew, deep inside, that the horrors continued on repeat, despite the changing faces of grief on television screens.

"No, I have other plans."

"I think it would do you good to see Imam Saeed today."

His ego hung about him in shreds. "Really? What good does that ever bring?"

Doris's gaze held his. She wouldn't tolerate any excuses. "Yusuf, you can't bury all your emotions. They will come out. Here, or worse, when you're on the trapeze or performing some other trick. Go, today. For me. Simeon has left us all raw."

His voice broke, and he hated himself for it. "The circus needs me. I need to check on Emir."

"I can do that. We need *you* to be whole." She held her warm palm over his hand on the table-top, as if she were the glue that held the pieces of him together. Age had slackened her skin.

A lump rose in his throat and he willed it away.

She pointed to a photograph on the windowsill. There stood a photograph of her husband, long dead, encased in a white wooden frame. "Life is full of risks, Yusuf. At every stage. Never forget how love is a force in this universe. It doesn't leave. It just comes to you in different forms." She hesitated, and tore her cotton-blue eyes away from her husband's visage. "Give Imam Saeed a chance."

It was easier to say yes than to fight. "Okay."

Yusuf set off as the sun climbed higher in the sky. A walk would clear his head. The confined spaces at the residences impacted his mood, one reason why he was happier in the big top. The route he chose took him through the park and past the memorial to the Soviet soldier, across tributaries of the stagnant River Spree and along carriageways heavy with traffic. The noise made him jump. In Syria, danger and fuel shortages had resulted in empty roads in the later years. A noise increase often meant a spike in death toll: fighting had resumed. In Berlin, he rarely strayed beyond the circus and the residences. Exploring the city took a confidence that still hadn't taken hold in this new place.

What would it take to make him happy here? Would it be securing the future of the circus, knitting their futures into the fabric of this society until no one could imagine them gone? How lucky he'd been to be chosen for the circus, when others had been turned away without the option of a fast-tracked status. Why did bitterness swirl in his belly together with gratitude? Silberling had never guaranteed the circus performers would always be protected. If the circus closed, they might lose their home together as a family, but he would still have the chance of citizenship. There were no safety nets in life, so why did he expect one?

He passed the building where he used to wire money to his mother. The troubles had advanced at such a rate he could no longer be sure she could access the meagre sums he sent her, and so he saved the money instead in a pile under his mattress. It belonged to her, his heart's wage, in lieu of being there to protect her. Allah forgive him.

A cry of pity escaped his lips, loud enough to draw attention.

A woman pushing a pram ahead of him turned to assess him, then crossed the road just before a bus hurtled past.

Perhaps he should grow a beard, or allow his skin to tan further. It would make him look more like the men they feared. Even now in daylight hours, men's hackles rose and women avoided him. Not one of them would choose to sit next to him in an empty train carriage. Fear against foreign-looking people had surged since terrorism visited Germany–the twelve deaths at the Berlin Christmas market, the axe attack on a train, the shooting in a shopping centre, and the Cologne sex attacks. Yusuf abhorred violence. He'd left Syria to escape his own horrors, but had somehow become tarred by association just because he happened to be a young immigrant man.

According to Doris, war refugees with a good chance of staying in Germany tended to avoid trouble. Still, who stopped to differentiate between different groups of asylum seekers when seething with prejudices? He knew what was said about people like him, how judgements fell based on the tone of his skin, the slight accent with which he spoke. Or was it his paranoia? Before he'd discovered the Arabic Library, he'd missed books, but had only once visited a German book shop. He'd found even a simple interaction like browsing books resulted in silent scrutiny of his tastes. He was a terrorist, or a sexual predator, or a thief. The world seethed with suspicion of his ilk, even here in the West, where they had everything and wanted for nothing.

It shouldn't bother him. Being an outsider was now part of his identity.

A voice punctured the invisible curtain he'd drawn around himself. "Hey, old man, wait up!"

Yusuf didn't slow, although he recognised the voice. He craved a peaceful walk, with just his own thoughts to accompany the tread of his feet on the pavement.

Someone thumped him on the back. A husky laugh filled his ears. Isaiah Beck's afro loomed into view. In his hands he carried a familiar case. Inside, graffiti cans clanked.

"Hey, Isaiah."

"I was calling you, man. You in a rush?" Bright eyes twinkled at him.

"Yeah, sorry," said Yusuf.

They fell into step beside each other. Isaiah's effervescence reminded Yusuf of a puppy, all bounce and boundless curiosity. They first got to know each other when Isaiah began volunteering at the residences, through one of Doris's initiatives to foster links between locals and the refugees. Isaiah led a monthly art club in the common room, and he'd been a hit with old and young people alike. With part-German, part-African heritage, he knew what it meant to be an outsider, and regardless, his personality made it possible for him to invite himself into conversations he had no part in. He had no sense of boundaries. In Treptower Park one night after the circus, where Isaiah had a standing invitation in exchange for his art class, he'd interrupted a conversation between Yusuf and Osman, and before long, this young man with the afro hair and cinnamon skin had blurred the lines between volunteer and friend. Isaiah often sought him out after that.

Isaiah studied him. "Wow, you're glum, man. Want to hang later?"

"You spraying?" said Yusuf.

"There's this sick new block. Got a wall that's begging to be baptised," he said, a mischievous glint in his eyes.

Isaiah took an interest in the world. He left a mark on it. He'd once confided to Yusuf that graffiti allowed him to etch his name onto forbidden places. He didn't believe in ownership or belonging. For him, fluidity equalled promise. Rules and boundaries were the antithesis of that.

"Not today. I have to get back to the circus." He needed to hold everyone together.

"Another time then." Isaiah grinned. "I'm off. Gotta wear my new trainers in."

He took off down a side street, fully at ease with himself. Yusuf envied the surety.

Yusuf continued, head down against the world. He reached the inner sanctum of the community centre early. A slap-slap of a ball against the walls rung out in the hall. There, he found Imam Saeed placing chairs in a round, ready for the session. Some of the younger boys, the ones who stayed with the Imam when their parents couldn't care for them, played handball in the corner. At the back of the room, a tray had been laid with crumbling biscuits the Imam paid for out of his own pocket and some dates that always reminded Yusuf of his mother as they were the first morsel of food she ate to break her fast in *Ramadhan*.

"I'm glad you came. I heard about Simeon," said Imam Saeed, extending his hand.

Yusuf shook it and looked away. He should have kept the boys safe.

"I missed you at Friday prayers."

The constant pressure to attend the mosque irritated Yusuf, when in Syria the routine had comforted him. How could there be faith in his life without family? "My intention is always to attend." The lie fell from his lips easier than the truth would have.

"It might bring you solace to come. In the absence of home, maybe you'll find you're not so alone."

"I have the circus."

"A place of fantasy and freedom, but does it nourish your soul? Here, we can speak Arabic. You can practice your faith."

"I can do that in the residence. We have a prayer room."

"Do you visit it?"

Yusuf flushed. "No."

"There is great power in congregations." He smiled kindly. "But no matter. I'm glad you are here today. Your brothers missed you."

Yusuf raised an eyebrow. "I doubt that, but thank you for the welcome."

The group trickled into their seats, and soon the session was in full throes. Yusuf listened to the debate, and wished that others from the circus had agreed to come. Instead, he sat here with a roomful of Turks who held German passports but still complained. Didn't they know how lucky they were? One man spouted venom about the lack of jobs and how German men thought it their right to approach Turkish girls.

Adrenalin flooded Yusuf's veins until he could not stem the tide of his anger. "Aren't you ashamed to sit here and complain when there are others in far worse situations? Do you think I wanted to be an acrobat? We do what we must to survive." His anger flamed.

The man's voice boomed in the sparse hall, the acoustics lending him an edge that he perhaps didn't intend. "I'm glad I don't have to flaunt myself in the costumes you wear. Who are you to lecture me? You arrived last of all. You know nothing."

Imam Saeed intervened. "That's enough, Solomon! If you can't listen to each other respectfully here, you leave."

The man ducked his head in apology.

Yusuf glared at him.

"You're not as different as you might think," said Imam Saeed. He kneaded his fingers as he spoke. "We are all displaced people. Some of us are angry; others are grieving. Let me tell you one thing." He skewered Solomon with a look and drew in a ragged breath. "There are over three million Turkish immigrants in Germany. Who do you think feels more alone, you or Yusuf? The circus performers are as welcome in this city as you are. Perhaps more so. Your family are economic migrants. His are refugees fleeing persecution. I won't tolerate discord between you." He banged a chair against the floor, showing a rare glimpse of his own fury. "You have a problem, you come to me. Otherwise, I expect you to stand side by side as brothers, without finger-pointing."

Solomon squirmed in his seat.

Imam Saeed waved his hand, the mis-step already forgiven. "We all make mistakes. It is when our community is hurting that we need each other the most."

The ill feeling hung in the air and Yusuf regretted coming. He shouldn't have been so honest. He'd grown comfortable with the masks of the circus, the nightly performances when he could pretend he was a different person. Being vulnerable made him an object of ridicule and pathos. His every instinct told him to leave the session, although it must nearly be over.

Suddenly, steps sounded at the entrance to the room.

"Our guest is here," said Imam Saeed, breaking into a smile. His *kufi* hat wobbled on his head.

Yusuf twisted around in his chair and there stood Ellie Richter. Was she following him? He stared at her. She laughed at something Imam Saeed said. Her fiery hair set her apart from the women he knew, along with her tinkling laugh. She possessed an innocence he would never have, and Yusuf resented it.

What was she doing meddling in his business? Didn't she have the decency to leave them alone after Simeon? How could her professional striving be more important than ordinary people's struggles to survive?

She turned in his direction.

He massaged the back of his neck to hide the heat staining his cheeks, and pretended she didn't exist.

11

Ellie travelled by S-Bahn a few stops away from the circus. Adventures waited around every corner. The hum of the train soothed her as an adult; as a child, it had excited her. The railway line clattered as she made her way to street-level, a few hundred metres away from where the Berlin Wall had once stood, to Imam Saeed's community centre.

It made sense that he would have set up shop here. Neukölln was home to a vibrant Turkish community, and more diverse than other districts in the city. Hermannplatz pulsed with life: loud, busy, weird and colourful. The streets teemed with kebab shops and Middle-Eastern goods, where corpulent, head-scarfed older women gossiped. It was a far cry from the polish of other Berlin districts, but in some ways it had more heart.

She arrived at the address that he had given her on the dot of 11 o'clock. The road traffic suddenly receded, and Ellie grew tense. She thought nothing of crossing through Neukölln late at night. Her street smarts usually bordered on recklessness, so the prickles that rose on her forearms as she entered the courtyard belonging to Imam Saeed surprised her.

The building itself looked innocuous enough, with no religious markings on the outside. In fact, it could have been a youth hostel. Illegible graffiti had been strewn across sand-coloured brickwork, and milky windows hid the inside of the two-storey building from view. Bikes and an old moped, as well as a miniature football goal, stood in the courtyard.

Alien environments didn't faze her; neither did the all-male environment Doris had alerted her to. She turned her magnifying glass on herself, as she would on a story. Was it the religion that disturbed her? She prided herself on her tolerance, but she couldn't be sure. The usual arbiters of choice–gender, class, sexuality, religion–made not one iota of difference to Ellie. As a child, it wasn't the flute or the violin, those most feminine of instruments, she had showed interest in. As rhythmically-challenged as she was, it had been the drums that had captured her imagination. She hadn't even winced when her father took her along to boxing matches as a child. It struck her as odd that her home city could still hide pockets that set her on edge. She prided herself on knowing every nook and cranny. Her personality and her job demanded it.

A voice startled her. "Frau Richter?" said a young boy.

"Yes." She adjusted the scarf she'd loosely arranged over her head, unsure as to whether her meeting with Imam Saeed would take place in a prayer hall.

"Follow me." Bare legs protruded from his maroon football kit. Thin wisps of hair dotted his top lip. He couldn't have been more than twelve years old. He pointed to the scarf on her head. "You don't need that."

Ellie stuffed it into her bag.

Inside, the quiet of the courtyard erupted into raucous chatter. She found herself in a shabby hall with unadorned windows and dove-grey cornicing. A motley assortment of chairs had been arranged in two semi-circles, and a man she assumed to be Imam Saeed held court.

"Our guest is here," said the man. He wore a mid-length white shift dress atop trousers in the Muslim way. A padded kufi hat sat on his head, and a grizzled beard covered the bottom half of his face.

The boy darted away, leaving Ellie alone.

"Come, join us. You can take my chair," said Imam Saeed. His shoulders stooped and his eyes gleamed with kindness. "We're nearly finished here."

The seated individuals, whose backs had been turned to her, swivelled in their chairs to take in the stranger, revealing young men of differing ages. Yusuf Alam stood out amongst them, and her heartbeat sped up at his scrutiny. Wary recognition flashed across his chiselled face. His hair curled around slightly protruding ears. She marvelled at life's synchronicity; four times in as many days they had crossed each other's paths.

Ellie sat and, for the first time, considered that she could be the alien, even here in her own city. Who were these men gathered here? Did they consider themselves Germans or foreigners? Did it matter?

The Imam turned to the men. "Before we end, let me remind you of your duty as revealed in the Holy Qur'an. Where is the charity we should find in our hearts?"

A voice piped up. "Are we to show charity when we are shown none?"

Ellie strained to see the speaker.

Around him, the crowd nodded.

Imam's Saeed's voice soared above the rest. "That is the will of Allah. He alone has the right to judge."

The man stood. He had closely shaved hair and a goatee. "I understand what you said about the refugees, really I do. But why can't we be angry? Why is the German man better educated than me? Why is he richer? I was born here too. Why does he have a job he wants whereas I must be grateful for the scraps? Showing charity is a privilege for the powerful."

Men and boys rose to their feet to thump the speaker on the back, raucous and unwieldy. Ellie looked around, assessing her safety in this room full of strangers. Tempers had flared, but there was no real danger.

Imam Saeed stepped forward. "I understand your anger, Rifaat. I feel it. And yet, how can we let our sorrow colour our futures? Blame is never a tool for progress."

The group muttered amongst themselves.

Imam Saeed tried again. "Look at Özil or Gündoğan. Who would have thought that Muslim Turks could play for the German national team and be some of our best players? Özil even won a BAMBI award. What a sign of acceptance."

In the back row, a boy with a ski-jump nose and soft, almond-shaped eyes spoke up. "Always Özil as an example. He is an exception to the rule, but even him, when he posed for a mere picture with Erdoğan, found his fans turned on him. Enough about footballers. The rest of us have to find our own place in history."

"Interesting points, Ahmet. That's enough debate for today," said Imam Saeed. "I'll see you on the pitch tomorrow or at Friday prayers. No excuses."

Ellie waited, soaking up the curious mixture of familiarity and discord while the group said their goodbyes. She waved to Yusuf, hoping he might come and speak to her, but he slipped out of the exit without a word. The Imam shook hands with some men and slapped others on the back. Rifaat, who had been the angriest, received a brief embrace. Some of the boys stacked the chairs.

When they had gone, Imam Saeed dragged a chair over to where Ellie sat. He sighed.

Ellie placed her phone on the ground between them. "Do you mind if I record our conversation?"

"Not at all." The spirit he had shown moments earlier had fled, and he suddenly appeared older.

"That was impressive," said Ellie.

The Imam glanced up in surprise. "Really? It was a fraught session. Some of the Turkish boys feel the refugees are making it worse for them here."

"You didn't shut down the debate."

"Well, no. Their anger needs space to breathe."

His German was accent-free, and Ellie wondered whether his birthplace had been Germany. "How long have you been running this group?"

"Five years perhaps. The mosque has a football team. When I first started getting involved, I used to coach the team, and the boys would confide in me. 'Things are tough at home,' they would say. 'There are no jobs,' or, 'I was insulted today.' I thought to myself, their experiences are getting worse, not better. It was going the *wrong* way. In some cases, the boys felt more like outsiders than their parents did when they first arrived in Germany as guest workers. They needed to talk to me about it. Maybe to shield their parents, or their parents didn't understand. My group makes them feel less alone."

"It is open to all?"

"All Muslim boys. In the summer, I host barbecues for the wider community. It's important to mix. But the boys also need a chance to blow off steam. I know they say things they don't mean sometimes, and that's okay."

"Are girls allowed too?"

"Not in this session, but if there was interest, I'd arrange another."

"I see." Ellie didn't really see at all. Was it a religious requirement to keep the genders separate? She filed the thought away to ask Doris.

"I noticed the boys laughed at you when you spoke of Özil," said Ellie.

A wry smile twisted his lips. "To them, Özil is a unicorn. He has a life they can never imagine achieving. He earns millions doing what he loves. He is invited to all the best parties. All it takes is a good performance for the newspapers to fawn over him. Or at least that was true until the recent debacle at the World Cup. To me, Özil is more than a pair of golden boots. His achievements are worth more than what community leaders and politicians can bring about in a lifetime. He shows them what is possible, what to aim for."

Ellie nodded. "There were more Turks here today than circus performers, am I right?"

"Yes."

"Are the performers regular attendees here? How do they fit into your work?"

"My work is one and the same, Frau Richter."

Ellie threw him a quizzical glance. "And yet the Turks are naturalised Germans. They are better integrated, wouldn't you say?" Heat rose in her cheeks at what might be perceived to be a stupid question.

"The refugees have additional trauma that arises from war: loss of family members, flashbacks to the fighting, a sense of injustice that accompanies forced transition." His hands moved as he talked, as if to keep pace with his busy thoughts. "The children of the guest workers are by and large born here and are holders of German passports. But many live what you might consider to be an immigrant life: isolation, lack of integration, poor German language skills, low employment prospects. Their colour, too, marks them out as different."

"You don't think the Government did a good job integrating the Turks?" Ellie scribbled in her journal. "May I quote you?"

Imam Saeed laughed. "Do you think it did? The failure of government policy with the guest workers is no secret. It's only in the past two decades that it's improved somewhat. The government always thought the guest workers would go back home. Their labour contributed to the boom in West Germany and yet there was no investment in their lives: no language lessons, no engagement, no integration with wider society." He sighed. "Military coups in Turkey made it unsafe to go home so the workers brought their families to start new lives here. They moved out of dormitories and finally unpacked their suitcases. What did the government do? It offered money to entice the guest workers to leave. Schools provided Turkish lessons to prepare the children for life in Turkey. The children ended up feeling like they belonged neither here nor there."

"And you think this safe space you have created here at this centre can make a difference to the lives of the refugees at the circus?"

"When you leave your home, there is nothing more important than a safety net to catch you. In some ways, that's what the circus is. That's what Rex Silberling understood. A place to call your own, a purpose, it is everything. This place too–these four walls–may not be much, but when you are at sea and everything is changing, these places are important. So yes, I think I can help this community–the Turks and the people at the circus."

"Although, forgive me, Imam Saeed, but your dream of helping the circus performers seems premature when they scarcely attend."

He reddened. "Yes, that is true." He paused. "Would I like more circus boys to attend my sessions? Yes. Would I like them to play football with us? Yes. But I cannot force them to attend. They haven't always been made to feel welcome here, but there is only one of me."

"Has there been friction in the past?"

"There's not always acceptance of newer members of the group. It's a luxury to help others if you yourself are in need. The first wave of group members has their own problems. They don't want to think about someone else's. I don't agree with their behaviour but I do understand it. I felt the same way. Sometimes I still do."

"Then why are you here?" said Ellie.

Tired brown eyes met her clear green ones.

"To be their anchor when no one else is. We might not be there yet, but I sense the potential of this community to heal at Friday prayers when we are all under one roof, making the same movements with our hands, prostrating to Mecca. Then, I am hopeful. It is only in the cold light of day that sometimes things seem impossible."

12

The night's performance had been cancelled out of respect for Simeon, who fought for his life in a white-washed hospital ward, but also for Dawud, whose guilt weighed like a millstone around his neck. The refugees understood violence, and how it could suddenly bloom then subside, even in children. They knew how the absence of primary relationships and stability warped the mind. They had long recognised that fairytales didn't exist for the likes of them.

Yusuf and a small group attached signs apologising for the closure on the route from local train stations, and on the tarpaulin of the circus tent itself. He didn't anticipate any trouble: advanced ticket sales had been meagre. On their return, the circus family carried out their chores amidst low-level chatter, too disheartened and superstitious to be raucous lest more misfortune befall them.

"He will be okay, won't he?"

"We should pray."

"Leyla's cooking up some treats for when we are allowed to visit Simeon."

"Dawud's eyes are red-rimmed. I'm scared of what he might do next."

"What if word gets out of the violence here?"

On and on, round and round, the thoughts carouseled in their minds as they worked on tasks assigned by Emir: the trainers tended to their animals and the rest secured exits and reset the arena for the evening thereafter. The routines usually soothed Yusuf but not tonight. The day's grime sat heavily on his skin. He stayed at the edge of them all until Emir approached.

"Son, we need to clean where it happened last night. Can you help?" Emir motioned to the corner behind the bandstands.

I don't want a reminder of Simeon laying there, thought Yusuf, but he nodded, bile rising in his throat. With an elevated pulse and a wash of grey noise in his ears, he fetched a spade and a bucket to remove the blood-red sawdust. The two men worked together until the red became gold, and the remnants of the night's events had been washed away.

When the chores had been completed to Emir's satisfaction, he called the performers into a round, and they prayed there for Simeon, right where they stood in clothes musky with sweat. The words came to Yusuf on auto-pilot. Anxiety crusted his soul and left him rigid and unmoved. After prayers, Emir tipped his top hat at them, incongruous with the tracksuit he wore from the neck down, and dismissed them for the evening.

Yusuf walked into the night, his footsteps heavy. The night wrapped itself around the big top and blotted out the stars. He breathed out slowly, releasing the toxins from the day, the way his mother had taught him to do as a child. An eerie silence stretched across the residences when he returned.

He fell into bed and shuttered out the world.

Little Mirjam tumbled through the door and switched on the light. Yusuf groaned, and lifted his head from the pillow, feeling as heavy as a humpback whale. He couldn't have been asleep more than an hour.

"Mirjam, what is it?" He rubbed his eyes. "Shouldn't you be asleep?"

The urgency in her voice pierced through his drowsiness. "There's loud noises coming from the tent. Emir Dada is there. Papa has gone to check everything is okay. He asked me to call you."

A clang sounded. Yusuf listened hard. The wind whistled through the thin walls. "It's probably nothing, little love."

Another bang, followed by a flurry of shouts.

"Did you hear that?" said Mirjam, eyes wide with worry. She'd only been calling Zul *Papa* for a few months. It tugged at Yusuf's heart that she'd finally given a name to their emotional connection after the hurt of losing her biological parents.

Yusuf sat bolt upright, his nerve endings tingling. There could be no sleeping if his friends needed him. Mirjam was counting on him to keep her new daddy safe. "Zul's there, you said? And Emir?"

The little girl nodded.

He slipped on his shoes. "I'm going to check on them, but I need you to go tell Doris what has happened. Can you do that for me?"

She grabbed his hand. "Can't I come?"

"No, you stay here." He bent down to her and pushed a soft toy into her hands. "Remember this? My elephant? My mother made it long ago. Look after it for me while I am gone. Take it to Doris. I won't be long."

He shut the door behind him and pushed her towards Doris's flat before jogging down the corridor, through the exit and out into the park. Outside, he met Osman and Zul.

"Mirjam woke you?" said Zul, torch in hand.

Yusuf nodded. "Just the three of us then? We could have asked Najib."

"You want a man like that at our side when trouble goes down?" said Zul.

"You're right," said Yusuf.

Zul pointed towards the tent. "Emir's got to be in there."

A horse darted past them.

Osman jumped, and put up his hands. "What on earth? Woah there, boy!"

The animal paid no heed, and galloped into the distance under the indigo night sky, with one of Esme's doves right behind it.

"Didn't you lock up?" said Zul, swinging his torch beam in the direction of the fleeing animals.

"Sure I did. The horses, doves and two goats in the barn tonight. The other four are in with me," said Osman, brows knitted together. "What's going on?"

Yusuf looked towards the barn, and the big top just beyond it. The house lights had been extinguished only an hour before when they had said their goodbyes. Now, it shone like a beacon. His pulse accelerated as they picked up their speed. Yusuf reached the barn first, his chest heaving with exertion. The door, usually padlocked overnight, had been prised open. He flicked the light switch and it buzzed on. Inside, he discovered that only one horse remained. Esme's bird cage stood empty.

Zul came up behind him, puffing heavily, his face a blotchy red. He looked inside. "Heaven help us."

"I don't understand," said Osman. "I checked them myself earlier."

From the circus tent came the clang of instruments, discordant notes and arrhythmic drumming that revealed an amateur's hand rather than the skilled house band.

Yusuf gulped. "Emir!"

A renewed sense of urgency filled them, though they had only just caught their breath. The trio sprinted towards the big top.

"Kids maybe?" said Zul, eliciting no response.

They reached the tent, and though the main entrance was still sealed, the tarpaulin had been slashed to create a crude doorway. They stooped to fit through the gap, and coarse laughter met their ears.

From inside the tent, they heard the roar of Emir's voice. "Stop that!"

Inside, the house lights blazed, and the stench of faeces infiltrated Yusuf's nostrils. Litter lined the stands, and instruments lay discarded in the sawdust. Fairy lights had been ripped from the lining of the tent.

In the centre of the ring, five men rolled Emir between them in a barrel. Malevolence shone from the faces of the men around him.

Fear tightened like a vice around Yusuf's chest.

Back and forth, back and forth went Emir in the barrel, like a ping pong ball. His face glistened with beads of sweat and flooded with relief as he saw them. He tried to speak, but the words shrivelled into a cough.

Yusuf turned to Osman and Zul. "We have to try and help him."

"Wait," said Osman. He fiddled for a moment and slid a metal rod from the stands.

The tinny sound of metal on metal attracted the attention of the men in the ring. They glowered and started forward.

Yusuf, Osman and Zul strode towards them.

"Well, well, what do we have here?" said the brains of the group, stopping the barrel with his foot. There could be no doubt this was their leader, judging by how the other men followed his every move.

Yusuf's voice trembled, as if he were not man enough to protect his loved ones. "Let him out, please. His heart is weak."

Behind him, Zul and Osman stood in formation.

"Let him out, please," taunted the chief thug in a sing-song voice that chilled Yusuf to the bone.

"You don't want any harm to come to him," said Yusuf. "He is old."

"We didn't put him in there for his health," said the man, showing perfect, pearly white teeth.

The men with him sneered.

Zul and Osman stood still, ready to spring into action. Yusuf's mind whirred through the options. It would be better to talk their way out of this situation. To persuade or flatter the men into leaving them alone. They would all willingly take a beating for Emir, if it came to that.

"The police will be here soon," said Yusuf. Beads of sweat coated the back of his neck. If Mirjam had relayed the message to Doris, perhaps help would follow.

The man gave a great big belly laugh and clutched his stomach as if Yusuf had just told a particularly good joke. "You think they would put a bunch of immigrants ahead of *real* Germans? You're the last in line for help."

Emir spluttered, his eyes pleading with Yusuf for help.

Yusuf signalled to Osman and Zul to stay in place and walked forward with tentative footsteps, his hands raised. "I'm just going to help my friend."

A bellow erupted from the chief thug. "You do what I say."

Yusuf glanced at the strangers. He took in their humourless, determined faces, the clenched fists and triangle stances that showed they were prepared to fight. Emir and Zul both lacked the physicality to fight. But Yusuf and Osman could land blows if that was what it took. There didn't seem to be another way.

He took a deep breath and ran at the ringleader, landing a punch on his cheek. The man groaned. Someone kicked Yusuf's shin, and he buckled into the sawdust. Emir wriggled out of the barrel. The muffled sounds of Osman and Zul fighting their attackers reached his ears. Blows landed on Yusuf's body from all directions. Emir tried to pull one attacker away, but within seconds he lay sprawled in the sawdust. A man with closely shaven hair chased Zul through the stands, and was nearly upon him. Only Osman, the giant man that he was, stood valiant, his gentle face transformed with ferocity, his arm swinging the metal bar wildly, meeting flesh and causing his attackers to recoil.

A wail of sirens cut through the rush of blood in Yusuf's ears.

The chief thug lifted his foot from the small of Yusuf's back. He gripped Yusuf's face. Passionless eyes raked over him. "This isn't over. You have powerful enemies, my friend."

The men scattered and ran for their makeshift exit.

Osman dropped the metal bar and it landed with a dull thud in the sawdust.

Zul lit a roll up. The performers huddled together in silence, bruised and tender, each trapped in a hell of their own.

13

Ellie returned to the office to empty her thoughts onto the page. She powered up her computer and fetched herself some tea. Then she slumped in her chair and blocked out the ring of the telephones, the shuffle of papers, and the chatter of the news environment. It took a minute to realise her phone oscillated on her desk.

"Ellie? It's Doris Kaun from the circus residences. There was a break in last night in the big top. Some of the men took a beating. I thought you should know. It paints a picture of some of the abuse this community deals with."

This entailed precisely the sort of information that would win her brownie points with Marina, but as Ellie listened hard to Doris's tale, she found her natural sympathies lay with the refugees. But how could she disregard the research Marina had provided her with that seemed to correlate a spike in crime with the arrival of the refugees? What was more, Marina's warning couldn't have been starker. Could there be any way for her to ignore Marina's explicit instructions and protect her own skin?

When her conversation with Doris ended, Ellie hung up without offering the assurances the warden would have liked about the article she planned to write. So much had unfolded in the past few days that her mind had become saturated with unfiltered information. After a few moments, she started to write without knowing where her words would take her, as if the meditative quality of touching the smooth keys and hearing the accompanying rat-tat would propel her towards a decision and help her carve out the direction of her argument. Her fingers splayed across her keyboard, and she paused only to blow her fringe out of her eyes.

Marina would have her assignment before long.

That evening, Ellie shunned after work drinks and packed her journal and laptop into her bag, intending to finish her article from the comfort of her sofa at home. Her feet carried her in the direction of the circus before she knew it. She arrived a few minutes before showtime, and Doris slipped into the seat next to her.

"The crew managed to repair the damage?" said Ellie.

"The show must go on," said Doris. "The tent was the least of their worries."

"How's Yusuf?"

"It wasn't just him who got hurt."

Ellie flushed, embarrassed at how easily the older woman sensed her softening towards Yusuf. "Of course."

"The men are bruised and the animals are jumpy. It took hours to coax them back and one of the horses strayed as far as the train—"

The light dimmed and Emir strode into the ring in his top hat, his moustache groomed to perfection. He stood in the spotlight, warming up the crowd, flicking his hat into the air. It whizzed up like a rocket and he caught it with a flourish, but lacked his usual sense of joy.

Ellie found herself searching for Yusuf amongst the performers, her heartbeat elevated.

Enough tickets had been sold for the stands to be two-thirds full and the stars in the lining of the tent twinkled so fiercely that Ellie shielded her eyes. Still—although the band's infectious beat took hold, performers twirled and leapt and flew through the air, and the animals did as commanded—somehow the show didn't quite transport her to another fantastical world, as if the performers were somewhere else entirely, on an astral plane with Simeon, or willing the show to be over.

An invisible thread linked her to Yusuf. Her eyes followed him, taking in how he interacted with the other performers, checking to see if he walked differently following his altercation with the thugs. She thought he perhaps favoured his right leg, but that couldn't be, because when he performed he made no mistakes.

Tonight, a mist of rain fell in the tent as he performed. His costume glistened, moulded to every part of him. He sprang from the trapeze, corkscrewed through the air, his body a whirl, though he seemed to require more effort than usual. He hesitated at the top of the bar, and winced when he landed.

She couldn't look away from him, whether he stood in the ring or outside of it. As if her body had been filled with electrical impulses that buzzed when he neared and made him stand out amongst the colourful costumes and the diverse acts that vied for her attention. The sheer physicality of her reaction paired with her curiosity about him was not lost on her. She'd enjoyed past flirtations with men, but had never been enthralled by one.

Ellie excused herself from Doris after the show had ended in an explosion of colour and song, and hung back to speak to Yusuf once the crowd drifted away. As she approached, she found him checking a tear at the far side of the tent.

"Hi," she said, tucking a lock of damp hair behind her ear. "It never stops for you, does it?"

He turned and his nostrils flared. "You? Stop hanging around like a bad smell."

"Oh." She wanted to fall into the ground. She should have stayed away. Why would he be so angry when she had helped the boy? "I didn't mean to step on any toes."

His grey eyes glowered. "We've had enough trouble around here. Things are complicated enough without journalists involved. And I know the calibre of your newspaper."

Ellie raised her chin, piqued by the question mark he'd raised about her integrity. Why was she here, spending all her time on this story, when she could be at a bar with Tom, or reading a book, or doing anything but standing here talking to a man with a planet-sized chip on his shoulder? Yusuf must know she'd never use her words to cause harm. "I don't know what anyone's said to you, but I only write what's fair."

"You expect me to trust you?" Up close, beads of rainwater and sweat pooled on his skin.

"Why wouldn't you?" She fixed her eyes on his face, on the hazel flecks dancing in their depths, and the crescent shadows beneath.

"People say things all the time. It doesn't mean they're true. The minister said this would be a glittering new start, but he was wrong." He gestured to the tent. His voice caught, and he pressed on through the weakness. "It all turns to dust."

"The crime the circus attracts must take its toll. It can't be easy, but there are people who want to help you." She took in a deep breath. "You were happy enough to accept my help with Simeon."

"I had no choice." He met her eyes and didn't flinch. "Now leave us alone. We don't need your attention, or your charity. We definitely don't need your meddling."

He disappeared into the black velvet tunnel exiting the tent. It swallowed him whole, leaving Ellie behind, reminding her of how much rode on her article for them all.

"This?" Marina threw the article at her in disgust.

At the top of the page, the draft headline stood out:

A CIRCUS FOR US ALL
By Ellie Richter

"This is what you've come up with? What is this? A bloody arts review? A piece of multicultural bullshit? What's wrong with you?"

"I'm sorry. It's just–" said Ellie.

Marina scooped up the article and her eyes resumed darting across the page. "Where's the eye witness account of the stabbing? The universe presents you with an opportunity and you forget to include it?"

"I didn't think it was appropriate or fair to the victims," said Ellie.

Marina screwed up the page. "There was one victim and one perpetrator, Ellie. You wouldn't have named them, but you could have written a lead article. Instead, you balls it up again. I warned you–"

Ellie held up her hands. "Wait a minute, just wait, Marina. I wrote two articles, but that's the one I want you to use."

Marina simmered with annoyance. She threw down her pen. "You did what?"

"I wrote two articles. I didn't want you to think I didn't listen to your instructions, or I didn't want to put in the hard miles. I'm willing to graft. It's just, the story you wanted–which is right here in this file–didn't sit right with me." Ellie handed over the second draft.

Marina huffed, and glanced over the second sheet.

Heat curled down Ellie's spine as she waited. The tension in Marina's office had leapt up the scale within seconds of Ellie entering. She must have done enough to show her commitment to the job. But she refused to abandon her principles. How was it that despite her best intentions, Ellie always managed to fall foul of authority? She'd been up until the early hours tweaking the first article. It was good. She knew it. The second one she'd written as an afterthought, feeling like a puppet to Marina's puppet master, although she hoped with a fervour that Marina would see the journalistic integrity in the first account.

Marina flung the copy aside. "You've spent about three minutes on this Ellie. There's no meat in it. And the first one..." She grimaced. "It's simply not what I asked for. How are your instincts so wrong? You've severed your chances at *BAZ*. Your word craft is impressive for someone just starting out, but you have a problem with authority. I can't work with someone like you." Marina's hand movements grew more and more erratic.

Ellie's adrenalin spiked. Marina questioning her character stung. How had she managed to mess up again? Surely, she'd not entirely missed the mark? She stood her ground, despite wilting inside.

"I stand by the first article. Maybe read it again? See what you think."

"Are you incapable of listening? It's a no, Ellie. I'm not running it."

"I'm sorry I didn't include the stabbing. I can write that in if you like. I just thought readers wouldn't have stomached that over breakfast."

"Our readers love gore and tragedy. It brings them back for more. You know what your problem is? You want to crack the mould open every time you write."

Dread gnawed at Ellie. The situation had spiralled out of control. "I think you're wrong. Readers are more intelligent than you give them credit for."

"Enough, Ellie. I've no time for this. Even with all your issues with authority, I thought you could be my protégé. I was mistaken," said Marina. The passion bled out of her voice, leaving her cold and haughty.

"Marina–"

"I don't want any excuses. I hope you have something to fall back on, because you're out on your ear. Good luck finding something else. Jobs like these are few and far between. You blew it."

Ellie took a deep breath. She couldn't understand why Marina was being even more rigid than usual. Yes, she'd messed up in the past, but she'd tried really hard to find the heart of this story. Why couldn't Marina see that? "Marina, please. If I just explain why I wrote what I did, the stories I found, the humans underneath..."

"I asked for a crime story!" Marina banged her fists on her desk and stood, glowering across the short distance between them.

Ellie's mouth twisted into a grimace. With all Marina's faults, she usually listened with a more open ear, even if eventually she decided to follow her own instincts. Today, her prickles had become claws. But what choice did Ellie have? The crime story brimmed with dishonesty and lacked understanding of the wider issues. "You know, if you got to know them, came with me to the circus maybe, you'd see–"

"I'm answerable to the board, Ellie. How do you think this all works? I've been in newspapers all my life, and I have never, *never*, seen someone squander this much talent. Do the hard miles, *then* maybe one day you can call the shots. The only reason I'm taking any time to explain anything to you is because you're just starting out. Now, for the love of God, just get out of my office, pack your things and don't come back."

"Marina..."

She pressed the intercom. "Tom, get in here."

Ever the eavesdropper, Tom fell through the door.

"Ellie's failed her probation. Escort her out of the building, please. Everything stays...her laptop, her mobile. She's no longer welcome here."

Ellie went, quiet and ashamed, while her colleagues looked on. Tom waited, sympathetic, while she put her things in a tote bag. Beyond her coffee cup and a favourite pen, there wasn't much else.

"I can't find my journal," said Ellie.

"Go, please, before Marina yells. I'll send it on," said Tom.

She nodded, and he cupped her by the elbow.

Ellie burned with humiliation and remorse while they waited by the lift. Perhaps she shouldn't have pushed so hard to have her way. She'd blown it, but something else was at play. Why would a story that would usually be buried on page ten or eleven of the newspaper have gained such importance for Marina? And why had her approach been so rigid? Yes, Ellie had been warned to better heed instructions, but she could have sworn that Marina's bark was worse than her bite. Either her impression of Marina had been mistaken or something lay hidden beneath the surface.

Ellie could have walked away, but her nature wouldn't allow it; every instinct told her to stay with this story. She dug her heels in and resolved to find out the truth.

14

The circus tent dominated the cloudless sky, almost as if the swirling chaos had been a fragment of Yusuf's imagination, as if the demons had been obliterated by the rising sun. He blinked into the streams of sunlight, and dust particles danced in his vision.

"That's tough, man. I'm sorry you had to go through that," said Isaiah, hearing about his encounter with the neo-Nazis.

"The police made us look at photos of known troublemakers. I recognised the leader of the group–Karl something or other–but with the CCTV footage erased and them escaping, there's not much that can be done."

"Same old, same old," said Isaiah.

Yusuf touched his ribs and flinched. His t-shirt hid the mottled bruises on his skin, a swirl of mustard, blue and green. He longed to forget the chaos surrounding the circus. Speaking to the others whose anguish mirrored his own only led him further down a dark path, and he definitely didn't need to speak to the journalist. Isaiah's offer of a kick about had been a blessing. Yusuf kicked the ball. It curved away from his friend and became tangled in undergrowth.

Isaiah snorted. "You're not much good at this, are you?"

Yusuf fetched the ball. "Damascus has a great team. Or it did."

His friend raised an eyebrow. "Really? I bet Hertha Berlin could kick their arse. Maybe you should come to a game. All you do is perform, see to your chores and attend your language lessons. I know you have Doris and your circus friends, but there's so many others, bro. Look how much fun Old Sayid has out on the town. Not all people are bad, you know. When was the last time you came spraying?" A cigarette hung from his lip. He barely puffed on it. "I've got so much to show you in this city, man. We'll start with the humble kebab or pancakes dripping in raspberry sauce. Or maybe *currywurst* made thick with ketchup or Turkish *meze*. It's up to you. Just say the word."

Yusuf's stomach rumbled. The thought of eating with the circus folk didn't appeal. They'd lived in each other's pockets even more than usual these past few days, clearing up after their attackers, rounding up the animals–although not all of Esme's doves had returned–and fretting about whether they prayed enough. Perhaps they'd attracted the evil eye or the ire of a malevolent spirit to have such misfortune befall them. At least Simeon had recovered enough to be moved to a ward which permitted regular visits. Besides, the police would do their work, and the brutes would never bother them again. Or would they? He just had to close his eyes to taste the sawdust in his mouth and hear the ringleader's warning.

This is not over. You have powerful enemies, my friend.

Could he have been referring to the journalist? He kicked the ball again and this time, it flew past Isaiah's shoulder. Maybe Isaiah was right. Maybe his world had become too small.

"Okay, you're on. Where are we going?" said Yusuf.

A slow smile spread over Isaiah's sun-kissed face. "I know just the place."

Isaiah tucked the ball under his arm, and they walked across the park and under the railway bridge. Underneath, the square footage had been divided between tiny food outlets selling pungent Middle-Eastern wares in tin foil and polystyrene trays. Yusuf rarely strayed this way.

"You'd rather eat here?" said Isaiah.

Yusuf wrinkled his nose. "No." He longed for the scent of his mother's homemade bread and pickles, for the recipes she'd made which had been passed down from his grandmother, and his great-grandmother before that. Food that tasted of home and brought back the nostalgia of his childhood.

"Let's hop on the S-Bahn for a couple of stations," said Isaiah.

Yusuf reached into his pocket for change. "I'll just get a ticket."

"Nah, you'll be fine."

They leapt onto the S-Bahn and the train hummed to its next stop, making their bodies sway as they held onto a central railing.

"What if we get caught?" said Yusuf.

Isaiah grinned. "We run. You got the metal?"

"Don't worry about me. I'll be miles ahead of you." Their energy reminded him too much of his relationship with his own brother. Yusuf gulped down the lump in his throat. "I wish I could be more like you. I need to inject myself with your carefree spirit."

Isaiah motioned in the direction of a man slumped in the next carriage, in pipe-thin trousers with a curved back. "Believe me, you don't need to be injecting yourself with anything. You seen the dopeheads around here?"

The S-Bahn jolted to a stop and they exited onto the platform, where the whiff of baked concrete drifted skywards. Isaiah tossed the ball ahead of him and kicked it. The ball soared through the air and thudded against a station bin. Startled passengers turned around.

"He shoots. He scores!" Isaiah ran a loop in mock celebration, right there on the platform, his arms spread like an aeroplane. He collected the ball and took the steps to street level two at a time. He bounded forward, his enthusiasm infectious. "This way. I tell you, man, you're going to enjoy this. The doners are stuffed full of meat and the garlic sauce is to die for."

"So this is a Turkish delicacy?" said Yusuf.

Isaiah guffawed. "Not quite."

"It's been passed down through the generations?"

"More like an invention for people who want a taste of the exotic that isn't too alienating. It's for people on-the-go, for people who like to party, to soak up a hangover, you know?" He paused. "You don't drink, do you?"

"Nah. I mean, maybe I would. I don't know. It's not allowed in the Qu'ran, you know."

"Yeah." Isaiah pointed. "So, I work in the Hip Hop record store over there, at least until I find something my Ma is pleased with. I like it. I'll take you in there sometime. I get to browse the records for hours, talk to the patrons. It's a hub for the Afro-German community." He slowed in front of a shop with a smeared glass front and shabby sign, and pushed a door open. "This is the kebab place."

Inside, two men roasted meat on vertical rotisseries. They worked deftly, offering toasted pitta bread or wraps served with the sliced meat with an array of salad and sauces. Isaiah made his way to the counter.

"A lamb doner with all the extras and garlic, please," he said.

"Same here," said Yusuf, deciding it easier to follow suit.

"Eating here?" said the man serving, dressed in a white apron.

Isaiah nodded. "Yeah."

"Great. I'll bring it over," said the man.

They slid into one of the four-person booths along the wall. Yusuf ran his fingers over the sticky table, slick with grease. A newspaper had been cast aside.

He unfolded it and sucked in his breath.

There, with Ellie Richter's byline sitting proudly underneath the headline, was a picture of his circus family, himself included, against the backdrop of the blue and bronze circus tent.

Isaiah whistled, low and long. "Oh, man. What a headline."

REFUGEES BEHIND SOARING
TREPTOW CRIME RATES
By Ellie Richter

Yusuf's grasp of written German lagged behind his spoken language. Nevertheless, as he scanned the words, a fury took hold in the pit of his belly. The words hurt. He didn't understand them all, but he understood the subtext, the dog whistle call of blame and alienation.

In Ellie's article, Simeon and Dawud had become distorted versions of themselves. She wrote neither about the wars and famine that had destroyed their day to day lives nor the provocations the circus and its people had endured. She'd painted the performers as broken individuals who couldn't be fixed, who presented danger just by their mere existence.

His skin crawled. She had spent time with them. Why didn't she have any sense of justice or balance? His gut churned at the omissions and manipulations presented in black and white.

"She pretended to be on our side." He spat the words. "She disgusts me."

Their food arrived and Yusuf pushed his plate aside.

Isaiah raised his eyes in surprise. "You know her?"

"She was poking around the circus." Yusuf thumped his fist on the table. "I warned her to leave us alone."

"Let it go, bro. She's one person."

How could Isaiah understand the fragility of an immigrant's place in the world? Yusuf's German came out clumsily, the cadences twisted apart by his climbing fury. "*BAZ* has a huge readership. We're front page news. Our faces are going to be in every bistro in this city, in homes across the nation, pushed through thousands of letterboxes. She's painted us as monsters."

"Breathe, bro. You got to give people more credit than that. Not everyone will fall for it." Isaiah leaned back against the worn red leather of the booth. "Know what your problem is? You think you're alone."

"That's not true. I know I'm not alone. I have the circus. I have…." Yusuf stopped short.

"Forget the circus. I'm not talking about them. I mean, there are good people here, here in this country. Kind strangers. This woman-this Ellie Richter-so what if she's a bad egg? Stop feeling sorry for yourself. There are others who want you here."

Yusuf looked at the newspaper in disgust. "Look at yesterday. We don't belong here. Where am I to go? My home doesn't even exist anymore, not like I remember it." He jerked up, no longer feeling bonded to this stranger who challenged him.

Isaiah's passion reached across the table. "You're going to let some arseholes tell you where you belong? Why give them the satisfaction? Why would blending in make you any happier?"

The air in the booth stilled. How easy for Isaiah—a man confident enough to graffiti his surroundings, to etch his mark onto walls built to keep him out—to spout this. "Look at the colour of my skin," said Yusuf. "Isn't it obvious I don't belong here? As fluent as I've become in German, my speaking voice holds rhythms that weren't made in the West. I stand out like an ogre in a land of princes."

Isaiah's tone sharpened. "You're being ridiculous."

"Am I?"

"We gravitate towards our own kind when underneath, we're the same. Is Cameroon more my country than Germany just because I can trace my father's ancestors there? You think I don't feel like you when my family tells me my afro is the reason I didn't get the job I went for last week?" He harrumphed. "As if my personality changes with my hairstyle, like some sort of Samson. As if I'm a disrupter just because I wear my hair big and curly and not shorn down like some sheep. Shit, it's not like black Germans are anything new. We've existed since the colonies. They dominated us, and still it feels like we're the ones who have to apologise." He pulled at his hair. "You know what my afro means to me? I worked for it. It's my badge of dis-honour, my don't fuck with me sign, my I-know-who-I-am Batman signal."

"What's wrong with wanting to fit in?" said Yusuf.

Isaiah poked at his food, his buoyant enthusiasm mellowed into thoughtfulness. "I've got an auntie, one of those aunties every family has. She's crazy. She taught me to be real because she tries so hard to fit in. She's black like the midnight sky, with hips as broad as a bus, and couldn't be any more different to the whiteys around her in Prenzl-Berg. You should see her at the baker or the butcher. I cringe. It's like she's a Doppelgänger. She has a special voice she puts on. It sounds more German to her. She hardens her syllables and always uses the same idiom. The one a German explained to her once, but the context is all wrong. She sounds like a clown," he sighed. "You know, the Germans laugh behind her back. The funny thing is, at home, she's the best story-teller, with a lilt to her voice that reminds me of long summer days under the African sun." He flicked the newspaper with distaste. "I don't care where you're from. I don't care about the colour of your skin, and I sure as hell don't care about your funny German. To me, language is at its best if it's not rigid. If it can be different things to different people. That way it's authentic. Real. What could be wrong about that?"

"You make it sound so easy," said Yusuf. "But not everyone is like you." He picked up the newspaper again. "This hurts. It hurts all the more because I've tried to be what they want me to be. Since I left Syria, it seems like I change my skin like a coat, just to fit in. But you, you're so accepting and unafraid of change. I envy that. I don't know who I am anymore."

Isaiah tucked into his food and soon, lettuce, shreds of meat and garlic sauce dotted his chin. "It comes from roots, man. Yours have been pulled out. But you know, look around you, why are you so scared? You think you landed somewhere perfect? That their shit don't stink? I got white German friends. They get things wrong too."

"Yeah?"

"Hell, yeah." He put down his kebab. "Like when someone in the supermarket queue strikes up a conversation and says, 'Where are you from?' Because with this skin colour, they assume you can't possibly be German. Or when I used to get asked in history class for my perspective on race because, of course, I must speak for all black people if everyone else is white. Or worse, when my friend Markus came into the record store, slapped me on the shoulder and called me nigger, as a *joke*." He palmed his face. "That's not okay, man. You can't use that word if you don't share our history."

"Did you call him up on it?" said Yusuf. Part of him wanted to see Ellie, to demand why she wanted to bury them in the rubble of her lies.

"Nah. It's not worth it. How do you shrink centuries of history into something that teaches but doesn't offend? I ain't no professor. I'm just trying to live my life. It's not like it was the first time, either. Once, he got carried away and sang Kendrick Lamar at me in a club. It was awkward, bro, believe me, however cool he felt in the moment, with his black man's dance moves and the lyrics flying off his tongue. He's still my friend, though. I've grown up with this shit, but he hasn't. The universal experience is white. Where do you start explaining?" He drifted off. "I don't know, maybe I should have said something. Without honesty, that friendship is worthless."

"Maybe. Still, why should a white man have thought about race?" said Yusuf. Why should Ellie Richter have any idea what it was like to be him? Maybe it was too much to expect compassion from someone so different from him.

"The white man is the alpha. He has the penis and the alabaster skin that makes him the kingpin. You're taking away your own power by excusing him."

"Come on, give me a break. Not everything is about politics," said Yusuf, although his mind strayed to Old Sayid, and how he'd been an outcast in his home town because he preferred men to women, and how even at home the structures had served to keep men in line if they deviated from the mould.

"That's where you're wrong, bro. In some ways, Markus is just as bad as the white men right at the top or the neo-Nazis that attacked you yesterday. He's complicit. He benefits whether he realises it or not. A black man has to be a genius to compete with an average white man because the game's rigged. At some point, we have to decide. Do we want to fit in or stand out? If we stand out, will they knock us down? Do we want to disrupt, to make this world ours, or do you want to squeeze yourself into their perceptions of what a brown man should be?"

Yusuf glanced at his friend and realised that, in the space of a few minutes, their friendship had deepened. For a moment, the rest of the world had faded away. The smell of grease and charred meat, the footfall of customers and the clang of the till had retreated, to leave just him and Isaiah and this connection on a very human level. In some way, their conversation had restored his sense of self and eroded some of the shame he carried since leaving Damascus. He'd lost dignity during his time as a refugee, but perhaps the time had come to take it back.

"This city...this city has promise, man. It can let you fly, if you escape the jailers, the ones who want you to stay in your box to make them feel safe."

Yusuf swallowed down his food in huge mouthfuls. "I'd better get back and warn Emir about the article. Three hours 'til showtime."

Isaiah wiped his mouth with a tiny paper square of napkin and they left, taking the football and the newspaper with them. Isaiah tackled him for the ball and flicked it, so the ball bounced up once, giving him room to swing his leg and propel it high up into the air. It spun before descending, a white sphere against the cobalt sky.

"You know, my Ma always told me not to let them cut you down to size. Blast them with your dreams and one day, maybe they'll thank you for it."

Yusuf folded up the newspaper and tossed it where it belonged, in a dustbin overflowing with half-eaten food, gloopy sauce and fat-soaked paper. Ellie Richter wouldn't ruin this new life for them. She could burn in hell. A small seed of hope sprouted in him, of all that he could achieve in this city.

"Tell me you broke up your friendship with Markus?"

Isaiah grinned. "Nah, he's fun. And has a decent car. That's mostly enough."

"But not always."

"No, not always."

15

Ellie woke in a cold sweat with the bedsheets tangled about her. The radio droned next to her, its dial blinking 7 a.m. She pressed her face into her pillow before the preceding day's events came flooding back: she'd been fired. With a groan, she decided it was too late to return to the sanctity of sleep. She raked back the hair from her face and swung herself upright.

Her mornings usually consisted of scanning the headlines on her phone in bed, preparing a packed lunch and riding her bike to work with her freshly-brewed coffee sloshing in its flask. Not one to rest on her laurels, this newfound freedom from work disoriented her.

Her day didn't begin in earnest without hearing her mother's voice. It formed part of her routine like scrubbing her armpits with a washcloth or brushing her teeth. But she swallowed her instinctive reflex to call her mother. Shame bloomed in her chest about being fired. She couldn't imagine her parents ever suffering any setbacks. Their belief in her, which once made her so strong, now made her weak and willing to withhold the truth.

She didn't want to disappoint them.

Hiding from the world wasn't an option, not for her. Even at weekends, Ellie rarely stayed home. Come rain or shine, she gravitated towards the city for a cultural hit: to the sprawling National Gallery, Museums Island or the open air cinema on the lush lawns of Berlin parks. Or if she longed for relaxation, she visited the misty women's hamam in the Chocolate Factory in Kreuzberg, practiced hot yoga in the gym near her flat or met her college friends in the bars on Oranienburgerstraße in the soft glow of the Jewish Synagogue, where they would fritter away time over deep glasses of red wine, talking about the future. She'd never been any good with the brakes on. However rotten she felt, she needed a plan. She threw on a pair of threadbare jeans and a t-shirt, grabbed her private phone, and headed out. She'd tell her parents about her work predicament later, once she'd salvaged something of the situation.

Over the years, Ellie had learned to follow her bulldog instincts. The more she analysed Marina's arguments and her reactions, the more certain she became that she'd missed a piece of the jigsaw. With renewed energy, she strode into a café in Prenzlauer Berg. Inside, plain brick walls and polished floors formed a moving canvas for an assortment of furniture and paintings on sale to customers. Patrons could buy the very seats they sat on. It was a concept typical of hip, ever-changing Berlin, and made this café one of her favourites. She nodded hello to the owner, a woman in a tassled top and space buns. Then she found a table and ordered coffee.

She pulled out her phone and dialled Tom at *Berliner Allgemeine Zeitung*.

"*BAZ*. Tom speaking."

"Tom. Has my journal turned up yet?"

He whispered down the line in staccato beats. "No, not yet. Are you okay?" His voice dropped a notch lower still, until Ellie strained to hear. "You shouldn't be calling–Marina's office door is open. I was going to stop by and see you later."

"I'm fine," said Ellie, breezily. What did he think? It hadn't been the greatest moment of her life, being hauled out of the office like a piece of furniture. She focused. "Maybe my journal slipped under my desk? It's packed full of my thoughts. I'd hate to lose it."

"I'll look, okay?" said Tom.

"Thanks." Next to her, a waitress splattered orange juice on the floor.

"You made the front page. Have you seen it yet?" He paused, and she clocked the note of anxiety in his voice.

The office had been too full of vanities and rivalries for friendships, but Tom was the exception. She could read him like a book.

"I'm on the front page? Which article?"

He didn't respond.

At the café, the coffee machine churned.

"Oh, God," said Ellie.

Her chair scraped against the wooden floor as she pushed it back. She waved at the waitress, left a couple of Euros on the table, and made a beeline for the nearest newsstand. She found the paper in seconds. There, next to her byline, splashed across the front page, stood a headline she had never intended to be published.

Ellie sucked in her breath.

REFUGEES BEHIND SOARING
TREPTOW CRIME RATES
By Ellie Richter

"Are you there?" said Tom, his voice so far away he sounded like a cardboard cutout of himself.

The whisky muskiness of her voice disappeared, leaving a hard edge. "I'll call you back."

She stuffed the phone in her pocket and her eyes darted across the page. Marina had used the second article, the one Ellie had written as a gesture of willingness to obey, the one that had been destined for the wastepaper basket. How could she have been so stupid? A knot formed in her stomach and she tightly clenched the paper.

The vendor coughed. Ellie glanced up and pressed some change into his outstretched palm. He faded away. She stood in the middle of the street, poring over every word. A photo of the performers accompanied the article. Ellie searched their faces, guilt rising like a wave in her stomach, making her nauseous. She'd had a connection with the circus and its people. Marina had pushed her into the role of villain and Ellie hated her for it. Every fibre of her being flooded with remorse and she railed at the unfairness of having this alien voice thrust upon her.

She rang Tom. "Oh Tom, how dare she? She knew I didn't want this printed. What on earth have I done? It's all here, and my fault, a deliberate blurring of the facts under my byline. What am I going to do?"

He sighed. "Damn, I'm sorry. I thought as much after listening to the fireworks yesterday. Look, you wrote the words while you were employed by the paper. You've not got a leg to stand on."

"I thought she'd tossed my work out along with me. What will the circus people think of me? It's not what I intended. I've got to put this right."

Voices boomed on the other end of the line and he hissed into the receiver. "I can't talk here. Can we pick this up later? I'll come-"

Ellie's mouth turned dry. She'd lost her job and her integrity. "No, Tom, please, there must be something I can do. There has to be some reason why this stupid story is so important to her."

Silence, then a pause. "Look, there might be nothing to it, but recently there's been a few meetings blocked out in Marina's diary, ones she's been cagey about."

Her wind whirred. "What do you mean, 'cagey'?"

"I don't know." He dropped his voice a notch until she strained to hear. "You know what Marina's like. She likes me to be on top of everything. Her coffee, her meeting notes, her contacts file, even her hair appointments. So when she blocks out a calendar entry, it makes me wonder."

"Maybe she's having an affair."

He cackled. "You can't be serious. You know she's married to her work, and she doesn't have eyes for anyone except Tina."

Ellie stepped back from the bustle of the street and lowered her voice. "Okay, so you think she has something to hide."

"Possibly."

Something inside Ellie clicked, like the switch on a train track. "I need you to do me a favour."

"I've said enough. I can't promise anything."

She took a deep breath and it whistled as she blew into the phone. She couldn't leave things as they stood. She had to understand why Marina would go so far to bend a narrative out of shape. "I need access to Marina's office and your work pass."

Tom spluttered. "Are you insane? You were escorted from the building. There's no way I'm letting you back in."

Ellie thought fast. "Remember that time I hooked you up with Paul?"

"Yeah."

"And all the time we've gossiped over buckets of red wine at the end of a long day?"

"Yes."

She smiled, despite it all. Nearby, bikes whooshed past in the wide Berlin cycle lanes, ringing their bells at errant pedestrians. "How about the time I covered for you after your monster hangover?"

He groaned. "I remember."

"I can't do this without you," said Ellie, crossing her fingers like she'd done as a child. Next, she'd be digging out the four-leaf clover she'd pressed between the pages of her favourite Murakami novel.

"Do what exactly?" said Tom.

She thought of Doris, Yusuf and Osman, and how they must hate her. If he said no, she'd have no way in. "I need to find out what's going on."

"I'm not giving you my pass. I'll ring when everyone's gone and meet you. It'll be late. If you're going to be this stupid, the least I can do is help."

"You don't know what this means to me." A calm washed over Ellie, cleansing her. Her anger pulsed at Marina's brazen disregard for the normal rules of etiquette, but perhaps Ellie could recoup something from the debacle. "One more thing. Is my laptop back with IT?" In all probability, it had already been wiped.

"I haven't had a chance to return it yet," said Tom.

"Good. I need a copy of the hard-drive." She'd sweated over those words. They were hers, as sacred to her as her own thoughts.

"This is ludicrous."

"It's the right thing to do." She felt the familiar tingle in her bones, when the truth lay just beyond reach and she could almost piece it together.

He lingered, not saying goodbye, and in the space between his words, she realised how much she had asked of his friendship.

"I can't lose my job. Wait for my call." He hung up.

Ellie stuffed the newspaper into her bag, way down, so nobody could see it, and headed for the S-Bahn, darting past street musicians who had hauled a whole drum kit out into the open. She'd seen a copy of BAZ in Doris's apartment, and there could be no doubt that her article had been discovered at once. She hoped to explain to the circus performers that her words had been twisted, and that she didn't mean them, but when she arrived, she found the big top quiet. At the residences, try as she might, Esme refused her entry.

"I heard what you did. I think it's better you stay away," she said, slight shoulders drooping, and her cheeks tinged with red.

"Can't I come in? Maybe I could speak to Doris or Osman?" said Ellie, worried about angering Yusuf further. Her instincts told her the former two would give her a fair hearing.

Esme shook her head, and her pretty scarf rustled at her shoulders. "Not today."

So, Ellie returned to her flat with the newspaper, and gazed morosely at the headline she had created. Then she dug up her battered old laptop from her university days. The computer, with its inch-deep casing, was a relic. No matter. She set herself up at the kitchen table, ignoring the missed calls from her parents, unplugged from the world and got to work piecing together the puzzle of her errant story.

That evening, after the sun had dipped beyond the horizon and leaden clouds gathered in great swaths over the streets and parks of Berlin, Ellie arranged to meet Tom. She waited for him a block away from the office, lingering on the wide expanse of pavement with its pink and grey cobbles, where canopies of linden trees stretched heavenward. When he didn't immediately appear, she reached into her pocket on impulse and called her mother.

Her mother picked up on the first ring.

"I didn't wake you, did I?"

"Ellie, thank God," said her mother, although she didn't believe in anything so other-worldly. "We've been trying to reach you all day. Your father's here, keys in hand. He insisted he was coming over to see you're all right. We've been worried."

Ellie toyed with a cigarette butt on the pavement with her boot. The tone of this conversation already put her on the defensive, as if she were more child than adult. "I don't have long but I wanted to check in."

"Is everything okay, darling?" said her mother, no longer admonishing.

Her gentleness disarmed Ellie. For a second, she wanted to cry. Her mother always knew how to pierce through her toughness. "Of course, why wouldn't it be?"

"Because, frankly, darling, that article you wrote wasn't like you." Omitting information in the course of a conversation with her mother took skill; lying, on the other hand, was impossible.

"I'm okay, Mama."

"Ellie..." There came that warning tone, the one she remembered from childhood. Her mother might as well have been a truth-seeking missile. Every inflection of Ellie's voice, every body movement provoked tireless scrutiny. Just like Katharina Richter's flamboyant outer persona with her pink hair and block colour power-dressing revealed her fearlessness, so her inner values embraced truth at all costs.

What good would it do, lying now? As alarmed as her parents would be about the firing, their liberal instincts meant the article Ellie had allegedly written would have given them equal cause for concern. She was, after all, the daughter of a woman who kept all the placards from her various marches over the years, though some had grown tatty with age: a *Love is Love* sign, an *Open Borders, Open Hearts* one, and Ellie's personal favourite, a giant vagina painted on a sign with the words *Women Against Fascism* in bold lettering above. While her parents would never force their opinions on Ellie, she knew they found significant deviations painful. As did Ellie.

So, the truth came out.

She braced herself. "Marina fired me yesterday."

Her mother's voice spiked. "What?"

In the background, her father muttered.

Her mother shushed him. "Be quiet, Martin. I can't hear. What was that, Ellie?"

"I was fired."

A long pause. "Oh, honey. I know how hard you worked. Was it that witch of an editor?" Her mother's colourful language had been a delight since she was eight years old. She'd let her feminist standards drop for an instant in solidarity with her child, and Ellie loved her for it.

"The article was mine, but I didn't intend for it to be published. There was another version, one I worked hard on but Marina found lacking."

"Oh, Ellie. What a mess," said her mother. She paused. "You didn't mean to tear that circus apart?"

Ellie bit her lip. "No. It was just a lack-lustre attempt to prove to Marina I could follow orders."

"I wish you hadn't written it. It sounds like you might be better away from that woman if she can railroad you into something like that. You've visited that circus so often, I couldn't think of a reason why you'd have taken that track. A project like that builds compassion, not enmity, especially when you peek behind the curtain and see the grief and hard work." Her mother had been a social worker for decades; care and empathy were integral to her sense of self.

A hand squeezed Ellie's shoulder. She spun to find Tom, huge eyes full of trepidation. Ellie hugged him, and whispered her thanks in his ear.

"Mama, I have to go."

"Call us later?" said her mother.

"Sure."

"We love you." Her words held no sense of expectation, no inquisitiveness about Ellie's next step or the career that might be floundering. Instead, her mother simply offered comfort.

"I know," said Ellie. She disconnected the call and nodded at Tom. "I can't thank you enough. Are you ready?"

"As I'll ever be."

"Okay, let's go."

16

In the aftermath of Ellie's exposé on the circus, Yusuf's sense of vulnerability increased. He ricocheted from one person to another, hoping to galvanise the community to push back against the slurs and untruths. But his friends retreated into their safe places, as a tortoise might do, and Yusuf resented the festering sense that the foundations of their new home crumbled before their very eyes. To his frustration, even Ellie's article and the repeated transgressions against the circus brought no tangible reaction. The circus community did nothing, other than blame themselves.

"Maybe we should try and fit in better," said Esme. "Our clothes make us stand out."

"We should improve our grasp of their language as quick as we can," said Osman.

"It's our food. It's delicious but perhaps too pungent for delicate German noses," said Leyla.

The injustice burned Yusuf. He grew irritated at their willingness to bend themselves out of shape, just to please passing strangers. He'd travelled to Germany out of necessity. He had no previous experience of a white man's land. But his otherness had come to him like a revelation, even in metropolitan Berlin. Even in districts such as Neukölln, Kreuzberg and Wedding, where the scents that pervaded the air differed from the tourist beacons of Mitte and Prenzlauer Berg. In Neukölln and Kreuzberg, the bustling, colourful immigrant communities lived parallel lives to native Germans, as if surrounded by an invisible gate. Like the Turkish barber he visited when his beard grew too unruly, where a string of young brown-skinned men waited in line.

Yes, ethnic businesses flourished–supermarkets, internet cafés and travel agents–but this was an inferior citizenship, underpinned by a singular notion of German culture, which excluded migrants. A whiteness washed over the city, silencing other perspectives with its vastness, rendering every other colour less important. Whiteness marched like a weapon. It encroached until nothing else flowered. Whiteness offered to save them all while belittling and disabling them.

It even attacked them.

There came the night when an angry man pushed Zul up against a wall, with little Mirjam nearby, and asked him about his faith and whether he believed in Allah. Zul denied his beliefs, and was ashamed of his own cowardice. The man punched the wall beside his head, and Zul soaked his trousers through with his own piss. When he reached the residences, he wept bitterly while little Mirjam wrapped her arms around him.

You have powerful enemies, my friend.

The neo-Nazi's words haunted Yusuf, and so did his friend's tale. He looked around for firm footing, for a recalibration of his mental state, for a way to control the future, but he found only platitudes. The stone of anxiety in his chest hardened with each passing day, until nothing brought solace: neither his circus family, practising his acrobatics nor Doris's mothering.

When he could no longer bear the weight of his worry alone, and his usual avenues for comfort had been exhausted, he trudged under grey skies across the wet park to the S-Bahn, hoping Imam Saeed might have some ideas to ward off his sense of foreboding.

"Your friend Isaiah is right," said Imam Saeed. "We may have enemies, but we also have friends. Don't forget that. Sometimes you just have to trust that Allah is on your side. Pray, and trust your fate to him."

Yusuf hid his scepticism in case he caused offence. How could Allah allow this much suffering for the innocent? How could He allow Death to wrap itself around the throats of young lovers, children and the infirm? The Imam's words made him doubt his intelligence. The older man had been in Germany for so long, it had made him soft. His instincts had faded, but Yusuf's hadn't.

Here, in the de facto capital of Europe, change was afoot. There was only so long the West could offer itself up as a saviour in the face of public opinion. The mood of the people had changed, and with it, the government's priorities. Now it would be the weak who paid, as they always did. Yusuf knew how quickly things could change. He'd lived it. He'd seen war break out between families when only a few pieces of bread remained and the acrid smoke of a chemical attack lingered in the air. He'd seen innocence and faith trampled before.

Yusuf returned to the circus to shake the cobwebs from his mind. He climbed the rigging until his head almost touched the starry velvet sky at the top of the tent. He reached up and touched a star, and it pulsed beneath his fingers, hot and tingling.

He'd walked the beams at the circus tent so often, he could do it with his eyes shut. In fact, sometimes he did just that during his act. A canary yellow silk blindfold, powdered feet stretched out in front of him, testing the beam before he transferred his weight, making the audience gasp with his daring.

For hundreds of years, spectators had been fascinated by those who risked their lives for entertainment. The possibility of death made his act exciting. Daily practice helped his confidence, and allowed him to hone his tricks or try new ones. It used to be his favourite way to start the day: the clean, quiet tent; the rise and fall of his breath; the time to take things slowly. Why then had his heartbeat begun to accelerate the moment he stepped out?

Ridiculous, really, for even basic beam-walking to frighten him. He focused, blocking out the sounds of other performers practising below, so there remained only him, the beam and his breath.

A memory hijacked his equilibrium. It ambushed him, unbidden, writhing demons in a sea of calm.

Flashes of metal through the sky: the red of the motorcycle and the silver.

His brother Selim's head, with its thick shiny brown curls, rolling, rolling.

Yusuf stumbled and toppled on the beam. His hands fumbled, and he ended up wrapped bodily around it in a koala hug.

"What's going on?" said Emir, calling up from the ring below.

Colour rushed to Yusuf's face. He knew better than to go on the circus apparatus with a clouded mind. It had been drilled into them time and again during their tutorial year. A distracted acrobat risked broken bones or worse. Safety nets and harnesses could only be relied on to a certain point. Without mental toughness, all the acrobatic skills in the world counted for nothing. One misjudgement could result in a fall or death.

Fall or fly, hadn't that always been the choice?

Yusuf scrambled to his feet. "Nothing. I just slipped."

Emir combed his fingers through his wiry hair. "That's not like you."

Yusuf skipped to the ledge, all bravado, though his heart hammered still. Underneath him, the safety net zoomed into focus. He closed his eyes and swayed. A memory gripped him like an assault.

The motorbike on its side. Selim's hands still gripping the rubber-clad handlebars, his head elsewhere.

Emir's voice reached him from far away. "Yusuf!"

Yusuf opened his eyes, half a heart-beat from disaster. His sight blurred.

"Get down here right now!" said Emir, urgent, harried.

Yusuf descended to the ground, his knuckles white where he gripped the ladder. His mother's screams rang in his ears. But that was then, wasn't it? Why could he no longer keep the nightmares at bay? His breath came in shallow puffs.

Twenty metres.

"Easy now, son, nearly there," said Emir from below.

Sweat covered his palms. How had his nightmares made a slow creep into daylight hours, until they invaded his thoughts even when he balanced on the beam or practiced trapeze tricks?

Sixteen metres.

Nausea rose, mirroring the choppy ocean. He lent his head against the rigging. He didn't want to be strong. How long had he been alone, even before the war? Everything changed when Selim died. In the space of a few moments, he was alone, without the love and protection of the brother he'd adored and who'd been a physical divide between him and their father's worst rages. The future had withered to a closed point, as if its possibilities had been swallowed overnight by that great monster: Death.

Twelve metres.

He hadn't known how quiet Death would be. The hush before the screams. As if the love and memories that had made a person had been sucked into a vortex, and the Earth was realigning itself on its axis. Remembering hurt.

Nine metres.

His flashbacks in the immediate aftermath of the tragedy had been debilitating. They would visit him in any situation, and he'd find himself on his knees, blinded by tears, calling out to prevent it from happening all over again. The horror felt so real in those moments, it cut him to the raw. Five years had passed and he'd grown accustomed to the flashbacks occurring only in nightmares when the world slept.

Until now.

Seven metres.

Below him, the ground spun. He dipped his chin to his chest and closed his eyes. In the hazy pink of his eyelids, a carousel of images whirred past: Simeon and Dawud; barrels and beatings; swines taunting him; furious headlines; and worst of all, his brother, again and again, broken, bleeding.

Four metres.

He bit his lip and drew blood.

Two metres.

Emir gripped his waist, steading him.

Yusuf sank to the floor and put his head between his knees.

"Thank Allah," said Emir. "What's going on?"

Yusuf shivered. "I'm tired."

Emir lowered himself to Yusuf's level. "Rubbish. I know you. I might be old but I'm not blind. You know more than anyone how dangerous it is to work at the heights you do. Talk to me."

Yusuf raised his head. "I'm fine."

Emir shook his head. "If you can't focus, you can't go up. What kind of ringmaster would I be to put you in danger?" He squeezed Yusuf's shoulders.

Yusuf grimaced. What would he do without the circus to ground him? "Emir, I felt dizzy, that's all. I must have a bug. I'll get some rest this afternoon and take some medicine. I'll be fine by tonight. Besides, it's too late to change the line up."

"Okay, if you're sure?" He searched Yusuf's face.

Yusuf nodded. He needed the circus to anchor him. Only on the trapeze did his troubles sometimes evaporate. Only there could he get caught in the moment, forget he was an adult and play like a child, unburdened and free.

"You'd tell me the truth?" said Emir, his moustache twitching as if he were a hound dog on a hunt for falsehoods.

"Of course I would. You can trust me."

17

A light drizzle fell over the city as Ellie and Tom passed under the halogen street lighting outside the glass façade of the *BAZ* offices and through the swivel doors. The rotating mechanism resisted as Ellie pressed her weight against it, and for a moment her courage failed her. Her heart thrummed like a hummingbird in her chest. She'd walked through this gleaming entrance hall a thousand times before, but never illicitly.

Still, her anger burned brightly at the injustice of the betrayal of the circus folk she'd come to know. She didn't blame them for not wanting to speak to her. Guilt about her role in the matter and shame about her unceremonious firing fizzled underneath the righteousness; they propelled her forward when anyone else might have reconsidered their plans. In her eyes, she had a free pass for duplicitous behaviour given the reasons for it.

Tom had checked the building had been emptied of news-hounds. Only a night duty manager and support staff remained–security guards, a lonely receptionist and cleaners–who knew the habits of the workforce so well that anything untoward could alert them to foul play.

They entered the lobby and she became Tom's shadow, so close that she clipped his heels. Undercover work had never been her forté, but they'd had a cursory discussion about how to avoid suspicion and detection. She wore a hat pulled down low over her ears and had tucked her hair into her jacket collar. Tom's tall frame shielded her from the security cameras.

Their footsteps echoed on the glistening marble floor as they approached the receptionist, who perched ramrod-straight on the edge of her stool, typing with tapered fingers edged with coral nail varnish. She threw them a cursory glance.

"She's with me," said Tom, stopping short and showing his pass.

Ellie stumbled into his back.

Tom's pursed his lips and his eyes flickered with irritation.

"Sign in, please," said the woman.

Ellie scribbled in the guest book using a school friend's name, taking care not to make eye contact, and received a visitor's badge. They reached the security arch, and a guard with ruddy cheeks nodded them through without incident. Ellie hurried to call the lift, and knew relief when the doors pinged open.

"Hold it together," said Tom under his breath, pressing the button for their floor.

The doors closed, and Ellie breathed out. Apprehension wound itself like a thread pulled tight around her spine. "I'm forever grateful for this, Tom. I'll need you to keep a lookout in case Marina comes back, but if I get caught, say what's necessary to keep your job."

"Deal... and please, don't thank me yet. Marina has a dinner tonight. The morning edition is off to print and there's barely a soul left in the office, but we'll still need to be on our toes."

Ellie nodded, sombre and focused. The lift jolted to a halt and the doors slid open. She held her breath, half expecting an ambush. Instead, the lights flickered on and the hum of computers on standby greeted them.

Tom lifted an eyebrow. "The last time I stayed this late, Remi and Paulina were doing it like rabbits in the copier room. Awkward."

Ellie stifled her laughter then pulled herself together. "My journal turned up yet?"

"No, sorry."

"You still have my laptop?" She dug into her pocket and pulled out a memory stick.

"This way."

They strode down the corridor to his desk, from which he retrieved her laptop. Within minutes, she'd powered it up and downloaded her work onto her stick drive. The lift chimed open.

Tom jumped and turned pale. When no one emerged, he exhaled. "Hurry, Ellie."

"I'm not going anywhere until I find out what she's hiding." No-one could cover all their tracks, especially if they considered their office to be a safe space.

He pushed a scrap of paper into her palm with clammy hands. "You'll need this."

She unfolded it, brows furrowed. On it, in Tom's messy scrawl, stood a jumble of letters and numbers. "Her password?"

His lips twisted in a wry smile. "My best guess. I've looked over her shoulder a hundred times while she typed it."

She wanted to throw her arms around him, but there would be time for that later. "I'll be as quick as I can. Any sign of trouble, leave."

Ellie opened the door to Marina's office with jittery fingers. Inside, darkness shrouded the room apart from a narrow sliver of light that fell through the blinds across the desk. Her feet padded across the carpet as she headed straight for Marina's computer terminal. How many times had she been at the other side of this desk, eager for approval?

She sank into Marina's ergonomic mesh chair and ruffled through a sheaf of papers. Nothing jumped out. In the corner of the room stood a tall filing cabinet, but if Marina was like her, anything that mattered would have a digital copy on her hard drive. Ellie tapped the keyboard. The monitor sprang to life, showing a bikini-clad Marina with her arms wrapped around her smiling partner in the Côte d'Azur. It was the first time Ellie had seen past the businesswoman veil Marina presented to the world, and for a moment she regretted this breach of Marina's privacy.

Osman's face flashed before her, and Yusuf's, and Simeon, bleeding into the sawdust floor. She couldn't afford to be soft now. The story demanded that she continue searching. With new resolve, she smoothed out Tom's note and typed in Marina's password, taking care not to make any errors, then pressed return. The screen flickered. It had worked.

She pulled out her phone, where she'd noted a list of dates Tom had told her might be of relevance. Dates when Marina had disappeared for the afternoon without telling him of her whereabouts. She worked in the glow of the computer screen, cross-checking with Marina's calendar, but her entries replicated Tom's. She failed to find any additional information of value.

Could it be that Marina was hiding a romance, and her cageyness had nothing to do with work after all? With every passing minute, Ellie's frustration grew, as did her fear of being discovered.

Tom, too, keeping watch, had likely crumpled into a bundle of nerves outside.

Next she delved into Marina's email inbox. Twenty minutes passed and she found only cutting missives to subordinates and fawning ones to superiors. She plugged in her pen drive, hoping to copy the contents of the machine onto her stick but a notice sprung up. The stick didn't hold enough memory.

"Dammit."

Even if she chose a limited number of folders, the contents would take a few hours to download. She couldn't risk that. She began rummaging through the documents, clicking through various sub-folders, unsure of what she was searching for, doubting herself. She wasn't an investigative journalist. Marina had experience and cunning on her side. There was no way Ellie could best her. The documents had been fragmented into sections: finance; advertising; editorials; arts; news desk; sport; recordings; human resources; IT.

The intercom buzzed and Ellie leapt out of her skin.

Tom's voice pierced the wall of silence around her. "What's taking so long?"

"I can't find anything."

"Damn. We have to go."

"Just a few more minutes."

She scanned the folder list again. Her eyes lingered on two, titled *Finance* and *Recordings*. She hit copy. The progress bar came up just as she heard muffled voices outside. Her heart thudded. A rush of blood filled her ears.

Ellie turned the screen off just as the door opened, sliding off the chair and into the space under the desk. She pulled the chair in after her.

The light flicked on and Marina's heels spiked the carpet as she headed for the filing cabinet.

"Really, Tom, I have no idea why you're still here. Everyone will think I'm a slave driver."

Tom's scuffed shoes appeared at the door. "There's nothing I can help you with?"

Marina turned towards the desk. "Go home, for Pete's sake."

Ellie's breath stuck in her throat. Marina was bound to notice the pen drive. Ellie curled herself into a ball, willing the moment to pass. A drawer clunked open, shaking the desk.

"There it is." Marina slammed the drawer shut, stalked to the door and turned the light off.

Underneath the desk, Ellie trembled, listening to their retreating voices. She stood and retrieved the pen drive with the copied files, thanking her lucky stars for her escape. A few minutes later, she left Marina's office with tentative steps, peeking around the door before proceeding. The coast had cleared.

Only when she reached home, eager to check the files, did she realise she'd misplaced the scrap of paper with Marina's password on it.

18

They came in their hundreds to protest against the circus.

Doris forbade Mirjam and the other children from going outside; she had less luck with the adults. She begged Yusuf to stay inside where it remained safe, but he didn't listen. What man would cower behind curtains when the enemy had come to his door?

By all accounts, a call on social media to wipe out the refugee scum had gathered steam. Yusuf had neither a mobile phone nor a computer, but the sheer power of the internet to spread messages struck him with fear. Ellie Richter's article had caught the national mood like wildfire. Disgruntled, hateful men–and some women–had come from across the country, and now only a line of thin-lipped police men stood between the refugees and the far-right radicals.

At the front of the line, partially obscured by the policemen, stood Karl, the jeering leader of the circus break-in and the attack on Emir. Sunglasses obscured his face, but Yusuf recognised him by the set of his jaw, the fringe that hung partially over one eye, the triangle stance and bulging tattooed forearms. On his cheek, he'd painted a German flag.

Schwarz. Rot. Gold.

The circus men grouped together in solidarity: Zul, trembling like a leaf, and Emir and Osman, comforting in their bulk. The women had come too: Leyla the cook, who wobbled when she walked; Old Sayid, his bouffant hair coarse and wild about his head; Najib, as pale as the slate sky, here when it counted, despite his trouble-making nature; Aischa and Esme, and there in the distance came Amena and Aya; circus hands; a subdued Isaiah with a small gathering of local supporters, men and women wearing bright colours to clash with the black worn by the neo-Nazis.

As Yusuf studied the protesters, he grew unsure that they could all be written off as the warped, abhorrent far right. A chill swept through him. Had everyday Germans joined the extremists in a common purpose? If mistrust of the immigrants had gained such ground that their ideology had seeped into the mainstream, then theirs was a lost cause.

Still, what could they do apart from stand their ground, as vulnerable as they were? They had nowhere else to go. He longed for a home, where a six-foot brown man could blend in if he desired it. Fate had not unfolded kindly, and so Yusuf stood, facing the hatred emanating from the faction opposite. Drivers slowed their cars as they passed by, eager to find out the cause of the disruption, some honking in support. Yusuf didn't know whose side they had chosen. His stomach churned.

The extremists played a techno tune from a ghetto blaster. They chanted a phrase he couldn't quite catch, jostling the crowd so that the policemen struggled to hold their line. Some of them held up Ellie Richter's godforsaken front page. One of them gave the outlawed Hitler salute, taking care to hide the act from the police. His dark eyes frothed with rage.

Yusuf hated Ellie. He blamed her article, full of lies and loathing, for stirring a nest of vipers, for putting his circus family in harm's way.

Why did loneliness diminish him when he stood here with his circus family? He sensed movement at his flank and glanced across to see the ranks of circus supporters swell. Imam Saeed broke the line to slip in between Yusuf and Zul. All this time, an overwhelming emptiness had engulfed Yusuf, and yet, when it counted, strangers and friends alike had come to their aid.

"You didn't think we'd leave you to fend for yourselves, did you?" said Imam Saeed. He wore his skull cap. He nodded to Rifaat and a group of Turks, all clad in religious attire. "I brought the whole football team. Let's show these buffoons who we are."

Around Rifaat's neck hung a sign:

MUSLIM.
ONCE AN IMMIGRANT, NOW GERMAN.
HUG ME IF YOU DARE

Yusuf would have laughed if the situation hadn't been so precarious. He touched Rifaat's shoulder, gulping down the lump burning his throat. "I'm grateful."

The Imam braced himself as the line swayed. Behind them, the circus supporters began chanting slogans of their own, in Arabic and Urdu, Pashto and German, and a smattering of English.

"Refugee rights are human rights."

"Liberty for all."

"We are one."

Imam Saeed raised his voice to be heard over the din. "Your parents might not be here, you might have lost your brother, but look around you, you have friends."

A shout drowned him out. "Speak German, you apes!"

The Neo-Nazis moved as one hive mind, their faces painted in anger, a sea of German flags held aloft. Some bared teeth or raised fists. Others had knotted scarves around their mouths and jaws, hoping to avoid recognition. All revelled in their show of strength, the thought of quashing their perceived enemy. Karl led the herd in their chants, a mix of expletives and rhyming that hit Yusuf with venomous force, words he couldn't decipher but understood only too well.

"Hey! Hey!" called Yusuf. "We're still standing, you arseholes."

Osman roared. "Why is a brown man so much of a threat? I should let the horses loose. That would teach them."

"An elephant would be better," said Zul.

"Shall we keep this civil?" said the Imam. "Why men feel the need to show brute force, I'll never know."

The rocking of the protesters became more violent, a thrusting to and fro that shook them all. Amena fell and cut her lip, and Aya took her aside. The protesters brayed in delight, revelling in her misfortune and their superior strength. Others in their ranks grew uncomfortable and drifted away.

"One, two, three," said Karl.

After a brief pause, he surged, and his ranks with him.

One of the policemen holding the line stumbled. His colleagues dragged him to his feet, their faces a grim canvas of exertion. With a blare of sirens, riot police suddenly arrived in booted feet with faces hidden by helmets. They crunched the mud underfoot as they slid between the crowds, working in formation, first reinforcing the police line, then cutting bodily through the masses on both sides.

Yusuf's vision swam, and the rush that accompanied his flashbacks overwhelmed him: the rising panic and constricted chest, the tingling hands.

Imam Saeed's voice reached him through the ruckus. "Breathe, boy. It will be over soon. Look, they tire."

Sure enough, the extremists' rage ratcheted down a notch, as if airing their grievances had punctured their fury, at least for now. They walked away, self-satisfied, shouting insults but taking care not to overstep the mark, lest the police make good on their threat of arrests. The police kept the two sides apart, taking names, shepherding the two groups into different segments of the park, frowning, threatening, encouraging remaining clusters of people to disband.

Finally, only stragglers remained to speak to the refugees, to confide that they had donated clothes and food to shelters, and to express fervent wishes that the group of trouble-makers not be taken as representative of Berliners. Yusuf checked on Amena and hugged his friends, then waited for Imam Saeed, who had stopped to shake Emir's hand, and to thank the police men and kind faces from the local community. Pearls of sweat beaded the Imam's forehead.

"You shouldn't put yourself in danger like this. There may be repercussions for you," said Yusuf.

"If I stayed behind my walls, I'd be a lesser man. Besides, it's never been more asked of us to show up as slices of ourselves in different places. I'm an Imam, but I'm also a father and a teacher. And I care deeply about this community."

"How do you do it? How do you carry on fighting? Some days, I don't know how to go on. One day, I am resolute that I'm going to make this work. Other days, my pity and anger floor me. I'm of a man made of fragments."

The Imam grasped his shoulder. "Grief and change are not the easiest bedfellows. Each of us needs an anchor we can drive deep into the ground. It might be the land, or a person, or even a purpose, but without those things, doubt sets in, and it can be like a storm swirling around us. Anchor yourself, son, before it's too late."

"And you? What's your anchor?"

"My faith and my calling. But I also find ways to remember my roots."

"How?"

"I listen to music from home. Prepare food from our culture. Home is all around us. You only need to look. Take the Konditorei Damaskus in Sonnenallee where the sweet scent of the Middle East washes over you. It has found fans across communities. You can indulge in sticky *mabrumah* with pistachios and exquisite triangles of *shaybiyat* pastry. Or the vegetarian *fatteh* and *toshka* sandwiches at Berlinaskus at Markthalle Neun. It will remind you that we never entirely leave our homes. We take them with us, and we bring that density of culture with us to new lands. It's human to let negativity linger, but open your eyes, Yusuf. Our culture is celebrated in this city in more ways than you have realised. I can spend hours looking at the collections in the Pergamon Museum: the Ishtar Gate, the Gate of Babylon, the Mshatta Facade, the clay tablets of Uruk, the Aleppo room with its bright wood panelling. I take solace from them and you can too. They remind me life has continued for millennia in some form and is destined to continue."

"What if that isn't enough?"

"It is for me, son. But only you can decide what brings you light."

The moon climbed higher in the sky. Yusuf lay sprawled on his bed, picking at the grooves on the pine frame. His mind drifted to the hot bricks of his childhood home on the outskirts of Damascus, the rose-coloured gauze at the kitchen window, the garden where he'd played basketball with his brother, the rolling hills and sprawling universities. He tasted the *booza* ice cream from Al-Hamidiyah Souq melting in his mouth. A wave of melancholy washed over him for all that he'd left behind. Perhaps he'd visit the patisserie Imam Saeed had talked of, and see if it eased his longing for what had once been.

The night hung heavy with recycled memories. His brother's green eyes twinkling with pride. Lean legs hugging the sides of the motorcycle. The engine revving. Selim's t-shirt rippling in the wind. Dust flying up from the street. A roar he couldn't fathom. A broken body in the coffin.

Yusuf opened his eyes and blinked, but the memories couldn't be erased.

A knock sounded on his door.

Yusuf heaved himself up. "Come in." Sleep never restored his energy anyway.

The door opened a fraction and Doris's unmistakable silhouette appeared, her sleek bob mere shadow play against the beige wall. She stepped into the room. "I wanted to check you are all right. There were ugly emotions at play tonight. We can catch up tomorrow if that's better?"

He could always count on Doris to be in tune with him. "No, come in." He said a silent prayer of thanks that she'd been allocated as their warden. He rolled out of bed and reached for a t-shirt and shorts to pull on over his boxers.

"I'll wait outside while you get dressed."

"Stay. I'll just be a second." He finished fumbling with the button at his waistband. His time in refugee camps and, later, the circus, had quashed any pangs of modesty. A body was nothing special.

"I have something for you." She tossed a bulging journal on the bed.

He picked up the book and smoothed out his bedcovers so they could sit down. Doris sank down beside him as he leafed through the pages. He turned to Doris. "What is it?"

"I think you should read it."

The journal had been filled with dense, messy jottings, half-thoughts and unfinished sentences. Doodles and post it notes, questions and quotes sat side by side. He tore himself away from a page with a drawing of a man who looked eerily like him. "I don't understand. Whose is this, Doris?"

"Ellie's."

Yusuf thrust the book away as if he had been scalded. "That woman's trouble. Why do you have this?"

She held up her hands. "I found it in the circus tent, and then the article came out and I was too busy firefighting to give it back to Ellie, and I was angry too. I'd introduced her to dozens of you. I felt used. And then I read the journal, and I realised, that article can't have been hers, and it all finally made sense. I knew she couldn't have betrayed you. How could she, knowing your stories?"

Yusuf peered at the older woman. He trusted her. He always had. Even though his father had taught him to trust no one but himself. "What do you mean?"

"You need to see for yourself." She tapped the journal. "I'm overstepping the line giving this to you, but with everything that's happened around here, I needed to show you that nothing is black and white." She walked to the door. "People make choices for all sorts of reasons, and we can never know what's bubbling underneath the surface, the secret longings and dark impulses. That's as close as you'll get to reading Ellie's mind, and maybe it can be a lesson to us all that most people are inherently good, despite their actions."

She closed the door gently behind her.

Yusuf flung back the covers. The journal fell open at the drawing of him. He turned to the first page, realising that they'd stumbled through a record of Ellie Richter's most private thoughts. The journal presented a jumble of unfiltered information, logic vying with emotions. Here, she worked through her innermost feelings, as well as her work assignments. Prying this way seemed sacrilege. He should close the book and return it to its rightful owner, but like Doris, his intrigue won out over his honour. Besides, hadn't she betrayed him first?

He read slowly, deciphering her handwriting, savouring every word although reading in German was not yet second nature to him.

He discovered that Ellie had always loved the immigrant circus.

He read stories he didn't know, about Osman and his sons.

He read anecdotes about Zul and Mirjam that told him as much about the observer as the objects of her scrutiny.

Zul the Clown: extravagant and bumbling in the ring. A master of gruesome facial contortions and slapstick. Beyond the clown persona, he is gentle and unassuming. Nothing more important to him than Mirjam, who he has made his daughter. Plain to see he mourns his family. Prays daily for his dead son but also eager to walk into the future with Mirjam. Plucks her flowers from the park. Tells her bedtime stories from his own imagination.

Mirjam: 9 years old. Teases Zul about how quickly she has learned German compared to him. Scraped her knee and ran to Zul in full clown costume. A wisp of a girl, comforted by her new father. Hope their futures ease the shadow of their past.

The hours passed and he cherished this private window into Ellie Richter's soul, a woman he'd written off to be heartless. Since the attack in the big top, he'd taken to segregating strangers in his mind, marking them out as either friend or foe, depending on how they spoke, what they wore and their demeanour towards him. But Ellie's journal showed she was an ally after all.

> Can't reconcile what Marina wants me to do with my own take on the circus. Can't be normal for journalists to bow to the will of their editor against their morals, can it? Will be hell to pay if I disappoint her again but maybe I can somehow convince her that my viewpoint is valid. Who am I kidding?

He absorbed Ellie's deep sympathy for the refugees and the firm hand of her editor, and her gradual realisation that she couldn't do what her editor had asked of her. The pages revealed her to be soft and strong, compassionate and brave.

He read until the early hours.

Inside, deep in the parts of him he had kept hidden, a seed flowered.

19

Some might have accused Rex of a certain amount of arrogance, self-satisfaction even. They couldn't, however, dispute his efficiency. He thought of himself as a master chess player. There hadn't been a time he could remember when he'd failed to secure what he wanted. As for his plan to dismantle the immigrant circus, events had been unfolding just as he envisaged. Karl had done a magnificent job. Not even the most beautiful putt on the golf course compared to the feeling of manipulating events on the national stage. The thrill never wore thin; it was why he'd entered politics in the first place.

He swatted the hand of the make up artist fussing with a powder puff on his nose. She ignored his rancour and swept a brush of some sort across his forehead. Studio make up irritated him, but it was a necessary evil. Oily skin on camera had truncated many a career. His vanity might have allowed it, but the sheen could too easily be confused by viewers as indicative of nerves or worse, deceit. The show was everything.

"And we're on in 3, 2, 1…" said a voice in his earpiece.

Rex cleared his head of distractions. All that mattered was his ability to convince the electorate–and the party–that he possessed a steady pair of hands. Despite the twists and turns of fate and circumstance, despite policy U-turns, they must think he belonged in the halls of power. It was his life's calling. He would bend to the will of the people, but they must not desert him.

A light blinked at the top of camera one, and the presenter looked straight into the lens to introduce him. "In the studio today is Rex Silberling, Interior Minister, responsible for the government's drive on immigration. He's here in light of the recent protests in Treptower Park, where policemen in riot gear were needed to bring the crowds under control." The presenter swung his chair towards him. "Minister, were you dismayed to see the scenes of chaos yesterday?"

Rex had always found this particular man's voice to be rather nasal. He smoothed out his features to project sanguine concern. "Public protests are part of democracy. I regret, however, the heightened tension in our communities. And of course, we owe the men and women in our police force a great debt for maintaining order."

"Tell me, Minister, our viewers want to know, is Germany putting the rights of immigrants ahead of its own people?"

Rex waited a beat before responding. Rehearsed answers wouldn't convince the public; experience taught him that stumbling over a few words or pausing for thought sounded more authentic. Presentation mattered just as much, if not more than, content. "This Government will always meet the rights and needs of its own citizens before any other groups, but there is of course, a clear distinction between the term immigrant and refugee under international law."

"And what do you say to the people concerned about the high numbers of immigrants flocking to Germany? Government policy here is more generous than those of our neighbours in the European Union. Are citizens right to worry about crime levels and new arrivals who refuse to integrate?"

Rex was nothing if not meticulous. Short, sharp sentences made for the best sound bites. They'd be repeated on the twenty-four hour news cycle, gaining him maximum exposure. "Of course, it's not good for our country to accept vast numbers of unskilled migrants. Refugees are rehomed according to our legal processes, and in liaison with federal states. We want people here who will integrate. Who will be successful. Who will live the German way. Who won't struggle in our country or rely on the state."

The presenter nodded. "Why is it, Herr Minister, that the very flagship project championed by you has fallen flat on its face? The Government has failed to protect citizens in Berlin-Treptow from the spike in crime, an increase, I might add, driven by the very refugees your aides handpicked. As we know, low-level criminality is often a path to greater transgressions."

The camera panned closer. Rex sensed sweat on his upper lip. "The papers of the refugees in question have been expedited. That doesn't mean we are without recourse should any criminal behaviour be taking place." He looked directly into the camera. "Any criminals will find their applications halted. I will send each delinquent home, from the first to the last. That is my promise to the German people."

"Are those empty assurances, Herr Minister? It is, after all, only a few years since innocent Germans lost their lives in the Berlin Christmas Market tragedy, an attack perpetrated by a failed asylum seeker. Isn't it true that the Government has invited the enemy into the very heart of our communities?"

On the edge of the pool of hot studio lights, Corinne flapped about like a bird. She'd warned him this wouldn't be easy. Rex resisted the urge to tug at his collar. He had plenty of practice at avoiding traps laid by journalists. He just needed to keep a clear head. A swerve here, a side-step there, a glimpse of good humour and a firm steer, and the people would stay in the palm of his hand. He'd listened to their concerns about the immigrants, and they would be as malleable as putty.

He only had to tell them they were being attacked, and that he was their saviour.

"We live in very dangerous times. In today's world, a car can be used as a weapon. An adult can masquerade as a child to win asylum. A child can blow up a train. But you have my word, this Government will stamp out any violence against our citizens, even if we have to use water cannon and weapons on the streets of our cities. We have both the intelligence and the means to protect ourselves."

The journalist took the bite. "And do you speak for the Chancellor in the use of unprecedented force where it is necessary?"

"This Government speaks as one."

Rex smiled in satisfaction. He'd showcased his strength, lest his enemies think the felling of the immigrant circus happened to be a stain on his resumé. What is more, he'd used the oldest trick in the book-negotiating by media-to bend the Chancellor to his will. She might have more liberal instincts than he and balk at the use of water canon on the streets of Germany, but a show of power always garnered respect from the electorate. Agreeing with him would be a more palatable prospect for the Chancellor than admitting her team included a loose cannon.

All in a good day's work.

The sky hung like a dense blanket as Rex left work, a black whirling mass without even stars to puncture it. Earlier in the evening, his wife had visited his office with the children for a picnic supper of sausages and pickles. The children jumped up and down on his sofa, to the dog's excitement, and pleaded with him to return home before their bedtime, but his mountainous workload stood in his way. He sent the dog home with them as a consolation prize, his heart heavy with the missed family moments that he traded for career progression.

He'd not long left the shadow of the Interior Ministry when a firm hand cupped his elbow and pulled him into a side street.

Rex spun and found himself looking down on Karl.

"What are you doing here? If you have any requirements, contact my assistant–discreetly," said Rex through his teeth.

Karl's words tumbled out at nineteen to the dozen. "I've held up my side of the bargain. Immigration is now a national talking point, and tensions have flared. My sister–"

"Carry on walking. We're too visible here," said Rex, signalling for Karl to follow him into a café.

Inside, mocha paint and oil paintings in miniature lined the walls. Rex nodded at the owner's greeting and led the way to the lavatories at the back. He knew this part of town like the back of his hand. The toilets smelt of dried urine and bleach. He wrinkled his nose. Once he'd ensured nobody lurked inside the cubicles, he turned to Karl.

"How stupid can you be?" said Rex, curling his lips in disdain. "I asked you to get in touch with Corinne should the need arise. You risk too much coming here."

"I'm risking too much for you, you mean," said Karl. "The thing is, Minister, I keep expecting to see the police around every corner. I just need to know you'll make arrangements for my sister if something happens. You must be pleased with the results so far."

"You didn't need to rough them up."

"You didn't give precise instructions," said Karl, his hackles rising. He took a deep breath, suddenly contrite. "I need to be sure you'll keep your word before I'm behind bars," said Karl.

Footsteps sounded outside the lavatory door before petering off.

Rex held his hands under the drier to trigger it. Air rushed out, providing him with noise cover before he spoke. He couldn't afford to be caught having a tête-à-tête with the likes of Karl. "It's funny your love for your sister didn't keep you out of trouble in the first place. You're not finished just yet. Let's see if you can rile the performers just a bit more. Ideally, they'll misstep and that'll bring this whole sordid tale to an end."

"A few more days then," said Karl, next to the urinals.

"A few more days. Give it five minutes before you follow me out."

The hand drier came to the end of its cycle. Rex stepped over to the mirror above the sinks to adjust his suit jacket and tie. He grimaced. His hair had thinned of late.

He left the toilets without a second glance at the younger man.

Rex had been summoned to the Federal Chancellery within minutes of the interview airing. It didn't faze him. His political manoeuvring might be an irritation, but it by no means placed him on the guillotine. Not yet. The most he had to fear was a verbal warning.

Early the next morning, the press secretary ushered him into the Chancellor's wing, where modernist furniture in white wood sat alongside amber accents and an array of bookshelves.

The Chancellor grimaced as he entered. "Leave us," she said to her press secretary.

The door clunked shut.

"Rex. This won't take long. I take it you know why you are here?" The Chancellor's displeasure could be measured by the depth of the grooves in her face. When she approved, her eyes twinkled and her skin remained smooth. A little deviance from her expectations, and the lines in her face showed a range of emotions from exasperation to rancour.

He didn't wait for an invitation to sit down. "I understand you must have reservations."

She arched an eyebrow and knitted her hands together, refusing to sit herself. "The scuffles in the park were bad enough. You went on national television and announced to the country that refugees are to be feared. You stated the Government will use force on our streets. That is without precedent in peace time. What were you thinking?"

Rex's talent as a politician lay in his ability to marry capitalism with social need, but underneath the sparkling rhetoric and full coffers, the stench of opportunism lingered. He had something of a used car salesman aura about him that he tried to hide under fine clothes. If he sensed the political headwinds were changing, he had no qualms about abandoning his position with utter charm or ruthlessness, as the situation demanded, and following another direction.

"Let's not be coy," he said. "You've seen the polls. Alternative for Germany won a 13% share of the vote in the last election. Polls show even more of the electorate have sympathy with their aims now. They have supporters amongst the rich and they have already sold themselves as the pro-workers party. How do we compete against a party that wants social justice but only for native Germans? We're on a back foot here."

The Chancellor's hand flew up like a whip, cutting shapes in the air. "You think I don't know all that? This Government doesn't govern on a whim. The polls change with the wind. You're not our campaign manager. Leave that to Baier."

Rex's nature didn't allow him to be slighted. "Do you really expect us to stand firm when the people turn against policy? When immigration has become a byword for forgetting our own people? You and I both know that the root causes of these problems are ordinary people losing jobs to technology, them seeing their neighbours and friends buy bigger houses and cars when they are stuck in the same place. But what are you going to do? The wheels of Government are slow. And fury needs to be fed, otherwise it will consume us all. Would you put your body in the way to protect your ideas like Jo Cox in England or Mayor Hollstein? To be attacked with a kitchen knife when you least expect it?" He slammed his hand on his knee to emphasis his point. "Nothing can stem the tide of anti-immigrant sentiment sweeping across Europe."

The Chancellor didn't flinch. She stared at him in disdain. "I see you. Men like you are a dime a dozen. Tread carefully, Rex, and be sure not to slip or you'll force my hand. You bound the Treptow refugees to the circus. You convinced me of the merits of the project. Together, we opened our arms to refugees in need of a safe haven and we won't turn them away easily, however you posture and prostrate before the nation. I won't have the lives of these men, women and children on my conscience. Since when is good media coverage more important than our track record? Your ambition has turned you into a shell of a man." She pointed her finger towards his chest and jabbed at the air. "Fix this."

He nodded, feigning humility. This woman was nothing without the men around her. "Of course, Chancellor. If that's what you want." She didn't realise the favour he'd done her. There was a time to reason with the public, a time to cajole, and a time to bow down to primal instincts. The Chancellor didn't understand that if the government didn't address the fears of everyday people, they would choose a strongman to give them security instead. To hell with morals and beliefs. Politicians needed to be changelings. Without listening to the public on immigration, the whole house of cards would come tumbling down and they'd be an opposition party. Only those with a firm hold on power had the luxury of idealism.

He took his leave.

The Chancellor began flicking through her next briefing paper before he'd even left the room.

The ball was already in motion. For all they knew, his intervention today could be the turning point in the campaign cycle. He'd given the people the impression he'd listened to their concerns. The *BAZ* article might have been fake news, but it heartened those who feared the immigrants, in the strange way that bad tidings could buoy someone, if they gave legitimacy to long-held suspicions. The article plumped up the tail-feathers of readers marginalised by governments ignoring their needs. It gave them someone to blame for their own failings, and helped stop the grumblings that one day might have turned into an anti-establishment revolution.

The Chancellor might have hauled him over the coals but she would thank him later.

20

Ellie sprawled on her sofa long into the night, forlorn as the images reeled across her television screen. Scenes from the Treptower Park protests dominated the news cycle. Guilt prickled under her skin, a vague sense that without her, the refugees would have remained under the radar. The *BAZ* article had acted as an enabler, ruffling the undercurrent of dissatisfaction amongst the have-nots. It had lanced a boil, releasing a river of pus made from hostility and fear.

The night had held monsters, but surely it had been an anomaly? The city of sorrow and anger Ellie had witnessed didn't marry with Berlin's real nature. Berlin had been remade, leaving Nazism and Communism in the past. It was resilient and free and full of possibilities.

Her Berlin never failed to delight her. It brimmed with surprises, even though she'd lived there all her life. The city changed from season to season. What one person loved about Berlin could be completely unknown to their neighbours, and possibly gone before anyone found out about it. This city thrilled like a kaleidoscope. It consisted of puzzle pieces, tiny mosaics of colour and possibility that had been stitched together. Her Berlin was half-litres of beer and bottomless wine, parks blanketed in green and half-pipes covered in graffiti. In its arms, cultures intertwined, giving birth to streets where bakeries with pretzels and sourdough sat alongside patisseries overflowing with Turkish delicacies and Vietnamese noodle restaurants whose spices caused her forehead to bead with sweat. From pop-up theatres, festivals like Fête De La Musique and the Carnival of Cultures, independent fashion labels, beach bars, and nightclubs which pulsed with house music or swayed with jazz, to the life-size Berlin bear mascots with their unique artwork, and people that made the city home, she loved every inch of it.

Her Berlin couldn't be a lie.

The next day, she rang her mother before the morning sun had warmed the soil, looking for the comfort that only she could give. They arranged to meet at Potsdamer Platz. As she rode the S-Bahn on her way there, fellow travellers clad in S&M gear reminded her of Berlin's celebration of those on the margins, of the changelings and transformers. Berliners didn't bat an eyelid at the couple with their peep-hole trousers, spiked collars and leash. There was no judgement for punks or women kissing freely on the streets. The freedom beckoned strangers into its embrace. It was why David Bowie, Iggy Pop and Nick Cave had gravitated here, why creatives and techies from across the continent chose this city as home, and why students at Berlin universities longed to stay. Berlin spoke to who you were and who you could become.

But she'd been shaken by what she had unearthed on her pen drive over the past few days. It had taught her that shadows gathered all around us, even where the sun shone. Even in her Berlin, in what should have been a beacon of democracy.

She stepped off the train at Potsdamer Platz and followed a stream of people towards the main square where her mother waited, transfixed by a topless man in a monkey mask playing the drums. The man danced, blissed out by the rhythms he created, and the crowd around him grew. After a few moments, Ellie pulled her mother away and they meandered towards a patisserie nestled between high rises and a multiplex cinema. Ellie hooked an arm through her mother's as tourists jostled by. Katharina, a social worker and force of nature, whose hair had been strawberry pink since David Bowie's Ziggy Stardust days, was a hippy at heart. At the ripe age of sixty-nine, she still painted her toenails with midnight purple nail varnish. They lamented about the riots the night before, and the nasty side of Berlin that had been swept away by the new day. Ellie couldn't resist telling her mother about Yusuf.

"He's sad and lonely without his family, I think, but he's like a cog in this circus. They depend on him, you can see it. And when he's on the trapeze, the audience holds its breath. You've really got to come with me, Mama."

"Well, I'm glad you have something to distract you from your employment status," said her mother with a dry chuckle.

"I'm being serious. He's really talented," said Ellie.

"What did you say his name was? You should bring him home, you know. This circus boy whose spell you've fallen under."

Ellie flushed. "I wish, for once, you'd–"

"Nothing wrong with giving my girl a helping hand," said her mother, enjoying herself far too much. "You wouldn't know romance if it hit you in the face."

"There's nothing going on."

Her mother waggled her drawn on eyebrows. "Of course not, but there will be. Don't forget the condoms, darling."

Ellie threw up her hands, exasperated. "I give up."

"Wise, dear. Very wise." Her mother cackled. "Wait 'til your father hears about this."

"Has he been drinking much?"

"Oh, let's not talk about your father. The acrobat is much more interesting."

"Seriously, Mama, I didn't come here to tell you about him."

Heavily made up eyes met hers, channelling innocence. "Then why did you start?"

They arrived at the patisserie and peered at an array of cakes before settling into plush seats in a quiet corner. Her mother scooped the cream off her hot chocolate with a teaspoon, and soon, she'd forgotten her mirth at Ellie's expense and listened intently as her daughter recounted the tale of sneaking into the *BAZ* offices. As she reached the apex, her mother's spoon clattered onto the dish.

"You snuck in? What were you thinking?"

Ellie shrugged. "My anger blocked most rational thought. I feel so bad about the article."

"For goodness sake, Ellie. You could have been caught."

"I almost was."

Her mother sighed. "Well, I guess I've done worse in my day."

Ellie laughed. Her mother always knew the right thing to say. "I was up all night combing through the files I stole."

"And?"

"There's been three transactions ostensibly for an open democracy project the paper is supposed to be leading. *BAZ* is hosting a conference engaging young minds, holding elected representatives to account, that sort of thing."

"Well, that's nothing out of the ordinary," said her mother, slurping her coffee.

"The figures were inflated, significantly so, and the money seems to have gone directly into our failing advertising revenue."

"I see. So Marina's trying to fiddle figures for the board. Are you sure?"

"There's more. The money is directly from the Government, and the Interior Minister's footprint is all over it. It's like a wormhole. Marina had filed away a cache of emails from his assistant, and I found voice recordings from a meeting with Silberling himself. I compared his voice to YouTube clips. It's definitely him. Silberling bought off Marina so she'd bury the circus. Everything points that way."

The hot chocolate stood forgotten to the side. Her mother grasped the edge of the table. "This is too dangerous, darling. You don't even work at the newspaper anymore. They'll just think you're a disgruntled employee. Are you sure you want to pursue this?"

Ellie ignored her. She was her mother's child. When had either of them ever backed down from a challenge, from doing what they knew to be right?

"What I don't understand, Mama, is his motivation."

"When do politicians ever need a reason other than their own interests? Think, Ellie. What can you see around you?"

Ellie cast an eye across the café.

"Not here, you idiot, think bigger," said her mother.

"I don't know," said Ellie.

"The tide is changing across Europe. The people aren't happy. They are scared and disconnected from the ruling elite. Immigrants are feared, as they always have been. They corrode national identity. They are a burden accepted by the state."

Ellie shook her head. Credit where credit was due. How could her mother be so critical? "Germany accepted more than our fair share of refugees. We're exemplary."

"At what cost?" The older woman toyed with the brass triangles threaded onto her necklace. "Brave governments have taken in refugees and paid the price with their popularity. But it's not enough to invite in vulnerable groups of people without shaping the narrative that surrounds them. My work tells me that. It's come straight from the mouth of the people I care for." She counted on her fingers. "Like the older Sikh man I visit, who has been repeatedly confused for a Muslim since 9/11, or the Afghan who works in Lidl and has been spat on in the street for taking German jobs. Or the young woman studying computer science at Freie Universität, whose peers assume she is under the thumb of her husband or father, simply because of the headscarf she wears. Or the vulnerable child many assume to be older than his years, given the ample stubble on his face, even though his papers prove he is fourteen. Such is our fear and mistrust of immigrants. And you, Ellie, even you, with your humanity and openness and quest for the truth, even you walked off an S-Bahn when the bearded man next to you happened to be reading Arabic."

Ellie rolled her eyes. "This isn't about your politics, Mama."

"I love you, darling, but you're wrong. We're all pawns. Minority rights are still in an infant state here. We might give the appearance of acceptance, but look under the surface, our culture is homogenous." Her cheeks glowed, and her eyes sparkled with passion. "Mark my words, the connection you're looking for is plain old human ambition. The Government's popularity is tumbling. Even the brave are forced to make concessions against their ideals. Against that backdrop you have a politician and an editor who want to keep their jobs at any cost."

"I don't believe you. Silberling initiated this project," said Ellie. "Besides, we're better than that. This is Germany, after all, not some a rogue state."

"Don't let your idealism trip you up." Her mother paused, and scraped back her pink hair from her face. "Do you remember that family trip up to the Baltic Sea, and how uncomfortable we felt when that big group of Muslim women splashed about in the sea in their burkas? If we look inside, every one of us has a seed of resistance embedded in ourselves that strikes out against those different from us. Real change takes effort. It's much easier to change tactics than it is to push against the mood of a nation. If you can't control the people, you persuade them. If you can't persuade them, you distract them. It's simple, really. An age-old trick."

Ellie's spirit sank. Perhaps her Berlin amounted to nothing after all. What if her Berlin was a pipe dream? What if her Berlin was unrecognisable to those in pain? What if her Berlin had a dark underbelly that birthed monsters? Her eyes clouded, and she shifted her chair around the table so she could lean against her mother. They sat together, silent, dewy skin against a powdered cheek.

"In the end, it's all about resources, isn't it?" said Ellie. "We come from nothing and we return to nothing. We're meaningless specs on a floating rock in the galaxy. There are countless planets and a perhaps a sea of infinite universes, and yet still people think where we are born is a measure of our value or power as humans."

Her mother hugged her. "Don't be disheartened. Democracy is fragile. We have to work for it. And for heaven's sake, call the circus and make them hear you out. Apologise. You'll feel much better for it."

Ellie sighed. She couldn't fix everything, but she wasn't giving up without a fight.

Haunted by the need to make amends, Ellie called the circus residences the moment she stepped out of the patisserie. When Doris agreed to see her, she wavered between relief and apprehension, wondering how to frame her regret and culpability. On a whim, she asked her mother to join her, feeling foolish for needing the support.

Broken bottles and discarded waste littered the expanse of park as they neared the circus. Not a soul lingered there. Just beyond, the flat-pack residences stood deflated against the cloudy sky. When Doris answered the buzzer, her puffy eyes revealed her sleepless night.

"Thanks for seeing me," said Ellie.

"It's no problem," said Doris. "But who is this?" Her eyes darted between Ellie and her mother, and realisation dawned. She broke into a reserved smile. "Why, of course. I see the resemblance. Frau Richter, I presume?" The sun reflected on her sleek silver hair as she opened the door wider to let her visitors through. Her pleated skirt swished as she closed the door.

They hovered in the dim hallway, with Doris neither extending a warm welcome nor directing the conversation.

Her mother stood to the side, awkward and silent, a third wheel.

"I feel responsible for what happened," said Ellie, nibbling on her bottom lip. She would find a way to fix this. She didn't like the feeling gnawing at her, that she'd come up wanting. She hadn't ended up pleasing anyone: not Marina, the refugees, her parents or herself. She'd bottled the thing that she'd always known instinctively to do: to pick a corner and stand her ground.

Doris studied her face. "The people here are poor. They've faced loss like I've never known. They shouldn't have to face hatred, too. But my gut tells me you're more friend than foe."

Heat stained Ellie's cheeks. She chose her words with care. "I never intended for that article to be published."

"I thought as much."

"My editor played me for a fool."

Doris softened. "We live and learn."

"I have a plan to set things right." Ellie paused, looking over Doris's shoulder for signs of life in the residence, for Yusuf. Perhaps she could tell him all she had learned and swear him to secrecy. "Can I talk to the residents?"

Doris made a steeple of her fingers. "I don't think that's a good idea right now."

Ellie felt the keen sting of disappointment. But she could be patient. Compassionate journalism meant a balance between the infringement of privacy and a story's need for oxygen. She could build her story brick by brick and gain the trust of its main actors. There would be an opportunity yet to make amends.

"Perhaps the three of us could have a coffee together, since you've made the journey," said Doris.

Her mother beamed. "That's very kind of you, Frau Kaun. And please forgive my daughter. She meant no harm."

Doris nodded. "Follow me. I might have a slither or two of banana cake as well."

The three women walked along the winding corridors to her apartment, with Ellie alert to every sound behind the closed doors they passed, hoping for a glimpse of one of the refugees, if only to convey with her eyes that she regretted her part in the article, that she truly was their friend.

Inside her apartment, Doris put the kettle on and ushered Ellie and her mother to the table, where they sat in uneasy silence, listening to the whistle of the kettle and the clank of kitchen utensils.

Her mother spoke first, tapping her hips. "You know, we've already had a treat today, we really shouldn't have any cake."

"Nonsense," said Doris. "There's never a bad time for cake."

Her mother's eyes lingered on a picture of a man on the windowsill. "Your husband?"

Doris swung a cupboard door shut, and brought a tray of coffee and cake to the table. "That's my Hermann. When he died, and with our boys grown, I was so lonely. The circus gave me a family again."

"It was a brave choice," said her mother. "You could be enjoying your retirement."

"I'm not brave compared to the other people here," said Doris, carefully dishing out a slice of cake for each of them. "They've suffered trauma and loss, and are stigmatised. You saw what happened on the news yesterday. Some would have them return to their lands of origin, without a second thought for what awaits them there."

Her mother leaned forward, her pink hair a halo around her head. "You have a lot of spirit, Frau Kaun. Many of us become resigned as we age. One of the hardest things about growing older is knowing we can't fix everything. You know how it goes. The young have ambition and ideals, and we have perspective. You can't save everyone."

Doris played with the golden rim of her porcelain cup. "I was a little girl during the war. The lessons we learned will stay with me forever. It's our responsibility to never forget the past. We have a duty to examine every decision through the lens of Nazism. I applied for the job at the residences because it's my choice to stay soft rather than go hard. My father was a *Mitläufer*. I remember him in his party uniform and it shames me. This was my way of making up for the past. Of testing my humanity."

The two older women retreated into their own thoughts for a moment, lost in the grooves of history and the future they hoped to see.

"We try to teach our children to be compassionate, to share, to appreciate the opportunities they have and the hardships others face. But the structures around them don't do the same," said her mother.

Ellie spoke up, eager to prove her colours to Doris, to wash away the residue of her mistakes. "We should have open borders and be done with it. In little more than a generation, all this nonsense, all the wars, will be a thing of the past."

A flash of surprise crossed Doris's face. "Really? However would governments plan infrastructure if comings and goings were so unpredictable? You can't run a country without knowing who's coming in. The state even struggles to react to small changes. Think about how even non-Berliners buying second homes in this city has caused rents to spike for ordinary people. Opening up our national borders would be a tsunami we just wouldn't cope with."

Ellie furrowed her brow. "We trust that things find a balance, as they do in nature. Nothing that's worth anything is easy. If we don't take any risks, things will only get worse. Look at the role of dark money on the internet. How there's these silent forces stirring up trouble."

The older women looked at her blankly. This was a war they'd leave to Ellie's generation to fight.

Her mother spooned some cake into her mouth. "Most people aren't evil. Their politics are shaped by the lives they haven't lived. That doesn't mean they're heartless or stupid, just blinkered. I've seen how those on the bread line live. They don't have the luxury of caring about anyone else; they are fighting to survive. As for the far right, they can swim in their own delusions for all I care, but we'll imprison them in our open, tolerant, brave society. That's the Germany I believe in."

"For now, the most we can hope for is the neo-Nazis to go back underground and not be so brazen," said Doris. "In a few short years, white nationalism has gone from a conversation you hold in whispers in the bathroom to one heard at the dinner table and even in bars. It's too much to hope for that everyone celebrates difference, but the far right mustn't feel emboldened to threaten or harm others. What happened here yesterday can't become the norm."

"I was horrified when I saw the coverage," said Ellie, pausing. "Look, I want to be honest with you. I don't think Minister Silberling is the friend you perceive him to be."

Her mother threw a sharp glance in her direction, a wordless warning about treading carefully without airtight evidence.

Doris raised her eyebrows in surprise. "Well, he's too untouched by reality to really understand those in need, of course, but the circus was his idea, so he can't be all that bad."

"Frau Kaun," said her mother, with a light touch. "You know as well as I do that all politicians are slippery eels."

"Well, yes, but when you're as old as us, you realise there's neither one type of politician nor one type of immigrant," said Doris.

"Goodness, look at the time," said her mother, catching sight of a wall-clock and setting down her fork in horror. "We must get on and leave you to your day, Frau Kaun. We've intruded on your time for far too long."

"It's been an unexpected pleasure to see you both today," said Doris. "I do hope to see you soon at the circus." She drew back her chair, and the two women emulated. She turned to Ellie. "Thank you for your apology. Perhaps you can find a small way to set this right."

"Of course," said Ellie, feeling a rush of love for the wise women she crossed paths with, and the world they built piece by piece.

21

Yusuf meandered through Treptow, having visited the supermarket and the local ice cream bar. He'd bought a cone on a whim and the remnants of stracciatella gelato lingered on his taste buds. Cranes littered the sky line, symbols of a city striding into the future, busily building for its citizens.

After a few moments, he picked up the multi-pack of water and continued on his journey back to the residences. His hands hurt where the plastic carry loop dug into his skin. Doris might be as bright as a button, but at sixty-eight years of age, the weekly shop could be a bit much. Yusuf liked to help with heavier items. The weekly ritual brought him pleasure, and he carried it out without pomp or ceremony. He appreciated the constant reassurance she provided, and this was a way of repaying her.

Sometimes Doris would request sparkling water, other times she'd need washing powder or wine. Each time, she insisted on paying him. He never bothered checking the amount. He'd have preferred Doris not to be such a stickler for returning precise money to him; his pride would have benefited had she been more lax. How wonderful to pretend he could afford to be generous about trifling sums. In fact, finances were tight for both of them. The halls of age and twists of fate cared little for dignity.

The laughter of the children playing in the park drifted on the wind, tinkling in his ears like the wind chimes his mother loved. He reached the abandoned Spreepark, where once brightly coloured dodgems, dulled by rust and the elements, waited to be brought to life with a melancholic beauty all of their own.

A rustle reached his ears, louder than the stirring of the wind-blown trees.

Yusuf whipped round.

There, with his arm looped casually around the rod of a dodgem, stood Karl, eating crisps.

His eyes flashed malice. "I've been waiting for you, acrobat. I'm a patient man. It doesn't matter how many people you surround yourself with, where you hide, or which route you take. I'll find you."

He scrunched up the crisp packet, tossed it to the floor, and sauntered over to Yusuf until they stood nose to nose. Up close, Karl was all sallow skin and taut angles. Salt granules dotted the corners of his mouth.

"You stuck your neck above the parapet for your friends, and then again at the protest. That wasn't clever. You're a marked man." He prodded Yusuf's chest with his finger, and Yusuf resisted the urge to cave in submission.

"What have I ever done to you?" This man, with all his posturing and accusations, was so different from Doris and Ellie. Surely Karl could tell just by looking at him that Yusuf wasn't a threat? Didn't his attire alone–too short trousers and frayed t-shirt–evoke sympathy? Didn't his demeanour–the one that marked him out as lonely and grieving–attract compassion? How could he be hated so much by a stranger?

Karl removed his sunglasses and considered him a moment. An aeroplane pinned to the lapel of his leather jacket glinted in the sun. His pouched slate-grey eyes flashed antipathy. "It's not hard to understand. It's fun, taunting you like this, seeing your confusion." His hands looked like meat cleavers. "If you really want to know, this isn't your home. You can roam the Earth with your belongings on your back, or set up home in a hovel far away from here. I couldn't care less. As long as it's not here. Filthy Muslim." He placed two hands on Yusuf's chest and shoved hard.

The injection of space between them was a blessed relief. Yusuf became aware of every sound: the grinding of his own teeth, the inhale and exhale of Karl's breath, the clicking of beetles not far from where he stood. Yusuf scanned the vicinity, wondering how to make his get-away, how to escape without bruises or an injury that would prevent him from taking to the trapeze that night.

"Well, I'm not wrong, am I? I'd know your lot anywhere, turban or no turban," said Karl.

Yusuf frowned, shaking his head. "Muslims don't wear turbans."

"Well, are you one or not?" He fished out a shiny piece of metal from his pocket and slipped it onto his fingers. "I'd like to know."

Before what? Why did he need to know? Why should his religion make a difference?

"Muslim terrorist," said Karl.

It was always the same questions, the same suspicions post 9/11. As if the world had been rocked on its axis and in an instant, billions had mutated into zealots and murderers.

In Yusuf's hands, the water pack weighed heavy. A rush of light-headedness blurred his vision. He thought of Zul the Clown, and how he'd denied his faith. Yusuf wanted to be different. He should have said he believed in Allah; he should have admitted he was a Muslim.

Later, when he replayed the conversation in his mind, he imagined he stood strong and resolute, and ripped the sunglasses from Karl's face to stare into his eyes, unflinching. "*I don't debate religion with atheists. You have your belief system, and I have mine. You have no patience or understanding for the culture and richness that accompanies my faith.*" Or he would say, "*Madmen have hijacked my religion. True religion does not sit in the same house as terror.*" He would explain to Karl, "*There are vast differences between different groups of Muslims in their beliefs and practices, differences that are geographical, historical, cultural, familial,*" and then he'd recommit to his faith a thousandfold, comforted by the fact he wouldn't accelerate his spiritual demise, as Karl had his.

But his mind betrayed him, and so did his runaway tongue.

Inside him, his identity cracked like a splintered bone that would never heal. His relationship with Allah had been complicated by all he'd seen and suffered. It was a small jump to deny his faith. An instinctive understanding kicked in, an outsider's understanding, of when to speak and when to remain silent.

"I'm not a Muslim."

The denial lay on his lips like a stone. He'd sinned. His mother sprang to mind, head-scarfed and devout, mumbling as she read the Holy Book, rocking on her prayer mat as dawn came.

Karl snarled, more animal than man. "You think that will save you?"

It happened in an instant.

Nobody waited in the wings to protect Yusuf; nobody needed protecting, either.

Yusuf was free to act or react, to fight or flee.

He chose to fight.

Karl lunged, and this time, Yusuf was ready.

His training kicked in, the limber feet, the agility and the strength. He ducked, avoiding Karl's metal-enforced fist. He swung the four-pack of water at Karl. The litre bottles thudded against Karl's side.

Karl's feet shifted under him, and he flew across the air and landed with a groan.

"Oomph."

Yusuf sprinted over, and kicked him for Emir. For Zul and Osman. He kicked him for himself and for Allah, who Karl had forced him to disown. When Yusuf finished, he found that his gratitude for Doris had been replaced by shame and wretchedness, but also a sense of power.

Karl lay sprawled on the grass like a rag doll, one hand on his nether regions. His pinched face told of his pain, though he didn't make a sound. The knuckle duster glinted in the sun a few yards away. He'd recover soon and there would be hell to pay.

Yusuf panted as he bent to scoop up the water, dented from the blow, and ran the remaining stretch back to the residences. He keyed in the password at the main entrance, looking over his shoulder, expecting his attacker to appear at any moment. His heartbeat jumped in his throat as the device buzzed twice, indicating he'd entered the wrong number. Again. His fingers fumbled with the keypad. Finally, the door swung open and he darted through, following the corridor around to Doris's apartment.

She answered his knock immediately with a grateful smile before relieving him of his burden and pressing coins into his hand.

"Next time bring a pack that isn't so bedraggled, if you can," she said, only half-teasing.

"I ran into trouble."

Only then did she take in his pale complexion, the sweat lining his forehead, the shame in his eyes.

"Whatever's the matter?" she said, setting down the shopping.

"Karl–from the protest and the break-in–was waiting for me behind the dodgems."

She grasped him. "You're not hurt?"

He shook his head, not admitting he'd been the one doing the hurting. "No. I got away. I was quicker than he expected, I think. Being alone made me faster." His mind flashed back to Emir in the barrel and Zul, running, running through the bandstand in a desperate attempt to evade a beating.

Doris frowned. "You have to stay away from trouble. Your citizenship process depends on it."

"I know, but what could I do?" His adrenalin surge had subsided, and a tiredness overcame him. "Let him beat me? Run, hoping he wouldn't catch up? Bring the trouble to our doorstep again?"

"I don't know, lad. I'm sorry." She reached for her telephone, her body curved like a bow, weary, defeated. "We should report this."

"Leave it, please." He didn't want to open this can of worms. Not that it had helped last time anyway. In any case, who knew how police would evaluate the events? Maybe he'd be seen as the aggressor. His behaviour hardly marked him out as blameless.

"Yusuf, this man can't go unpunished. You have a responsibility."

He snapped, his shame at renouncing his religion morphing into incandescent rage. He didn't explain to Doris what had happened or why his anger burned like a fire. Instead, he let his emotions loose. "Why? Why do I have a responsibility? Why is the burden on me to do good when others can behave like beasts? Why do I have to jump through loop after loop, scale the heights of acceptable requirements, just to be safe? Why can't it be someone else's turn to be the saint for a change?"

Doris listened, and when he'd finished, she reached out her hand and squeezed his.

"I'm tired of being scared. I'm tired of being weak."

She stroked his hand with her calloused thumb as if she comforted a child. "I know. But from where I'm sitting, he's the weak one."

They sat in silence a while, neither knowing what to say but not wanting to end the conversation without comforting words to wash away the residue of his ire. Yusuf's mind drifted to words scratched into a page that should have remained private.

"You were right, you know," he said.

The corners of her mouth lifted. Her magnanimity taught him how to be a better human. "About what?"

"Ellie's journal." He held her gaze, channelling neutrality, when all the while his heart raced.

"Interesting read, wasn't it?" said Doris. She nudged him playfully, and in her eyes he discerned the young woman she'd once been. "You saw the drawing of you, then?"

His mouth twitched. "Oh, yes." He still wasn't sure what to make of it.

"Good thing she's coming by tonight then. She retraced her steps and called to ask if I'd seen it. I'll send her straight to your room and you can return it to her yourself."

He held up his hands. "No, no, you return it. What would I say?"

A mischievous smile lit up her face. "Whatever you want. You're a grown man. But after this morning, I dare say you might enjoy it."

That evening, Yusuf spied Ellie in the circus tent, marvelling at the acts as if she'd never been before. She'd always been objectively beautiful with her inquisitive green eyes above the freckles that fanned her nose and the fiery hair she impatiently brushed from her face. She hung at the edge of her seat, not caring she was there alone, as comfortable in her skin as he was wretched in his.

The magic of the circus took hold. Horses galloped on a bed of clouds and when the girls danced, the tent filled with the scent of dense rainforest, with the musk of exotic blooms and humidity in the air. Zul outdid himself with a comic rendition of a love song while fawning after Esme, who shimmered like an apparition. All the while, Yusuf hid in the wings, as close to Ellie as he dared, watching the shadow play and emotions dart across her face.

She'd inhabited his thoughts these past few days, and he knew pangs of guilt that he'd treated her badly when they last met. He heard her voice in his head in quiet moments, snippets taken from her diary, as if the journal had stripped away any sense of artifice between them. He'd travelled away from his initial instinctive distrust of her, and she'd become a balm to soothe the negative sentiment that swirled around the circus. The irony of her involvement in the headlines was not lost on him, but he still felt drawn to her, and had, after all, been tasked by Doris to return her journal.

He'd hardly been a gentleman the last time they met, and she would be well within her rights to insult him. He worried she'd be angry at his intrusion of her privacy. His heart drummed a raggedy beat, knowing merely holding the journal would arouse suspicion that he'd read it. Perhaps she'd be sanguine about how he'd come to read it, but he couldn't know how she'd react, or even if he'd feign ignorance of its contents.

The confetti fell at the end of the show, as it always did, and this time the foils warped and wriggled until they became tiny birds which circled above the heads of the crowd, who shrieked in delight at the transformation. When the final guests had filed out and the last throes of Old Sayid's band had soared through the tent, Yusuf searched for Ellie and found her seat empty. He swept the tent for a sign of her, but she had gone. It disappointed him that she'd left without speaking to him. He'd built up the conversation in his head, playing out different scenarios. In one, she flung her arms around him in gratitude for finding the journal; in the other, she tore it from his hand, deaf to his apology.

At ten o'clock, just as he considered turning in for the night, a knock sounded on his door, a knock so rhythmical it could have been a piece of music. He'd been flicking through the journal once more. He gulped and placed it on his side table, taking care to make sure it looked tidy in case the visitor was Ellie after all. His hand grasped the cool steel of the door handle, but he stopped short, and changed his mind about the placement of the journal. He shifted it to the corner of the room, as if he'd never touched it in the first place and it had lain there, forgotten.

The door reverberated again, this time more tentatively as if the visitor didn't want to rouse him.

"Just a minute," he said, smoothing down his t-shirt.

He swung the door open, and there she stood, drenched to the bone, her hair dark with rain and flattened to her skull.

"What happened to you?" he said, surprised, without even a hello.

"I had a meeting with a source." She shrugged. "It poured and he didn't even show up. I didn't even have an umbrella." A rain drop rolled down her nose to the tip. She wiped her face with the arm of her jacket, but that, too, was sodden with water. "Can I come in?"

He'd been so distracted by the sight of her, he'd blocked the threshold. "Of course." He moved inside and beckoned for her to follow.

"It's not too late? I wasn't expecting to be so long. Doris did tell you to expect me?"

A towel hung on the radiator. He offered it to her.

She accepted it with a smile and began patting herself dry, not knowing where to start. After a few minutes, she became aware of her surroundings, and turned a full circle in the room. "It's so small in here."

"I don't need much," said Yusuf. After the camps, it struck him as a luxury to have a door to close, to feel safe from thieves and worse, to be clean, to have friends nearby and not worry about head lice and food rations. No bombs fell out of the sky here to turn his nightmares into reality. By any measure he knew, he had much to be grateful for.

She grew sombre. "Yusuf, I've been meaning to say sorry to you, for the trouble and hurt my article caused. Those words didn't reflect what I think, and I didn't intend for them to be published."

"You could have refused to write it." It disappointed him the ink had been hers after all, but it took courage to stand there before him and admit her error, and he found he was willing to give her a chance. Her journal had removed all pretence between them.

"I was worried about my job," she said, holding his gaze, willing him to understand.

He nodded, pensive, thinking of his father and the war. "We are all at the mercy of people more powerful than us."

She breathed a sigh of relief, and he realised it meant something to her that they reconcile. He didn't understand why she cared, but it made him feel valuable.

"I have something for you." He pointed to her journal in the corner of the room.

"Oh, I've been looking for it everywhere." She made a beeline for it. "I can't believe you found it!" She hugged it to her chest and he soaked up the sound of her joy. "I've squirrelled away my thoughts in it, and the thought of losing it was terrible."

"You have it back now."

"Did you read it?" she said.

He paused. The truth lay on the tip of his tongue, waiting to spill out.

She shrugged. "I would have. It's in my nature always to look under the covers." She coloured.

The energy between them pulsed. She'd been honest with him, and he didn't want to lie to her. "Okay then. Yes, I did."

He ducked as she flung the wet towel his way.

"You rascal."

"I'm sorry."

"No need to be. Makes me feel better about the other thing." She looked at the journal again, thumbing through its pages. "Well, thanks again."

She turned to leave, and he wanted to stretch out the moment because with her, he forgot his loneliness.

"Ellie?"

"Yes?"

"Would you like to go out with me tomorrow?"

She stopped, her hand on the door knob, and turned to face him. A hint of colour touched her cheeks. She nodded.

He grew embarrassed. "I don't know the city very well but maybe we could go for a walk or some food?"

"I'd like that a lot. There's some really nice places by the river. Berlin is beautiful in the open air at this time of year. Or there are some rooftop bars. I could show you."

"I'll meet you at the Ferris Wheel after the show."

"Okay." She tucked a lock of hair behind her ear, waved goodbye with an awkwardness that endeared her to him, and closed the door behind her.

22

Over the years, the once proud Ferris wheel in Treptower Park had become wrapped in trails of ivy. Even Yusuf, with his experience of heights, regretted climbing it now. It had seemed such a good idea from the ground. Safer, somehow, than braving a new environment, but still with the open air and views that Ellie had seemed so keen on. He took her hand and pulled her up after him, swinging from the steel structure with ease, teasing her about her hesitation.

"You're enjoying this, aren't you?" said Ellie, breathless from exertion, her cheeks a rosy hue.

Yusuf grinned. "Maybe a little."

"I should have forced you to come dancing with me, even though I have two left feet. Anything would be better than this."

Her hand slipped. He steadied her then manoeuvred himself so he brought up the rear. "Take your time. I'm right behind you."

When they reached the top, they clambered into the nearest pod. The night had cooled, and goosebumps sprung up on his bare arms. A crescent moon and blanket of stars studded the velvet sky. Beneath them, the city lights glowed.

Ellie absorbed the view and sighed. "Okay, maybe it was worth it." She turned to him. "You do know the story about the old lady a few years ago? Ninety years old and she decided to have a go on the Ferris wheel. Except the wind carried her up and she had to be rescued by the emergency services."

Yusuf's laughter rang through the air. "I like the sound of her."

"Me too."

They smiled at each other, and he realised how close they sat. It had taken him a while to discern the real Ellie, and knowing her a little through her journal made him want to know all of her. He couldn't be suspicious about the motives of people who crossed his path. If he armoured himself against hurt, he risked missing out on joy. She'd been the motor for his realisation, and he was grateful for it.

"I really shouldn't have read your journal. It was wrong of me. I can't believe you got fired for standing up for the circus. For us."

"I've never been good at doing what I'm told. It was the last straw. And, please, don't feel bad about reading my journal. I spend my life digging into other people's affairs. I understand."

"That's letting me off the hook. Ask anything of me, and I'll answer," he said.

"Okay. You're on," said Ellie, eyes like glassy moonstones, unreadable. "Tell me who you are."

Yusuf's heart hammered. "I wouldn't know where to start."

"How about I ask you three questions and you decide what to share."

He could cope with that. There was a heady intimacy to sitting in the pod of the Ferris Wheel, thigh against thigh, up amongst the stars. "I'll try."

She rested her chin on her hand, considering her options. The cab rocked. In this light, she had the sheen of a marble statue in profile, and he experienced a sudden impulse to touch her.

"What was your childhood like?" she said.

"I was born in the suburbs of Damascus. My mother, she's the best. My favourite days were filled with games and simple food. Corn on the cob with a sprinkling of chilli. My big brother Selim would challenge me to see how much chilli we could eat without burning our tongues. We'd run for water to quench the fire in our mouths."

Speaking about his brother didn't hurt as much as he thought it would, as if by focusing on happy memories, Selim was, in some way, alive again.

"The days were hot and dusty. The climate is nothing like here. We played hide and seek often. I remember how gleeful I'd be to find a new hiding place. We'd play on the streets of our town, running past topsy turvy houses with heavy thatched roofs covered with mud and old men smoking hookah pipes who stank of tobacco. We'd play basketball until the sun went down or my mother got cross. Selim was old enough to have his own friends but he looked after me, protected me even. I worshipped him."

"He sounds nice. The perfect brother, or at least to me. I don't have any siblings. What did he need to protect you from? The war?" The intensity of her gaze unsettled him.

His secrets had been his alone for so long. Not even his circus family knew these little details, the memories of home he clung to. In the common room at the residences, too often they steered clear of the past, like talking about it would open a trap door of sorrow or lead to a domino effect in which they infected each other with grief. But Ellie was whole and strong. He needn't fear sharing his burden with her. Sharing his history held meaning for him. It marked her out as special, but he couldn't be sure what was developing between them.

He batted her away, his voice playful. "Hey, no follow up questions."

"You can't add rules halfway through. You had my journal for three days, Yusuf. Three whole days!" She swatted him and inside he thawed a little more.

"Our father worked long hours as a hotel bellboy in Damascus, and when he returned, he would be irritable. Anything would anger him: food he didn't like, a pair of sandals out of place, or simply disagreeing with him. Even then, I was interested in gymnastics. I was naturally flexible and strong. I'd do cartwheels in the house and my father would catch me by the ear and haul me to my feet. He didn't think that sort of pursuit manly enough. He'd argue with my mother about how wild we were. I should have been doing my schoolwork or playing basketball. After the sun set, sometimes he'd take a belt to us, but Selim would push my mother and I out of the way and take the beating. In the morning, Selim would smile and tell us not to worry, but I saw the welts my father left, and how Selim would rile him on purpose just to prove he hadn't been broken."

Ellie's eyes filled with tears. "Where's your brother now?"

Yusuf looked out across the city. "Dead. He's dead."

Her voice seemed far away. "I'm so sorry."

"He's buried in our town, and my mother won't leave him. Not even for me. She said she was too old to travel here, but really, it's because it breaks her heart to think Selim will be alone." He rubbed his arms briskly, suddenly feeling the chill. "He was so proud in those last moments. A boy from a neighbouring village offered to let him ride his motorbike. Selim promised our mother that he would be careful. The other kids were so envious. Cars were rare and motorbikes even more so. He wouldn't even let me ride with him. He made it a few hundred metres down the throughway before an explosive device ripped him apart. He died instantly. I don't remember much after that, just the screams: my mother's, and my own, the highest pitch of all." His grief scalded him, as though time and distance had no impact.

Ellie shuddered. "An explosion? I don't understand. Who would do such a thing?"

Yusuf shrugged. "Does it even matter? He's gone."

She leant her head on his shoulder, and the gesture was just small enough for him to bear. "It matters."

He was grateful for the dark that lent his grief cover, for the cab that prevented her from looking him directly in the eyes. "I don't know if the bomb was meant for Selim. The war was starting. Selim was foolish, too open about his views. He'd sit on the steps of the masjid after prayers, his green eyes full of fire, discussing his dreams for our town. A Syria where all opinions were valid, where the government put its citizens first, regardless of creed, where our mother would have her own means and not have to stay with our father. When Syria would be a bustling hub of culture and industry, and draw in tourists and dollars from across the globe. Above all, he dreamt of a time when, with Allah's grace, the powers that be, the United States of America and Russia, would look to Syria and view it not as a pawn, but as an equal. He believed in the impossible, and I think that's what made my father more angry than anything else."

"Your parents must have taken it hard. How did they cope?" said Ellie.

"Last question?"

She nodded. "No more questions about your past. Not until you're ready."

"My father wasn't there that day, but he drank himself into a grave after that. A man, who'd never touched a drop of alcohol before. He blamed himself, I think. At least that's what my mother says. He blamed himself for explaining with his belt rather than his tongue. He could have taught Selim not to be so open, to chain up his dreams. The thing is, Selim was so strong. Who knew he needed protecting too?"

"You've lived horrors I can't even imagine," said Ellie, looking up at him. "Your poor mother, losing you all."

"After Selim, she changed. Her infectious laughter dried up overnight, as if it had been blocked by a bath plug. She wore only black and prayed Qur'an more than ever. And our house, it was like all the joy had been sucked out, as if Selim's death created a vacuum where nothing existed but a raw ache. Now I'm gone too. And all she has is their graves."

She grasped his hand, but their fingers sat awkwardly, as if they didn't quite belong together, so she released it. "She has you."

"Maybe I'm not enough to balance out all the pain," said Yusuf. He'd voiced his deepest fear, that he was unlovable or somehow not enough, for his mother or for the people in this land. It hung in the air between them and the gulf between them widened.

"Maybe she's just not ready to let go," said Ellie. She drew her coat close around her and buried her chin in her cranberry-coloured scarf.

He wondered if he'd been right to exchange his home for this strange land. He ached to hold his mother once more. "Maybe I should have stayed. Part of me thought this is what Selim would have done. He would have left."

"Who knows what the future holds, Yusuf? You can only make the choices in front of you. Maybe your mother would choose differently too. Maybe she'd come if you asked again."

"Perhaps it was Allah's way. She was too old to make the journey. It's hard even for the young. In a few years, when I have the right to stay permanently, I'll convince her, and we'll do it the right way, with tick boxes and forms, not on the seas or in the back of a truck praying not to be found..."

Ellie took his face in her hands, and for a moment, there, high up above the trees, they swayed in the wind. She planted a kiss on his cheek, and it comforted him. They drew apart. The twinkling lights of the city stretched for miles, and the thud of soft house beats drifted over to them from a makeshift bar underneath colourfully lit trees a few hundred metres away.

"I envy the roots you have here, how comfortable you are," said Yusuf.

"Cities are always changing, even if you've lived here all your life. I've seen sides to Berlin recently I didn't expect."

"You mean you've seen the dark side of people. Cities are just bricks and mortar."

A sad smile played on her lips. "Yes, I've made sense of it now. Cities are made up of people. They are made from the sweat, tears and dreams of the people who live there."

"You still love this place. I can hear it in your voice, it's clear in the way you look down at the specks of light," said Yusuf.

"It's my home."

"Can it be mine?" He knew that no place could be everything to everyone. There were always losers and winners. Places changed with the wind, and they changed with leaders, and with the weather, and with external forces. So much lay out of his control, but he wanted reassurance.

She leaned into him, and her body warmed his. The silken strands of her hair tangled in her scarf. "Only you can decide that, but you are not the first refugee to make your home here, neither will you be the last. The majority of Berliners welcome new faces. It is a young city. A city full of dreamers and artists. You can find things here that would be unimaginable elsewhere, like the Syrian man performing burlesque to great acclaim on the other side of town, or the man in Friedrichshain with an armoury of rings piercing his nose and his whole body tattooed save the whites of his eyes."

Yusuf laughed.

"I'll let you in on a secret. This city is real. There is no artifice." Her fingers glided over the rusty steel of the safety bar, the dents in the cab and the peeling paintwork. "Show this city and its people the shades of you, the dark and the bright, all your hidden colours, and it won't abandon you. Make yourself vulnerable, and the city will catch you if you fall."

He wished he had her faith. "I'll think about it." He couldn't be certain he had any more to give.

She stood, and the cab jerked. "I don't think I'm going to make it down again." She gripped his arm in panic.

"Come," he said, standing and holding out a hand to her. "I'll help."

They climbed down with care, each lost in their own orbiting thoughts. When they reached the ground, she took off her boots and stood barefoot in the grass.

"It feels good to be on the ground again." She tugged at him, and pulled him in the direction of the river. Fireflies zipped past them, yellow pinpricks of light in haphazard flight, like fairies just out of reach. When they reached the river bank, water swirled beneath them, dark and shallow. "I want to give you something."

"Oh?" said Yusuf.

"Some good luck. It's a custom here in Berlin. You need to spit in the River Spree. I'll go first."

To his surprise, she took a deep breath and lobbed a ball of spit into the water below.

He hooted with laughter. "You didn't."

She raised her eyebrows. "I did. Your turn."

He spat, a great big gloop of saliva, and when he was done, he wiped his mouth with the back of his hand.

She looked at him approvingly. "Now sleep. Your luck is about to change. You just need to trust."

They hugged goodbye, and when she had shrunk to a small dot in the distance, he missed her.

23

Some grown up children chose to build their own
lives far from their parental homes. Others never quite bring themselves
to be entirely free, bound by the double calling of duty and love to a
small corner of the world, because their family resides there.

It took a gentle nudge from Ellie's parents to turf her out of
the family home in Treptow. She rented a flat in Friedrichshain,
despite her father's misgivings about vandalism there and her
mother's worry about the increasing gap between the rich and
poor in that particular district. Ellie loved the hodge-podge nature
of Friedrichshain, the punk scene that had never died, the gritty
streets with their stench of art and dog mess that insisted on
realism rather than an illusory sheen. She loved her flat, too–an
airy one-bedroom filled with Cézanne and Monet prints–but her
childhood home remained her favourite place to be, despite her
father's drinking.

Her parents had met on a march towards the end of the
swinging sixties. Back then, Katharina had slept with both men and
women. Hunger pangs had made the usually cheerful Katharina
grumpy on the march. A stranger beside her called Martin Richter,
swigging beer from a bottle he'd stashed inside his jacket, caught her
eye. He offered her an apple, and by the end of the day, Katharina
realised her loud mouth and quirkiness didn't faze this quick-witted
man. They fitted together as snugly as two spoons.

Every week, unless they happened to be travelling, Ellie's
parents cooked Sunday lunch. Each time Ellie slotted her key into the
door, she breathed a sigh of contentment to know what awaited on
the other side…as long as her father hadn't started drinking too
early. This Sunday was no different to any other, except that Ellie

had invited Yusuf to join them. She imagined curtains twitching at the sight of the tall, bearded man she'd brought home with her.

Ellie paused on the threshold and smiled at Yusuf. "They won't bite, you know."

"It's been a long time since I've been inside a family home."

She'd invited him here almost as a reflex to his sorrow, an involuntary need to share her safe haven with him. Before lunch, she'd rung her parents to ban talk of politics from the table, and warned them to avoid mentioning Silberling. She'd decided not to confide in Yusuf just yet. It shamed her that German politicians could act this way. Yusuf's fragile faith in the country had already been damaged; she didn't want to add fuel to fire.

She unlocked the door, and Yusuf hesitated before following her in. Inside, the air wafted with the smell of a nut roast with a burnt undertone. Low voices hummed in the kitchen. To her right, the hallway opened up into a living room bursting with her mother's penchant for all things tactile: a faux sheepskin rug stretched across the ageing wooden floor, cushions in velvet and satin lay strewn on sofa, oil paintings of warm summer landscapes adorned the walls, and surfaces were awash with framed family photographs and travel mementoes.

Ellie stumbled into a blue stone buddha blocking the doorway. "Ouch!"

Yusuf side-stepped it with ease, and threw her a sympathetic look.

"There you are!" Her father pulled her into his arms. He smelt of soap and coffee, but the sour whiff of excessive alcohol consumption seeped through.

She tensed, then relaxed into him. Now wasn't the right time to challenge him.

Her father held out his hand to Yusuf, and his eyes lingered for a nanosecond on Yusuf's beard. "We've heard a lot about you. Welcome."

Yusuf shook her father's hand, stiff with nerves. He pulled out a small bouquet of daffodils from behind his back. "These are for you."

"Oh?" Her father smiled. "Katharina will be pleased. Me, I don't know the difference between real flowers and plastic ones."

Ellie swatted him. "That's not true. Don't believe a word of it, Yusuf. He's teasing you. Papa could make a rainforest grow in a desert."

The grey of Yusuf's eyes swirled to unfathomable depths and Ellie's heart skipped a beat.

Her father beamed. "If you say so. Lunch is ready. Your mother was talking so much she burnt the roast, but it's edible." He waggled his eyebrows at them, indicating they were probably in for a rotten meal.

Ellie stifled her laugher.

Her mother emerged carrying a steaming plate of carrots and peas, an apron tied around her round hips. Her pink hair stood on end like a scarecrow's. She spoke fast, her speech garbled. "Yusuf, come in, come in. We're so happy to have you here. I'm sorry I'm such a mess."

Yusuf's eyes didn't move from her animated face, the hair that hovered in the air by design. He smiled.

Her mother reached up to kiss Ellie's cheek. "Grab the sauce, won't you, love? It's on the stove. If we drown the food, it might taste okay."

They sat at the table in the dining room, the three of them and Yusuf, still and silent. All around them, the jumble of artefacts her parents had collected over the years could be found, the ones that showed how at home they were in the world, showcasing their view that it was possible not to be threatened by other cultures. A tiny family of Sri Lankan elephants had been arranged trunk to tail across the midline of the dining table. A wall hanging depicted a Masai woman, her long neck encased in jewellery, her elongated earlobes heavy with adornments.

It pleased Ellie to widen their usual gathering to make space for Yusuf. Too often since she'd started the circus story, she'd locked away the recurring thought of her parents' creeping age, the deepening wrinkles on their faces. She'd always been content, it being just the three of them, and besides, she'd arrived so late for her mother that another child had been out of the question. But the refugees had woken her sense of mortality, and she didn't want to imagine a time when their circle would be broken. Widening it distracted her. It made her feel less alone.

She shook her head and her morbid thoughts scattered like arrows.

Across from her, Yusuf struggled to make conversation while her mother dished out the food and her father acted as assistant. His eyes lingered on the floor to ceiling rack of wine bottles.

"That's quite a stash," Yusuf said.

"I have a splendid bottle of Riesling," said her father. "Would you like some with lunch?"

"Yusuf's Muslim, Papa," said Ellie.

"Oh, of course." Her father paused. "So you don't drink at all?"

Yusuf coloured. "No, I'm afraid not," he said in half-apology, as if his refusal were somehow a slight.

Ellie stepped in. "What's that buddha doing by the living room, Mama?"

Her mother scooped some carrots onto Yusuf's plate. "We spotted it in Thailand last year and couldn't resist. It's taken an age to arrive. Lost in transit, apparently."

"We're lucky it's still intact," said her father. "When your mother disappears upstairs for one of her scented baths, I can pop it on the sofa next to me and I won't even know she's gone."

Her mother rolled her eyes.

Yusuf glanced at her parents, and Ellie's intuition told her to be wary, that perhaps instead of soothing him, her family environment brought his own into sharp contrast: the rages and beatings his father had inflicted on him, how there could be no recasting of personal relationships now his father had died.

She suddenly grew ashamed for her good fortune. Yusuf couldn't know her father, in particular, had his vices. Discord appeared in the Richter household, but it disappeared quickly. Her father would retreat to his office, fester a while, and soon enough return to hug her mother, whose irritation subsided as soon as it peaked. She wished sometimes that her mother would challenge her father on his drinking more, but she seemed blind to his faults and reared up like a lioness to protect him if Ellie ever tried to make an intervention. He wasn't a mean drunk, thank God, but alcohol transformed his mild manner into childish exuberance and made him prone to sudden impulses. It was not uncommon for him to splash money on gifts for them when in a stupor and for them to return home to mounds of clanking bottles in the living room.

Still, the demons in her family seemed manageable in comparison to what Yusuf faced, and without Yusuf knowing her more intimately, it must seem like her life sparkled with joy compared to his.

They ate, ignoring the charred bits, and her mother turned to Yusuf. "You must miss home."

Her father coughed. "Give the boy a second, Katharina, before you come at him with all your questions." Kind· eyes shone underneath grey eyebrows that grew bushier by the year.

Yusuf plastered on a smile. "Yes, I miss home, Frau Richter. I miss it a lot. But the home I knew isn't there anymore. I have a new one now."

"I hope you've been made to feel welcome. Your German really is very good."

"We have language lessons a few times a week at the residences."

"Are they enjoyable?" said Katharina, struggling to chew her mouthful.

"Yes, although we find that amongst ourselves, the refugees have adopted a mix of languages. We reach for whatever word we find first, that will be understood by our conversation partner. It's like a constant language exchange."

"How marvellous."

Yusuf's eyes twinkled. "Of course, sometimes it leads to misunderstandings. Like the time one of the kids wanted to tell me the shower had run out of hot water, and he used the term 'holy water' instead. On the whole, though, the kids are picking up the language faster than the adults. They've even been holding little clubs, learning the lyrics to songs by the Fantastischen Vier and Udo Lindenberg. The German teacher finds it funny to hear them try."

"That sounds like great fun. It's been awhile since I've put together a mixed tape. Maybe I could do one for the children?"

Yusuf took sip of water. "They'd love that."

"How long have you been in Germany, Yusuf?" said her father.

"Almost two years now."

"It must have been such a wrench leaving everything behind." Her mother was all warmth, practicality and activism rolled into one. She bloomed at the thought of taking another person under her wing. Caring for others amounted to her life's work.

"A wrench?" said Yusuf, knotting his brows together.

Ellie chimed in. "Difficult."

He rubbed the back of his neck. "Yes, there have been difficult moments, but I'm grateful to be here."

Her mother ploughed on. "Luck plays such a big role in how our lives unfold. I'm sorry this happened to you."

Yusuf's expression hardened and he put down his cutlery, leaning forward, his voice a velvet casket of grief. "I don't believe in luck. When civilians are bombed, someone is responsible. It's not just luck."

"Of course. I'm sorry to be so clumsy," said her mother.

"What people have endured there is inexcusable, son," said her father with a longing look at the contents of his glass, as if he wished the water would transform into wine.

Yusuf's olive skin turned a motley red, as if he feared his outburst had ruined lunch, and he couldn't fathom how to rewind the past few moments. "Even now, I feel powerless to stop the suffering that continues there. There's a weight you carry with you," he said, his fingers tracing the beads of condensation on his water glass.

Her mother pushed aside her plate. "It's hard, being somewhere new. You must miss your mother."

Her mother's sensitivity radar had gone awry: she'd hit the bullseye she should have known instinctively to avoid. His own mother.

"Why don't we talk about something else. Yusuf wanted to invite you to the cir–" said Ellie.

Too late.

Yusuf set down his cutlery. It clattered against his still full plate. "I'm sorry. Can you excuse me?" He pushed back his chair.

Her mother lips turned downward. "Yes, of course. Yusuf, I hope I didn't offend you."

"Oh, it's nothing Frau Richter. I just need a minute." He walked into the back room.

Her father rose, but Ellie shook her head.

Yusuf had his back to her when she approached him. She placed a hand in the small of his back and stood for a moment, watching the dust particles dance in the air, waiting for him to compose himself. When he faced her, an emotion she didn't recognise sparked in his pale face. His fragility surprised her and convinced her she'd been right to hide Silberling's machinations from him.

"She didn't mean anything by it, I promise," said Ellie.

"I know. I'm embarrassed. Maybe it was too soon to see this happy family life." He drew in a shaky breath. "Look around you. Every corner of this home is filled with memories. What remains of my family, I can fill a shoe with."

They stood in her parents' library. Keepsakes from her childhood decorated a small desk in the corner. Medals from teenage swimming competitions hung from overflowing bookshelves. Ellie shrivelled. Had she been unfeeling, inviting him here without knowing how he'd react? She should have known the permanence of her roots only made his own rootlessness more pronounced.

She reached out to him, and he pushed her back.

"You have everything, but I'm not even sure you know it," he said. "If I were you, I'd be on my prayer mat every day, giving thanks for what I have."

His willingness to point fingers at her just to make himself feel better angered her. "My good fortune isn't my fault, Yusuf, just like your poor fortune isn't your fault." She refused to be his punchbag, but she wanted to comfort him, still. "Please don't push me away. I want to help." She held her hands out to him, palms upturned.

Her parents could probably hear every word. Just behind him, her mother's placards from marches leaned against the wall. It had always soothed her to march with her mother, but even at twelve years old she'd been aware of the foolishness of marching only to absolve yourself of the need for any real actions. She'd always believed in fighting injustice. It constituted the main reason why she'd pursued journalism.

"I'm ashamed, Ellie. That's how I feel. This isn't the man I'm meant to be." Pride emanated from the set of his shoulders and his flashing eyes.

"You think I don't know that? Your story isn't finished, and you have more control than you think."

"You're wrong. It's so easy for you to say."

She paused, uncertain of how far to push him. "You're not the only one with problems."

She intended to make him feel less alone.

It backfired.

"You think you have problems?" he said, his body coiled tight like a spring. "Go on, Ellie, tell me your problems."

"You know what? It's not all about you." She didn't care anymore about being overheard. She could express herself without the lag that came from a foreign language, and she pressed home her advantage. Her heart pounded. "As privileged as I am, I'm allowed to feel sorry for myself too. I'm grateful for my life, but that doesn't mean I have to be satisfied the whole time. It's okay to want more."

"You in the West, with your culture, your foreign holidays and the world at your feet. You always want more." He shook his head, deflated. "Don't you see? Just having enough is no bad thing. I would die for that."

It cut her to the quick that he thought so little of her.

"I have no right to expect the world at my feet, to be exempt from suffering. But I have the right to point out entitlement when I see it," he said, stumbling over his words, slowing down so that each syllable drilled itself onto the fabric of her mind. He stepped away and rearranged his hoodie, all brisk movements, his tone like ice. "Please say sorry to your parents for me. I shouldn't have come."

His words stung.

She let him go.

24

The police came around, asking questions about a fight between two men in the park. Fear sparked in Yusuf when one of the officers closed in on him, and he found himself retreating from the common room, leaving it to Doris to smooth things over. He couldn't be sure of the police agenda, or how Karl might have twisted the story of that afternoon, so his lips remained sealed about Karl's repeated provocations.

Terrors began to fill his sleep once more. He couldn't decide what the trigger had been: Simeon's stabbing, the clashes at the circus, the argument with Ellie, or his growing suspicion that perhaps the Interior Minister wasn't a friend to refugees after all. Fragments of Silberling's television interview had filtered through to the circus folk, unsettling them, revealing the fragile footing they stood on in this new home of theirs.

If only he could reel back time. If only Selim hadn't died. If only the war hadn't started. If only his mother was there to believe in him when he didn't believe in himself. If only he hadn't come to this place. Why did everything good in his life crumble to dust?

He'd been unable to sit still since his argument with Ellie. Once he'd dressed, he headed to the circus tent to practice his skills, hoping the physical exertion would dull the whirr of thoughts in his head. The midnight blue and bronze tent quivered in the wind, as if it was a real, breathing person. Yusuf followed the tunnel into the ring and inhaled the scent of circus life: the sawdust that grounded him; the sweat of the performers; the lingering salty musk of popcorn.

He longed to practice alone, but an air of concentration pervaded the tent. A handful of performers toiled, deep in the throes of their routines, despite the early hour. Only repetition and rehearsal kept them sharp; rusty skills formed the surest route to injury. Witnessing their exertions brought him no pleasure this morning. He wasn't himself. He recognised the patterns that revealed inner turmoil. Zul clowning about on the trampoline made him cringe rather than laugh. He squeezed his eyes shut in response to Aischa's clumsy dismount from her galloping steed. Time and again, he'd observed variations of the acts, but his mental arithmetic of the timing of jumps or the crescendo of a set piece seemed off, as if his judgement was impaired.

As if he couldn't trust himself.

He crossed his arms across his chest and retreated to the stands to wait. More performers arrived, skipping into the ring, calling out hello. Being here, surrounded by people, made Yusuf feel more alone than if he'd stayed cooped up in his flat. He pressed his lips together and scrubbed a hand over his face in frustration, restless, eager for his own turn.

Ellie lingered in his mind: her downturned lips, tearful eyes and the voice that sought to soothe him but fell short. He'd ruined everything. Even his friends in the circus couldn't scale the walls he'd erected around himself.

Leyla approached, a cotton headscarf framing her sweaty face, an apron tied around her plump middle. "You look pale. You need one of my pastries to give you strength."

Whatever the ailment, food was Leyla's answer. She'd offer treats to a man on his deathbed, long after he'd given up physical nourishment.

"No thank you," said Yusuf, dull-eyed and cold.

The pastries glimmered with egg-white. She leant forward with the tray, and he resisted the urge to up-end it. "Take one. I promise, it will help."

She irritated him for an instant, the way she smelled of the kitchen and her exertions, the powder crusting her fingers, her eagerness to serve him. He couldn't bear any more attempts to cheer him up, the innocent queries after his well-being. "I said no."

She moved away, surprised and downcast. Remorse hit Yusuf, a plummeting of his stomach, knowing he'd hurt her. He was as bad as Najib. A word of encouragement wouldn't have harmed him. Instead, he'd caused offence with his disinterest, his monosyllabic refusal. He should have learned his lesson from how he'd lashed out at Ellie. No amount of backtracking could undo words uttered in haste.

What was happening to him?

His breath came in rasps.

Tremors rocked his body.

In the corner of his eye, his dead brother loomed, but when he turned, he saw only a stuffed bear in a top hat and bowtie marked up as a raffle prize.

He stared at his feet, throat thick with tears, overwhelmed by the instinct to hide away like an animal in a burrow. Just until he'd regained his composure and control. His seat clattered shut as he rose to his feet. On the way out of the tent, he forced himself to make eye contact with Emir, wave goodbye to Leyla and shower encouragement on Esme–who blushed at his attention–teaching her doves a new trick. He acted on autopilot. His mind had already shuttered.

In his apartment, he crawled underneath the covers, seeking refuge in the arms of sleep.

"Roll up! Roll up! Get your tickets here. Witness the skills of far away continents right here on your doorstep!" said Emir into the megaphone, a gleam in his eye.

You couldn't keep a good man down. Far from despairing about the racism they had encountered, Emir had been energised since the protest, buoyed by the support of Imam Saeed, and even more so by the kindness of individuals in the community.

The day after the protest had seen letters of support arriving in great big sacs. Even Dawud had been delighted by the pictures children had drawn. They'd offered their drawings to their favourites: Esme had been reimagined as a princess; Osman as a friendly giant; the horses as unicorns underneath a pyramid of girls. Dawud received a superhero cake from a chattering girl in pigtails. Neighbours brought typical German foods to share with the circus folk, much to Leyla's joy. There'd been hot plates of strudel, tiny halal sausages with curried ketchup and great balls of potatoes with a lingering papery taste.

Even today, though the crowds didn't reach capacity, a palpable sense of good will filled the air. Children skipped and squealed in excitement. The dissenters, too, seemed to have stayed away. They couldn't count on it, of course: this could be the calm before the storm. In fact, Doris had raised the question of whether the circus required security, but Emir had pooh-poohed her. Why should they change arrangements? Wouldn't that be a victory for the thugs? There could be no reason for the performers to travel to and from the residences in pairs. Any incidences had been mere flashes in the pan. Everything would settle down. The circus folk just had to believe.

Yusuf harboured doubts but his voice remained in the minority. Only Zul backed him up.

"There is naivety and there is stupidity," said Zul in hushed tones as they tidied flyers in racks at the entrance to the tent.

"What can we do? Parole the grounds ourselves?" said Yusuf, shaking his head.

Zul nodded. "You had good form the other day against Karl. I know I'm not the strongest, but maybe you can teach me to defend myself better."

Yusuf waved off the compliment with a flick of his hand. "I love you, man, but you're not a fighter. And I was lucky. We don't want our own mini-war here, with rival groups squaring up against each other. We need to put an end to this once and for all."

Zul dug his hands into the pockets of his billowing clown trousers, dejected. "Maybe we should speak to Doris."

"She's as helpless as us. She's our friend but she doesn't have the authority to make real change," said Yusuf.

"How about Silberling?" said Zul, gnawing on his fingers in mock terror. "His assistant is here tonight. The one with the crazy curly hair. We should speak to her, suggest putting a council together. We could come up with ideas on how to impress Berliners more, to win a place in their hearts."

A vein throbbed in Yusuf's neck. "His assistant is here tonight?"

Zul nodded. "The usual seat."

"I don't think she'll help. The last time Silberling was here, he told us to sort ourselves out. Like it was our problem, not his. This is their project. No one from the ministry has even visited Simeon in hospital. You're clutching at straws, my friend." Yusuf stacked the last batch of leaflets and straightened his costume. Ten minutes until showtime. "I'll think of something."

"Like that Western film my son used to like. What's it called?" Zul fumbled to grasp the name from the buried memories of his son. He smiled. "The Lone Rider?"

Yusuf poked him in the ribs. "Very funny. The Lone Ranger." His brother had loved that film too, one of the old American exports they'd become aware of on a time lag.

In the ring, Old Sayid's band swung into its final song before Emir took to the ring to warm up the audience. The beat of the drum and jangle of the tambourine instilled a sense of urgency in the two men. They knew their cue.

"Break a leg," said Zul.

"Yeah, and you."

They dashed to the ring and Yusuf glanced at the audience. Sure enough, Silberling's assistant, the nervous woman with the yellow corkscrew curls, watched morosely from the front row. Emir stood centre stage, beckoning the audience to move forward, making for a more intimate experience. Zul jumped into action, borrowing Osman's most docile goat, as they had practiced in rehearsals, pretending to chase it across the ring as the crowd howled with laughter, and Emir shushed him. The goat ran circles around Zul, and he fell repeatedly, transformed from the worried man he'd been just minutes before, his energy electrifying the audience.

Once Emir had chased Zul off the stage, who in turn was hot on the heels of the goat, he returned to tip his top hat to the band. Old Sayid, playing the trombone, riffed for a delicious few minutes, then laid down his instrument.

Quiet reigned in the tent. Only a medley of coughing pierced the silence. Yusuf snuck a glance at the front row, and his nerves ratcheted up as he took in the boredom evident on Silberling's assistant's face.

Emir's voice filled the tent. "Now, ladies and gentleman, I have a rare treat for you tonight. Esme's doves are ready to debut their ring of fire trick. She'll be guiding them through ever smaller rings. Such is their trust for their mistress, they will subvert their fear to obey her. Rest assured, no animals are harmed here at the Treptow Circus. Not one feather on these dear birds will be singed in this performance - however much you enjoy chicken wings!" He tossed his top hat into the air and a chalky substance flew out, which transformed into seven doves hovering in a semi-circle about his head. The audience pointed in delight.

Zul relinquished the spotlight to Esme and Osman, who assisted her in this trick. The two performers worked in harmony, little and large. Esme with her doves, he with the rings looped around his arm. The rings had been coated in flammable liquid, and Osman hung them from a simple skeletal frame, suspended above their heads. The band struck up a thrilling beat, and he lit the rings one by one. The rings flared to life, and the audience, up close to the action, instinctively moved back.

Fire burned.

The flames danced and transported Yusuf back to the bombs.

To the woman who couldn't bear the loss of her child in a chemical attack, who set herself alight, an enflamed ghoul.

To Selim, the explosion of light and fuel that left him as blood and gore on the street.

To his mother, burning incense at the graves he'd left behind.

Waiting in the wings, Yusuf didn't see Esme's act. His memories trapped him. He pressed his fists to the side of his head, but they wouldn't stop. The fire roared. The sound of it swelled in his ears and became a primal scream. He dug his nails into his palms, whimpering as he drew blood. The applause sounded far away.

Zul's face loomed near, ghastly white. "Aren't you in the wrong place? You're up next."

Yusuf jerked away, disoriented. The lights seemed garish, like a technicolour alternate reality, not the circus he knew.

Zul cocked his head. "Are you okay?"

A clammy sheen coated Yusuf's skin. "On my way," he said.

He darted towards the rigging that served his trapeze. His hands burned where he had clawed them.

Emir announced his ascent and the speakers boomed, too loud for Yusuf's ears. "Here comes our flying man, the extraordinary, über-talented, fiendishly handsome man himself, our resident acrobat, Herr Yusuf Alam! Let's clap him, shall we?"

The clapping echoed like thunder through his head, corresponding to each step he climbed. Yusuf bit his lip and focused on the task at hand, willing the images that haunted him to stay away. The metal rigging cooled his palms. He exhaled as he reached the top, then stretched out his feet and ran across the tightrope before his thoughts could catch up with him.

At the end of the tightrope, he steadied himself, then leapt like he'd done a thousand times before. He aimed for the bar but instead of joy, fear pulsed through him. Somehow, he miscalculated the space, or his body did, and he dropped like a stone in a well. He closed his eyes, and Selim's face seared the pink of his eyelids.

Far away, on the periphery of his consciousness, Emir's voice rang out, a cry of terror.

The crowd gasped as he crashed against a pole.

Funny, he wasn't scared anymore. He twisted, like a broken bird, ricocheting through the air, and falling too fast for it to end any other way.

Silk caressed his cheek–his mother's touch, perhaps–then darkness enveloped him.

25

Ellie's scream died in her throat as she watched Yusuf fall. From the third row where she sat, heads obscured her view. She leapt to her feet, covering her mouth with her hand and prayed for a miracle, though she was atheist and always had been. Yusuf's body, usually taut and precise, had become a floppy, discarded piece of flesh that slammed into apparatus as it descended.

He'd never worked with a safety net during his performances. He'd never make it.

"Don't look," said her mother.

The two of them clutched each other, heads bent together.

Wild cheers erupted.

Ellie tensed, listening intently. She gathered her courage and lowered the hand from across her face. The air had thinned, and her legs became jelly. She unravelled herself from her mother's grasp and inched forward as the crowd whooped.

There stood the folk dancers Amena, Aya and Aischa, resplendent in dresses, holding a vast expanse of blue silk. The fabric shimmered like the ocean and spanned the centre of the ring. It had been stretched taut between them.

In the middle, lay a man curled like a foetus.

Ellie released her pent-up breath and bolted for the ring. She didn't care if she interrupted the show. She needed to know Yusuf had survived, that he'd live and they could talk again. The straggly old maestro sprang into action and struck up a joyous tune, as if there could be no doubt that Yusuf was fine. But Ellie had grown accustomed to the smoke and mirrors of the circus. Projections wouldn't fool her; she needed to see Yusuf up close, to prove he was intact. Flesh and bone.

He stirred by the time she reached him, and Ellie's body sagged in relief. The girls lowered him to the floor, these slight things who had saved him with their strength and quiet grace. He blinked, eyes detached, as if his mind was still on a different plane. Ellie soaked in the angles of his face, the pale sheen of his skin as Emir helped him to his feet and he stumbled over the folds of the fabric.

"Bow, son. Lean on me, but bow," said Emir.

They bowed and the crowd cheered again, buoyed by the drama that had ended well after all.

There, underneath the spotlight, side by side with the circus folk, Ellie had never felt so vulnerable or so human. Her chest ached for these people and herself. She squirmed as the audience applauded, and ran off stage first. Emir and Yusuf followed at an agonisingly slow pace, the younger man's breath still uneven.

Ellie peeked into the ring, where the atmosphere became euphoric. The band changed gear, and an exquisite melody drifted out of the sousaphone, with the fiddle, tambourine and lute intertwined so that the audience couldn't help but tap their feet. Amena, Aya and Aischa worked as a team to whip up the silk, and weaved a magic all of their own, creating mesmerising waves, skies of infinite blue. They clicked their tongues in unison three times, and a thunderclap reverberated across the tent, bringing forth a phoenix with spiked feathers that soared ever higher and disappeared in a cloud of ash above, only to reappear and dive back into the skies again.

Emir's top hat cast shadows over his face, but his eyes found hers, and they flickered with disquiet. "We could have lost him. I've seen enough death," he said.

Yusuf slumped heavily on Emir's arm, and could hear every syllable.

Regret soaked Emir's voice. "I have to go back on stage. Look after him, will you?" He dipped his head to chest, as if drawing on reserves of energy. "Silberling's assistant is here tonight, you know." He strode away, leaving her alone with Yusuf.

Ellie guided Yusuf through heavy velvet curtains to the performer area, to protect him from prying eyes. There, she helped him sit on a crate. Shivers racked his body.

"Let me take you to the hospital."

He shook his head.

"Let me see, then." She tried to peel his costume down.

He flicked her away. "Water, please. Over there."

She followed his gaze to a fridge. A moment later, she'd retrieved a lukewarm bottle of water. He accepted it with a murmur of thanks, broke the seal and gulped down its contents. Then he collapsed into himself, a wretch of a man, his concave body a shell that curled around his heart. Ellie didn't know how to make him feel whole again. She perched next to him and placed an awkward hand on his knee, letting the heat from her palm seep into his skin through the thin material of his costume. He sank into her, his hard chest against her soft one.

In the main tent, the acts continued and performers scurried past, giving them a wide berth, as if the area around them had been cordoned off, as if they were lovers and not something as yet undefined.

Ellie stroked Yusuf's back and felt the tension evaporate from his neck and shoulders. Too much pressure on his left shoulder caused him to flinch, and she realised his body would be covered in unholy splotches by the morning. He was foolish for not seeing a doctor, but who was she to insist? She couldn't even be sure they were friends, so she continued soothing him with her touch, offering comfort but not demanding anything in return.

After a while, he drew back. His colour had returned to normal and his voice no longer quivered when he spoke. "I can't believe I fell."

"What happened?"

He grimaced. "I lost focus."

"You must have been so scared."

He evaded her eyes. "I felt relief."

She scrutinised his face, puzzled. He'd fallen over fifteen metres. His escape had been miraculous, bruises or not. "I don't understand."

His voice was an empty vessel, his energy spent. "I've feared that moment for so long. Falling. Now the worst has happened."

Ellie shook her head. "You're lucky to be alive."

"I have the girls to thank for that."

She looped her arms around his neck and leant her forehead on his. He didn't resist her embrace and her heart leapt a notch. "I'm sorry we fought."

"That doesn't matter now. The circus is done for. Silberling told us not to mess up, and after all the chaos, the protests and violence, now I've fallen. What have I done? What if I'm the last straw? I've handed Silberling the excuse he needs to shut us down." He crumpled into himself.

Ellie averted her gaze. Her feelings for him compromised her ability to herald the truth. The secret she'd held about Silberling's duplicity weighed on her, leaving a bitter taste in her mouth. Yusuf deserved to know, but she didn't want to crush him, not after the knocks he'd sustained.

She strained to hear his words above the din of Zul's clown act. His breath fanned her face. "Have you been watching the news? All that talk of citizen's rights. Don't refugees have rights? We jump through loop after loop and still the ground shifts. All these cycling highs and lows. How do some people have it so easy, or does everyone end up in the dirt and have to claw their way out?"

Ellie didn't have an answer; she remained silent.

"I used to daydream as a child. I'd see my life mapped out in front of me in beautiful symmetry: a smooth road with only small deviations for adventures. I didn't doubt that I'd be happy. That I'd have my family around me. In my dreams, my father worked elsewhere, but my brother and my mother sat around a table. We lived in a big house altogether, and I had a beautiful wife and a Jaguar the neighbours envied. I was important." He shuddered. "I remember the child I was, and recall my dreams, and wonder, is it my fault I didn't get there? Is there still time? Can I force the life I want to live or is it my job just to wait out the cycles? Somewhere, maybe there's a version of me living that life. I can almost taste it. It's just beyond my reach."

She hugged him. "You aren't responsible for life's knocks, Yusuf. Sometimes we just need to weather life's storms and be kind to ourselves." Her chest tightened, knowing that if she lied to Yusuf now, he wouldn't forgive her. That the truth must always come first. She closed her eyes. "I have something to tell you."

His body grew still. "Yes?"

"Silberling's not the friend you think he is."

Grey eyes narrowed into slits, deep shadows beneath them. "What do you mean?"

"I've been doing some digging. The spike in attacks on the circus, my editor's pushiness, turfing me out on my ear–none of it felt right. And I found something out. He wants the circus to fail."

Yusuf's brow furrowed. "He was the driving force behind this project. Why would he want us to fail?"

"He asked my editor to write a story that would fuel negative feelings. I have proof." A thickness coated the insides of Ellie's throat. How could her timing be so off? She didn't want to hurt him, especially not now, but she couldn't let him blame himself. "Can't you see how tensions are escalating? How it doesn't seem like a coincidence? He's behind it. My gut says that he's going to shut you down."

Yusuf leaned on the crate as he heaved himself up. Wild hair framed his pale face and his clenched fists hung stiffly by his side. "Why would he do that?"

The ground trembled under their feet as the performers and their animals took to the stage for the finale. Emir beckoned Yusuf to join them. Yusuf held up a hand, signalling he'd be right there, and turned back to Ellie.

"Why, Ellie?"

He couldn't use this new information tonight. They needed to concoct a plan. If he acted before they were ready, he risked blowing their advantage and ruining the story. She worried his emotions would overshadow his good sense, compel him to do something stupid. "Officials from the Interior Ministry are here tonight. Please, you can't say anything. Not until we're ready."

Yusuf grew still, like the quiet before a storm. "Tell me why he'd do that, Ellie."

"He thinks the public has given up on you. He wants to force it to a head so it's buried before the election."

Yusuf flinched. His eyes darted back and forth as he pieced his thoughts together. "You're lying."

"I have proof." She closed the distance between them. "I want to help."

A vein pulsed in his neck. "And how are you going to do that? You have no job. You're as powerless as me." He gritted his teeth, attempting to restrain his anger, choosing her as a target because Silberling lay out of reach.

"I can help, Yusuf."

"I don't need a white saviour. I don't need your charity. Don't you see? You're all the same. I'm never sure if you want to keep me small or see me fly. Whether you want me to be your pet or your equal. The rules you play by are always changing. Just leave me be."

Ellie recoiled. She considered the two of them to be equals; why didn't Yusuf? She opened her mouth to explain, but shut it again, and the moment for her to smooth things over passed.

"Acrobat! Acrobat!" came the call of the crowd.

"Your grief is so raw that you're confusing your friends with enemies."

"My grief makes me strong. Grief is love. Love for my country, for my people."

The crowd clapped and stomped their feet.

Yusuf pushed through the curtains without a backward glance.

26

Ellie pressed through the crowds to her mother, and they headed out arm in arm under the moonlit sky to find their bikes. Their shoes slapped the path as they walked: the thud of Ellie's Dr. Martens and the squelch of her mother's trainers.

"I really thought that was going to end badly. What a relief he's okay," said her mother.

"He's fine," said Ellie, lost in a jumble of thoughts.

"You made up then, after last time? I was sorely tempted to come after you when you ran into the ring."

They located their bikes: her mother's stately one in apple green with its wide handlebars and woven basket up front, and Ellie's, neon amber with a high bar and extensive gears for the speeds she liked to ride.

Her mother secured her purse in the basket and mounted her bike. "It's a pity I couldn't say hello. I hope there aren't any bad feelings."

Ellie tied her hair into a bun. "He had other things on his mind, Mama," she said, swinging her leg into place and pushing off.

She smarted from Yusuf's rejection. It lay at odds with her own depth of feeling for him. She had no idea how to scale his walls, or if she should give him up altogether. How often had she shown him they were on the same side?

Let him wrap his sadness and anger about him if that's what he wants.

One thing had become clear: the truth needed to come to light. She needed to write her version of the story, with or without his blessing.

She rode next to her mother at a comfortable pace along the edge of the park. Firs and oaks rustled as they passed, and the musky scent of the damp night lay on the leaves.

"You're quiet, love. It was quite a shock, seeing Yusuf fall. The circus is so joyful, it's easy to forget the risks the performers take. And then, with you knowing him, it makes it harder."

Being with her mother left no room for morose thoughts. Every moment with Katharina Richter thrummed with curiosity. She couldn't help but set the world to rights, to question and fill voids. It both exhausted and lifted Ellie.

"Still, all's well that ends well."

"Except it isn't," said Ellie, glancing over her shoulder as the big top receded into the distance. "Yusuf decided he didn't need saving, not by me or anyone else."

Her mother's laboured breath punctuated her sentences. "Quite right too. I imagine him being pushed and pulled all over the place, poor lad. He must have been all up-ended after that tumble–a proud man like that. Give him some space to make his own decisions."

Ellie cycled faster, suddenly craving space. Part of her wished to turn her back on the whole sorry affair. She could move. Barcelona beckoned. Or she could resurrect her school French and head to Paris. No, maybe not Paris. She preferred Berlin's laissez-faire flair to Parisian chic. Besides, Paris had its own problems with multiculturalism and the march of the far right, and Ellie considered herself most at home in tolerant, hopeful places. Researching possible destinations would give her something to get her teeth into. A new start always brought opportunities. She kidded herself that her parents needed her, that her mother required support with her father's drinking. They were grown adults. She'd never flown far from the nest: it could be the best decision she'd ever made.

Except Ellie never ran from problems. She ran into them, and she wrestled them until she won.

Her mind shuttered back to Yusuf, cowed but proud before her, stubborn and brave but determined to be alone. His siege mentality would get him nowhere but he needed to find that out for himself.

In some ways, they were alike. As adventurous as she was, she'd always needed her touch points, the places and people who anchored and understood her. There could be no thought of traversing the world alone, with her thoughts bouncing about her head with no one to listen. Even tonight, there could be no question of returning to her flat with its silence and stark walls. She'd boomerang back to her parental home like a migrating bird following its instinct for preservation.

She'd return to the cocoon of her family home, and attack this story anew, whether Yusuf wanted it or not. But bubbling beneath the surface, something niggled: a sense that her journalistic mettle hadn't been tested enough to unravel a story this big.

She slowed her bike to let her mother catch up. "Can I come home with you tonight?"

"Of course, darling. Your father's probably snoring on the sofa, but what a lovely surprise for him."

How lucky she was to have these two humans raise her. How easy to take her stable environment for granted, and how she'd never been subject to the tyranny of war.

"Am I too much of an amateur to get this story out? Just tell me straight. I can take it."

Her mother's voice boomed, filled with passion. "You can't be serious? Ellie, this is your story. You've done the legwork. You're passionate about it. Why would you think you're not good enough to write it?"

"Maybe Marina was right, starting me on filler stories. I was chomping at the bit, but what if I'm not ready or experienced enough?"

They rolled around a corner and onto a bike path, riding alongside each other. Above them, street lights hummed on the quiet streets.

"Darling, do you think a man would second guess his abilities? Yes, experience counts, but so does fearlessness, and plain old guts, and the willingness to risk looking stupid. Do you think masters of their field get there just by experience? It takes so much more to be a supernova. Don't dim your own light. There are plenty of people who will do that for you. You're like me. You always need a purpose. Just because you don't have a job, it doesn't mean that internal need stops. Just write the story — that's your talent — and the rest will fall into place."

"You make it sound easy. What about when I've written it? What then? It's not like I have the mechanisms to get the story out."

"Blogs are all the rage, you know that. Especially controversial ones." Her mother chuckled and the sound fell like pearls into the open expanse around them. "Or use your contacts. If the story's good enough, it'll stick. The most important thing is deciding a course of action. Anyway, enough shop talk. I've never quite seen a clown like the one tonight. He was magnificent, wasn't he? So expressive. How he was able to twist his face into those positions, I'll never know. I must take your father."

Her mother knew when to retreat. She had quashed Ellie's doubts and buoyed her, but now she stepped back, allowing her words to linger. The wind ruffled their hair while her mother told her about the acts she'd missed, about how she could still feel the remnants of the music in the echo of her chest, how the ringmaster had forged ahead despite the scare, and the animals had delighted the crowd.

They pulled up to the apartment block and dismounted. Her mother wheeled her bike into the rack in the courtyard and secured it. Then she retrieved her bag. She reapplied her lipstick, smacking her lips together, before shaking her pink hair free of its clasp. It remained curled upwards in a peculiar fashion.

"Come now, let's scare your father awake."

Ellie stored her bike and trudged up the stairs.

Just write the story. It sounded like a mantra.

Truth didn't just appear. It required advocates and trail-blazers, heroes and heroines to herald it.

Silberling and Marina deserved a comeuppance.

It did Ellie good to be freed from the constraints of editorial requirements. She made herself comfortable at her father's desk, switching on the light with its dusty, fringed lampshade. Then she prepared herself a steaming mug of coffee, tucked a blanket over her knees and powered up her laptop. When the home screen had finally flickered to life and she had managed to connect to the internet, she spent a few minutes drafting an email before ringing Tom.

He answered on the second ring. "Hi, trouble."

She smiled. "Hi, you. Fancy coming over for some beers next week? I can make you some of my veggie pasta, and we can sit out on the balcony."

"Or we could just hit the town for a burger."

"Sure." She hesitated. "I have a favour to ask."

Tom groaned. "Doing favours for you is like going into battle. I'm not ready for another round yet."

"Have I scarred you for life? You really were very brave, trying to distract Marina."

"I almost soiled myself. Let's just say I'm not cut out to be in the spy game."

The vapours from the coffee drifted into the air. "Do you have your laptop nearby?"

"Hang on," he said. The sound of him rummaging filtered through the phone line. "Got it."

"I'm sending you over a story outline, for your eyes only. It can't go anywhere." She hit send on her email app. "You should have it any second. I'll wait while you read it." She undid her ponytail and rubbed the sore bit on the back of her head.

"Okay, here it is," said Tom.

She sipped her coffee and sank into the sensation of heat travelling through her body.

Tom emitted a low whistle. "*That's* what you found out? Holy hell, Ellie."

Her hands jittered and she set down the cup. "Could you send me the name of a few editors who might be interested?"

"Are you sure you want to go down this route?" said Tom. "As your friend, I need to warn you, these are powerful people."

"The truth will speak for itself. It has to," she said simply. Without that one belief, her whole world would tilt. She lived by the values of truth and justice. There could be no question of hiding or ignoring what she had uncovered.

"If you're sure."

"I am."

He sighed. "I'll get you a list by tomorrow."

She exhaled. "Thank you."

"Good luck, trouble."

She set her phone aside, and stretched her fingers out over the keyboard. Her father's persistent snore reached her through the walls. Before long, her childhood home had faded from around her. She added flesh to the lead story she had outlined for Tom, her biro leaving a trail of messy ink as she swept her hand across the page. She had to bring Silberling and Marina's deception into sharp focus and hope that an editor of another national paper would pick it up. Her story needed to grip the consciousness of the nation, creating waves, and not disappear into the cracks.

When she had finished, she read over her work, and the bare bones of the lead article seemed lacking to her, as if it were merely a skeleton and it needed to be brought to life with the colours and back stories of the circus. Ellie resolved not to cut short the story; the refugees' voices deserved to be heard, not silenced or squeezed into the space a news desk could spare for them.

She wrote a supplementary piece, and then another, and another, that she eventually decided would become a blog series. As she wrote, the centrifugal forces of the story took shape beneath her fingers, growing it far beyond the story she had initially submitted to Marina. At first, she didn't know who her audience was. Then she realised her ideal reader had to be someone like her. Someone who had fleeting interactions with refugees but might not have had cause to know them better. A reader who had the capacity for compassion, if only Ellie could show them that the aches and needs of the refugees were not far removed from their own.

She had to humanise strangers, to awaken sympathy, to portray them not as a faceless group of outsiders, but as individual people. She had to define the real monsters: poverty and war, corruption and fear. Her thoughts lingered, in turn, on each of the individuals she'd met at the circus, considering the heroes and heroines of her story, and the villains. She had little hope of convincing those who disliked immigrants of their value. Instead, Ellie targeted those who wavered; she addressed those in the swollen middle ground whose minds remained open. Those who might stumble onto her blog after reading about the Treptow Circus in the nationals.

She bled her ideas onto the page until the early hours, and when her eyes blurred and her fingers ached, she gathered up her work into a neat pile, and curled into a ball on her parents' sofa, exhausted.

27

At dawn, when tangerine fingers of sun sliced the sky, men in boots came. They rammed the door to the residences. The building shook as if it were made of paper, waking the performers wrapped up in bed. Half-dressed people stumbled into the corridors to investigate the commotion. They gathered together in groups, leaving their doors ajar. Others barricaded themselves in, terrified, their instincts primed to fear the worst.

The men sought Dawud.

"Who told you? Who told you it was me?" said Dawud, a scream tearing from his throat.

Dawud had once been as strong as a tree, sturdy legs and lean arms, early signs of puberty shadowing his cheeks. Over the past weeks, the guilt about Simeon had withered him, and it showed in his sudden weight loss, gaunt crescents underneath skittish eyes, jerky movements of a boy ill at ease with himself and the world around him.

"Tell me! Does no one love me?" he said.

The men took him, bodily, as if he were a thing and not a person. As if his feelings and thoughts counted for nothing, and only theirs did, or rather the papers thrust into Doris's hands.

Dawud struggled, no longer a man-child, but a broken boy who kicked and screamed in the arms a of tall blond man going about his job with ferocious intensity.

The man barked. "Quiet! Be still."

Yusuf placed a hand on Dawud, seeking to inject calm.

"Stand back," said the man.

The boy writhed still, his face painted in terror.

"Where are you taking him?" said Yusuf, eyes wild in his search for Doris or anyone who could stop this culling.

"Frau Kaun has all the information."

Doris stood to one side, ashen-faced, her dressing gown tied hastily at her waist.

Yusuf turned to her. "Doris? What's going on? Why now?"

She shook her head, but her eyes lingered on Najib, who stood sullen against the wall. "There's nothing I can do."

"Simeon didn't want to press charges."

She held her head high but her chin quivered. "It's not Simeon who spoke. It doesn't matter now. The order came from the top. I can't protect you anymore."

Behind them, the men dragged Dawud along the corridor.

"I'm sorry!" he screamed, choking on his tears, beating his fists against his captor's chest.

Osman stormed forward, and all around, emotion flared, but Doris placed herself in between the two groups.

Yusuf clenched his jaw. "We can't just let them take him."

She met his eyes, openly weeping, her mouth slack. "We have no choice."

Around them, the refugees touched Dawud as he passed in his captor's arms, as if it were his funeral and the finality of his death had already been written. As if he wasn't a live body, but a casketed one, and this was their last chance to say goodbye.

Demons crawled through the performers' nightmares. The following day, practice started later than usual. The performers clung to one another in the common room over hot spiced tea and eggs whipped up by Leyla, rehashing the traumas of the night before, clinging to one another, wondering whether Dawud would return from the detention centre, worrying that they might be next.

A clawing guilt attached itself to Yusuf, weighting each step he took so that his body seemed to press into the earth with the burden. He should have done more to help the boys; the responsibility for their fate lay at his feet. His mind conjured up flashes of a blade at his wrists or a cocktail of drugs bought from one of the layabouts at the edge of the park, whose deep pockets might be filled with stashes of white powder. The thought of oblivion beckoned, until he remembered Selim. Suicide would be an insult to the brother who should have lived.

The immigrants' dream of Berlin still existed. The one he'd chased while at the mercy of the smugglers. It couldn't all have been in vain.

None of the performers supported active measures to help Dawud, nor did anyone question Najib and the prickles that revealed his guilt. The minutes passed and their anguish, worn initially for all to see, transformed, burying deeper and deeper until by early afternoon, Dawud had been all but expunged from their vocabulary. They were helpless to change his outcomes, so what could they do?

Enough compassion remained in their well to smother Yusuf with concern after his fall from the trapeze. Emir had forbidden him from practice and performance until further notice. It stung Yusuf to be away from the blood and sweat of the circus ring. How could he exorcise his demons without it, or contribute meaningfully to the circus with a ban? He was a grown man, not a child to be told he couldn't participate. The ban became like a scab or a knot of scar tissue that didn't heal. Every time he answered an inquiry about his health, the scar opened up. He hated repeating the same assurances about his well-being. Being the centre of attention away from the stage embarrassed him, especially in light of Dawud's fate, rotting somewhere far away from the people he knew.

They deported Dawud.

Yusuf refused to give up. His anger at Najib pulsed red-hot beneath his skin. The Judas had thought only of himself. His fingers twitched with the need to strike Najib, to demand he exchange places with the boy. To tell him that Dawud was worth a hundred of him. But to fracture their community even further in fraught times would be unwise. Neither would it help Dawud.

"There must be something we can do or say to bring him back to us," said Yusuf.

Esme slipped away first. She'd grown accustomed to wearing trousers and Wellington boots for practice sessions, and teamed with her headscarf, it looked an odd ensemble. "I can't think about this anymore. I need to check on my birds," she said.

Emir threw dark looks at Najib, but he agreed with the others that they had to let Dawud go. "For our own sake, Yusuf. I wish we could help, but how? Maybe if we were different people–richer, whiter, more powerful–maybe then we could save him, but he set the ball in motion when he hurt Simeon. Violence has its own path."

Inside, Yusuf railed at Ellie, holding her partly responsible. If only she'd revealed the truth about Silberling sooner, he could have protected Dawud. He would have known this was coming.

Now it was too late.

Doris's anger pulsed, as palpable as his own. "Dawud's just a boy."

Even so, she offered no solution, as if the driving force of her nature, a staunch practicality and resolute courage, had somehow been diluted by circumstance.

"I'll try and find out where they are taking him, but our hands are tied," she said.

Yusuf bristled. "What good will that do without the means to be there for him? He has no-one. Who will tell Simeon? How will he feel to know that Dawud has suddenly gone, without even a goodbye, because of what happened that night? Don't we all carry enough guilt?"

She lay a hand on his shoulder, and leaned into his ear, motioning to Najib. "There are others here who will find their sanctuary short-lived if I have anything to do about it."

When Esme returned with a pale face, trailing mud from her boots all over the common room, Emir tutted.

"Take off your boots, child," he said. "Have you finished seeing to the animals already?"

She ignored his instruction, and her stricken face drew the eyes and ears of those around her. "There are government men at the circus putting up signs, and some walking this way."

Emir and Doris drew closer.

"What signs?" said Doris, disquieted.

Esme thrust a white page with red and black lettering under Emir's nose. He smoothed it out with his square, hairy hands. As he read it, his face twisted in despair and he slumped into the chair behind him, wheezing. Leyla and Yusuf hurried to his side. The old woman whispered softly into her husband's ear.

Yusuf unpeeled the page from Emir's hand, and sucked in his breath. He stammered, reading the sign out loud, for all to hear.

TREPTOW CIRCUS
FIVE DAYS UNTIL CLOSURE

Gasps and a flurry of chatter swept across the room. Even the children stopped playing and came to stand with their guardians.

"They asked me to give this to you, Doris," said Esme, handing over a sealed envelope. "It's a copy of a letter sent to your email address last night."

Doris flushed. "There was a lot on my plate. I didn't check my emails last night."

"Open it now," said Esme.

Doris tore open the letter, fingers clumsy. Her voice stretched out across the common room, clear as a bell, cutting through the whispers.

> *To whom it may concern,*
>
> *Following a thorough evaluation conducted by officials in my department over the past few months, I have come to the conclusion that the refugee programme at Treptow Circus is no longer fit for purpose.*
>
> *I have not come to this decision lightly. Multiple violent and disruptive incidents in and around the circus have convinced me that closure of the circus is the best possible outcome. The recent fall during an acrobatic performance highlighted health and safety implications that cannot be ignored. Furthermore, as Interior Minister, I am unable to sanction the use of state funds for a project that has lost its bearings.*
>
> *While there is only a small fraction of the funding that remains, I have instructed my officers to release it for your use. The final performance of the Treptow Circus will take place on 5 May. After this, the circus tent and its furnishings, as well as the animals, will be sequestered.*
>
> *Despite your inevitable disappointment about this decision, I would like to congratulate you on your role in contributing to the Treptow Circus project over the past two years. While your service falls short of the tenure required to secure the permanent right to reside in Germany, rest assured that your applications will continue to be assessed through the normal channels.*
>
> *Please address any issues about the next stage of your applications to your warden Frau Doris Kaun, who will be*

acting as liaison in this matter, and who will be providing you
with information on interim accommodation upon closure of
the residences.
  Regards,
  Rex Silberling
  Interior Minister

Emir leaned forward. "What does sequestered mean?"

"Taken away," said Doris, her voice small.

May the fifth.

That left five days.

"How can he do this?" said Emir. "Does the man have no honour? And to think, in two weeks, it's the start of *Ramadhan*, and here we will be with our prayer mats but no home, no family to call our own. What have we done to deserve this?"

Yusuf's anger twisted inside, a swirling storm that controlled him. He should have known better than to trust Silberling. His instincts had always told him to be wary. All this time, he'd wanted to prove to Silberling that the circus folk were good enough to merit German citizenship. What a fool he'd been.

They had travelled great distances to escape war, but sometimes it appeared as though war had followed them, or they'd carried it within them, a raging beast caught within living carcasses. It hit him then, that maybe Allah had imposed a penalty on him for escaping, for severing the tether to the land of his ancestors and to his mother while true Syrians stayed to die or suffer.

Maybe none of his circus family deserved to be happy.

They had squandered their chance of a new life together.

In five days, their family would be torn apart.

28

Later that afternoon, Doris convened a meeting for the circus folk in the common room, in an effort to smooth over the tensions and offer solace following Dawud's detention and Silberling's letter. She fluttered like a bird, anxious about their well-being but completely at the mercy of the department she worked for but didn't agree with. Her careful words of comfort stopped short of concrete assurances for her charges, and Yusuf discerned her helplessness in her whitened knuckles when she gripped the table, the eyes that darted from face to face, wishing she could do more.

The performers splintered into groups based on nationalities, frightened, talking in their respective languages rather than the broken German they had come to use as a group. Even Emir and Zul, who had believed the project would work and who'd thrown their whole energy into it, grew silent, as if their fight had been drained.

"We'll close the circus with dignity," said Emir, placing his top hat on his head. "We'll give Berlin a week of shows it will never forget."

"Maybe they will change their minds," said Zul, lacklustre, already defeated.

"The decision has been made," said Doris, crestfallen. She hung her head in her hands as if the closure were her failure, as if she hadn't toiled to make her home theirs.

Five days and it would all be over.

The passivity riled Yusuf. "Come on! There must be something we can do." How could they sit here so calmly when he itched to retaliate against someone, anyone, for the lies they had believed? They had been promised safety and opportunity, and instead, their lives crumbled once more. What an illusion security was for people like him. He'd been separated from his mother for nothing. All that time apart, and he had nothing to show for it. He wouldn't pretend he could accept this outcome. He wouldn't pretend the Germans harboured only good will.

Someone had to pay, but instead, his friends sat around talking.

Yusuf stood, knocking back his chair. "I've got work to do."

"You're not staying for Isaiah's art class?" said Esme.

"No. Not today."

He headed outside to do chores, hoping to dampen the unease in his mind. He'd been hard at work for an hour, mucking out the stables, when Isaiah startled him.

"Esme said you were in here," said Isaiah, wrinkling his nose as he caught a whiff of manure. "I know that look. Girl trouble?"

Ellie flashed into Yusuf's mind. The warmth of her hand on his knee, her eyes wide with concern, their foreheads touching. He shook his head to wash away the thought of her.

"Nah. There's no girl."

Isaiah clapped him on the shoulder. "I was joking, man. Emir filled me in on Dawud and the circus closure. I'm so sorry. I don't know what to say."

Yusuf set down his shovel. "It's not your fault."

"It sucks, bro. When the chips are down, I like to let off steam."

Yusuf sighed. Isaiah could be so young sometimes. "I don't want to come spraying."

"Not to kick a brother when he's down–your body might be a work of art but your spraying skills are awful."

"Thanks."

"I was going to ask if you wanted to come to Witches' Night tonight? There's a sick warehouse party my friends are going to. Or how about Kreuzberg for the May Day protest tomorrow?"

"I don't know," said Yusuf. His hair flopped across his forehead. He pushed it back with impatient fingers.

The stallion whinnied and nudged him with his muzzle.

Isaiah stuffed his hands deep into his jeans pockets. "Looks like the horse thinks you should come."

"I remember seeing the May Day images last year. It was chaos," said Yusuf. There'd been burnt out cars and even Molotov cocktails.

After his fall from the trapeze, when he'd looked back on what happened, he'd been sure the fire in Esme's act had triggered the flashbacks. It couldn't be sensible to expose himself to heightened stress right now, but when had being sensible ever helped him?

"There's the May trees celebrating Spring, there's concerts and girls and beer, and the workers' protests. It's the one day the bulls go easy on us if we cause a bit of mayhem. How about it? Fancy tagging along before the straitjackets go back on?"

Mayhem. No rules. A loss of control.

Yusuf's internal voice that told him to beware.

A heaviness settled in his stomach.

"Aren't you tempted to show the white boys and the bulls how you feel? You need to live these protests. Just once. You don't know Berlin until you've experienced it. It's a day for the oppressed. It's for anarchists, feminists and anti-capitalists. It's for all shades of the left. It's for punks. For the people who feel wronged or want more. Come on, bro." Isaiah's gaze swept around the stables and out to the circus tent standing erect against the sky. "They're shutting this place down. Aren't you angry? Don't you want to show it? What do you have to lose?" He punched Yusuf's shoulder, not in jest, but as a challenge.

Yusuf winced. His body still ached from his fall. Under his shirt, bruises in bright green and deepest mauve danced over his olive skin.

"Seriously man, we have anxiety as people of colour to justify our space. To be good. To not be a burden. Even when our luck is down. When our home is in peril, and our brothers are dying. Even when those who have it all don't want to help us."

He was riffing now, a young man in the throes of his beliefs. Not someone who should be trapped in an empty record store, but someone who inspired and could drive change.

He slowed down, rubbing his neck. "We don't even vote, bro. We sing. We rhyme. We march. But we don't vote. But there's one day, one day we can take up space and the police make way. One day when we can protest and let our anger soar. Are you in?"

"Of course you can vote," said Yusuf. "You're a German citizen, aren't you? Voting is a privilege."

"No, it's rubber-stamping. Who on the podium speaks for me?" Isaiah dug into his pocket and pulled out a thumb-sized iPod with tangled headphones. "Listen to the first playlist. Focus on the lyrics, bro. Tell me they don't speak to you. And if they do, meet me at Plänterwald S-Bahn at 10 a.m., and we'll go into the fray."

Yusuf took the iPod. "And do what?"

"Be what they fear."

Isaiah's playlist consisted of an eclectic mix of rap, blues and soul music from America and Germany, songs that Yusuf had heard on the radio in the common room, in addition to gems Isaiah had most likely discovered at the record store where he worked. Yusuf listened blind: the iPod lacked a display and his knowledge of Western music fell short beyond Michael Jackson and Prince, whom Selim had loved. On some tracks, he struggled to unravel meaning from the lightening fast vocals.

Even so, one song in particular moved him. He lay in his bed with the headphones vibrating in his ears, staring at the beige walls with *Talkin' Bout a Revolution* on repeat. He spooled it back until the lyrics became an anthem and fanned out in front of him, a banner, a flag of his own.

A spark flared inside him, dangerous and wild. Following the rules had brought only disappointment and despair, so why bother at all?

For all the West's talk of opportunities, it failed to deliver. Germany would never accept people like him, not really. The West knew only carrot and sticks, reward and punishment, never understanding or acknowledging how innocents had been wronged. Even so called progress showed the rot to the core. People of colour had witnessed and internalised the backlash in the USA after Barack and Michelle Obama strode into the White House amidst fanfare. What should have been a high-point for race relations unravelled quicker than a moth-ridden jumper.

Yes, he'd meet Isaiah. After all, when had the state ever protected him, here or in Syria? Hadn't his father taught him that violent people get their own way? Hadn't Silberling shown once again that even in the hallowed West, under the mask of democracy, the corrupt pulse of power throbbed?

He didn't recognise the rage in himself, the dormant power inside that had woken.

His whole body pulsed with the need to discard his demeanour of calm and burn up the rulebook.

The thought electrified him, a contagion.

29

The moon faded from the sky and the birds chirped, and still Ellie tapped away on her computer in her father's study. She'd spent the whole night locked in one position. Her neck had grown stiff, and she rolled her shoulders back in an arc, and doubled down again to wrestle the words into existence.

In the morning, Tom came through with a list of editors and their contact details, men and women who commanded the respect and attention of millions of readers. At first, Ellie balked at approaching them. Her ousting from *BAZ* had knocked her confidence, and she shied away from the possibility of further rejection so soon. Still, to publish without the umbrella of *BAZ* or another newspaper would be an act of self-sabotage and diminish her credibility as a journalist. There could be no way that the new WordPress blog she had created would take off overnight of its own accord. She needed the patronage of an editor to draw attention to the story. Fear of rejection couldn't stop her if she wanted to make up for her previous error and rally people in support of the circus. Maybe then her own prickles of guilt would subside.

She drafted a cover note to accompany the story outline and the evidence she had collected, then she sent an email to the editors of her three favourite publications on the list, together with her credentials, asking them to respond to her within two days.

When she'd finished, she flopped on the desk with her head cradled in her arms and fell asleep as a train of words continued to trail across her mind, kernels of thought she couldn't quite capture.

The buzz of Ellie's phone pierced through the fog of her sleep. She woke to find her mouth had crusted with saliva, and swept her sleeve across it. She reached for the phone, her body slow and heavy and not yet replenished.

"Hello?" Her fingers rubbed the side of her face where a circular motif in the metal desk had imprinted itself on her cheek.

A voice like a purring engine met her ears. "Frau Richter? This is Simone Mayer from *Die Welt*. I received your email. Can you talk?"

"Of course." Ellie sat bolt upright and tossed off her blanket. She looked at the grandfather clock in the corner of her father's study. She hadn't expected a response so soon.

"So, Marina Schmidt is up to her neck in it? These are quite some allegations you're making. You can send me the proof?"

Ellie's hand quivered on the handset, but not one note of hesitation crept into her response. "I have everything ready."

"The article, too?"

Please, please, let me be doing the right thing. "Yes."

A grunt of satisfaction. "Good. We'll pay you our usual freelance rate for one article, and additional money for any follow up pieces. This is in exchange for exclusivity. We'll email you a contract once I have received the piece. Sign the terms immediately, and we'll run the story this week, assuming I'm satisfied with your work."

Ellie thought fast. "I'm intending to write a connected blog series about the refugees. Will that impact exclusivity?"

"Big news is ours first. Run anything you need to by my assistant before you post it to your blog," said Simone, reeling off the instructions with a butter smoothness that commanded respect. "Welcome to the big time, Frau Richter."

Ellie gulped, said her goodbyes and called up her gmail account to send Simone the promised work.

Half an hour later, her father found her staring into space and placed a fresh coffee next to the stale remnants from the night before.

"You're working too hard," he said.

She grasped the mug in her hands and ignored his concern. "Thanks, Papa."

Her father looped his arms around her shoulders and she could see his grainy reflection on the screen of her computer. "You making much progress?"

"I think so." She softened her voice, willing him not to get prickly. "You've been drinking less recently."

"Yeah, well, I know when my girls need me."

She reached up to kiss his stubbly jaw.

He rubbed the prickles against her face like he used to do when she'd been a little girl. "Being cooped up isn't good for the soul, Ellie. How about I treat you to a champagne brunch in Hackescher Markt?"

"Are you sure a drink this early is sensible? You know what you're like," said Ellie. She longed for a leisurely walk in wet woods to clear her head, not a family tête-à-tête, and certainly not alcohol first thing in the morning. No doubt her father would start as he meant to go on. "Besides, I've got something I need to wrap up."

She filled him in on the conversation with *Die Welt* and his eyes grew wide with pride.

"See, you can't keep a good woman down," he said, delighted. "Are you sure we shouldn't celebrate?"

"Don't you have work?"

He ruffled her hair and she grimaced. "Sometimes you forget who's the father and who's the child. Don't worry about me. I can go in late today."

"Is Mama coming too?"

Her mother popped her head around the door, a haze of pink, with a felt-tip in her hands. "I've been making up signs for the march tomorrow, but I'm almost done."

Ellie brushed her thick fringe out of her eyes, and smoothed out her crumpled t-shirt. "Look at the state of me."

"We'll give you half an hour to get ready," said her father.

"Okay. I'll do the brunch, minus the champagne."

He patted her shoulder, and left her to it. Ellie lingered a moment, then hit publish on her blog. She pinged a few journalist friends on Twitter. After that, she pushed her anxiety away, deep into the darkest recesses of her mind, where it simmered.

Twenty-five minutes later, Ellie had showered and changed. She slipped into the cool leather interior of her parents' Audi.

"Ready, love?" said her mother, turning around in the front passenger seat.

"Ready," said Ellie, tying her damp hair into a knot at her nape and plugging in her seatbelt.

Her father drove across the city and, before long, he'd parked and they entered his favourite brunch restaurant in the tourist trap of Hackescher Markt. The chandeliered ceiling, cornicing and art nouveau paintings adorning the walls were a far cry from the laidback shabby chic charm of the restaurants Ellie favoured in Friedrichshain and Prenzlauer Berg.

They ordered their food and coffee, and her father requested three glasses of Prosecco. Ellie's scowl at the early alcohol soon gave way into smiles as her parents toasted to her success.

"I knew you'd fall on your feet, darling," said her mother.

"I bet they're paying you quite a fee," said her father, with a wink. "Maybe you should be treating us today, and not the other way around."

Ellie laughed. "Hold your horses until I've signed the contract at least."

They watched tourists amble past, through rain-splattered panes of glass. Soon, the waitress returned, balancing plates laden with scrambled eggs, sausages, Dutch cheese, avocado and toast. Her mother cast an envious glance at Ellie's bowl of natural yoghurt and pomegranate.

"Maybe I wanted something healthy after all," she said.

"We can share. I need some stodge after the night I've had, especially if we're going to be walking miles tomorrow," said Ellie, helping herself to some cheese.

"Are you sure you want to go to the May Day march?" said her father, downing his drink. "Wolfram was at the *stammtisch* last night. He told me the police expect a bit of trouble this year. Maybe you should stay away."

"Wolfram getting in a flap really isn't going to sway us," said her mother. "We're battle-hardened Richter women. We can handle ourselves."

Her father rolled his eyes.

"If you're really worried, Martin, why don't you come?" Her mother flashed her most winning smile.

"And miss the game?" said her father.

Her mother sighed. "You really are impossible."

Her blew her a kiss. "As are you, darling. I wouldn't have you any other way. Just promise me you'll be careful, and for goodness sake stay on the edge, won't you, in case you need to make a quick getaway."

Her mother nodded.

Her father raised his hand for the waitress. "Time for another glass of Prosecco?"

"No!" said Ellie and her mother in unison.

30

In the morning, a light rain fell from the sky, the kind that coats cities in a grey mist. Yusuf stuffed a few Euros into his pocket, packed a satchel with snacks from Leyla's kitchen and slipped out into the park before anyone noticed. A flock of birds swooped overhead in a great heaving mass, turning one way then the other. He longed to be that free. He'd start over, but it took too much energy. Before long, the grass had muddied his trainers. Wet strands of his hair curled around his ears. He pulled up his hoodie and began the walk to Plänterwald S-Bahn, past a portrait of Marlene Dietrich graffitied on a wall, Isaiah's playlist still blaring in his ears.

On days like this, Berlin was not merely a city; she became a life force all of her own. She had many faces. Perhaps time had made her the most accomplished city of them all. She could soothe with her green spaces or be a city for lovers, a musician's bolthole or a creative opioid. But in the same breath, she could also be a window to dark days of human history, with bullet holes carved into her, a seat of power, and sometimes, a nihilist's dream.

Today was such a day.

Isaiah and Yusuf veered into the crowds. Hardcore electro music pumped out of an underground nightclub a few metres away, drawing drunken revellers towards it. Yusuf ignored the swell of sound. They hadn't come for beer or music.

"It's disgusting, really," said Isaiah, shaking his head. "Music should be about freedom, not about control. The coppers sponsor all these street parties, the concert stages, the food stalls. It's all to dampen the protest itself, to keep trouble-makers from rioting. It even gives them a reason to say we can't demonstrate on certain routes."

They made straight for Kreuzberg, an inner city neighbourhood, which encompassed both Little Istanbul and remnants of the Berlin Wall, stretching over a kilometre to Friedrichshain. The ensemble of murals stood as a monument to fall of the Wall and a reminder of the Berlin's complex past. It featured the work of more than a hundred national and international artists, including the kiss between Brezhnev and Honecker, which Old Sayid always tried to recreate in art class.

"I love this part of town," said Isaiah, pointing to the side of a building covered entirely in a black and red rose motif. "Amateur street art sits alongside well-known artists such as Victor Ash, Blu and El Bocho here. The art is like a life cycle. It's constantly scrubbed out, painted over, embellished and altered. The face of Kreuzberg is always changing."

They rounded the corner, and met a wall of people.

Yusuf sucked in his breath.

The demonstration stretched for kilometres ahead of them, despite the drizzle. A sea of placards and obscured faces swam before them. Many wore hoodies, like Yusuf, and some wore ski masks. He hadn't known what to expect, but inside him, a seed of destruction had taken root, and he hoped for a chance to express it.

"This is awesome. Can you feel the buzz in the air?" said Isaiah.

"I can feel it, man," said Yusuf, exhilarated.

A wave of euphoria blanketed the crowd, as if they'd been made giddy by the prospect of change, by the semi-illicit nature of this type of civic participation. Taking control of the streets could be more powerful than merely wishing for change or marking a cross in a box at the polling booth. The signs held aloft bore no hint of compromise. Stark letters turned heads and invited discussions. Strangers smiled at one another and bumped fists.

CAPITALISM KILLS
WE ARE MANY
WE ARE ONE

"It's time," said Isaiah, zipping up his bomber jacket and digging into his pocket.

"For what?" said Yusuf.

"For these." He handed over a piece of cloth, and unravelled one of his own before pulling it down around his neck then up over his nose and mouth. "They're from my spraying kit. Just in case we need to hide our identity."

Just in case we need to hide our identity.

A mask turned a man into a stranger, and sometimes into a monster. The same could be said for a uniform.

Isaiah leaned closer, his eyes sparking, his sonorous voice muffled by the mask. "Ten years ago, the May Day riots spiralled out of control. The demonstrators weren't satisfied with the usual fare. My auntie told me they went wild. Just picture it plastered all over the front pages, bro-a policeman running, his riot gear in flames. It's urban legend. Usually, it's the black man running." He pointed at the mask. "So, you going to wear that or what?"

Yusuf nodded and pulled the mask on. It felt alien on his face. On any other day, a man such as he would be more likely to be attacked if he appeared to have something to hide. Just like a black man in the USA feared a bulge in his pockets could be construed as an illegal weapon, reading the wrong book or growing a beard could attract trouble for Yusuf. Isaiah had assured him he had nothing to fear. Today, donning a mask meant he'd be one of the crowd. A part of the whole.

They marched alongside seasoned and sanguine protesters holding recycled banners against a silver sky. They marched next to timid first-timers and bored kids from the provinces. They marched with the weary unemployed and angry students. They marched with gays, punks and feminists inspired by Red Rosa. They marched with Erasmus students high on their first taste of a demonstration, and with bemused tourists, untied to any philosophy, eager only to amass photographs and recount their stories at home. They marched side by side with brash young men, nudging those in front of them, elbows out, impatient for trouble. They marched in sight of the Wall, where families had been separated and lives taken.

Yusuf marched, and he waited for the promised violence to ignite. Inside, he stilled the voice of his mother-*never forget who we are*- and heard only the drumbeat of anger.

When the change came, it swept through the crowd like a virus. First, the pace of the demonstration became stilted, as if an unpractised hand lay on the throttle of an engine. The crowd grew agitated with the sudden stops and swells. Demonstrators set fire to wheelie bins; they flared and fizzled like litmus paper, and smoke bellowed into the air. Respectful chanting gave way to cat calls and anti-state venom. The police fanned out across Kottbusser Tor as the remaining crowd grew more and more unruly.

"Down with the pigs!"

"Capitalist scum!"

Isaiah adjusted his mask. The earring high up on the cartilage of his ear glinted in the light. "It's about to kick off."

A megaphone called for calm in the background. Some marchers responded, sensing trouble. Families, especially, moved away in alarm. A hard core group of a hundred men and women with fire in their bellies and in their eyes took the megaphone announcement as an invitation.

They leapt over the specially erected barricades. "Stupid bulls!"

"Stay back!" said the policemen, batons raised.

A police dog bared its teeth and barked at a group of drunken, jeering men, who taunted its beer-bellied owner. A lone tourist held his selfie-stick up high to get a better shot.

Yusuf absorbed the scene around him, narrowly avoiding injury when a bottle whizzed past his ear. It exploded feet away, near a fire hydrant. Blood pounded in his ears, and he was transported back to falling bombs and children covered in rubble. He clung to the present, his feet planted wide apart, the veins in his neck straining against his skin. Next to him, Isaiah's eyes had widened, the whites of his eyes in stark contrast to his black mask.

After a brief pause, like the pendulum before a clock strikes midnight, mayhem erupted all around them, within the ranks of the protesters and the state apparatus, as if they had crossed an invisible line.

Masked youths barged towards a bank, throwing rocks and beer bottles that cracked panes. Sirens blared. People zigzagged across the street, searching for pockets of safety or property to destroy. Yards away, a man crouched on the floor to let off a firework and the side of his face took the blunt force of a police baton. A group of men ran riot, flipping over bins, targeting cars and looting shops so that the streets became strewn with filth and fragments of glass. The police numbers exploded, and soon the streets had become a battlefield of pepper spray and batons, improvised projectiles and ferocious strangers. From balconies nearby, phone cameras flashed.

The scenes intoxicated Yusuf. This wasn't war like in Syria. There was a barely there civility, still, to this deteriorating demonstration. He felt alive. Uncaged.

He grabbed Isaiah's arm and together they ran into the stream of troublemakers, shoving their way through. Some fool had parked a sleek black Mercedes on the roadside. A man next to him drop-kicked the wing mirror, cracking it. Then he and Isaiah joined others rocking the car, heaving with all their might until it rolled onto its roof like a beetle on its back.

Yusuf thought back to all the times he or Selim had fought with their father, and how every angry word left a welt on the soft flesh of his heart. Better to strike the enemy, to land blows before someone else did, to protect yourself by being the attacker, the bully, by taking what should be yours.

He thought of Simeon and Dawud, Silberling and Karl. Most of all, he thought of his mother and his dead brother.

His anger helped him soar.

Power surged through him as if he was in the eye of the storm.

A policeman swung his baton in their direction and Yusuf elbowed the man in the windpipe. The policeman's knees buckled, and he fell to the ground, winded.

Yusuf paused, suspended in time, while around him men threw punches and shouted themselves hoarse, hurled broken bottles, and stumbled through the white whirling vapours of noxious gas. He turned a lens on himself and saw an alien, someone he didn't recognise, as if he'd splintered into shards of his former self.

Could a person fragment and still make their way through the world? How had his identities become so layered? What had once been fluid and seamless had become a complex negotiation, skins chosen or attributed to him in different times and places: a small, loved Syrian child; a brown man; a refugee; an alien; a terrorist; a lost man; a thug. He'd tired of the nimble feet required to stay upright on his path.

Next to him, Isaiah helped a woman to her feet. They swarmed forward together, finding release in their delinquency, in the disregard for law and property. He didn't have anything anyway–not really–so why should he care about others and their things?

Selim had envisaged a world that could never exist.

The real world wasn't soft and round, but made of jutting glass and force.

Lines blurred, and the hairs on his arm stood on end. Perhaps he and Karl weren't so different after all.

31

Attending the May Day protests with her mother had become an annual ritual for Ellie. She'd been nine years old when her mother had first taken her on a march, on the proviso that she'd walk the entire way herself. Ellie had marched until the blisters on the soles of her feet oozed, but she hadn't complained. Since then, they regularly pounded the streets together, placards in hand, feeling empowered and alive, their fingers resting on the pulse of the nation and not on the keypad of a phone.

Today they ambled along with their signs held aloft, both designed by her mother. *The Future is Female* read one, next to an elegant silhouette of the female body. *Justice for All* read the other, beside a boxy gavel in charcoal black. They walked along with the crowds, making the odd friend and greeting old ones. Her mother relished these opportunities to refresh her social justice credentials and to talk to like-minded people.

When the trouble first flickered to life, making itself known in jostling and bottles tumbling through the air, her mother insisted it would be a flash in the pan that the police would control.

"These aren't people who are here for the cause. They come to make trouble. You know that, Ellie. The police know how to deal with this. They won't be caught unawares."

Her mother liked to protest peacefully. She placed the blame for violence firmly at the feet of a small proportion of demonstrators. Violence, for her, ruined the impact of a march, making more enemies and derailing progress. She tutted at those who marched without a sense of togetherness. But Ellie had become less complacent. Her experiences with the refugees had taught her how violence could erupt from deeply buried wounds, suddenly, slipping into spaces like a cat burglar, leaving trauma in its wake. She'd seen how the police, too, could use disproportionate force, and how quickly a situation could escalate.

The tear gas came from nowhere.

Ellie grabbed her mother's hand and didn't let go. They ran, dropping their placards in their haste, tripping over themselves and barely managing to stay ahead of the cloud of smoke.

"There was no warning. I can't believe it got so ugly so quickly," said her mother, her breath heaving. They found a place outside of the immediate circle of trouble and she sat heavily on the kerb to catch her breath.

"Papa's going to be furious," said Ellie, crouching down beside her.

"Worried, more like. We'd better call."

Ellie shook her head. Her hair fell in dishevelled waves around her face. "Best we leave the area first. Let's head towards Checkpoint Charlie."

Police sirens and shop alarms sounded a few hundred metres away. Shouts and the pounding of feet punctuated the air. Her father had been right: they should have stayed home. They looked ridiculous: she, with her patent boots and a cranberry bandana; her mother with her *Nasty Women Make Herstory* t-shirt and mascara streaming down her cheeks.

They composed themselves, patting down their hair and clothes, and stood.

"It's a shame about the signs," said Ellie.

"I'm hardly Usain Bolt," said her mother. "Can you imagine how slow I would have been if we'd held on to them?"

They laughed, in spite of it all, just as a group of men came tumbling through the smoke, spluttering, eyes streaming. Ellie stared, taking in a young Afro-German in skinny jeans and a bomber jacket. He pulled down his mask and gasped for air. Behind him, a taller man strode through the smoke. He, too, pulled off his face covering, itching at his bearded face. He bent over, leaning heavily on his knees.

Her mother jerked her in the direction of the U-Bahn. "Let's go."

Ellie watched the man, transfixed. "Wait."

The man glanced over his shoulder into the cloud of smoke then lurched forward, scrubbing at his face with the back of his hand, coughing. Their eyes met, and a jolt of electricity travelled up Ellie's spine.

"Yusuf!" What was he doing here, in the midst of all this trouble?

He dragged his friend towards them.

"I can't breathe. My eyes are burning," said Yusuf, clawing at his face. His olive skin had turned a blotchy red.

His friend vomited, splattering the pavement. Her mother, alarmed, tended to him.

"Come with us," said Ellie.

The four of them hurried away from the trouble, a motley crew. Ellie's heart thudded in her chest, and she looked furtively around, worried that the police might appear, or thugs intent on exploiting the situation.

"What on earth were you thinking?" she said, staring at Yusuf.

"You're here too," he said, his breath raspy, heavily leaning on her. He could barely open his eyes. "And your mother."

Ellie raised an eyebrow. "My mother is more of a hell-raiser than you or I will ever be."

His voice cracked. "Isaiah, meet Ellie Richter and her mother."

Isaiah's mouth fell open. "You're the journalist?" He whistled low, before spluttering again.

Ellie nodded and supported Yusuf as they took laborious steps down into Kochstrasse underground station, where the comforting, familiar smell of iron and grease hit her. Her mind worked overtime. Yusuf had told his friend about her. That had to mean something. But what was he doing caught up in the riots?

They sat bedraggled in the U-Bahn, paired into twos: Ellie and Yusuf, slack and wordless; and across the aisle, her mother and the man Yusuf had introduced as Isaiah. The cab swayed as it moved out of the station and away from the city centre towards Tempelhof. Yusuf and Isaiah washed their eyes with water and slumped on their seats, drawing curious glances from fellow passengers. After ten minutes, their symptoms eased.

"They're going to shut the circus," said Yusuf, his knuckles white against his knees.

His words hung between them like an axe.

Ellie took in the tone of his voice and the shadows on his face. She'd known it was coming. It had only been a matter of when. Her heart twisted for him, but she recognised something else inside of herself: a belief in the power of her work. She'd done good work on her blog, and her *Die Welt* article lay just around the corner. It could make a difference in the face of powerful people like Marina and Silberling, as long as she had her wits and the people stood with her. She'd never relinquish the dogged stubbornness ingrained in her every cell.

"You're not going to just accept this?" she said.

"What else can be done?"

Her mother, ever the fighter, leaned forward, fixing her gaze on Yusuf. "Listen, why don't you both come and get cleaned up at our apartment? It's not too much out of your way." She nudged Ellie unceremoniously with her foot, a signal for Ellie to work with her to persuade Yusuf.

Her mother's eyes twinkled. "How about you, Isaiah? I bet you have some stories to tell about today. We're in Treptow, not far from the circus residences. We even have cheese cake."

"I'd like that," said Isaiah. "I live with my mother and aunt in a high-rise around there." He seized the mask Yusuf held, and stuffed it deep into his pocket with his own, as if they had something to hide. Then he turned to her mother. "I'm sorry for the vomit. I like your hair, by the way."

Her mother beamed, leaning towards him conspiratorially. "Why, thank you. And never mind the vomit. You haven't lived if you've never vomited in public." She turned her attention to Ellie and Yusuf. "How about it, you two?"

Yusuf's tired eyes searched Ellie for a hint of whether he'd be welcome. She nodded at him, willing him to say yes. There could be nothing worse than them parting ways now, without her trying to lift the cloud of defeat that hung about him. She was her mother's daughter, after all.

"Count me in," said Yusuf.

Her face broke into an involuntary smile. A warmth spread through her at the thought of spending more time with him, at convincing him that the fight wasn't yet over.

At Tempelhof, they gathered up their things and changed lines. Isaiah and her mother chatted, at ease in each other's company, as though age and background formed no barrier to friendship. Ellie and Yusuf followed awkwardly.

Her mother swivelled to speak to Ellie. "Give your father a ring, won't you, love?"

They both knew turning up unannounced would be a mistake. While mostly a mild-mannered drunk, her father would keenly feel the loss of dignity. Should they arrive with guests and find him reeking of alcohol and surrounded by empty beer bottles, he'd never forgive them.

Ellie delved into her bag for her phone. She'd switched it onto silent during the march, and had reached for it only to take the odd photograph before the march spiralled out of control. "I'm just going to let my father know we're safe. He'll have heard about the riots on the radio and will be worried."

"Of course," said Yusuf.

She blinked looking at the display, gawking in wonder at hundreds of social media notifications on her screen.

"Your father?" said Yusuf.

She stopped on the platform to scan the messages. Her fingers trembled as she scrolled through an avalanche of responses to her blog series.

"Ellie?" said Yusuf.

She kissed him, hard.

He pulled away, surprised, then gathered her to him.

His beard prickled against her skin. Heat pulsed between them.

"What was that about?" he said when they drew apart, searching for an answer in her face.

"I have something to show you," said Ellie. "Not here. At my parents' apartment."

Judging by the way her phone continued to vibrate, she'd reached far more readers than she'd ever imagined just with the human stories she had painted of the refugees on her blog. She'd wanted to present a narrative that countered Marina's, and she'd succeeded, even before the publication of her article in *Die Welt*. She couldn't wait to share the news with Yusuf.

Perhaps the world would swing in their direction after all.

32

Ellie reminded Yusuf of the man he wanted to be. In the midst of the tear gas, he'd grasped Isaiah by the collar and thrust him forward, out of the billowing cloud of smoke, away from the madness where men scrambled for the upper hand. They pitched forward onto a street where the air cleared and their lungs fought to eject the poison, but the sky above them hung heavy and leaden.

He glanced up, checking if they were safe, and there Ellie stood, her red hair and bright scarf conspicuous against the grey Berlin street, as if the earth would bend itself in half so they could encounter each other. As if chance were a fool, and Allah had written down his plans for each human in the most exquisite detail.

Kissing Ellie gave him a taste of a life just out of reach. Now, in Ellie's parental home with the hallmarks of civilisation all around them, from the fine wallpaper to Ella Fitzgerald's voice soaring from the age-worn vinyl on the record player, his conscience clawed at him.

He and Isaiah had been lucky to escape without injury or arrest. The symptoms of the tear gas had now entirely dissipated, leaving them both bleary-eyed and eager for rest. Isaiah wolfed down his cheesecake. Yusuf toyed with his, pushing it around on his plate with a fork. Animated voices travelled from the kitchen where an exuberant, alcohol-fuelled Martin Richter questioned his wife about the demonstration while she replenished the coffee.

Four days until his circus family would be torn apart.

"This is some record collection," said Isaiah, marvelling at the gems he discovered amongst Ellie's father's most prized belongings.

"You really shouldn't have been there today, Yusuf," said Ellie. "I know you're angry but the circus closing doesn't mean that you won't find a home in Berlin. Any trouble could put a nail in your chance to stay in Germany permanently. You know better than anyone what Silberling is like."

"It's my fault. I persuaded him to come," said Isaiah, looking up from scraping the crumbs off his plate. "And after everything Silberling's done, the government deserved what it got today."

"Yeah, well, there are other ways to hit back other than going full out cuckoo," said Ellie, rolling her eyes. She prised the fork from Yusuf's fingers, placed his plate on the coffee table and tugged him to his feet before motioning to Isaiah. "Want to come?"

"I'll be there in a minute," said Isaiah, his eyes drifting to Katharina Richter fussing around her stumbling, ruddy-cheeked husband. "I'm going to help your parents clear up first. A nap would be really good right now too." He eyed up the sofa with its deep cushions and the throw folded neatly over one arm.

Ellie sighed, and the green of her eyes deepened as she took in the scene in the kitchen. "Suit yourself."

Yusuf trailed after her to the back of the apartment, aware of her every movement.

She caught his eye. "Papa's not always like this, you know. He's a good man."

"It's not for me to judge," said Yusuf. "But for what it's worth, I like him. He's worth ten of my own father."

"The drink has always been his vice."

There were enough vices for men to fall prey to, without alcohol being one of them, but some flaws were more forgivable than others. Martin Richter didn't beat his family, nor seek to mould them in his own image. He wondered what drove her father to drink, but didn't think it his place to ask. Perhaps one day, but not yet.

Ellie dragged an extra chair towards her father's desk so they could sit side by side, their thighs inches apart. He longed to touch her and drive the worry from her face, but he held himself in check.

Her voice twisted into something more hopeful with a shy undertone. "I've been working on something to make up for the *BAZ* article."

She powered up her computer, biting her lip as she pulled up a screen, drumming her fingers on the mouse pad. He'd not seen her nervous before, and found it ignited a reciprocal anxiety in him.

The website she revealed puzzled him at first. He wasn't one for computers, but he understood their possibilities and that she could reach a big audience with the click of a button. When he read her blog posts, he could hear her voice, the one from her journal that had captivated him and revealed her true self. Here on her blog, she'd written about each of them: about him, Emir, Zul, and Osman; about Aischa, Aya and Amena, who had been strong enough to flee Yemen, and to catch him when he fell; about Simeon, stitched together in a hospital, his lung punctured, without a mother to piece him back together again.

Her pen pictures didn't skim the surface; they dove into history, personality and dreams, weaving together facts and emotional insights. Refugee narratives had become so common against a darkening patchwork of news that included terrorism and threats of nuclear war, displacement of people elicited less empathy. But Ellie had uncovered the beating heart of all of them, building a story not of strangers, but of a community that deserved recognition. As if she had a microscopic understanding that allowed her to zoom in on their value as people.

She watched him as he read, anxiously, repeatedly brushing her fringe out of her eyes. Every now and then, he asked for the meaning of phrases he didn't understand.

"What is reconciliation?"

"And degradation?"

He understood the compassion behind her words without needing to unravel their precise meaning. He asked to reassure her. To give him a chance to drill down to the minutia of the words that helped him rediscover his sense of worth. To buy time while he found the words to express how he felt.

In the end, after he'd absorbed the comments that strangers had left on the articles, ones that made him feel perhaps Germany could be his home after all, he said simply, "You have all the words, and I have none. Just thank you."

Ellie shrugged, as if her courage didn't deserve praise, as if her compassion was a thread running through everybody rather than something special. "I was looking for a way to correct the damage done by Marina's article. I couldn't bear for my name to be attached to those views. They aren't me. This is me."

His eyes kept drifting to her mouth. He forced them away, stubbing the floor with his socked feet, trying to focus. "What I don't understand is why you've only written about us as people, and not about Silberling and Marina, and the part they have played in this story. Why can't you publish the recording of them you found on her computer? The emails she exchanged with his assistant?"

She met his eyes and hers beamed with a quiet pride. "Because that part of the story is being picked up by *Die Welt*."

He whooped and punched the air; it felt like justice. All he'd ever dreamed of was a fair chance to make something of himself. "I can't believe it. That's incredible, Ellie."

"There are still some pieces missing, and the editor at *Die Welt* thinks so too. Marina and Silberling are dangerous people to take on. I need the full story," said Ellie, "and secret recordings are illegal, unless they are made in the overarching public interest. What I really need is for us to establish, beyond a shadow of a doubt, that Silberling fell below the standards of his office. We need more."

Yusuf set his shoulders back, sucked air into his cheeks, then released it slowly. "Then let's get it."

Yusuf's exhaustion settled into his bones, and fatigue played out in shadows across his friends' faces. He, Ellie and Isaiah had been mulling over options for hours, working out a plan about how to catch Silberling out and force him to make a mistake.

So far, Silberling had made all the running. He'd enlisted Marina's help, he'd got out ahead with television coverage and the circus closure. *BAZ* had even bagged an exclusive on the closure letter. Its online edition carried a barrage of support for Silberling in the online comments, and Yusuf understood that this had become a war of perceptions between the haves and the have-nots, between those who despised mass immigration and those who tolerated it.

Soon, he'd have to leave for the circus, and every breath took him closer to his circus family losing it all. He and the circus folk were just collateral, unless they managed to steal a march on Silberling. Unless Ellie's blog and *Die Welt* article could change the narrative.

They all agreed the surest way to keep the circus safe was to discredit Silberling so they weren't at the whims of his plotting. Surely his successor at the Interior Ministry would have more of a conscience?

It was down to the three of them. And Ellie's mother, who wouldn't be kept out of the melee.

"This is so exciting! A whole operation out of our apartment," said Ellie's mother. She eased herself onto the rug of the library where Yusuf, Ellie and Isaiah had sprawled. She'd showered after the demonstration and now wore a flowing zebra-print dress. The jewellery around her neck clanked. "And it's May Day, too. The perfect day to stand up to the state."

"We should rifle through Silberling's bins and get one of those DNA tests done. I bet his heritage is as mixed as mine," said Isaiah, only half in jest.

"I can't get Karl out of my mind," said Yusuf, cupping his hands behind his head and staring at the swirling plaster on the ceiling.

"Oh?" said Ellie, chewing on a pen.

"He told me I have powerful enemies. More than once, I think."

Ellie's eyebrows shot up. "That's what he said? You haven't mentioned that before."

"It was in my statement to the police after the break-in at the circus. They didn't seem to find it significant."

She called up the latest incarnation of Karl Klein's race-baiting website. Her research had listed at least five different websites that had existed over the past three years with links to him. "God, look at this," she said in disgust. "The internet could have been something special. We could have had a classless, genderless, raceless utopia, where it didn't matter if you are gay or trans or have a disability. Everyone could be equal there in the ether, but instead, the internet amps up polarisation. It's just a way for arseholes to find out about other arseholes."

"Maybe Karl was just trying to get under my skin. People like that don't need an excuse to cause trouble."

"I think there's more to it. His baiting of you has to mean he's linked to Silberling. My goodness, what if Silberling put him up to it? What if Karl was part of his plan?" Ellie kneaded the back of her neck. She paused. "How about we turn this on its head? Get Karl to come to us. If we can somehow prove he and Silberling are connected, that would blow this thing wide open."

"Would it? Be careful what you wish for," said her mother, frowning. "Just make sure you're ready for what you set in motion."

Ellie paid no heed. She flicked her fingers on the space bar of her computer.

"What are you doing?" said Isaiah.

"I'm dropping a big hint to my followers that this story will appear in traditional print under my byline. I'm also posting an update about the circus closure. Who knows, it might trigger fans into fighting for it. And most importantly, I'm letting it be known that I'm interviewing Yusuf just before showtime tonight."

Yusuf's throat tightened. Emir still hadn't given him the green light to perform. He ached to be up in the rafters with a bird's eye view of the circus tent. Up there, nothing was complicated. "How is that going to help?"

"Here's the spiel. If my instincts are right, Karl will be watching, and he won't want any good publicity for you. Not if 'powerful friends' have tasked him to cause trouble. We just need to lure him out and trick him into making the link."

What had he let himself in for? What good could come of inviting trouble? Selim surfaced from his memories: curly hair, sloping shoulders Yusuf had ridden on as a boy, his smile when he talked about the world he believed in. And Yusuf knew, then, that he had to find his courage.

33

Ellie's spine tingled with nerves as she, Yusuf and Isaiah approached the circus. Gusts of wind whipped up her hair. Mammoth trees loomed around them, veined with mystery and knowledge. She met Yusuf's eyes; so much rode on tonight.

The scent of caramelised peanuts drifted on the air towards them. From fifty metres away, she recognised Osman's bulk balanced precariously on his stilts. Next to him, circus children zipped about on unicycles. The Ferris wheel shone with hundreds of fairy-lights, as if the performers refused to go gently into the night. The blue and bronze tent, too, had been embellished with streamers that danced in the wind.

Ellie dipped her hands into her bag and her fingers found her phone. She withdrew her hands, keeping them deliberately free in case they were surprised by Karl or his crew. She'd done her homework on him. He was a nasty piece of work, and they couldn't afford to be complacent. Beside her, Yusuf's jaw jutted out and his eyes scanned the park, looking for any sign of trouble.

"Half an hour until showtime," he said. "If Karl is here, he could be anywhere. Are you sure you don't want me to get Zul and Osman?"

Ellie shook her head. "No. The more people involved, the greater the chance that this spins out of control. Just stay close and be on the alert, both of you. Yusuf, you're the bait. Isaiah, you be ready to call the bulls. My job's to try and get him to spill on Silberling."

Isaiah rolled his eyes. "As if the bulls would get here in time to stop anything."

Yusuf shot him a warning glance.

"Okay, okay," said Isaiah. "You know, sometimes I wonder who is worse, the ones who pretend they aren't racist under their masks or the ones like Karl. It's a relief to know what men are really thinking, to know the colours of their heart, not to have it all hidden away."

They passed underneath a group of chestnut trees reaching out from an undergrowth of moss and flowering shrubs, casting a deep bay of shadow. Raised voices came from behind the stable block just beyond.

Yusuf's features hardened and his mouth flattened into a straight line. "I'm going to check that out."

"We stick together," said Ellie.

They approached the stables with cautious movements, the sound of their footsteps absorbed by damp grass. Backed up against a brick wall stood Doris, her blue eyes troubled, her stance wide as if she were bracing herself. A short, muscular man had positioned himself too close for comfort.

Doris stumbled over her words. "It's not migrants who put a strain on resources. The strain comes from increased life expectancy. What do you propose to do about that? Kill me? I'm old enough to put a strain on resources. None of this is the refugees' fault."

"God Almighty. Stop talking, bitch." The man spat at Doris's feet and she flinched.

Yusuf swore under his breath and darted to her side without waiting to consult his friends. "You stay away from her!"

Ellie bit the inside of her lip.

Next to her, Isaiah tensed.

Karl Klein.

Karl laughed and sized up his opponents. He reeked of beer. "I thought I'd have some fun while I waited for you. I tried to have some fun with one of the pretty dancers but she wasn't having any of it, so I found the old lady. We're only having a chat. I should have known this one would be a dirty sympathiser."

"Doris?" said Yusuf. "Are you okay?"

"I'm so relieved you're back," said Doris, pale and disoriented. "Osman told me you were off at the demonstration. I've been worried. I've been out looking for you. Then this young man found me."

Karl shifted his weight from one foot to another, itching for a fight. His lips curled back when he noticed Isaiah. "Oi, mulatto.

How's it hanging?" He chuckled. "The old lady's been trying to convince me to go easy on you lot." He swung to Ellie. "And you. What's wrong with you? Your own kind not good enough? Do you have to go spouting that rubbish online? There's no need to rile up support for these losers. We all know their shit show is about to close."

"If you're so sure, then why are you here tonight?" said Ellie.

"Yeah," said Isaiah.

Karl thrust out his chest and snorted. "What, are we six years old now, trading infantile insults in a park?"

Ellie ignored him. "*Your kind* always needs someone to pick on. What next? People who are chronically ill, single mums?"

Behind Karl, Yusuf cupped an arm around Doris and led her away. The older woman let out a groan, and Karl whirled around.

"Where are you going? We're not finished here," he said with an ugly twist to his mouth.

"This is between me and you. Leave her out of it," said Yusuf, urging Doris away.

A slow smile spread across Karl's lips. "You both belong in a ditch." He stepped forward, fist raised, and Doris whimpered.

Yusuf raised his forearm up to block any punches, but it didn't matter anyway.

"My arm hurts," said Doris, slurring her speech, as though opening her mouth widely took more energy than she could spare. She slid onto the floor before Yusuf could catch her, her breathing erratic.

Yusuf dropped to knees beside her. "Doris! Doris, what's wrong?"

Her eyelids flickered shut. A clammy sheen covered her forehead and upper lip.

Yusuf checked her airways. "Doris, please!" He slapped her cheek, gently at first then with more force.

She remained motionless.

Yusuf crumpled over her, his face drained of all colour. He cradled her, whispering into her ear, kneading her fingers.

"Isaiah, call an ambulance!" said Ellie.

"Oh shit," said Karl, taking off at a run.

Isaiah spoke into his mobile, his voice low and urgent.

Ellie grasped Yusuf by the shoulders, shaking him. "Move, Yusuf. She needs CPR. She needs it now."

He staggered away, curling his arms over his head as if he were a child.

Ellie's hands quivered as she pulled Doris's legs so she lay flat on the lawn. The older woman's trousers had travelled up one leg and she had grass in her hair.

Ellie turned to Yusuf. "Follow Karl. He can't get away with this. Follow him!" She heard the pounding of Yusuf's footfalls as she started CPR, hoping that her memory of First Aid training would suffice. She placed the heel of her hand on Doris's chest, wincing as she pressed down, deeper than seemed natural, compressing Doris's chest, feeling her warmth, the slackness of her skin. One–two–three… She counted until she reached thirty then tilted the older woman's head and pinched her nose before blowing into her mouth. A second rescue breath brought tears to her eyes.

Isaiah knelt down next to them, his brown eyes pools of sorrow. "They're on their way."

Ellie nodded. Doris's life was in her hands.

Yusuf might not admit it, but anyone could see how close the two had become. Doris had been a mother to him; Ellie couldn't fail either of them.

Doris's chest rose and Ellie started the compressions again, willing help to come.

34

Yusuf dashed after Karl, although every fibre of his being wanted to stay with Doris. Karl might have been strong, he might have had a head start, but Yusuf's legs were longer, and he gained ground with every metre. He regulated his breathing as he flew forward helter-skelter through the park, squinting to locate Karl. The memorial to the Soviet soldier dominated the skyline. A person-sized Berlin bear shaped out of foliage loomed into vision and startled him. He hesitated, then picked up his pace once more, deciding that Karl must be running to the S-Bahn. Sure enough, he made him out in a narrow underpass a few hundred yards from the station.

Karl had hunched over, hands on his knees, and panted heavily. He glanced over his shoulder. If he'd continued like a horse with blinkers on, galloping on irrespective of the foes behind, he might have slipped Yusuf's grasp.

He didn't.

The years of training and the practice ring had made Yusuf tough. He'd grown accustomed to pushing his muscles further than he should. His affection for Doris and fury at Karl drove him on as adrenalin coursed through his veins.

He leapt and landed on Karl, unsure of whether he wanted to drag him back to Doris or beat him to a pulp. The two men barrelled into a recycling bin, sending bottles and aluminium cans clattering all over the ground.

Yusuf clutched Karl's collar, glaring at him.

Karl's eyes flicked from Yusuf to the empty expanse behind him, checking to see how alone they were, whether he could call on help. He turned startled eyes back to Yusuf. "I didn't mean the old woman any harm, really."

Heat surged through Yusuf's body. "Why should I believe a thing that comes out of your mouth? You came after my friends, you came after me, you deliberately intimidated Doris–" His voice caught in his throat.

Karl spluttered. "I wouldn't hurt an old lady. I swear. I was putting it on. I wasn't going to do anything."

The light had grown dim, and in the distance, an ambulance siren wailed. Yusuf's mind flashed back to Doris, lying motionless against the grass, the stink of the horses just beyond. His anger spiralled upwards, and he tightened his grip on Karl's collar. "You won't get a chance to hurt anyone else."

A green bottle clanked against his foot. He bent to pick it up, hauling Karl with him. At the last second, he changed his mind, picking up an eroded brick instead that had become dislodged from the underpass.

"What are you doing?" said Karl, ashen-faced in the flickering light.

The night had cooled and goosebumps ran along Yusuf's neck. Selim had dreamed of a better world. His mother had dreamed of a fresh start. Even Doris wouldn't want him to protect her this way; there wasn't a violent bone in her body.

Who was he doing this for? To what end?

He tossed the brick aside, and relinquished his hold on Karl. The brick bounced, disintegrating further. Both men slumped, exhausted.

"I'm sorry," said Karl.

Yusuf glanced at him in surprise. "Are you?"

Karl eased himself to a sitting position, his back curving against the round edge of the underpass. It reeked of piss.

Yusuf followed suit, tentatively at first, then with a reckless disregard for letting his guard down. He should be at Doris's side. He should maintain his anger against this man, but he'd grown tired of divisions. "Why do you hate me?" he said without any hint of recrimination. He simply wanted to understand.

"Hate?" said Karl, his brow furrowed. "That's such an ugly word. Don't be soft. I'm passionate about what I believe in, that's all. I like a man who knows his mind. None of this dancing around…men need to tell it straight."

Vibrations shook the underpass from a train passing overhead. Yusuf's anger subsided like the ocean at low tide. "Something must have happened to make you this way," he said.

Karl huffed. "Look, if you want me to tell you I've changed my mind, that I want your kind here, you're going to be disappointed."

"What have we ever done to you?"

"You think I'm racist?" said Karl, puffing out his chest.

Yusuf's breathing had returned to normal and he exuded calm. "Well, aren't you?"

"This country used to be something. And now we're so keen to make up for our past, to be a world leader, that we are opening the floodgates to anyone that knocks. How long before Germany is unrecognisable? It's not racist to think your country can't sustain mass immigration. It's not racist to vote for slowing population growth. It's not racist to reject open borders."

"And yet when you look at me, your lip curls, your fists clench, my skin colour sets off a reaction in you that I have no control over. I wonder, when you look at me, what do you see? Do you see me as an alien? Do you see me as scum? A rapist, a job-stealer, a benefits-tourist?"

"No, a terrorist maybe, you being Muslim and all."

"Maybe the problem is you and your friends, not me and mine," said Yusuf, flashing a cold smile. He wouldn't be intimidated by this man anymore, despite the tattoos in old German on his skin. "Tell me, do you seek out the sun to tan?"

Karl rubbed his arms absently. The underpass had grown cold. "What kind of question is that? Everyone likes a tan."

Yusuf emitted a scathing laugh. Couldn't Karl see his hypocrisy? "You tan yourself darker, but my skin bothers you. In some countries, women bleach their skin lighter. My own mother worries about her skin tanning, instinctively thinking that white is better. What a world this is."

Karl clambered to his feet. "Get of your high horse. It's not just your skin. It's your background, your accent, the smells, your culture, your difference. I don't want us to be lost in a multi-racial soup. I see how your kind are systematically erasing the white gene. The Germany I love won't exist when you are finished with it. It makes me sick, all of you coming here. We aren't one *Volk*. We're a joke."

Yusuf sighed. "You can't really expect immigrants to turn their back on their culture. Don't you ever tire of the outrage?"

"What would I have without my anger? Everything's changing. There's not enough jobs for people like me. There's not enough people who care about what I'm going through, and yet here's the Chancellor, willing to take a chance on you, giving you housing, giving you benefits, a job. What about the German women who choose you over me? I see you with all those chances and I think, 'What about me?' This is my country."

Was it even possible to convince Karl to think another way? Yusuf tried a different tact, and for once, his German flowed so he didn't have to overthink which words to grasp from his limited vocabulary. "What do you know about me, Karl, apart from the usual clichés, the stereotypes blown up to make it easy to herd us into groups, to erase our individuality? Have you ever wondered what it's like to be a brown man? Have you ever thought about what lies underneath my skin? About my memories, experiences and dreams?"

Karl laughed like a drain, clutching his belly, then stopped abruptly. "Have you, acrobat? Have you ever wondered what it's like to be a white man at the bottom of the heap? For a person like me who everyone looks down on? Have you thought about what lies under my skin? What about my worries? What about my ill parents, high rents, scant work? I don't want to bump along drawing money on *Hartz IV*. I want more for myself. What about the little sister I have to feed and clothe, the fact I can't afford to take a woman on dates let alone raise a family of my own?"

Yusuf raked his fingers through his hair. His body ached. He needed sleep, but he also craved resolution. There must be a way to set to right all the wrongs of the past, the ones he had suffered and the ones this man had too. A reset button that erased the past and built a new future. Yusuf understood anger and disappointment; rage and violence were also part of him. In another lifetime, another world, could he and Karl have been friends? No one had a monopoly on virtue or on sorrow. They all just wanted to survive.

"Look, Karl, I'm not a scrounger. I'm not an illegal immigrant. I'm just here to build myself up after the war. I don't want to take anything from you. I want to contribute. When I first came here, I was willing to change every cell in my body to please this country. I was so grateful to be here. Even today, I'd bend myself into a different shape to fit into the mould."

Karl's jaw was a hard line silhouetted against the brickwork. "As if you could conform to German values. Your kind will creep into our schools and hospitals, just like the Turks did. You, with your Allah and your *jihad* and your bloody virgins."

Yusuf's faith might be in flux, but he tired of the judgements of those who didn't understand it. His Islam was his mother's religion: one of knowledge, peace and community. Yet many in the West, including those with liberal and educated backgrounds, viewed it as a religion of rigidity and violence.

"How are German values any different to mine? Don't you think I am scared of terrorists, too? And who are you to cast a stone? You think *I'm* a terrorist when you act the way you do? What would you have me do? Go back to Syria with bombs falling out of the sky while the international community grapples with how to get monsters under control? Do you ever think of the immigrant children washed up on the beach? The ones crushed by rubble?"

Cold eyes over gritted teeth. "It's not my problem."

"Context is everything. You pluck out my otherness without thinking of the reasons behind my journey here. I didn't come here for money. I came to be safe. Even now, if I left for Syria, I'd carry pieces of Germany with me. I love both places. This city, its trees, its parks, its possibilities have become mine. Could you live with all the circus folk being sent back to their countries of origin, even though it might not be safe, just because fate decided to make your country of birth safer than my own?"

Karl hesitated, and this time he sounded less certain. "You don't belong here."

"I can be someone here," said Yusuf.

Karl slumped down next to Yusuf. His rubbed his hand through the close-shaven sides of his hair. "I'll always be nobody if you stay."

"Why can't we both shake off our shackles and just live the lives we want to lead?"

Karl buried his head in his hands. When he looked up, all anger and bravado had been stripped bare. "Because the police came for me today, and I'm living on borrowed time. I'll be in prison before you can sneeze."

Yusuf jerked his gaze to Karl's, and a fraught connection fizzed between them. "Are you serious?"

"Deadly. It was only a matter of time." He paused. "It's a public holiday and everyone is celebrating, or demonstrating, and then there's me, evading capture and scaring old women to death. It's not fair. I'm not a bad man. I've got the courage of my convictions. That's got to count for something."

Did Karl really believe that he could act with abandon and evade justice? "Tell me. Did you tell the police we fought in the park?"

"Do you really think I'd go to the bulls? Draw attention to myself after what I just told you? Admit publicly that you'd bested me?"

"I guess that's a no." Yusuf tired of the missiles back and forth. He quelled the pangs of sympathy he'd begun to harbour for Karl. Doris's ghostly-white face haunted him, her slack limbs against the emerald grass. He stood up.

"Wait," said Karl. "The thing is, there's this man. He promised he'd take care of my sister when I go to prison, but he's as likely to keep his word as I am to land a holiday in Florida."

Yusuf's heart skipped a beat. Could Karl be talking about Silberling? He stilled his expression, lest too much eagerness resulted in Karl clamming up.

"The man's a weasel. I can't trust him." Karl paused. "I might not like you, acrobat, but can I trust you?"

Yusuf's voice echoed through the underpass, a rekindling of hope. "I guess neither of us have anything to lose."

35

By the time the ambulance crew arrived, the circus was in full flow. Ellie pressed on with chest compressions to the sound of Najib's muffled beat-boxing and the distant stamping of the audience. She didn't know if it would be enough.

Isaiah guided the paramedics to where Ellie crouched over Doris with her knees in the dirt.

Ellie stepped aside, relieved to entrust Doris to the crew's superior skills.

They administered oxygen and stabilised their patient with a shot in the thigh, but still Doris's eyes remained closed, her skin tinged blue, her pulse weak.

Ellie clambered up into the ambulance behind the stretcher, leaving Isaiah behind to relay the news to Emir and look out for Yusuf.

The ambulance rocked as it sped towards its destination.

She squeezed Doris's clammy hand, urging her to pull through.

At the hospital, a team of doctors and nurses met the ambulance, and Doris disappeared into a ward.

Ellie collapsed into a chair, where a nurse offered her a glass of water and took Doris's details.

"I'll be back soon to tell you how your friend is doing," said the nurse, checking her paperwork.

"Thank you," said Ellie, numb and disoriented.

The nurse hurried away and returned a few minutes later to find Ellie pacing the corridor. "It turns out Frau Kaun has been in for a minor ailment before, and we have her next of kin details. A son in Munich, and another in Stuttgart. They're on their way but it will be hours before they reach the hospital."

"Oh."

"Will you be staying here until they arrive?"

Ellie nodded.

The nurse squeezed her shoulder and continued on her way.

What had happened to Yusuf? Why hadn't he made it back to Doris? Images of the past few days swirled around her head: her head slumped over her computer; the ugly May Day demonstration; the threat to close the circus; baiting Karl Klein; pumping Doris's chest, desperate to keep her alive.

Ellie swallowed her panic before it overwhelmed her. She was good in a crisis; she didn't lose her head. She needed to focus on the practical. Her fingers crept around her phone. She dragged in a shaky breath and dialled her mother. "Mama, can you come to the hospital? We're at Charité."

Concern coloured her mother's voice. "Whatever's the matter, darling? Are you okay?"

Her mother's voice anchored her and kept the loneliness away in the white-washed ward. "It's the circus warden, Frau Kaun. I need you to stop by the residences to pick up some of her things."

"Your father's out cold, but I'll leave a note and will be right there."

Two hours later, on the ground floor of Charité Hospital, not far from the Brandenburg Gate and the Palace of Tears exhibition on life in divided Berlin, a doctor in scrubs with a stethoscope around his neck sought out Ellie and her mother. Ellie scrambled to her feet.

"You're here with Frau Kaun?" said the doctor, raking a hand through the grey hair at his temples.

The nurse who had been kind to Ellie hovered in the background, shoulders deflated.

Ellie suddenly felt light-headed. "Is she all right?"

"Of course she is," said her mother. "Women like us are tough old birds."

The doctor focused his attention on Ellie. "I understand you accompanied her in the ambulance, but her next of kin is yet to arrive?"

Ellie's voice trembled. "Yes."

"I'm afraid Frau Kaun passed away a few minutes ago from the stroke she suffered. We did all we could. I'm sorry." Grave eyes met hers.

Ellie sank into a chair.

At her feet, Doris's possessions spilled out from the tote bag her mother had picked up from the residences: soft cotton pyjamas, a button-up blouse, a pair of slacks, her toothbrush and a comb, with strands of silver entwined in its teeth. A bunch of grapes wrapped in a brown paper bag now seemed pathetic.

Ellie covered her face with her hands, willing the clock to reset. If only they had intercepted Karl before he and Doris had crossed paths.

The doctor rocked on his feet. "I'll be happy to speak to her family when they arrive."

What about Yusuf? Ellie kneaded the muscles in her sore neck. She stood. "Thank you for all you did."

"I'm sorry it wasn't enough," he said.

"Can we see her?" said Ellie. She didn't like to think of Doris all alone here, without a friend or relative to mourn her in the hour of her death.

The doctor's tired eyes glazed over. He was already thinking about the next patient. "Only for a few moments. I'll ask the nurse to take you through when they're ready."

The nurse led them through to Doris's bedside. How pale and small Doris looked, compared to the energetic woman Ellie had come to know in her role at the residences. Her sleek grey bob, which had been as straggly as a scarecrow's stuffing in the ambulance, had been returned to its former glory, as if a kind nurse had wanted her to look her best. Her body lay cocooned under neat sheets. No tubes pierced her skin. Halogen lighting revealed her puffy face; the left side of her mouth drooped slightly. A serene expression adorned her gentle features.

Ellie collapsed against her mother and sobbed.

Her mother held her close. "I'm sorry it hurts, Ellie. I wish she'd made it."

"So do I." She pulled away from her mother and turned to address the dead woman in a whisper. Perhaps she could still hear. "I'll try my best to fight for them, as you did."

Then she bent slowly, ceremoniously, to leave a kiss on Doris's parchment cheek, and wished her well, wherever her spirit may be.

That night Ellie stripped off her clothes and made a beeline for her kitchen to make herself a cup of Earl Grey, heaping in two spoonfuls of brown sugar when usually she would have taken only one. She'd needed her own space despite her mother's invitation to stay over at their family home. Inside, she knew she had work to do.

A wave of sadness washed over her for Doris. Her sons must have arrived at the hospital by now. She wondered if they had found out the news by telephone or in person. The weight at the centre of her chest expanded to think of receiving a similar call.

Every inch of her body ached with the excesses of the day. Her palms had been stamped with the memory of Doris's brittle ribcage as she willed her to live. Ellie kneaded the back of her neck and returned to her bedroom. The clock had long since struck midnight but she couldn't afford to sleep, and her mind wouldn't still without work. The tea slopped dangerously in her mug when she placed it on her side table. She switched on her night light, pulled on an oversized t-shirt and grabbed her laptop, then sat cross-legged on her bed with the bedcovers tucked around her.

She still hadn't heard from Yusuf, but he didn't have a telephone and she'd never given him her number. At first, she held hopes he'd turn up at her flat but her mind had been jumbled after leaving the hospital, and now she remembered that while Yusuf had been to her parents' house, she'd never invited him to her own place.

Her mind flashed with the image of him lying bruised and broken in the deepest recesses of Treptower Park with Karl Klein standing over him.

Ellie sucked in her breath and turned on her computer, calming herself by running her fingers over the keyboard, thinking about her next steps. Her father had taught her that trick: worry and melancholy didn't help anyone, least of all yourself; having a plan of action was a way to leapfrog over it.

Her Twitter was awash with questions about the circus. Some Berliners had taken a chance on the circus only after uncovering its story on Ellie's blog. Others sent questions asking why the promised interview with the acrobat hadn't been posted. More still pledged to visit the circus before it closed.

Could it be that her Twitter comprised only an echo chamber, and she wasn't influencing anyone at all? She needed to persuade readers outside her circle. Her frustration grew at the decision to wait for more evidence before publishing her story at *Die Welt*. Time had become their enemy. Soon, there wouldn't be a circus to save. Their plan to trap Silberling had ostensibly failed, judging by the lack of contact from Yusuf. How could she draw out supporters for the circus, but also establish beyond a shadow of a doubt that Silberling was unfit for public office? Morality played less of a role than it once had in matters of state. Perhaps she merely required a powerful emblem to rally support.

Could Emir be that emblem, the resolute, big-hearted ringmaster with his shabby top hat?

Or Zul in his clown alter ago? No, that wouldn't work. She needed someone more relatable to sway the masses.

The answer came to her like lightning.

Of course. Doris was that emblem. She always had been.

The synapses in Ellie's brain fired up as her fingers flew across the keyboard. She made a mental note to herself to express her condolences to Doris's sons and ensure she had their support in invoking their mother's memory. A calm washed over her as she drafted a blog post. It helped to write in a world that often felt destructive. It brought her clarity and a sense of immersion. A power surged through her as she channelled her thoughts. At no other time did she feel so poised and uncompromising, so in charge of her destiny. She could make a difference with the words and paragraphs she pieced together, just as surely as if she erected a soaring tower or planted a forest. She made waves with her words, she always had. Even in a void, on a desert island, on a distant planet without the slightest chance of being read, Ellie would write.

UPDATE ON THE TREPTOW CIRCUS

You might have visited the circus. Or maybe you've
noticed it when you wandered through Treptower Park,

smelling the meat from barbecues, with warm beer slopping from your bottle. You probably know it as the immigrant circus. This label has stuck, although it doesn't differentiate between economic migrants, students, or refugees who have fled war and famine.

The threat to the circus is no longer a theoretical one. Soon, it may no longer exist.

A nation with our history can't afford to be complacent about the rights of minorities. The eyes of the world are upon us and judging us still. Germany must uphold the highest standards of democracy and integrity. I hope soon to be able to reveal to you the corruption I have uncovered, but tonight, let me tell you about a woman called Doris Kaun, the warden at the circus residences, who suffered a stroke and lost her life tonight. Doris spent her last few moments defending the Treptow Circus to a neo-Nazi.

Let's take a leaf from everyday people, such as Doris, who believe in the right for all humans to have a chance of a better life. The onus is on us to refuse artificial divisions, the lines in the sand, the clashing flags, when we are all skin and bone. Let's celebrate the circus because it enriches this city. Because it widens our understanding and brings our life colour.

Stand with me. Come to the circus tomorrow evening with your hearts and your banners, and show the Government the fabric of this country. Without people to stand behind these words, they will evaporate, and so will our resistance.

#SaveTheCircus #TwoDaysToGo #BeADoris

It didn't matter that Ellie sat alone in the dark, full of fear. She could still reach outside of herself and touch others. She just had to believe.

36

Sometimes May the first could be a
headache for the Government. Rex liked to keep a tight rein on
outcomes, and the May demonstrations were notoriously
unpredictable. Keeping the public order was their priority. Still,
compared to the riots in 2007, this year had been a breeze. Yes,
the use of tear gas was unfortunate and there had been some
harm to businesses and public property, but within an hour, the
police had cleared the area around Kottbusser Tor and made a
dozen arrests.

Rex smiled. Corinne had called earlier to say the coverage in
the papers cast the Government response in a fair light. Of course,
the liberals had been riled by the use of the gas, but in a world full
of fear, coming down hard on crime won favour with the silent
majority. Not only that, but Corinne had identified the acrobat in
at least two separate reels of footage that had appeared on the
news. She had yet to corroborate his participation in the rioting,
but things were looking rosy. Rex recognised the narratives the
media spun: there was always a push and pull between who
would be depicted as the hero and who the villain. He very much
preferred the role of hero. The day really couldn't have played out
any better.

He poured himself a whiskey in his study and turned on the hifi,
ignoring the briefing papers on extra funding for the current crop of
Olympic and Paralympic athletes on his desk that Corinne had
requested him to look at. The opening bars of *What a Wonderful World*
drifted out of the speakers, and soon he'd settled back into his
leather armchair, listening to the croaky magnificence of Louis
Armstrong's voice.

The intercom buzzed and his wife's voice filtered through. Jessy cocked her ears. "There's someone at the door. Can you get it, darling?"

Rex swallowed his disappointment at the interruption. "Of course, darling." Although often absent from family life due to the demands of state business, he took pride in being a more affectionate husband and father than his own father had managed.

He peered into the flickering grey-scale security monitors, squinting over the half-moon glasses he wore at home, to discern who might be visiting at this late hour. White-hot rage flared inside him when he recognised Karl Klein on his doorstep. He flung his glasses on his desk.

"Jessy! With me." He stalked to the front door to unhook the latch with Jessy on his heels, her amber eyes glowing in the dark. "You dare to come *here*? It was bad enough at the Interior Ministry, but home is sacred." Inside, his wife sat helping their son and daughter with their homework. Any second now, Sara's violin teacher would arrive. They had high aspirations for their children.

Beside him, Jessy growled, and Rex hooked his fingers around her collar.

"Can't you quiet that mutt?" said Karl.

Jessy bared her teeth, and Karl took a step back.

"Sit, Jessy," said Rex, patting the dog's smooth flank. She responded at once. "Why are you here, Karl, and how on earth did you find me?"

"I tailed you a few weeks ago," said Karl. "You're always out with that dog. It wasn't difficult."

Unkempt hair hung in Karl's face, and grit blackened his fingernails. He emitted a nonchalance that irked Rex. What had changed? He should be quaking in his boots; he'd risked Rex's wrath coming here. He had to know that.

Rex stared down his nose at him. "It was a mistake to come here. Your services are no longer required."

Karl didn't even react. "The police came after me today," he said, cocking his head to the left and glancing behind him.

Rex didn't care. He wasn't this man's father. Did Karl expect a shoulder to cry on? He'd warned him about the net closing around him and how he wouldn't interfere. The man had dug his own grave. Regrets wouldn't change the path of his life. How ridiculous and simpering some men could be when their choices had been their own.

Still, he couldn't afford a ruckus here on his doorstep. The neighbours might be watching, or his family might come out. He took out a notepad from the chest in the hallway and ripped out a sheet before scribbling a number on it, and pushed it at Karl. "Here. My aide's number again. She'll see to it that you get cleaned up and advise you on how best to turn yourself in. You might cut a few months from your sentence that way. Now get lost."

Karl clutched the note between dirty fingers.

Rex pulled Jessy back and made to close the door, but Karl jammed the doorframe with his foot. Jessy leapt forward, baring her teeth in menace and attached herself to Karl's foot.

Karl yowled, and behind Rex, his wife peeked into the hallway. "Is everything okay, darling?"

Rex tugged back the dog, inserting his fingers into her jaw to prise it open when she didn't relent. She released her grip. "I'll just be a minute, Agnes. Go back inside, and take Jessy with you."

His wife threw him a questioning look, but whistled for the dog all the same. Rex shoved the dog towards her. Jessy whimpered, but obeyed.

Rex turned back to Karl, who was nursing his foot. "What the hell do you think you're doing?" he said, between gritted teeth.

"There's someone here who wants to speak to you."

Rex's eyebrows shot up.

A man approached from behind the bush Rex's gardener had painstakingly trimmed into a cone shape.

The acrobat. He searched his mind for the man's name. Yusuf Alam.

A roiling heat spread through Rex's belly, and for a moment, he regretted sending Jessy away. What were they doing at his house together? Could it be that Karl had somehow revealed their deal? He didn't think it possible that he'd been betrayed. Karl had far too much to lose. He surveyed the men from under half-lidded eyes, calculating how best to extricate himself from this situation.

"Herr Alam. This is an unlikely collaboration." He fought to maintain some kind of gentlemanly composure. They'd shaken his equilibrium by bringing the sordid edge of his business to his doorstep. It placed him in danger, and he hadn't yet grasped what they expected from him. "I'm afraid if you're here to persuade me to overturn my decision to close the circus, you've set yourself up for disappointment. Accosting me on my own doorstep is never going to end well. You'd do well to respect my office and all that it stands for."

"I'm not here to ask anything of you," said Yusuf, his accent careful. It struck Rex how proficient he'd become in German since they'd first met. "I know you've been playing God, that you're behind the swell of hatred towards us. I know what you promised us, and what you delivered, and the gap in between."

Rex reared up. He smarted at the accusations that his project had come up short. "You think I wanted you to fail? I was on your side, but nothing stays the same, boy, and nothing comes for free."

Yusuf snorted. "Not even for you, with your birthright, your education, the privileges that fell into your lap by chance?"

Rex struggled to find a way to turn the situation to his advantage. His mind hurtled through a myriad of options. Police would attend his call in minutes, of course, but he couldn't be sure how the scene would play out. How awkward for Sara's violin teacher to witness it all, and how cumbersome to field all the questions from the government or, God forbid, the media. This was home. It wouldn't do to sully it, or to expose his family to the ugly side of his job. No, it was best to extricate himself without outside help.

Still, he'd imagined he understood Karl and the acrobat's motivations and strengths, but here they were together, and he couldn't unravel what they would achieve from being in cahoots with one another. They were like chalk and cheese. Rex was unaccustomed to being challenged. He shoved his hands into his pockets, projecting power, as if the two men on his doorstep were mere insects.

"Who are you to lecture me? I gave you everything. I gave you a fresh start. It's not my fault you made nothing of it. Look at what I've made of the opportunities I had." He beat his fists against his chest. "This—" he swept his hand across the façade of his house with its vaulted ceilings and manicured lawn, "I earned this. Me. Without handouts."

Karl had grown silent and stared impassively at a speck on the wall.

Yusuf's skin flushed. "You think ambition and hard work got you here, Minister?" The last word hung heavy with sarcasm. "Have you ever given thought to where you were born, and to whom? Have you ever considered what impact your education and networks have had on you? Have you ever thought how different it would have been if you hadn't been born into money or this place?" Yusuf shook his head slowly in disbelief. "Don't you see? We internalise the roles written for us by others. The circus was our ticket to stay here, and we were so grateful. But you fooled us. We taught our bodies to do incredible things, but you don't care–we can fly or fall–it's nothing to you, as long as you come out of it intact. You reduced us. You colluded with Karl and you colluded with *BAZ* to rile up sentiment against us."

Bile rose in Rex's throat. His daughter's tinkling laugh seeped out into the cool air outside, and his protective instincts kicked in. He'd had enough of this nonsense; he wanted to end it. He ejected his words in sharp, staccato beats. "My first duty is to the German people. How long do you expect me to be your champion? Resources aren't finite, and neither is time. You haven't been in my position. You don't know the skill it takes to balance priorities for the country, how citizens bray for your skin when they sit in their armchairs criticising your every move. Maybe you should stop holding me responsible for problems that I did not create in the first place. Hold your President responsible, the one who created the conditions in your country of origin, rather than grasping me by the neck."

Yusuf pinned him with a fiery gaze, and his voice soared into the night. "You talk a fine game, Minister, but I see in your eyes that I am nothing. You think you're my better. But you're mistaken. I am something. I will prove to you that even with all your tools and all your scheming, I'm in charge of my destiny."

Rex didn't have to argue with this ungrateful man. It changed nothing. The circus would still close, and he wouldn't have to hear about this sorry affair ever again. "Get out of here, both of you, before I call the police. They would be here already were I not amused by these games."

The men exchanged glances.

Rex stepped back on the threshold. He longed to send these two scurrying away with their tails between their legs. "What a mess you've left your poor sister in, Karl," he said, adopting a jaunty tone designed to wound.

The corners of Karl's mouth drooped and Rex felt not a shade of pity. He might have helped the girl had Karl kept his side of the bargain, but that ship had long sailed. Favours couldn't be extended to all and sundry; they had to be earned with blood, sweat and loyalty.

"We'll see," said Karl. He turned away, and even from behind, he looked deflated, as if the air had been sucked out of his sails.

Rex watched, loosening his tie, as their backs retreated into the night.

He reached for his phone even before the door clicked shut to tip the police off to Karl's whereabouts. If Corinne confirmed Yusuf's role in the riot, he'd alert the police where to find him also.

His whiskey and Louis Armstrong waited.

37

A slither of moon cast a dull light over the street as the two men moved away from Silberling's grand house, their hearts racing from what they had dared. A third man joined them, and the three of them couldn't have been more different from one another in appearance, background and outlook.

Yusuf slowed the thoughts galloping about his head and turned to Isaiah. "Did you get all that?"

Isaiah's fingers navigated his phone menu. "We'll have to lighten the footage. Even with the lantern at his door, shadows obscured his face, but–"

"Have we got what we need?"

Isaiah grinned. "Bro, he admitted he knew Karl. He taunted him about his sister. We've got him pinned naked against a wall."

Yusuf whooped, springing up into the air. He'd felt so small standing on Silberling's doorstep, but they now had the admission Ellie needed on tape. Yes, the recording had been made secretly, and therefore might not be admissible, but surely it was in the public interest?

Perhaps they'd managed it; perhaps they'd saved the circus.

Excitement bubbled up inside him at the thought of telling Ellie and Doris.

Doris.

He'd heard an ambulance, but what if she'd not made it? Despair filled him at the thought of everyone he loved being taken away one by one. How could it be fair that some people had so many to love, while others had their joy stolen or never experienced love at all?

Karl revolted him. He may have helped tonight, but he hadn't fooled Yusuf. Nothing but self-interest motivated him. But even

Karl had a sister he would sacrifice himself for. Yusuf's mind skipped back to Selim on that dusty street. The freedom of the motorcycle ride juxtaposed against his all too human body torn apart by the explosion.

At his side, ghouls chased across Karl's face in the half-light. "We stuck our heads in the hornet's nest. Silberling's going to send the bulls after me, I know it. What have I done?" He shot Yusuf an imploring look. "Promise me you'll find a way to take care of my sister."

Yusuf nodded. He didn't know how but he owed the man that much. He'd find a way.

Behind them, a din of sirens approached. The police cars skidded to a halt a few metres away, and men in green uniform leapt out, barking orders.

Karl flinched. "I'm not going to run this time."

He hovered, waiting for the men to reach him, his hands in plain sight. His sad eyes met Yusuf's. He needed comfort, but the walls between them were still too high. The strange night stretched out men's dreams and fears, but in reality, he and Karl would never eat from the same table or fight the same battles. They occupied different trajectories and Yusuf was glad that his own brimmed with hope, not hate, even when it appeared all the light had been turned off.

The policemen shouted, still, demanding that Karl put his hands behind his back. He yielded, a wretch of a man caught in a trap. They cuffed him.

"Let's go, bro," said Isaiah. "He got what was coming to him."

The boughs played tricks with Yusuf's mind as he pressed on through Treptower Park; the trees crowded him, appearing human and unbending, villains of their terrain by moonlight. At this late hour, shadows shrouded the bright colours of the big top. The tent and the assorted buildings nearby seemed buttressed, erected in such a way to maintain boundaries between the circus folk and everyday Berliners.

As he passed the stable block, the horses whinnied. He lingered there a moment, although Isaiah had told him the ambulance had long since taken Doris to hospital. At the residences, he entered the key code and, seeing the communal areas cloaked in darkness, trudged to his room, though he longed to wake someone for news of Doris and Ellie. He'd never forgive himself if Doris hadn't survived. He'd abandoned them both.

In his room, he flicked on the lamp and cast his eyes on the floor in case someone had pushed a note under his door. Nothing. He sighed.

Isaiah had entrusted him with the Silberling footage. Yusuf plucked the memory card out of his wallet with great care, and wrapped it in a piece of paper. Then he reached for the stuffed elephant his mother had made him long ago, and found the little chink in the cotton of the trunk, where the stuffing sometimes escaped. He pushed the card into the hole and returned the toy to his chair.

Remnants of the day floated through his mind in disparate pieces. There could be no hope of sleep now. The day's filth lay heavy on his skin, and so he undressed to his smalls, grabbed the towel on his chair, and traipsed to the shower.

The tap screeched as he opened it, and soon, scalding water cascaded over his head, down his back, over his bruised rib cage and aching calves. He stood still, head bowed, hands splayed outwards, reluctant to adjust the temperature though it seared his skin. After a few minutes–excessive showering risked waking the others and drove up the bill–he soaped and towelled himself dry before scooping up his underwear.

A rap of knuckles sounded on the door, followed by a whisper.

Yusuf slung the towel around his hips and opened the door to find a bleary-eyed Emir standing there, wearing too small shorts and a threadbare white vest, his moustache spiking in different directions.

"I thought I heard something. I've been waiting for you," said Emir. He shook his head. "I didn't think we'd see troubles like these again." He took a deep breath and his stomach shook with emotion. "Ellie called with news of Doris. I'm sorry. I know you were close. At least she wasn't alone, *shukkar*."

The ground swayed beneath Yusuf's feet. His chest constricted, and he needed to be out in the park, anywhere but in this small space where demons had found him.

"She's gone?"

"I'm sorry, son," said Emir, embracing him.

"What happened? Why couldn't they save her?" His voice was that of a child, not a grown man.

"I don't know much." He paused. "I have something for you." He handed Yusuf a scrap of paper.

Yusuf gripped the paper, knuckles white. "What is it?"

"Ellie's mobile number. Her mother stopped to collect Doris's belongings on her way to the hospital. She wanted you to have the phone number. Ellie might have the answers you're looking for."

"How can Doris be gone? What will we do without her? I miss her already."

"The sands of time don't wait for anyone." Emir set his shoulders. "Doris believed in the circus, son. She was a part of this family. I know you don't want to think about this right now, but we need you on the trapeze for our very last performance. Let's change up the routines a bit. We'll put on a show this city will never forget. We'll do it for Doris."

Though his insides churned with the loss of his friend, a slow resolve crept up on Yusuf. He wouldn't let Doris die in vain. She'd want him to fight on. The circus ring beckoned, and even if it all were to end, there was nowhere he'd rather be than with the strangers who had become his family.

And Ellie.

He needed to call her, listen to her voice and hear about Doris's final moments. He needed to share his grief with her and to borrow her strength. In light of Doris's death, the Silberling recording amounted to a joyless victory, but Ellie needed to know what had happened.

Emir manoeuvred Yusuf out of the bathroom, like a father fussing over his child, and switched off the light. "We can sit together in the common room for a while and talk about Doris, if you like."

Yusuf's words garbled. "It's late. We should probably sleep. Perhaps we can meet in the morning? There's something you should know." His fingers jittered around the scrap of paper.

Emir, tufts of hair visible on his back, retreated down the corridor. "As you wish. Then I will save my energy to say my prayers for Doris. Everything else can wait until the sun rises."

The rawness of Yusuf's sorrow accompanied him as he dressed in a fresh t-shirt and shorts, then padded to Doris's apartment in bare feet. He knew he shouldn't be there, but his instinctive need to be close to her overrode logic. Her unlocked door didn't surprise him; she had always welcomed whoever came to her door. He picked up a family picture from her windowsill, feeling like a thief, and sank into her sofa. Tears pricked his eyes as he memorised the angles of her face, the happiness of this memory of a young married couple with their teenage children, before ill health and death stalked them.

Once he had composed himself, he replaced the photograph, eased her apartment door shut behind him, and headed to the common room. A phone booth with minimal lighting hung on the adjacent wall. Tangy smoke drifted over to him, a telltale sign that Old Sayid had been smoking shisha.

He hovered for a moment by the booth. Some of the circus folk called their relatives, but Yusuf hadn't spoken to his own mother in over a year. The telephone nearest their family home had been blown apart in an air raid, and the one next to that also, and so Yusuf had stopped hoping to hear her voice.

It was enough to hope she lived.

Someone he loved had to live.

One day, maybe he would see his mother's face again, and say sorry for leaving her, and trace the outline of her face with his fingers, and give her the money he had saved for her in fistfuls under his mattress.

One day, his guilt and fear would dissolve like salt, leaving no residue.

One day.

He lifted the receiver and cupped it under one ear, and dug in his pocket for a few Euros. The machine accepted his money greedily, and the receiver emitted a series of high tones as he dialled Ellie's number.

Her voice seeped through the phone, distracted, sleepy. "Hello?"

"It's me." Stupid man, thinking in his arrogance that she'd recognise his voice.

She tripped over her words, suddenly alert. "Oh God, Yusuf, I'm so sorry. I wanted her to make it so badly. I can't believe this has happened."

Her grief didn't add to the weight of his; it comforted him instead.

His voice caught in his throat. "I'm sorry to have left you both alone. She deserved better."

"She knew you loved her. She loved you all. I understood that from the moment I met her." She slowed. "How did you get my number? What happened with Karl? Where have you been? I thought you might have been hurt...I was worried."

He drew in a ragged breath, soaking up the sound of her voice, the signs that he was special to her. He'd forgotten what it felt like to be important to someone; not just as one of a number, but more special than others. To her, he said only, "I need to see you."

He knew it to be true even before he vocalised it. It was about Doris, and two people providing a balm to each other after loss.

It was also more than that.

His admission hung in the air between them, a weight that meant something, not a throwaway comment, and in that moment, it was only the two of them and nothing else mattered. He held his breath, holding on to the sparks that flew between them, the promise of what could be.

"Can I come over?" she said.

He imagined a shyness to her voice, but the Ellie he knew brimmed with courage. She could never be hesitant or timorous; his nature was full of fear, but hers shone like the sun, regardless of what life threw at her. He thought of Doris, her body cold with no hope of warmth. He thought of his mother, and whether it would be improper for Ellie to visit when respectable men and women slept at this hour.

How could he say no to Ellie?

He wanted to say yes. So he did.

"Shall I meet you at the S-Bahn?" he said, pleased that she couldn't see how he'd twisted the phone cable round and round his wrist I n his nervousness, how it had caught fast. How his emotions had become so muddied that he could no longer form a coherent thought.

"I'll take a cab. I'll be there in twenty minutes."

"I'll wait at the door," he said.

She hung up, and Yusuf untangled the cable, his thoughts ricocheting through his mind, like wayward bullets failing to find their mark. He waited at the door for her, grounded by grief but expectant, as if the night held intimacies that the day couldn't offer. Close to half an hour later, he glimpsed headlights in the distance, and sure enough, Ellie came darting across the lawn with a satchel across her body, using her mobile phone as a torch.

He opened the door and she tumbled into his arms as if it were the most natural thing in the world. She smelt of spring grass and daisies. Her breath came in rasps from how she had hared across the park.

"I'm so sorry about Doris," she said, lacing her fingers with his and squeezing.

"I need to know she was at peace," he said, searching her face for the truth.

Ellie bit her lip. "She looked beautiful."

He took her satchel from her and led the way to his room. They walked in silence, lest they wake anyone. Neither wanted to explain themselves, nor invite anyone else to join them. When they reached his room, Yusuf fumbled with the door, distracted by the pressure of Ellie's thumb on his palm and how her body pressed against his side. Inside, he let her satchel fall to the floor and heard a thump.

She winced. "My computer."

"Sorry."

"Don't worry."

They sat on the bed and she told him about Doris's final hours. Her story soothed him, as did her presence. Although Doris hadn't been with family or even friends, she'd been surrounded by kindness. That had to count for something.

Ellie unbuttoned her cardigan, a verdant green that contrasted with her fiery hair. Underneath, she wore a pale vest.

"Now your turn," she said.

He swallowed. "Excuse me?"

Ellie met his gaze, as if she knew, as if each of them held the knowledge inside of what would happen between them, as sure as a seed unravels and pushes through the earth to flower.

"Don't hold back. What happened with Karl?"

"Oh." He jumped up and retrieved his stuffed elephant.

She smiled. "When I came here tonight, that's not really what I had in mind."

Heat flooded his cheeks. He used his forefinger to hook out the memory card and offered it to her.

She unravelled the folds of paper, and held the memory card with care. "What is it?"

"Take a look."

Understanding dawned and her voice rose an octave. "You did it? Did you really do it?"

"Shhh, don't wake anyone up."

Her mouth fell open as she watched the video. "I can't believe you managed this. It's brilliant. Is that Karl? Oh my word, we've got the sucker. We've got him!" She threw her arms around him and planted a kiss on his lips.

Despite his sadness, or perhaps because of it, a quickening overcame him, a stirring that he'd long forgotten.

He didn't understand these signals. He knew from movies that Western girls differed from the ones at home. Ellie didn't wait to be kissed; she took what she wanted. He stood in awe of her passion, the way she presented herself to the world. He'd realised she was special as soon as he found himself confiding things to her only his brother had known. With her, he became the man he was always meant to be: bold and valiant, not a blot on society.

Esme hadn't acted this way when she had been sweet on him. She'd taken extra care to look pretty and had looked at him from under long lashes. She'd brought him treats she'd made with Leyla, and had gone quiet when they were alone. He'd pretended not to notice how Esme had felt because he thought of her as a sister. Still, wouldn't she have been the better fit for him?

Spiky thoughts weaselled forward from the back of his mind. Wouldn't he be more suited to someone more like Esme, someone who had replicated his experiences? Ellie made him feel less alone but she didn't share his history or culture, or a knowledge of the sights and sounds, peculiarities and tragedies of his life. He knew the term *coconut* for those who seamlessly adapted to the West and forgot their roots. But didn't Doris prove that differences in culture and origin could be bridged, and that only love mattered? His heart lingered on the stills in his mind that captured his mother and Selim. Was walking through this door with this woman a sign that he'd abandoned the people he loved best?

Perhaps he was only an adventure for Ellie. Perhaps this was her way of relaxing at the end of the day. Western women gave themselves more freely than the women he'd been accustomed to. Worse, maybe he'd become an extension of Ellie's liberal upbringing; perhaps her affection for him was a masquerade, less about his individual qualities than about symbolism, a notch on her bed post, a brown man to taste but not to love.

He wanted love more than anything.

He wanted Ellie to love him, because he knew–from how his breath caught in his throat, how his thoughts drifted to her when they were apart, the way she made him face her fears, and how his fingers itched to comb the tendrils of her hair away from her face– that he loved her.

She peeled off her vest and there could be no doubt what she wanted.

Refusing her would make him seem less of a man somehow.

He didn't want to resist.

Together, they stumbled to the floor, there, in his meagre room, in a paper thin building populated with broken souls. His lips found hers, but he shut his eyes to hide his emotions. Their closeness healed the fractured parts of him. She straddled him, tangling her fingers in his beard, dusting feather-light kisses on his eyelids, her breath warm on his cheek. He held still, worrying about his beard scratching her soft skin.

She stopped, and when he opened his eyes, he found her studying him. Suddenly, the dull glow from the table lamp bothered him, as if it highlighted his vulnerability.

"Shall I turn the light off?" he said.

Ellie shook her head, stopping to untie her hair so it fell across her breasts.

He couldn't take his eyes off her.

She tugged at his t-shirt and he wriggled out of it. He didn't tell her that he'd hardly done this. He didn't need to. They fell into the dance together. Her hot palms explored him, and his fingers brushed the pink peaks of her breasts. She entwined her fingers in his hair, more roughly now, writhing against him until neither of them could bear the clothes that still separated them, until they craved skin on skin, breath against breath and entangled limbs. A language all of their own.

They shrugged off their remaining clothes. He gasped when she touched him, then there was only her and him, and no-one else. She guided him to her and it took a superhuman effort for him to pull away.

"Wait. A condom," he said, fumbling to put one on before reaching for her again.

He kissed her, tugging at her bottom lip with his teeth until she opened her mouth to his tongue. Then he entered her, and she arched her back to meet him, and it had never felt this right. He didn't know what the morning held, but it didn't matter.

Only this mattered. Ellie and him.

Their bodies moved as one, and although she was protected from pregnancy, he imagined his seed pushing through the dark burrows of her body. In his mind, her womb became a cave with soft blossoms underfoot, where new life took root.

If this moment created life, it would be a clean start. The child would be full of potential. The world would lay at her feet, and no one would harm her. No brutes would come for her. No wars would steal her childhood. She would know the privilege of growing older.

They rocked together and his urgency took over, his need for Ellie, for her softness and her scent, and the scraping of her nails against his back.

When it was over and they had crested the wave, he held her to cushion her from the cold floor, and his melancholy mixed with something earthier, as if he were finally rooted to this place and its people.

38

At some point in the night, after Ellie had fallen asleep in Yusuf's arms, he'd lifted her onto the bed and pulled the covers over her. But the bed was cramped, and she became claustrophobic under the covers, and so she woke to find him sprawled next to her, peaceful and serene in the lamplight.

She craned her neck to locate her phone. She'd tossed it aside when she entered the room, without a thought for where it might land, and now she cursed her recklessness. The notification light pulsed on top of Yusuf's chair. She lifted Yusuf's arm and extricated herself from his embrace before retrieving her phone and laptop. Then she slipped on his t-shirt, still warm from his body, and sat on the floor, propped up against the bed with her computer on her lap.

Half an hour later, she finished tweaking her article for *Die Welt*, and sent it to Simone. Inside her, a slow burn of excitement took root. Isaiah's footage had gifted the circus and its allies more than a fighting chance of survival. She wished she could share this news with Doris. With the deadline for the circus closure two days away, Ellie had no time to lose.

Yusuf's breath fanned her neck as Ellie checked her work. Tom had confided in her once that Marina had a Google alert on her own name; she expected any articles mentioning her to be printed out and placed in an urgent folder on her desk. He was sure to tell her of Marina's reaction to the exposé in *Die Welt*. With or without a Google alert, she'd find out: the publishing industry would ricochet with the ramifications. There could be no doubt that Marina would come for Ellie. There would be a *BAZ* editorial at the very least, in which Marina would see-saw between rage and victimhood, riling up the anger amongst her newspaper's readership.

Still, a small part of Ellie hoped Marina would develop a grudging respect for her, and perhaps even regret ever firing her. She was proud of the writer she'd become, having stepped out of Marina's shadow. She'd finally found her voice away from *BAZ*; it was fierce and uncompromising, spurred on by the injustices she'd witnessed. Marina would never have sanctioned her taking on the establishment; but then, Marina was in their pocket.

Let her come for me, thought Ellie. *I am ready.*

All she needed was for Berlin to show itself as the city she knew it to be.

Berliners were an open, tolerant people for the most part. They just required a nudge to step beyond their mind-your-own-business culture.

Ellie had faith; the alternative remained too bleak to contemplate.

39

Yusuf's sleep cocooned him. No nightmares slipped into his dreamscape, or jumbled memories of Doris, or Selim, or Simeon, or a snarling Karl draped in the German flag. He'd become accustomed to disturbed sleep since leaving Syria, and he marvelled at what had happened to soothe his subconscious. Perhaps in thwarting Rex, he'd finally conquered his monsters, scratching together enough power to rise out of his victimhood. Or maybe it was the night he'd shared with Ellie. The touch of another person, the warmth of bodies lying together, healed in a way that medicine never could.

He knew in his bones that when he stepped into the circus ring tomorrow, he would fly.

Even if it was the last time.

A wet towel interrupted his thoughts, hitting him in the face. Ellie stood before him, grinning, dressed once again in yesterday's clothes, her hair damp from her shower. He preferred her in his t-shirt; he basked in the intimacy of her borrowing his clothes.

After washing, he stole some bread and jam from Leyla's kitchen for them to eat together, and they walked in the park, piecing together their plan for rescuing the circus. Ellie spoke fervently, as if she could stop the closure by the sheer force of her belief. He spilled crumbs on his shirt, and she wiped away a dollop of jam from the corner of his mouth, at ease in his company, with no sign of regret about having slept with him. He relaxed into their togetherness and the sense that, for now at least, they belonged together.

A beep on Ellie's phone alerted her to the fact her *Die Welt* article had been included in that morning's edition. Simone, satisfied that Ellie's evidence had at last met her standards, had published it on what was otherwise a quiet morning for news. They rushed to a newsstand.

BERLIN'S CIRCUS DISCARDED BY
CORRUPT GOVERNMENT MINISTER
By Ellie Richter

On 15 April, a meeting took place in Mutter Hoppe restaurant in Berlin Mitte between two well known residents of this city: Rex Silberling, Interior Minister, and Marina Schmidt, Editor of Berliner Allgemeine Zeitung. What transpired in that meeting, and the actions that followed, go to the very heart of who we want to be as a nation.

Silberling, darling of the establishment and career politician, has enjoyed a meteoric rise in the Bundestag, and has a reputation for having his finger on the pulse of public sentiment. Two years ago, when he secured backing for a flagship project to help refugees, the public and politicians from major parties were behind him.

Once the project had been greenlit, a circus and adjoining residences were hastily erected in Berlin Treptow, in a forgotten corner of the park that needed regeneration. The refugees–many of whom suffer from post-traumatic stress disorder–set up a working circus. They trained hard to perfect their skills, learned to speak our language, began rebuilding their lives and grew together as a family.

After years of intense conflict in the Middle East, the number of refugees has swelled and caused much concern amongst the political establishment and voters. Minister Silberling, too, recognised the adverse impact on his electability given his close ties to the circus project.

Die Welt has gathered proof of how Minister Silberling has orchestrated a campaign against the very community he purported to support. We have handed over the findings–including two time-stamped recordings–to the police. In the first one, Minister Silberling promises BAZ funding, that he ultimately channelled directly from his departmental budget, in exchange for fear-mongering articles written about the circus community. In the second, the Minister is caught on film colluding with a far-right extremist.

In the past few weeks, Minister Silberling has used his office to offer inappropriate favours, deported a minor with no warning or due process, and issued notice of the closure of the circus without formal consultation.

Germany is not a kangaroo court; we do not believe in trial by executioner. We are a bastion of democracy, and ministers of state cannot feel emboldened to act with such impunity and bring their office into disrepute. History has taught us to beware those whose arrogance leads them down dark paths. Let's remind ourselves about who is fit to lead and who deserves our trust.

Ellie couldn't contain her excitement. Television stations had already picked up the story. Ellie thought it a real possibility that the circus could be saved, and although Yusuf himself knew too much about the nature of corrupt government to believe her, he refused to rain on her hopes.

"It's happening. It's really happening, Yusuf. There is no way the circus can be closed overnight now. Imagine if people respond to my call on social media to come to the vigil. Imagine if they show the Government they won't stand for this," she said, grasping the dense newspaper in her hands.

Yusuf enjoyed the sparkle in her eyes and the innocence and idealism that distracted him from his grief and the sense of foreboding that his world was about to change. He knew better than to give her words credence. Luck had never favoured him, so why would it now?

Two days until their family would be torn apart.

A serenity washed over him, at odds with Ellie's excitement. He'd feared losing the circus for so long. It had been a loss by degrees: a slow chipping away of security. He swallowed the sense of an approaching precipice and reconciled himself to the closure despite the turn in fortune. Reaching over to kiss Ellie, he determined to make the best of these precious moments with people he loved, the last few hours on the trapeze and the community he had found, in case it all ended.

The incessant peeping of her mobile phone irritated him. He itched to throw the device in the bin, and wanted her attention for himself, to enjoy the here and now.

Yes, he would fight for the circus in Doris's memory, as he'd promised Emir, but he'd also brace himself for its loss. Realism protected him from crushing disappointment.

Ellie's readers might coo with support from the comfort of their own homes, glued to their mobile phones, feeding off the drama of tragedy and corruption, but Yusuf would stake his life on the fact that no real action would ensue, no feet on the streets, no demands for resignations or a Government response. People liked to protect their own kind, not the likes of him.

Ellie was a rare gift, and he appreciated her, but she couldn't turn the tide by herself. He pulled her into his arms under an elm tree. The scent of his soap on her skin hit his nostrils.

She glanced at him, surprised. "What was that for?"

"For trying to help."

"You'll see. It's all going to be fine."

He gulped. "Emir has asked me to tell the others with him. About Doris." He saw her face in his mind's eye. His brain struggled to compute she was really gone.

"I can't imagine how hard that'll be."

He took a deep breath. "I need to get in the ring to practice today, too. Emir said I can perform tomorrow."

"How about you practice now, and I see you later? I really should get a clean set of clothes and answer some of these messages."

"Done."

He kissed her a lingering goodbye, her lips like a whisper against his own. On his way back to the residences, he stumbled across a jamming session in the big top, and the great folds of the midnight blue and bronze pulsed in and out, like the mouth of a speaker. The sound of the drums and brass followed him home through the tall grasses.

At the residences, he showered, taking care to soap himself well and wash his feet in particular, for he intended to pray. He dressed in modest white clothes and found his skull cap at the back of a drawer, smoothing it out before placing it on his head. Then he picked up his prayer mat and made his way down the corridor to join in morning prayers.

Some of the refugees had remained devout through the years, clinging to their faith like a lifeboat. Two prayer rooms existed alongside each other: one for the men, the other for the women and children. Yusuf walked barefoot onto the beige carpet, and took his place alongside the two dozen men and boys gathered there. He'd heard the congregation numbers had doubled after news of the closure, as if Allah might find a way to protect believers. The numbers would swell further once news of Doris's passing had been relayed to the residents.

He unrolled his prayer mat and quickly fell back into the natural rhythms of reciting the Qur'an: the bending of his body, the prostration in unison with his brethren, the humility that bloomed in him when he heard the holy words. He'd shirked his sacred duty to pray for too long. Palms cupped together, he gave thanks for the blessings in his life, and prayed for Doris, for Ellie, for the circus, and for himself. He vowed to hold fast to his faith, even when he felt weak.

After prayers had ended, the men embraced one another. Yusuf tidied away his prayer mat and removed his skull cap, and walked with the men to the common room for a breakfast of sweet tea and dense, seeded bread smeared with thick plum jam.

He waited in line for his cup of tea, knowing the news of Doris would soon be common knowledge, and that the atmosphere at the residences would grow more sombre still. He overheard a conversation between Osman, Aischa, and Aya at an adjacent table. They chatted, lingering over empty cups and plates dusted with crumbs. Yusuf's ears pricked when the conversation took a turn away from the circus closure and their uncertain futures.

"Did you hear?" said Aya, her smooth skin still crumpled from sleep. "Last night, Amena and I were walking past a gay bar in Warschauerstrasse and we saw Old Sayid through the window. I mean, I know he sometimes goes to Die Busche on Alexanderplatz, but this place was crazy. He looked wanton. It's unfitting in a man of his age."

Next to him, Osman and Aischa leaned into the story, their chairs creaking under their weight.

"He was wearing slim-fitting black jeans with a rainbow t-shirt, the one he wears when he attends the refugee group at the local gay bar," said Aya. He looked ridiculously happy, and plain ridiculous with his scrawny legs and huge stomach. And after a few minutes, he leapt on stage to sing karaoke with another man, and when his hand tapped the mic, we saw he even had on glittery nail varnish. He slurred his words. He'd definitely been drinking."

"It's like we leave our homes and we lose our morals. We have a responsibility to keep up our way of life, to not lose sight of who we are inside," said Aischa.

Yusuf joined their table. "I'm happy for him. He's more free now to express his sexuality than he ever was in his sixty years at home."

Osman clapped Yusuf on the back, and scooped up the plates cluttering the table, making room for him. "You are right, brother, who are we to criticise other people's happiness? It is a prayer of its own, isn't it, to leave people to their own choices?"

Aya's temper spiked, despite the early hour and her usually sweet nature. She swung around to Yusuf. "Don't think we don't know who stayed in your room last night. It's hard to keep anything secret with walls as thin as ours. Esme will be heartbroken."

"It doesn't become you to gossip." Yusuf held her gaze. "I'm a grown man. Last time I checked, I didn't need your permission for anything."

Aya looked down. "I'm sorry."

"No matter." He rested his palm on her hand. "I am glad you're all here. I have bad news."

40

Stars blanketed the heavens as Yusuf and Ellie walked hand-in-hand by the River Spree. In Ellie's hands, she clutched a handful of flowers the colour of ripe tangerines Yusuf had plucked from the park. He intertwined his fingers with hers to distract her from her nervousness about the vigil.

He, too, wanted the vigil to be a success. Not for the circus, but for Doris, who deserved to be remembered. His chest ached with her loss. The rest of the circus had also experienced the loss keenly: Doris had been their friend, a blessing for those who didn't trust easily and had been disappointed often.

"What if no one comes? I'll look so stupid," said Ellie.

She had every reason to be proud of herself. Her *Die Welt* story had spread like a wave to other newspapers. Even with a gagging order from Marina's lawyers, *Die Welt* refused to retract the allegations, so secure they were in the knowledge that their case was airtight. Information about the vigil had been retweeted thousands of times on Twitter.

Yusuf drew small, smoothing circles on the back of Ellie's hand with his thumb, eager to be touching her still. "No one will laugh at you. If they do, it's only because they envy your passion."

"Is that supposed to make me feel better?" She glanced at her wristwatch. "Fifteen minutes to go."

"Have you even thought about what you'll do if a crowd does turn up?"

She grimaced.

A man hurtled towards them in the distance, his clown trousers billowing like sails.

"There's a crowd gathering outside the circus. They look friendly. I mean, I think they do," said Zul, puffing with exertion. "Emir said you should come, both of you."

"Oh, God," said Ellie, paler than usual under the night sky.

She dropped her flowers when he grabbed her hand, and they hurried after Zul to the lawn in front of the big top, beyond the trestle tables, where a river of humans stood deep and wide, stretching out across the park.

Ellie froze.

Yusuf tightened his grip on her hand. He blinked, thinking this couldn't be for him, for the refugees, but their banners fluttered like ghosts in the sky, and there could be no mistake that this was the vigil Ellie had called for.

There was no uniformity to the crowd, and he made out Christians, Muslims and Jews, Turks and Afro-Germans, hippies and punks, students with their rucksacks and bikes, workers in crisp shirts, pensioners and children riding on their parents' shoulders. They had wrapped themselves in flags from across the globe, in rainbow flags and European ones, in the tricolour Syrian flag, so similar to Germany's own. The throng continued to build as they watched. This wasn't a rabble; this was a community. They moved like a shoal of fish, shaking hands, patting backs and sharing food.

Yusuf's breath caught in his throat.

There stood two young men he recognised from pictures in Doris' apartment: her sons. Alongside them were Ellie's parents, and Isaiah with some of his spraying friends, holding up a sign for open borders and *Be a Doris*. Just behind, Imam Saeed held one corner of a multi-faith banner aloft, adorned with the Star of David, the cross, the crescent moon and star, and beside them, the Om sign and the Dharmachakra. Soon, his circus family joined in: Emir in his top hat, Zul with his white face and red nose, Osman in a shimmering satin tracksuit, and the girls in flowing dresses.

Yusuf's stomach tightened at the sight of the hovering camera crews, along with the police patrol engaged to keep the peace.

Ellie danced on the spot. "We have to greet them," she said, jerking him towards the crowd.

Yusuf shook his head, still hovering by the big top, trying to suppress the hope that bloomed in his chest that everything would be all right.

She tugged his hand. Her eyes sparkled. "It'll be okay."

He followed her, light-headed, his stomach a bundle of nerves.

A hush descended as they stepped towards the masses, then the crowd erupted into cheers and cameras flashed.

Tears clogged Yusuf's throat as he read the signs and the welcoming faces around him: a mosaic of goodwill from all corners of the city.

A journalist from ZDF pushed a microphone under their noses and asked a stream of questions without pausing for breath. "Do you consider Germany your home, Herr Alam? Was this what you hoped to achieve, Frau Richter?"

Yusuf blinked into the glare of the camera light, his lips dry. "This is my home, yes."

Ellie leaned forward. "We're grateful for everyone who is here today. We're here in memory of Doris Kaun and what she believed in. We need to send a message to the Government." She pointed at the crowd. "*This* is who we are."

A man wearing a black t-shirt with a host of tattoos covering his arms approached, and commandeered the attention of the journalist and his cameraman. He squared up to Ellie. "We'll purge this country of people like you and him." A ball of spit landed on Yusuf's shoe.

The cameraman zoomed in, and the crowd grew still.

Ellie stepped closer to the man, arching her back, until her nose almost touched his.

"Leave it, Ellie," said Yusuf, placing a protective arm around her.

She shooed him away, shrugging her shoulder while the camera still rolled. "I've got this."

The man puffed out his chest, eyes ablaze, facing Ellie down, daring her to act. His body odour filled Yusuf's nose, even at this distance, but Ellie stood her ground. She didn't flinch.

"I want people like you to be outnumbered so you learn what it is like to be a minority," she said. "Look around you. You *are* outnumbered."

The man snarled, venomous, and Ellie stood tall and uncowed. Then she smiled despite the man's animosity and the hate that made him small.

Yusuf looked up, sensing a change in the current of the crowd. His heart raced to see friends and strangers, nearing thousands now, holding their mobile phones in the sky. The crowd became a sea of light amongst the dark shadows of the trees, and it didn't matter if one person, or many people, hated because the weight of love would always be greater.

A lone voice sang, and soon the crowd joined in, and the melody seemed far away. Yusuf didn't recognise the song, though he knew the spirit. Ellie knew it, and so did the man. He slunk away, and the camera whirred, taking in images of the vigil that would be projected on the national news, and also internationally, in countries where hope was in short supply, and others where they longed for Western aid.

The people continued to sing as the moon climbed higher in the sky, peeking at them from behind a group of leafy trees. A rugged man in shorts and loafers had brought his guitar, and soon, he stood on a trestle table, leading the crowd in renditions of Bob Marley and The Beatles, and when the police tired, they shooed him away, and the crowds dissolved into the night, leaving remnants of joy floating in the air.

Yusuf, wrung out with emotion, turned to Ellie. "Would you like to come back with me tonight?"

She looked up at him, radiating strength, and his heart skipped a beat. "Yes."

They walked the short distance to the residences and the balmy night hugged itself to their skin. The trees rustled as they walked through the park. He held her close to his side, understanding once more how much one person's love could hold storms at bay. Tonight, the circled dwellings seemed like a stronghold that no ill will could penetrate, although in reality he knew the circus remained under threat.

They crawled into bed together, and she slept within moments, her body curled into his. He drew the covers over her, matched the rise and fall of her body to his, and drifted into oblivion.

41

Rex, on a fishing trip with school friends near Potsdam, marvelled as the red perch writhed on the deck of the boat. The fish gasped for air and he could make out the welt where his hook had pierced its flesh.

"There you go, boys. That's how it's done."

He didn't like to gloat, but his haul always impressed. The water frothed next to their boat and the sun had barely risen over the verdant valley, but here he stood, with a magnificent catch already at the bottom of the boat, while his oldest friends still hadn't rubbed the sleep from their eyes.

Marcel punched his shoulder. "Not everything is a competition. Unless you want to test how many beers we can put away, that is."

Rex laughed. He relished these yearly trips away from the call of the city. The pressures of work and family receded into the background, leaving only man and nature, and Jessy, waiting in the shadow of a bush at the shoreline, her eyes trained on him. He would never admit as much to his friends, but he cherished these moments of simplicity with the men he'd known all his life. He rarely stripped back the layers of his prestige and intellect, but here, or later at their favourite fish restaurant that looked out over the bay, he could be himself and remember the boy he'd once been.

"How about another few hours here and then we break for an early lunch?" said Rex.

"You took the words right out of my mouth," said Marcel.

Joseph started spinning fast on his reel. "I've got something. I've got something."

They peered together at his catch, and when he brought up an old Wellington boot gushing with murky water, the expression on his face sent them into fits of laughter, rocking the boat.

Rex's phone sounded in his pocket, cutting short the moment. He preferred to leave technology behind on his rare weekends away from the city, but he promised his wife as his political career burgeoned that he'd always be accessible to her and the children, and the Chancellor had demands of her own. There'd been a number of missed calls from Corinne in the night, but he wouldn't think to ring her back at this early hour. It must have been urgent after all.

He wiped his hands on his trousers and reached for the phone, surprised to find the Chancellor's private office number flashing up on his screen.

He sighed. "Silberling."

Her voice reverberated through the telephone, as ill-tempered as winter frost. "I take it you've been keeping pace with the news?"

"I'm on a short trip away from the real world," said Rex. "Corinne informed your office I'm out of town until tomorrow night."

"I suggest you get up to speed. I expect you in my office at the Bundestag at two this afternoon," she said without pausing a beat.

The boat bobbed, and Rex's trio of friends listened with keen ears.

"Can it wait?" He rolled his eyes at them, signalling his irritation at the Chancellor's summons. Stupid, vapid woman still thought she knew best.

"It certainly cannot. It seems, in your arrogance, you underestimated the public mood."

He couldn't imagine what could have happened to make her so uptight, but he counted to three to calm his ire, then spoke with authority. "I'll be there at three."

"Two, Rex. No later." The line clicked.

He turned to his friends and his cheeks burned with shame. "I have to get back to shore."

They commiserated with him about his departure, but they didn't suggest cutting short the trip and finding another date, and it cut him more deeply than he allowed them to see.

Back at his Berlin house, Rex hugged his family to him, holding his wife closer than usual.

She glanced at him in alarm, and the children tumbled to the ground with the dog. "Oh darling. Is everything going to be all right?"

"Yes, there's nothing to worry about," he said, although his Adam's apple bobbed in his throat and his wife sensed the lie. She'd endured so much by his absence over the years, he liked to spare her worry when he could.

He retreated to his office with a stack of newspapers tucked under his arm that he'd picked up en route. Ever faithful Jessy shadowed him. He telephoned Corinne, asking for her to come to his house. When she informed him, her voice heavy with regret, that it would be impossible for her to return before nightfall, a sense of loneliness washed over him despite the warmth of the dog's sleek silver mass at his feet.

Deciding not to lower himself to reading a blog, Rex pored over the newspapers and noticed how Marina's journalist and the acrobat had been plastered over the front pages. His heart thumped. In a regrettable turn of events, the circus warden had died, ostensibly from heightened stress following an altercation with an as yet unnamed member of the far right. His skin prickled with the awareness of his own possible culpability. The broadsheets announced that his own political star declined, and declared him an unsavoury blight on the character of post-war Germany. The gutter press gushed over a possible romance between the journalist and acrobat.

Rex stared at their earnest faces and committed their names to memory.

"Pah!" He tossed the papers towards the wastepaper basket and it toppled onto the floor.

Jessy barked, her mood matching his. He ruffled her ears, leaving the mess for the cleaner to tidy up, then headed to the shower to wash the remains of fish, guts and saltwater from his skin. As the water pressure kneaded his shoulders, defeat washed over him, unfamiliar and stinging. When he'd finished, he dressed carefully and schooled his expression, knowing that the hacks would be waiting to crow over his fall, because there could be no doubt what the Chancellor intended.

His driver scrambled to open the car door for him as he descended the steps down from his house, for once leaving Jessy behind although he would have been grateful for her silent friendship. The engine hummed to life, and with the windows sealed and the city rushing past, it seemed to Rex he'd been entombed. He rolled down the window and leaned out, drawing in deep gasps of air, hoping to still the storm at the centre of him.

Even if the worst happened and he lost his job, he'd pick himself up. The Chancellor assumed that just because she happened to be party leader, she held all the cards. But he'd always possessed the ability to scope out the whole terrain, to find new routes where others would have been flummoxed. Even without the Christian Democratic Union party, there would always be other avenues open to him. He was a survivor.

As they approached the south bank of the Spree, the Bundestag loomed, with its imposing neo-classical stone columns, magnificent glass dome, and flags rippling in the wind. Sure enough, a member of the Chancellor's team had leaked rumours of his possible political demise to the news-hounds.

It didn't surprise him: he'd seen events such as these unfold countless times, and it was every man for himself. Or woman.

The cameras flashed and a horde of journalists rushed towards him as he emerged from the car, his lips set in a grim line, knuckles white against his dark blue suit. Rex nodded to acknowledge their presence though he refused to comment.

"Minister Silberling, is it true that your job is in danger?"

"Did you collude with neo-Nazis to aggravate tensions against Berlin's immigrant community?"

"Are you aware of the personal stories of the immigrants under your care, Minister?"

"Do you deny that you siphoned off public funds to pay the editor of *Berliner Allgemeine Zeitung* in exchange for favours?"

"Minister, do you believe in freedom of the press? How about democracy? Are you a law unto yourself?"

Rex ducked his head and pushed on, leaving the voices calling after him, incessant, like a wave about to submerge him. He'd stalked these halls of power, revelling in the deference and respect that came with an office of state. Every step now weighed heavy with humiliation. Not even the fine cut of his suit could lend him the confidence that Ellie Richter had stolen.

He seethed with rage against her.

This felt like a public flogging. He'd been so close to winning.

He swallowed, and his Adam's apple bobbed in his throat. There had to be a way to salvage the damage to his reputation. He could have tried to blame his rogue assistant, but by this point, Corinne had almost become family. He wouldn't sink that low. Perhaps he could talk the Chancellor around. He arranged his features into their most charming constellation, loosening the tension in his face, lifting his chin to lend firmer lines to his weak jaw, and pushing his shoulders back so that when he arrived in the Chancellor's inner sanctum, he'd be on the front foot.

He needn't have bothered.

She stood in front of her desk, her hair like a helmet, legs in a wide stance, arms folded, ready for battle. "You're late."

"My apologies," he said smoothly, keen to unruffle her feathers. A glance at his Raymond Weil told him it had only just passed two o'clock.

"Be under no illusion, this won't take long. My time is more valuable than yours."

Her combative mood didn't surprise him, but he still harboured hopes of winning her over, if only to save his job, not his pride. He motioned to a seat. "May I?"

She shook her head then seemed to waver, and gave him a curt nod. "Tell me, you sold me the idea of the circus, Rex. Why?"

He sank into the chair and decided to appeal to her maternal side, to dig out the child he'd been from the graveyard of his mind. Just to survive the meeting. "I loved the circus when I was a child. Some part of it must have stuck. I wanted to give the immigrants a chance to escape the usual structures. Give them a chance to shine."

In that moment, there was no artifice, and he wondered what it would have been like if he'd run away as a child. How his life might have been different if the stakes had been lower, if he'd done something physical with his body instead of relying on his mind. Even then, though, he'd been aware that circuses employed misfits, and that the word itself had become sullied by general acceptance, and Rex wanted more than anything not just to belong, but to dominate.

The Chancellor's scathing laugh echoed around her office. "What a pile of crock. Is everything a performance for you?" She stopped short. "They're refugees, Rex, not just immigrants. We owe them more than you've given."

"Well, yes—" He filled his face with contrition, but her virtue signals bothered him, her ability to paint everything in black and white, as if there weren't other considerations. As if it wasn't their job to be responsive to public opinion.

She continued, unabated, her face a black cloud of displeasure. "We need more trust in our politicians. I expect integrity. Not this whipping up of mob mentality by the very officials who are supposed to serve the people. I can't help but think you wouldn't have acted this way had you been a woman. You had close hand experience of the refugees and their stories. You had the means to help them. Why didn't you innovate? Why didn't you breathe life into those corners of despair? Instead you schemed and lurked and you brought my Government into disrepute."

My Government.

Her words fell like a whip about him, and he cringed, understanding finally that there would be no convincing her to let him keep his job. He shuddered at the thought of how his standing would be lowered in the eyes of the nation and his fawning acquaintances and his family. How many people would celebrate his downfall, or at least feel a frisson of schadenfreude?

How ridiculous for the Chancellor to have brought gender into it, but he didn't ostensibly react in case she wrested away the little power he had left. She would allow him time to draft a resignation letter, she owed him that much. Then he could at least manipulate the narrative, cast himself in a less damning light and prepare the way for a return.

He didn't know who he was without the mantle of power politics had given him, without the path to the top it had marked out for him.

The Chancellor rattled on, in full flow, and Rex sat inert and irrelevant, like a crumbling statue. "I won't do you the honour of allowing you to tender your resignation."

He sprang to his feet. "That is outrageous." His head spun. Inside, shame twisted him into a pathetic version of himself. "All this on the hearsay of what some journalist has concocted. Please, please. Maybe if you understood—"

She cut him off, her eyebrows knotted above stern, unforgiving eyes. "I sent in a team to scrutinise the finances at the Interior Ministry this morning. I understand plenty. You would only use your resignation as a means to repair your own reputation rather than atone. You're entirely without scruples."

Rex floundered for the words to create an advantage for himself before the window closed, but the Chancellor was in no mood to dally. Even now, her intercom buzzed and she rustled her papers, ready to dismiss him.

She arched an eyebrow and he recognised the ruthless streak in her that he'd always admired in himself. "I will issue a statement through my press office about your firing."

It was done.

His stomach rolled and a sour taste invaded his mouth, stealing his words.

"If I didn't fear for the stability of my own Government, I would order an inquiry into your department," said the Chancellor. "But that would be self-harm, and so, we'll sweep this under the carpet, and I'll make reparations to the refugees on your behalf."

"I see," said Rex, though fingers of dread greyed out the corners of his field of vision. She hadn't even shaken his hand or thanked him for his years of service. His bravado drained away. Her announcement would leave him in the political wilderness. How would he maintain the standards he had set for his family?

"Let's be certain of one thing. If you seek to challenge me, I'll make sure you never work in politics again, not even at local party level. Our colleagues in the party won't take kindly to a shark amongst their waters."

She looked him over, and he couldn't find even an ounce of sympathy in her expression, though he searched hard for it.

"You may go." She picked up her telephone.

Rex stood, buttoned up his suit jacket, and went to meet the cameras with a weighted chest and sealed mouth.

42

Following a workshop on their last ever show, the performers and crew exited the tent, leaving Yusuf alone to climb to the top of the rafters and savour the solitude. He vaulted and caught the trapeze, soaring, free of residue, as if he'd been baptised. Goosebumps raced along his skin with the exhilaration of reclaiming this part of his identity, and he noticed how each quirk of his personality meshed together to form a whole, how one part couldn't exist without the other.

One day until their family would be torn apart.

He'd known the big top carried a singular type of magic from the moment he had set eyes on it. Joy wove itself into the fabric of the tent, and he wondered how he'd feel if they tore it down, whether a small fragment of the performers' souls would be sucked into a crypt, waiting for the circus to be born again.

Something had changed in him.

Every nerve ending in his body fizzed with the anticipation of this very last performance, but it wasn't just that. He'd recast himself over the past weeks, despite the spectre of the circus closure hanging over him. It had been a gradual process, and he couldn't pinpoint whether his transformation had been internal or the result of a series of little impacts that had nudged him into this stronger version of himself. He'd finally figured out that in a shame culture, refusing to be shamed gave him power.

In the wake of the vigil, the performers had been heartened by an invitation to perform at this year's Carnival of Cultures. He'd dreamed of taking part in the carnival. Even with the looming closure, it was an honour to be asked.

Doris would have been so proud.

Silberling, with all his intelligence and influence, had failed to understand that circus is free-spirited. It could never be tied down by rules. He'd tried to trap the performers; but tonight, they would break free. They'd agreed as a family that the last show would not be the usual fare. It would be distilled from the essence of who they were.

Just like immigration, circus was about reinvention, but also about staying true to traditions. Some mistook the circus for frivolity, but to Yusuf, it had always been more than that; the circus acted as a window into the dark and an escape from it. He could close his eyes and imagine himself as a maharajah wooing a princess, or an English gentleman on a country jaunt, or a migrating bird with a plume of technicolour feathers. Or he could be himself and show the strength Selim had always believed he possessed.

So the performers prepared the final fanfare, under the tutelage of Yusuf, who inspired and cajoled them into showing the losses they'd endured, the journeys they'd made, the roots that twisted out of them to bind them to their countries of origin and their new home.

Peeking through the opening curtain, Yusuf trembled to witness a full house. Perhaps his return to prayer had convinced Allah to stand by him. Extensive news coverage drove new patrons into the tent. This time, neither top-hatted Emir, nor Osman on stilts, nor pretty Esme with her sweet wares greeted the crowds. Instead, a shy, wordless Leyla–whose kitchen duties meant she had no act of her own–sold tickets to patrons, stapled to a thank you note handwritten by the circus children.

Backstage, the performers huddled together in a circle, arms cast around each other.

"Remember, this is for Doris. For our family. We're telling our own story. A story without words. A story of resilience. One told with our bodies," said Yusuf. "Our story can't be understood from statistics, newspaper headlines or nightly bulletins. We'll show the audience the darkness, but also our strength and creativity, how our self-esteem has grown, and the love that bonds us."

They rested their heads against each other, drawing courage, then scattered to their positions.

Mere yards away, the audience proceeded into the hushed tent, only to be met with a tangible darkness. Yusuf insisted the fairy-lights remain dormant, and that Old Sayid wait until the very last spectator took their seat before striking up the house band. For this last performance, no child visitors were allowed. Even so, not a seat in the house remained empty. The sense of anticipation in the tent spiralled higher and higher, broken only by the whispers of the crowd.

In the seat once reserved for Silberling sat the Chancellor, flanked by a thrilled Imam Saeed on one side, with a nervous Simeon, newly discharged from hospital, and Leyla on the other side. The spotlight flashed over to them, and Yusuf didn't allow himself to consider why the Chancellor might be there or what it might mean.

His heart skipped faster as he spotted Ellie, her thick red hair piled on top of her head, with a grinning, excited Isaiah beside her. Marina Schmidt had taken her place a few rows behind them, all gracious smiles and earnest nods, as if to display her regret to Berlin society, although Yusuf could have sworn her contriteness was as false as her nails.

A man in the audience punctured the silence, quoting the hashtag, which had become the rousing pro-immigrant call on social media. "Be a Doris!"

The crowd cheered.

Yusuf prayed the risk would pay off somehow.

He signalled, and the spotlight swept to Old Sayid. With a flourish of his gnarled fingers, he instructed the band to play, his giant hair out of proportion with his wizened body as he moved in time with the music. While once the circus tent had appeared to lift with every note, this time, with each beat of the bleak melody, the big top compressed so patrons turned inwards not outwards. They listened, transfixed to the poetry of the oud and sousaphone, entwined like husband and wife.

Emir stepped up to the microphone, a discombobulated head in a pool of black, designed to disorientate. "Our dear Chancellor, ladies and gentlemen, welcome to the Treptow Circus," he said, twirling his moustache. "Our very last performance is a special one, in which we'll show you where we have come from and who we are."

He disappeared.

The spotlight shifted, capturing Zul the Clown, recognisable in his flared trousers and oversized shoes, but without his customary white clown face and rouged nose. He bowed low and deep, until his nose almost touched the sawdust, and when he righted himself, he meandered over to the Chancellor–ignoring the twitching of her security men–and reached into his sleeve to retrieve a paper flower for her. The flower glowed and bloomed from a bud to full blossom in her hands. Zul made a show of delight, then joined the Imam's hand with the Chancellor's to the tittering of the crowd, who craned their necks to see.

Zul skipped away to an ominous music score composed by Old Sayid. Darkness consumed the tent. The spectators fluttered with expectation, whispering to each other, still unsure of what to expect. With a clicking sound, a projector screen lit up the back of the tent, arranged by Isaiah and his technical contacts. The screen gleamed with news cuttings and documentary footage of the performers' home lands and their reception in Germany. The snippets were brief, and in between, the screen turned black, a rhythm of binary code, all or nothing, peace and turmoil.

Najib took centre stage with his goblet drum. Najib, whose lack of compassion had been responsible for Dawud's deportation. The lights strobed and settled high above, where Amena, Aya and Aischa balanced en pointe on a tight rope in barely-there harnesses. They skipped along it dressed in ballet shoes and white satin, as if they were children playing in the street. In swooped Esme's peace doves to fly amongst them, and for a moment, it seemed the girls had become majestic animals of flight themselves. The lights dwindled, and the girls became mere silhouettes on the tightrope.

At ground-level, Zul leapt into an ocean-blue clown car decorated with peace emblems and daisy chains. It spluttered as he drove around the ring, punctuating Old Sayid's dark score with sudden bangs reminiscent of the bombs that fell far away. All at once, the sousaphone wailed, like a bomb siren. Zul made no attempt at comedy. His face twisted into a grief so profound that it seeped out into the audience. Behind him, the screen displayed images of emaciated children, shell-shocked adults and parents numb with sorrow.

At Yusuf's nod, smoke sped into the tent so that soon, the lower levels of the tent became humid and steamy. This part they'd not practiced, but it played out better than he'd imagined, and for a moment, his throat constricted as he recalled the chemical attacks and the friends he'd seen fall.

A dazzling light bathed the tent. Up above, after a heartbeat to allow for the crowd's irises to adjust, Amena, Aya and Aischa unhooked their harnesses and leapt, catching bands of red silk. The crowd gasped as they plummeted, but deceptive strength lay in those small bodies, and they coiled the silks around their limbs and their flanks, red on white, white on red. Their routine defied gravity. Aischa launched herself at Aya, and Aya arched her back to catch her. Together they danced, a slow, sad turning and stretching in the air, helped by the smooth silk supporting their bodies. Amena twisted the silk and pirouetted, and when the next bang came from Zul's clown car, the girls fell, hurtling earthwards into the smoke like angels suddenly human, robbed of their wings, and there could be no doubt that this was war and the silk was blood.

They stopped just short of the ground, jerking upwards, before laying on the floor.

When the smoke cleared, they lay lifeless on the floor for three heartbeats against a backdrop of crumbling Middle Eastern architecture and culture that occurred when civilisations endured crisis. The crowd held their collective breath until the girls stood.

Cheers erupted in the tent, and some members wiped away their tears.

Only the Chancellor sat still and impassive–but she stayed.

Sweat glistened on Yusuf's skin as he absorbed the rapt faces in the stands. Part of him had feared a mass walk-out at the themes of this show, but that hadn't transpired. His relationship with Ellie had only improved once he'd closed the distance between them; perhaps this performance would tie his circus family to the fabric of this city.

Amena, Aya and Aischa skipped out of the ring, and in rushed the twins with the magnificent blue silk that had saved Yusuf's life. They mimicked the ocean that had carried the immigrants to their new home while the screen projected documentary footage of refugees making the journey across the ocean, of bodies washed up on beaches, of camps and poverty, aid agencies and officials in parliamentary chambers, debating over the fate of those who waited on their shores.

Next, Najib led a crew in break-dancing, and though Yusuf wished for Dawud to be here instead, for a moment their internal tensions ceased to matter. The troop filled the circus ring and split into two sides, dancing with ferocious intensity, a push and pull of policy and human need.

As the dance group exited the circus ring, Emir and Zul edged into the ring clad as a two-headed animal. Walls grew around it, made of twisting vines, an impenetrable maze. The creature stumbled around, wretched and mournful, its legs a muddle, and when the audience laughed, they did so at the woeful creature's expense, like you might titter at a circus freak or an outsider, secretly pleased not to share the same fate.

But the road they'd travelled hadn't been only of misery. The creature exited the ring. Old Sayid bounced and bounded, his face a picture of rapture, as the house band rocked itself into a joyous frenzy. The screen lit up with candid snaps of the circus family in the residences, and in the ring, just being themselves, practicing, performing, carrying out chores, laughing, eating and praying together. A lingering shot of a beaming Doris surrounded by her charges, with Mirjam on her lap, ended the presentation.

In came the crew to set up walls with stacked beams. Osman's horses cantered into the ring, majestic creatures shining with health: one nut brown; the other a shimmering grey. Each wore a magnificent garland, fashioned from the flags of the refugees' countries. At Osman's call, four of the goats whizzed in with German flags in their mouths. The horses and goats danced together at Osman's command, weaving lines through the sawdust, cross-crossing the ring, leaping over the beams in quick succession. The spectators cheered, delighted.

Only one act remained.

The animals filed out behind Osman, the walls fell away, and Old Sayid's score took on a classical feel, inspired by Muwash Shah in Aleppo, but overlaid with Najib's take on Berlin hip-hop. Deep base notes caused the ground underfoot to reverberate. A current of electricity ran through the crowd as they sensed the climax of the performance.

Yusuf, at the top of the circus tent, searched for Ellie, and when he found her, the nerves in his stomach settled. Above him, silver stars stitched into the tent flickered. He stood tall, reaching his arms up to the rafters, and arched one foot forward onto the hoop that had been secured there. Opposite him, Esme did the same. Her eyes searched for his approval and he nodded his encouragement. Their costumes mirrored each other, with the exception of the saffron yellow headscarf which adorned Esme's head and had been secured neatly at her nape.

They jumped, each onto their own hoop, hooking their legs through, hanging like bats, swinging with the force of their bodies, balancing precariously, unafraid and defiant. Yusuf ignored the twinges in his body that hadn't yet fully healed from his fall and the altercation with Karl. This was the pain and the cost of the life that had chosen him.

He and Esme built up their momentum, a swinging to and fro. He counted in his head, as he knew she did in hers. Partnering with someone on the trapeze engendered intimacy. Maybe they could have been something more to one another after all, if it hadn't been for Ellie. All at once, they released their grips, hovered in the air and exchanged places. This is what refugees and acrobats did; they flirted with death because their lives demanded it. Esme leapt towards him, and he caught her in a flash of saffron and black satin.

Together, they flew.

They flew, effortlessly, to the sound of the tambourine and fiddle and Najib's hiphop. Their bodies swished through the air, creating something from nothing. And Yusuf knew peace up there, with her life in his hands and the eyes of the world on him. His body pulsed with certainty that at this precise moment, he could manage any feat.

He released Esme, and she tumbled through the air, twisting, her arms tucked into her body. She landed in the sawdust and Yusuf leapt, finishing inches away from her. He grasped Esme's hand and together they bowed.

After a pause, the crowd went wild.

Esme leaned into him, quivering. "I didn't think I could do that," she said in her own tongue.

Yusuf replied in a mix of German and Arabic, and the words meshed. "None of us ever do, until we try."

The cheers crescendoed and Emir ran into the ring to join them. He clapped Yusuf on the back, beaming. The rest of their circus family followed: Osman, Zul, the twins, Amena, Aya and Aischa, Leyla, and Simeon from the stands. Every part of the family that had made him whole again. Only Dawud was missing. The crew filled the ring, leading in the animals: the goats, and the horses, and Esme's doves that settled on her shoulders, cocking their heads at the hullaballoo. The children—who had not participated in the final show, but who belonged as part of the celebration—followed. Mirjam led them in, blowing soapy bubbles across the audience. The bubbles floated upwards and burst, one by one.

A myriad of foils fell from the rafters. The foils became swooping dragonflies, flitting around the tent, looping through the stands, lending their fragile light to distant corners, and finally escaping out of the exit in jubilation. Yusuf's euphoria mixed with an aching melancholy at the thought this might be the last time, and around him, his family hugged one another, openly weeping through their smiles.

The Chancellor stood, absorbing the applause around her, and the faces in the circus ring.

Emir stroked his top hat as if it were a cat and grabbed the microphone. "Thank you for letting us make this our home," he said, and Yusuf smarted, because as long as weapons and the ambition to own and conquer territory existed, there would also be displaced people who didn't belong.

Old Sayid picked up his sousaphone and led the band in a jam, and soon the crowd danced in their seats, but not before the Chancellor's team ushered her away.

A few rows back, willowy Marina stood head and shoulders above those around her, fawning at the performance, although she must have been inwardly seething. She tossed her glossy hair, and for a moment, Yusuf wished one of Esme's doves could be trained to empty its bowels on her head. How satisfying for her to be here, to see the euphoria of this evening despite her scheming.

He didn't want this night to end.

When he left the circus ring, Yusuf's limbs seemed to drift of their own accord, but despite his exhaustion, he stood with the performers in a receiving line to greet the Chancellor. Imam Saeed conducted the introductions and the Chancellor smiled at them, asking meaningless questions. Her eyes shone with kindness, and when she reached Emir, she congratulated him on the home he had made for them all with no trace of hypocrisy in her voice.

To Yusuf, she said, "I enjoyed that very much. Tell me, Herr Alam, what would you do differently, if this project wasn't constrained by the rules of the Internal Ministry?"

"That's easy," said Yusuf. "I'd teach classes for local children, teach them all about what we do here, the focus, the strength, the creativity. But I'd also have street troupes, where the circus branches out from the tent, into the lives of ordinary people, brightening up the day of people in nursing homes and hospitals, in schools and on street corners. We'll send in the clowns, the musicians, the dancers and the acrobats. Community can save lives. Looking at things from different perspectives can save lives, too. It saved mine."

She nodded. A trail of thoughts sped across her face. "Will you come and see me tomorrow?" she said.

And he dared to hope.

43

Ellie darted between the rows of seats, hoping to spend a few minutes with Yusuf after the performance, but the Chancellor's security guards blocked her access to the performers-only section of the tent. Disappointed, she turned to locate Isaiah only to find herself facing Marina.

"Oh." Her cheeks flushed with warmth. "I thought you'd be hiding," she blurted out. It wasn't every day that you crossed paths with someone you'd rubbished in black and white. Ellie pushed her shoulders back and squared up to Marina. She wasn't a coward or a troll who threw insults at victims without ever intending to show her face. Ellie could defend her decisions.

Tom lurked behind his boss, sheepishly holding her enormous Louis Vuitton handbag.

"Oh yourself," said Marina. She combed her hand through her hair, drawing attention to her widow's peak and the stern lines of her face. "My lawyers advised me to give you a wide berth, but I had to speak to you. You know what I don't understand? After everything I did for you, how could you expose me like that? You made it seem so clear-cut."

"That's your complaint?" said Ellie, anger surging through her veins. "You accepted money for telling lies, Marina. You used my byline knowing I'd been forced into writing what I didn't believe in. I've handed over my recordings to the police and I hope they come for you."

"The board will have my head first."

Ellie shrugged. "You're probably right."

Marina's expression softened. "Maybe I should have taken the time to tell you before. The reason I've been so hard on you is that I see in you who I once was. Come back to *BAZ*, Ellie. You'll have a clean slate and a portfolio of your own. You're resourceful and determined, and your instincts are good."

Ellie's eyebrows flew up. "Are you serious? I was expendable then so why not now?"

"I haven't been scalped yet, and bringing you in-house could be just the thing to make amends. It's more than that, though. You're good, but you're just starting out. Don't turn up your nose at the chance of coming back in house. You'll get more readers than on your little blog, or freelancing for that matter. I take it that Simone hasn't offered you a staff role?"

Little blog. "I wouldn't go back if you begged me."

"Come now, I know it was you who raided my office." Marina tossed her hair. "I found the scrap with my password on it. Don't think I don't know how you got in. I could have you up on breaking and entering charges if I wanted."

A bitter tang filled Ellie's mouth. "Maybe, but something tells me you have more problems coming your way than going after me."

Marina set her mouth in a grim line.

"The answer is no," said Ellie. "If you want to make amends, how about using your editorial to eat some humble pie? Isn't news supposed to help people understand the world? Isn't it supposed to keep the powerful honest? You inadvertently became the mouthpiece for angry white men, who are anxious about their declining power. But that didn't matter to you. All that mattered was keeping Silberling happy and saving your own neck."

"Those angry white men you so scathingly refer to–they need a voice too. Would you silence them?" said Marina.

Ellie didn't know what she wanted. She just didn't want to give fake news a chance, and she certainly didn't want fearful people to warp public life with their twisting logic, but perhaps exposing flawed arguments to discussion was the cleverer route. Hadn't even Yusuf and Karl been able to come to some kind of mutual understanding?

She wouldn't give Marina the satisfaction of even moving a millimetre closer to her viewpoint. "They can't be silenced. Their voices are amplified by the algorithms of social media and search engines. It's our duty to challenge them. Why do you ride the wave and never crest it, Marina? Why not go back to old notions of journalism and hold power to account rather than be beholden to it? You mistake loudness for authority. The public trusts us with their minds. Every word we write holds power and you wield it with such contempt for the people we serve. We are in service. Not to the advertisers, or the gods of parliament, or the businessmen on diamond-crusted thrones. To the people."

Marina rolled her eyes, her body rigid. "It's not my job to educate the people. Your idealism will die with your youth."

"I honestly think you're trying to help me, so thank you." Ellie gave her a hard smile. "But your way is outdated. It's cowardice dressed up as wisdom. I see how in thrall you are to the purse strings. I don't see a role model in you anymore. I see a world that will be better when you move aside."

A few rows away, Isaiah waved at Ellie to capture her attention. She stepped past Marina without saying goodbye.

"Way to go," said Tom in a whisper as she passed him.

Ellie squeezed his arm. Despite her bravado, uncertainty plagued her about whether she wanted to be a journalist in a post-truth world. News had lost its link to the minds of readers and instead sought to rifle through their pockets. At any given moment of the day, a dozen breaking news articles competed for the reader's attention in a decontextualised screech which took no responsibility for advancing understanding. It served only to damage the reader's equilibrium or reinforce existing prejudices, like feeding an addiction.

Worse still, she recognised she'd failed to save the circus. Doris had been notified that contractors would be dismantling the circus within days, and the case files of the refugees were to be reviewed. The outcomes could not be guaranteed; some could find their status rescinded, and they would be separated from all they knew.

She weaved her way to Isaiah, fixing her brightest smile to her face, though she ached to sink into Yusuf's arms.

The next morning, a gentle wind washed over the city as Ellie dismounted from her bike in her parents' front garden. Her phone rang, startling her.

"Good morning. Is this Frau Richter?"

"Yes."

"The Chancellor would very much like to meet you."

Ellie lowered her bike against the fence and her bag spilled out.

"Frau Richter?"

She scrambled to pick up her things. "Yes."

"Can you come at four o'clock and bring Herr Alam? The Chancellor has a free window."

Her pulse raced. "Where should I come?"

"The Federal Chancellery. Please don't be late."

The man hung up, and Ellie's hands quivered as she reached for the number at the residences.

Tourist guides and locals had named the Federal Chancellory the Federal washing machine or elephant loo due to its unusual appearance. A sprawling study in curves and cubes, with trellises crawling up its walls and encircled with fountains and miniature trees, the Chancellory dominated the landscape. The building intimidated Ellie and Yusuf on their approach, and they released their grasp on one another's hands, as though romantic interaction might be improper here.

Once through the security protocols, they followed a slim man with square eyebrows and a clean-shaven face along long white-washed corridors. After a few minutes, he ushered Ellie into the Chancellor's office, leaving Yusuf feeling very much alone in the ante-room, judging by his downturned mouth and the way he fidgeted with his borrowed shirt.

Inside the Chancellor's office, sombre tones reigned. Dusky grey and yellow wallpaper covered the walls. A painting dominated one wall: a Paul Klee, perhaps. On the other side of the room, a serving table drew Ellie's attention: on it, three slices of lemon cake with tiny silver forks waited on exquisite bone china.

Nearby, a vast bookcase rose from floor to ceiling, on the left-hand side of a desk devoid of papers. Ellie scanned the books and found an assortment of political memoirs, encyclopaedias, newspaper cuttings and, stuffed in the corner, a number of feminist classics: some Virginia Woolf, *The Yellow Wallpaper* in its original English, and Angela Carter in translation. She wondered whether it would be against journalistic etiquette to reveal the Chancellor's reading choices to the nation.

Opposite the bookshelf, a colossal window frame looked into the distance in the direction of the Jewish memorial. Ellie pictured it: small black cubes of differing sizes, with tourists dotted in between. In Berlin, nothing was divorced from Germany's past. It coloured every decision made in the present. Germany's future was safeguarded by collective responsibility: each citizen contained a seed of shame for acts that had preceded their birth. Still, Silberling had shown that even in today's Germany, it was possible for minorities to be wronged in the most heinous ways.

All it took was one bad egg.

The Chancellor and an aide entered, interrupting her train of thought. "Sorry to keep you waiting, Frau Richter. First, let me offer my condolences on the passing of Frau Kaun. I understand she was quite a woman."

Ellie nodded, and stood to shake the Chancellor's hand. "It's an honour to meet you."

She took a sip of water, her mouth suddenly dry.

A benign smile washed over the Chancellor's otherwise stern face. "I very much enjoyed the circus yesterday. Quite something, wasn't it? And I must say–just between us–I never liked Silberling, that sneaky bastard."

Ellie choked on her water, then composed herself.

The aide hovered in the corner, holding a stack of files in the crook of his arm.

The Chancellor rounded the desk and settled into her chair. "I asked you here today to say thank you. The constraints of my office mean I must be guarded in what I say in public, but I wanted you to know how grateful I am to you for your spectacular work. What a sad and dark day when the powerful destroy lives in petty acts of ego."

Ellie couldn't help herself. "Chancellor, may I ask? Why did you make Silberling Interior Minister?"

"I thought long and hard about it. He always considered himself a shoo-in for leader, and it made sense to keep him close and flatter his ego. He's very resourceful, you know, but quite Machiavellian. But an internal party struggle is rarely in the interests of the country. It's safer to keep a man's pride intact. A humiliated man is rarely willing to admit defeat. He lashes out. And so I accommodated him and let him preen, allowed him to think I relied on him when he was simply mediocre. It was only a matter of time before he made a mistake." She gazed off into the distance. "You see, the men around me like to think they are cleverer than me, just by virtue of having a penis rather than a womb. They think I'm here by accident, rather than by design." A gentle smile played about her lips, but the crow's feet at her eyes and the pallid tones of her skin revealed her tiredness. "I can't tell you the steps it's taken me to get here. The slights I have endured, the waggling eyebrows I have ignored. What they forgot was that while I always knew what they were thinking, they never knew what I was thinking."

Ellie shifted in her seat, unsure of how to respond.

"Are you going to argue any differently?" said the Chancellor, amused.

"I know countless good men," said Ellie. "And I know many flawed women."

"Well, of course you do. So do I. But tell me, aren't good men more flawed than good women? Do they put a stop to the privileges that advantage them over women? Do they counsel their mothers to follow their dreams, or do they prefer them at the stove? Do they teach their daughters to be fearless or to be careful and safe and as pretty as a window ornament?"

"We want the people we love to be safe."

"Even if safety means they make themselves smaller to suit others? Amongst your friends, is there one of you who hasn't altered her behaviour or tempered her response to defuse tensions because a man might get the wrong impression or take offence? Power, Frau Richter, belongs to all, not just to the ones who seek it. Sometimes, it's the weakest in the pack who make the best decisions."

"What's going to happen to Minister Silberling?"

"I fired him. The scoop's yours if you want it."

Euphoria swept through Ellie. "Yes, yes, please." Silberling had charmed and manipulated his way through life. He'd land on his feet, of that she had no doubt. Still, she celebrated this reckoning, applauded it even, because Silberling's meddling couldn't have been the first time. She might even look into his past. Her journalist's brain ticked. "Will there be criminal charges?"

"Justice has its processes and it's an unwise leader who intervenes or seeks to influence it."

"Of course."

"How about *BAZ*? It can't be acceptable to vilify a group of people in the press, and to get away with it."

"A free press is one of the pillars of this democracy, Ellie. You played no small part in the salvaging of this fiasco. This was your story and others will inevitably look to you to lead the narrative. You *will* focus on the positives, won't you? It doesn't do to muddy the waters for too long," she said, all brisk and business-like.

"Yes, Chancellor."

"I very much enjoyed my visit to the circus. I've looked at its track record and that of its performers, and despite some isolated troubling incidents, I think it's been a success. I'd like Emir Karzai and Yusuf Alam to hold monthly meetings with my advisors, but I'm happy for the Treptow Circus to remain open."

Ellie's heart burst into colour, and she forced herself to quell the instinct to dart across to Yusuf in the next room to share the news. "Thank you, thank you," she said, jittery with excitement.

"Herr Alam will find no governmental obstacles to the classes and street troupes he dreams of. There was a small matter of his involvement in the May riots, but I have instructed my officers to lose the footage as a gesture of good will." She knitted her fingers together. "He would do well to steer clear of further trouble, or it *will* have a direct impact on his citizenship process."

"Oh." Ellie's throat tightened.

"Is something wrong?" said the Chancellor.

"It's just, I was hoping... I was hoping you could bypass the paperwork and..."

"Yes?"

"Could you grant the performers and crew citizenship? Like the French President did when a refugee scaled walls to rescue a child."

The Chancellor shook her head. "I'm sorry, Frau Richter, but you ask too much. I can't risk factions in my Government accusing me of bending the rules or being too lenient, however much I myself believe in the advantages of giving the downtrodden a chance. I know that within a few years, the refugees will pay more in taxes than the public purse spends on them. I know they enrich our land with culture and create jobs. I know our infrastructure is coping quite well, and our population has remained level since the 1990s. But I can't force that view on my colleagues or the electorate, and it would be stupid to take my position for granted." She shuffled her papers, signalling that the meeting would soon come to an end. "The polite political landscape of the post-war years is changing. We have openly nationalistic parties in parliament for the first time since the Second World War. There's more dissent than ever before, and the changes to our demographics are a challenge. Of course, we shouldn't swing to extremes in order to shore up votes. Policy debates belong in the open, however difficult they are. What I can't abide is this abstract fear of immigration. So I'm giving your friends a chance at citizenship, using fair process, and I hope they are grateful for that chance, because not everyone is so lucky."

A weight settled on Ellie, despite the good news about the circus, because this was perhaps only a temporary reprieve, and the spectre of impermanence must be difficult for her friends to bear.

The Chancellor stood, smoothing down the pleats of her skirt. "Now are you going to introduce me to Herr Alam? That cake's been waiting an awfully long time for us."

Her aide coughed.

The Chancellor looked to him, and turned swiftly back to Ellie. "Ah, of course. Frau Richter, is there anything I can do for you personally to thank you?"

Ellie beamed. "There is one thing."

44

As day tumbled into night, Rex adjusted the tie at his neck and strode out to greet the media swarm outside his house. His audience, there by Corinne's invitation, eagerly awaited him. Their cameras lit up the street, and soon perspiration shone on Rex's brow.

Behind him, Jessy waited at the living room window, wet nose against the glass, velvety ears cocked in puzzlement at the furore outside. Rex steeled himself, drawing on the stillness of his wife and children who stood to his left, not a hair out of place or a splash of spaghetti sauce to be seen. He hadn't taught his son to shine his shoes at the age of six for nothing. To his right, Corinne shifted from one foot to another and shushed the journalists.

It hadn't taken him long to make his decision.

When he'd asked Corinne to join him, she hadn't hesitated. It didn't concern her what he could offer her, only that she went where he did. He admired her blind loyalty, loved her for it even.

He drew in a deep breath. "The time has come for change. Today's citizens are plagued with frustration about the global order. They are mistrustful about the rate of technological progress. These are not problems that are going away. Anti-elite parties are springing up across Europe. Some will tell you to look down on these parties, that they will take you down a dark path. Let me tell you, these parties are the only ones willing to innovate. Today, the Chancellor asked me to step down from my role as Interior Minister–"

The media scrum broke into uproar.

"Herr Silberling is not yet finished," said Corinne, her forehead puckered. "Please hold back your questions until he is."

Rex held up his hands for quiet. "While I am saddened to leave this great office of state, I am heartened by new opportunities on the horizon. For too long, traditional political parties have dragged their feet in responding to the challenges of the day. This is why I have withdrawn my long-standing party affiliation with immediate effect. There are other parties which will appreciate my insights. No longer will the agendas of big business or foreign policy trump what the people need. That is my promise to the German people."

Rex unbuttoned his suit jacket as the journalists unleashed a barrage of questions.

So what if the Chancellor wanted to take him on? It might take some time, but with him chipping away from the outside, she'd eventually lose. He knew the strength of his charisma and resolve. His elastic values meant he could pivot in even the smallest space. Ideological contortionism was a huge strength; freeing himself from the chains of his current party membership allowed him a nimble-footedness the Chancellor lacked. She wanted to play by the book in a changed world, and would end up cannibalising her own government if she stuck to her guns. He had enemies, yes, but he also had allies. In the world of politics, allegiances shifted fast, and he wouldn't go down without a fight.

There was a section of society that wanted to believe he could solve all their ills. He might have overplayed his hand with the circus, but it didn't change how the cards had been laid out. Fear and conspiracies had more wings than facts. Politics at its best was simple, unambiguous, a call to arms. The modern world was so complex that the electorate needed men like him to simplify it. The promises he made would bring them solace and soothe their worries. The public had a short memory. His past indiscretions would fade away. It didn't even matter if he couldn't deliver on his promises. What mattered was assuring the struggling part of the electorate they weren't alone, that someone was on their side.

He'd give them what they wanted.

45

A week later, Yusuf and Ellie rocked in a pod of the Ferris wheel, pleased to be alone and without the scrutiny and needs of others. Jet trails threaded through the cobalt sky above them. A calm settled over Yusuf's soul to be here above the bustle of the city and the circus, where silence soothed him and allowed his thoughts the space to unfold. Here, no chatter or footsteps drew his attention, no march of the drums or chug of engines. He turned inward and found no shame, only familiarity and calm.

Ellie's body fitted snugly into the crook of his arm, and Yusuf marvelled at the change in and around him. Just days ago, up on the Ferris wheel, he'd felt as broken as the rusting frame. But despite the pain of his past, and the possible ruptures that littered his–and anyone's–future, Allah had not abandoned him. He wondered at his luck when some had none.

They'd managed to save the circus. Home wasn't just the buildings or the land, it was the people he surrounded himself with, the ones who fought for and believed in him. It was the ghost of memories, of loved ones who had protected him.

He kissed Ellie's brow, and she turned her face to his, and he discerned anticipation in her eyes. He laughed. "What are you up to?"

She shook her head. "Nothing. A girl doesn't always have to be plotting and planning, you know."

"That's a shame," he said. "Because I was hoping you'd help me get my circus classes off the ground. I could even teach you the trapeze. You might like it."

She shuddered. "You know what I'm like with heights, but I think I might be a dab hand with the clown car."

Yusuf laughed, then grew sombre. "I've been thinking about visiting Karl in prison. How do you think he'd feel about someone like me visiting him?"

Ellie sat up, and he missed her heat against his skin. "He's a convicted neo-Nazi, Yusuf. If he's in his right mind, he'll be grateful for your news. It was kind of you to ask the Chancellor."

"A promise is a promise, and besides, she was in a good mood. Maybe his sister doing well is just what he needs. Maybe it'll change him."

He missed Selim more than anything then, and thought of how his brother would never have wasted the chance of a life in a country like this, where opportunities teemed at every corner. Perhaps he'd have been a teacher, a professor, or even a government official, someone who could drive change. He gulped down his sorrow, because the clouds had cleared, finally, and he was determined to look to the future, not dwell on the past.

"I wish I'd been able to convince the Chancellor that Dawud belongs with us. I'm scared for him," he said. An involuntary shudder ran through his body, a premonition that the boy would not be okay. It hurt for Dawud to be gone. Simeon missed him, too. Yusuf worried that Dawud wouldn't survive alone. That he'd get caught up in violence or would try to end it all.

Ellie curled into him. "I'm so sorry, Yusuf. I wish she'd agreed. In her mind, the decision had already been taken."

"Where politicians direct their interest has power. I don't want him to be alone or forgotten."

"You could sue, you know," said Ellie. "Despite the circus being open, you could sue. Silberling's still trying to weasel back into the political scene."

Yusuf drew his eyebrows together, puzzled. He shook his head. "Why would I, and risk everything the state has given me? It'd be churlish. Besides, I'm not a saint. We all need a fresh start."

She collapsed into him again, pensive.

"I've come to love this country as I do my own. I don't need more than I have already."

He lied, because losing Doris made him miss his mother even more, but it seemed ungracious to admit in that moment, and Ellie was almost enough to fill the chasm. He loved her fiercely, for her intellect and her compassion and her willingness to question everything.

"I'm going to make something of my life, you know. One day, I'll hold one of those gold-embossed maroon booklets in my hand, and I won't have to worry about men turning up in the night and telling me I don't belong. I'll belong here. I'm going to work hard, pay my taxes, and be somebody."

"You already are somebody."

They looked out across the city skyline, at the high-rises and parks, the trail of railway lines and cars like ants. A plane passed overhead, and he thought of the future, and how perhaps one day his own children would travel back and forth, nonchalantly, simply because they could, because they belonged and would always be welcomed back. For them, travel would equate to joy and adventure, not fear and displacement.

He stared across the horizon, with Ellie at his side, considering how many decades might pass before a city like this considered people like him one of their own. How long it would take for his children, and their children, to feel rooted to this place? How long before men and women like him could know that they never had to worry about being bombed, or turfed out, or having bellies ache with emptiness? Why should some children be more likely to leave their mark on the world than his own just because of an accident of birth and a land's history? To ride on yachts and play violins? To dream and be protected?

A thought slipped through the net in his mind, and he centred on it, forcing it back. "You didn't tell me what you asked of the Chancellor."

Her green eyes twinkled. "You'll know soon enough."

He tickled her then, and she crumpled, gasping for him to stop.

They kissed, and her lips lingered on his. She'd kicked off her boots, too warm on this balmy night, and her bare soles idled against his calves. He longed for the moment to stretch forever, so when car doors slammed below and she pulled away, he grumbled.

"One day, your curiosity will bite you in the bottom," he said.

She didn't respond, but peered below, suddenly tensing. "They're here."

Yusuf frowned. "Who?" He followed her gaze, and spied a car below, not unlike the one that used to transport Silberling to the circus. He settled back into his seat. He didn't want to be distracted from Ellie, the way her fingers caressed his arm, and her hair that rippled in the wind.

She crammed her feet into her boots, grabbed his hand and pulled him up.

His brow furrowed. "Why the hurry?"

"You'll want to see this," she said with a gentleness in her manner that touched him, one he hadn't seen before.

He stood, and the cab swung precariously as they shifted their weight and eased out, clambering ever downwards until they reached the ground. Ellie had grown practiced at the descent, and she hurried this time, more careless and confident than she had been before.

At the bottom, he reached out his hand to her, and she tugged him across the short distance to the car gleaming in the early evening light.

He laughed, nonplussed. "What are you doing?"

"Trust me."

"Always."

His heart stilled.

Imam Saeed was there, and Leyla with her arm around a woman's shoulders.

The woman was frailer than he remembered.

He let Ellie's hand fall from his grasp and ran to her. His fingers searched her face, working their way across the shadows under the eyes, the deep fault-lines in her skin. Milky tears trailed down her face.

They spoke in their native Arabic.

"Maa. Do my eyes deceive me?"

"No, my son."

He studied every inch of her worn skin. "You had a long journey."

She wrapped her scarf closer around her head. "They treated me well."

"Is Selim's grave moss-green like he would have liked it?"

Her eyes became glassy with tears. "I tried."

Still he held back, holding on to his last shred of dignity in front of Ellie and Leyla and the Imam. "How did they convince you to come here, to leave Syria?"

"They told me you needed me," said his mother.

He crumpled into her embrace, and was home.

THE END

BOOK CLUB GUIDE

1. What are the main themes of the novel?

2. How does the book's title relate to its contents?

3. Which character would you most like to spend time with?

4. Which character did you most dislike and did that character have any redeeming qualities?

5. If you could hear this same story from another circus performer's point of view, who would you choose and why?

6. What made the setting unique or important? Could the story have taken place anywhere?

7. What does the circus represent within this story?

8. Do you think the nature of Selim's death had more of an impact on Yusuf than if he had died by natural causes?

9. How are Ellie's perspective and choices different from those of the circus women? Are there ways in which Ellie's Western privilege becomes obvious?

10. Was Marina right to fire Ellie?

11. What was your favourite quote/passage in the book?

12. Does responsibility for Rex's behaviour lie with himself or with society?

13. Does Karl redeem himself by the end of the novel? Could you be friends with him?

14. Which familial/romantic/platonic relationships are the most nourishing in the novel?

15. In what way do mother figures/strong women play a role in the novel?

16. Compare the father figures in the novel. In your opinion, who is the most perfect example of a father figure?

17. Which leaders did you consider to be good and bad in the novel?

18. What role does culture and otherness play in the story?

19. In which ways do the Germans help the refugees integrate? Could the state have done any more?

20. What prejudices do the characters deal with? Were there any parts of the novel that caused you to recognise xenophobia in yourself?

21. Are there any instances of xenophobia by people of colour in the novel?

22. Who has the most difficulties fitting in–Isaiah, Yusuf or the Turks?

23. Which artist would you choose to illustrate this book? What kinds of illustrations would you include?

24. What feelings did this novel evoke for you? Did it challenge your perspective in any way?

25. Will Yusuf and Ellie's relationship survive into old age?

26. How do you imagine the story continues for Ellie?

Acknowledgements

I hope this book reads as a love letter to Berlin and to people who keep their hearts open. I love Berlin and every visit there is like a homecoming. It helps to see it through the eyes of my husband, whose hometown it is, to have spent time in its parks and on its streets, and to know its fraught history and how it has carved out a place in the world. For me, it's always been a place to discover my true self.

Just like Yusuf on his trapeze, suspended between joy and fear, this book toyed with me. I was scared it was too political, and that readers would abandon it. When I wavered, I kept coming back to the Pericles quote: *Just because you do not take an interest in politics, does not mean that politics won't take an interest in you.*

My thanks to all of you who encouraged me: my readers, my critique group, and my beta readers Meg, Amira and Ross. You urged me on, challenged me and helped shape the book. I couldn't have done it without you. To Jess, Dale and the team at Evolved, thank you for helping me bring this story to life.

I owe both *The Good Immigrant,* edited by Nikesh Shukla, and *Circus Mania* by Douglas McPherson a debt of gratitude. They formed the backbone of my research. Tracy Chapman's self-titled album was the soundtrack to this book, together with 'The Circus', a song written especially for this novel by my creative sister Lindsay Crichton. While I wrote, two real life stories were never far from my mind: Eva Garcia, who fell from the trapeze and died in 2003; and the clown of Aleppo, who died in 2016. I imagine his story continues here.

Most of all, thanks to my family. Nana, you were so brave. You built a new world with little means and a big heart, and we still feel your ripples today. Mum and dad, you are the helpers, and sometimes, I think you carry a community on your shoulders. To J and our three musketeers, thank you for anchoring and inspiring me. Your belief in me and the little celebrations of my daily word count mean more than you know.

About the Author

Nillu Nasser was born in London, UK, to Indian parents.

She studied English and German Literature at Warwick University, followed by European Politics at Humboldt University, Berlin. After graduating, Nillu worked in national and regional politics, but eventually reverted to her first love: writing.

Nillu's debut novel, *All the Tomorrows*, was published in 2017, followed by *Hidden Colours* in 2018. Her third novel, *An Ocean of Masks*, is due to be released in 2019. Her stories often take place in rich settings and explore the search for identity from an outsider's perspective.

Nillu also blogs and writes short fiction. Her work can be found in *Mosaics 2: A Collection of Independent Women* (2016) and *UnCommonly Good* (2017).

She lives in South London with her husband and three children. If you fly into Gatwick and look hard enough, you'll catch sight of her in her garden office, working on her next story.

To find about her next release, sign up for her newsletter:

www.NilluNasser.com/mailing-list/

What's Next?

AN OCEAN OF MASKS
By Nillu Nasser
(Coming 2019)

Deceit is sewn into the fabric of our lives
long before our first breath.

Norah is all about tough love. As headmistress of a community boarding school in Brixton, South London, her job is to put children back together after their lives have derailed. She understands their anger because the same red hot fury pulses through her own veins.

When a lack of funding threatens to close the doors to her school, Norah's pupils act out their anguish in increasingly dangerous ways. As the fate of her pupils hangs in the balance, Norah accepts an invitation to join a mysterious society of masked women who might be able to help her. Little does she know, she's on a collision course to meet the mother who abandoned her as a toddler.

Some traumas never heal. With her carefully controlled world in turmoil, Norah fights to save her pupils and herself. Can she be an example to her pupils, not only of grit and courage, but vulnerability? Or will her single-minded focus on saving the school be her undoing?

More from Nillu Nasser

ALL THE TOMORROWS

This award-winning, critically acclaimed novel offers a compelling look inside a culture many in the west simply do not understand. For more information on this book, please visit Evolved Publishing:

www.EvolvedPub.com/ATT

Akash Choudry wants a love for all time, not an arranged marriage. Still, under the weight of parental hopes, he agrees to one. He and Jaya marry in a cloud of colour and spice in Bombay. Their marriage has barely begun when Akash embarks on an affair.

Jaya can't contemplate sharing her husband with another woman, or looking past his indiscretions as her mother suggests. Cornered by sexual politics, she takes her fate into her own hands in the form of a lit match.

Nothing endures fire. As shards of their past threaten their future, will Jaya ever bloom into the woman she can be, and will redemption be within Akash's reach?

"Replete with hard lessons, determined dreams, and illusions and realities surrounding love and relationships, *All the Tomorrows* is a gripping saga set under the sweltering heat of not just India, but hearts on fire. It's an involving story of the tides and trajectories of love which will especially intrigue readers looking for more than a light dose of Indian cultural insight." ~ *Midwest Book Review*

"*All the Tomorrows* is rich in engaging, realistic characters who grab readers' hearts and minds and don't let them go till all the story is told. And what a story it is!" ~ *Readers' Favorite Book Reviews*

More from Evolved Publishing

We offer great books across multiple genres, featuring hiqh-quality editing (which we believe is second-to-none) and fantastic covers.

As a hybrid small press, your support as loyal readers is so important to us, and we have strived, with tireless dedication and sheer determination, to deliver on the promise of our motto:
QUALITY IS PRIORITY #1!

Please check out all of our great books,
which you can find at this link:

www.EvolvedPub.com/Catalog/

Thank you!